W9-BRN-254

# THE YEAR OF LUMINOUS LOVE

*You'll want to read these inspiring titles by*

# Lurlene McDaniel

ANGELS IN PINK

*Kathleen's Story • Raina's Story • Holly's Story*

ONE LAST WISH NOVELS

*Mourning Song • A Time to Die • Mother, Help Me Live*
*Someone Dies, Someone Lives • Sixteen and Dying*
*Let Him Live • The Legacy: Making Wishes Come True*
*Please Don't Die • She Died Too Young*
*All the Days of Her Life • A Season for Goodbye*
*Reach for Tomorrow*

OTHER OMNIBUS EDITIONS

*Keep Me in Your Heart: Three Novels*
*True Love: Three Novels*
*The End of Forever • Always and Forever*
*The Angels Trilogy*
*As Long As We Both Shall Live • Journey of Hope*
*One Last Wish: Three Novels*

OTHER FICTION

*Red Heart Tattoo • Reaching Through Time • Heart to Heart*
*Breathless • Hit and Run • Prey*
*Briana's Gift • Letting Go of Lisa • The Time Capsule*
*Garden of Angels • A Rose for Melinda • Telling Christina Goodbye*
*How Do I Love Thee: Three Stories • To Live Again*
*Angel of Mercy • Angel of Hope*
*Starry, Starry Night: Three Holiday Stories • The Girl Death Left Behind*
*Angels Watching Over Me • Lifted Up by Angels*
*For Better, For Worse, Forever • Until Angels Close My Eyes*
*Till Death Do Us Part • I'll Be Seeing You • Saving Jessica*
*Don't Die, My Love • Too Young to Die*
*Goodbye Doesn't Mean Forever • Somewhere Between Life and Death*
*Time to Let Go • Now I Lay Me Down to Sleep*
*When Happily Ever After Ends • Baby Alicia Is Dying*

*From every ending comes a new beginning. . . .*

Lurlene McDaniel

# THE YEAR OF LUMINOUS LOVE

DELACORTE PRESS

This is a work of fiction. Names, characters, places, and incidents either are the product of the author's imagination or are used fictitiously. Any resemblance to actual persons, living or dead, events, or locales is entirely coincidental.



Visit us on the Web! randomhouse.com/teens
Educators and librarians, for a variety of teaching tools, visit us at RHTeachersLibrarians.com

*Library of Congress Cataloging-in-Publication Data*
McDaniel, Lurlene.
The year of luminous love / Lurlene McDaniel. — 1st ed.
p. cm.
Summary: Eighteen-year-olds Ciana Beauchamp, Arie Winslow, and Eden McLauren of Tennessee rely on their close friendship as they face serious problems the summer before they start college, from parents' illnesses, to cancer, to loving the same cowboy.
ISBN 978-0-385-74171-2 (hardcover) — ISBN 978-0-375-99020-5 (glb) — ISBN 978-0-375-98675-8 (ebook)
[1. Best friends—Fiction. 2. Friendship—Fiction. 3. Family problems—Fiction. 4. Love—Fiction. 5. Tennessee—Fiction.] I. Title.
PZ7.M4784172 Ye 2013 [Fic]—dc22 2012024904

The text of this book is set in 11.5-point Goudy.
Book design by Vikki Sheatsley

Printed in the United States of America
10 9 8 7 6 5 4 3 2 1
First Edition

*This book is dedicated to my longtime friend*
*Artie Pullen,*
*who lost her fight with cancer in 2011.*

# CONTENTS

# PART I

# 1

Something was wrong.

Ciana Beauchamp bolted upright in bed, her heart pounding and fear closing off her throat. What had she heard that had awakened her out of a sound sleep? Something was wrong. The noise came again, from outside, in the distance. She heard the horses locked in the stables neighing in alarm.

Her bedside clock read 2:00 a.m. The horses should be asleep. What was spooking them? She tossed off her covers and fumbled around for her jeans, which she had discarded in a heap on her floor before she had fallen into bed that night. Ciana tugged the cold denim on over her pajama bottoms, grabbed an old sweatshirt, and padded to her door. She opened it carefully, stepped into the hall, and listened for sounds from her mother's room at the far end of the hall. She heard Alice Faye snoring and knew that the horses' distress hadn't disturbed her mother. But then, how could it have? When Alice Faye fell into bed dead drunk every night, she could sleep through anything.

Ciana hurried through the house, through the kitchen, and into the mudroom. There she pulled out her work boots from beneath the old timber bench where she'd stashed them after feeding the horses and locking down the house for the night. She removed a rain slicker from a peg beside the door, slipped it on, and reached for the doorknob. She hesitated, then turned, opened a cabinet door, and took out the double-barreled shotgun. No telling what she might run into—a marauding coyote, a rabid raccoon, something more dangerous. She opened the cabinet over the bench and took down a box of shells and quickly loaded the pump shotgun. She went out the door, moving quickly, stepping through puddles left from yesterday's cold April rain. Her boots made a sucking sound.

The closer she got to the stables, the louder the shuffling of the two horses in their stalls. She squinted as she approached the door and saw that it was standing ajar. Fear prickled up her spine. No animal except the two-legged variety could have unlatched the door.

She stood still for a moment, taking deep breaths to slow her heartbeat. She missed her grandmother with an ache that made her knees weak. Olivia should have been handling this, just as she'd handled all the Beauchamp family issues over the years.

*Suck it up!* Ciana told herself. Olivia couldn't help. The ball was in Ciana's court now.

She eased inside carefully, knowing that the hinges needed oiling and their squeaking would give her away. Another thing to put on her to-do list. The scent of her caused the horses to calm somewhat. Still, Firecracker, her favorite riding horse, snorted and moved against the side of the stall, making the old boards creak. She commanded silently, *Don't give me away*.

She stood stock-still, listening for noise. Shuffling sounds came from the tack room. She heard the lid lifting on the oak chest where blankets were kept and heard the thump of a saddle as it hit the floor. Her heart squeezed as she remembered Granddad Charles's antique Mexican saddle with the sterling silver trim. Whoever was inside could steal it. The tack room needed a better lock. Maybe the whole barn needed a security system. There was so much for her to do. Too much.

Ciana swallowed against the lump in her throat formed partly from fear and partly from being overwhelmed. She stole to the door and saw a candle flickering and a man kneeling in front of the trunk, tossing out the contents, his back to her. The guy had lit the way for her and presented a broad target.

The shotgun had grown heavy in Ciana's hands. She'd shot it many times growing up and knew the damage it could do. But she'd never aimed it at a human being before. "*Don't ever raise a gun unless you're prepared to use it.*" Olivia's words came back to Ciana. Was she prepared to shoot? What if the man was high on meth? She'd heard stories that such people could charge like raging bulls. She raised the gun, pumped it, and with a bravado that came from holding the weapon, said, "What are you doing in my barn?"

The man spun, but the unmistakable sound of the shells being chambered kept him on his knees. The whites of his eyes were glowing in the light of the candle. "Don't shoot. Please."

Emboldened by his fear, Ciana aimed at his chest, her hands rock steady. "You stealing from me?"

He stared wide-eyed at the twin barrels. "Please, I'll go."

Now she had a dilemma. Fumble for a phone and call the cops? What phone? She fumbled for her cell and realized she'd left it in her bedroom. Let him run? He was a thief. "Cops in this part of Tennessee don't prosecute landowners for defending their property, you know." That wasn't quite true, since the man had no weapon she could see, but she wanted to keep him very afraid.

The man was shaking all over. "You empty out anything you've already put in your pockets," she commanded, nudging the gun toward his open coat.

He hurriedly obeyed, dropping a handful of coins she kept in a mason jar on the old scarred desk against the wall. He dropped matches and a few candle stubs. Had he been planning to burn her barn before he left, trapping her helpless horses and sentencing them to certain death? The thought focused her anger, melting away all fear. "I should shoot you!"

"No, no, please!"

She stood her ground for a minute, then finally backed out of the doorway and motioned with the barrel of the gun for the vagrant to stand and exit the small room. She stood far back, out of reach but with the gun still aimed at him. "Don't you ever set foot on my property again," she said in as menacing a voice as she could muster. "Because I will shoot you dead." She motioned with the barrel of the gun. "Now get out!" The man seemed frozen to the ground. "I said, out!"

He didn't need another prod. He sprinted through the barn door like a squirrel chased by a fox. Ciana took a deep breath and lowered the shotgun, for it had grown unbearably heavy in her suddenly trembling hands. She figured she should call the police and report what had happened, but she realized she couldn't cope with waiting for them to get out to the farm and fill out a report. She went to the stalls to calm the restless horses. She gave each a cup of oats, picked up the gun, and returned to the house.

She scraped off her boots in the mudroom, rehung her slicker, removed the shells from the shotgun and shoved them into her jeans pocket, and took the gun with her to her room. Once inside, she leaned against the wall, her legs rubbery, too quivery to hold her up. She sank to the floor, grasping the gun in her lap. It wasn't supposed to be this way. Olivia was supposed to be in charge. Ever since Ciana had been six and her father and grandfather had died in the crash of Granddad's single-engine Cessna, Olivia had been the backbone of the family. She had taken care of Bellmeade, the family farmland that traced its origins to before the Civil War.

No more.

Dementia and old-age frailty had claimed Ciana's beloved grandmother. She was in a continuous-care facility in downtown Windemere, fifteen miles away. As for Alice Faye, Olivia's daughter, well, she lived inside a gin bottle, unwilling and unable to take the reins. Ciana longed to talk to her friends, Arie and Eden, but it was almost three in the morning. She couldn't call them now.

Ciana began to weep as the tension of the night's confrontation began to leak out of her body. She might have killed or severely wounded the intruder. She muffled her sobs with her fist, her shoulders shaking hard with each racking breath. Just weeks before high school graduation, everything had fallen on her shoulders—the farm, the debt, caring for her mother and grandmother. It was all hers.

And she was only eighteen years old.

# 2

"Your CT scan looks good, Arie."

"How good?" she asked. Every CAT scan was a lesson in hand-wringing, coupled with hope.

"The spots on your liver are greatly diminished. They've shrunk to dots." Dr. Austin gave a self-satisfied nod. "We can remove your shunt."

Artemis Diane Winslow let out the breath she'd been holding. She'd spent her entire senior year going back and forth from this hospital in Nashville for treatments, longing to be normal, praying that the cancer she'd been fighting since age five and that had popped up in her liver last fall would be defeated. All she wanted was to be free permanently of cancer and medical procedures. Was that too much to ask?

"The sooner, the better," she told her longtime doctor. "I always feel like I'm climbing a cliff and just when I get to the top and stand up, cancer pushes me over the edge again."

Dr. Austin touched her shoulder. "You've fought hard, and better treatments come along every day. Hang in there."

He hadn't said, "*The worst is over. Clear sailing now.*" Disappointing, but with the shunt coming out and her latest chemo protocol over, she might have a normal summer—her last summer before starting college.

"Chosen a college yet?" Dr. Austin asked, numbing the skin around her shunt for the removal and stitching process.

"Middle Tennessee State University. I plan to study art history. It's close to home." She'd wanted to go away to college, but living at home would be cheaper. Eric, her twenty-year-old brother who worked with their father in his cabinetmaking business, liked teasing her about her love of art and ancient cultures. "Four years of college and you still won't be able to *do* anything," he'd say, and she'd answer, "I'll be a sought-after lecturer, and you'll be begging for my autograph." He always laughed, tickled her side, and dashed off before she could retaliate.

"We'll keep up the oral meds and check you again in two months," Dr. Austin said, smiling.

She'd take the pills, but Arie's pipe dreams included travel abroad to the great museums of Europe. *One thing at a time*, she told herself. *Today the shunt, tomorrow the world*.

"I guess I should let Mom come in to hear the news," she said, positive that Patricia was outside the exam room with her ear to the door.

"I don't know how you've kept her out," Dr. Austin said.

Arie had put her foot down months before over her mother or father haunting her every visit to the doctor. All she wanted now was to tell her best friends Ciana and Eden the good news, certain they would make plans to go somewhere fun and celebrate.

"Call her in," Austin said, "and let's get you out of here."

Riding home from the doctor's office, Arie felt renewed optimism about the future. She glanced over at her mother, driving with a smile and humming to herself. Arie hadn't insisted on driving so that she could talk and text. She called Ciana Beauchamp first, her best friend since the fifth grade, the one who'd cheered Arie through two other remissions, one at twelve and another through their senior year of high school. On the phone, Ciana first cheered, then said, "Come straight over. We'll go for a ride."

Nothing would make Arie happier. The feel of the sun hitting her face and the smells of freshly turned earth, newly mown grass, horseflesh, and saddle-soaped leather always comforted her. And without a horse of her own, she had learned to ride on Olivia's horse, Sonata, at the Bellmeade farm, Ciana's home. For graduation, Ciana had given Arie a glittery cowgirl jacket. "For the rodeo parade this summer," she had said. Arie had never owned a jacket so beautiful. Over the years, such jackets had been loaned to her by Ciana or bought at the Goodwill store and decorated by her mother with sequins and hot-glued rhinestones. Arie had cried when she'd lifted the jacket out of its box.

Next Arie called Eden, who'd joined their friendship in middle school to make an unbreakable trio. Eden worked in a fashion boutique in the downtown area of their small town of Windemere. "Awesome!" Eden said after Arie shared her news. "We have to have some fun."

Arie wanted to ask if Eden was sure she could break away from Tony, her possessive boyfriend, but she stopped herself. Why darken Eden's mood? "I'm open to everything! Come over to Ciana's when you get off."

"We'll do something bodacious," Eden said.

"Nothing that involves a police presence," Arie said with

a laugh. Beside her, Patricia glanced over with an arched eyebrow. Arie ignored her.

"I'll be there." In the background, Arie heard a bell jingle. Eden said, "Whoops, customer just walked in. See you later."

"What about *our* celebration?" Patricia asked as soon as Arie ended her call. "You know, your family? You may be eighteen, graduated, and all grown up, but we want to celebrate with you too."

Arie sighed. A party with her family meant crowds, because she had more relatives in the area than Cooter Brown had hunting dogs. "You and Dad plan the party and I'll be there, but for tonight, I just want to be with my friends. Please."

Patricia grumbled but followed it with a smile. "All right. Tonight with your friends, but a barbeque with the family soon. You'll be glad you came. Trust me."

She imagined a cake and balloons as in years past when she'd been pronounced cancer-free. There would be lots of good wishes, hugs and squeezes, mountains of grilled meat, casseroles, salads, molded gelatins, chips and dips. She'd hear congratulations, and she'd be toasted with sodas and beer. Her family loved her and she loved them—all of them, the entire army of them—but in many ways they still saw her as a little girl, a broken fair-haired, blue-eyed doll cursed to bear the burden of cancer through a life always on the brink of disaster.

After all, Arie was "the cancer girl," and the whole town had pitched in over time. They had held bake sales, placed collection canisters in stores, sponsored bingo nights at the veterans center, and held fish fries in church parking lots, all to help pay her mounting and finally overwhelming medical bills.

# 3

The house wore its emptiness like a dark cloak. Eden McLauren didn't need to go inside to know that her mother was gone. Yet despite being eighteen and grown, she felt like a four-year-old again. That was how old she was when it first began to dawn on her that her mother, Gwen, wasn't like other mothers. She had huge mood swings—one day erupting with the energy of a volcano and tearing around in a frenzy, then crashing for days with such depression that she couldn't get out of her bed.

Eden stepped through the side door in the carport and into the kitchen. Dishes were piled in the sink; cabinet doors were standing open. Gwen had left in a hurry, not even locking the door behind her. No way to tell when she'd left. No way to know when she'd return. The old run-down house seemed to sigh with a sense of abandonment.

Eden's gaze swept the room, taking in the ripped vinyl flooring, the worn-out table and chairs, and the egg-yolk-yellow walls. Eden had painted them out of spite once when her mother had left, knowing how her mother hated the color yellow—the color of the sun and daffodils and school buses.

Eden's old insecurities returned, along with the anger she felt toward her mother. Where did her mother go? Why did she run away? A child's questions, she knew, but ones that still haunted her even after all these years. She spied the paring knife on the counter and picked it up, staring at the tip, longing to bring it to the inside of her arm, press it into the scarred skin and slice. She imagined the thin line of blood oozing onto her skin and the sudden pain that would dispel the other pain that lived inside her head. How good it would feel, this release, this freedom to bleed. Fighting the urge, she laid the knife down.

Maybe her mother hadn't run off. Maybe she'd been called in to her cashier's job at Piggly Wiggly grocery and rushed out the door, carelessly leaving the door unlocked and forgetting to write a note. Eden went upstairs into her mother's bedroom and checked her hope at the door. Contents from drawers were heaped on the floor, closet hangers picked clean, making it look as if a burglar had ransacked the room. Eden stared at the mess, hardly able to breathe. She glanced to the closet shelf and saw the blue duffel bag was missing. She remembered they'd had their first screaming fight over it when she'd come home from school at age eleven and found Gwen furiously packing it.

"Where are you going?" she'd asked, standing in her mother's bedroom doorway, mystified.

"Away. I have to go away."

"Go where? Why?" Fear. Confusion.

"I can't say. Just away. For a little while."

Eden had thought she was accustomed to her mother's weirdness and had adapted to it, her "ups" of all-night activity and "downs" of days of retreating under her bedcovers, unable to function, but Gwen had never packed and left before. "I'll go with you."

"No! You have school."

She watched Gwen zip the duffel closed, hardly able to breathe. "But . . . but when will you be back?"

"Um . . . a few days."

"What about me?"

Gwen had dropped to her knees and taken hold of Eden's small shoulders. "You're such a big girl. I left money for you in the kitchen drawer for lunches. You can get ready for school all by yourself. You'll be fine, honey. Just fine."

"But . . . but I'll be alone. I don't want to be alone."

"I'll be back soon," Gwen promised. She stood and picked up the duffel bag, then started to the door.

Eden ran and grabbed the handles of the duffel bag, trying to rip it from her mother's hands. "Don't go, Mama!"

Gwen won the fight, pushing Eden onto the bed and stroking her black curly hair. "You'll be fine," she said. "If I leave, the bad things will follow me and not bother you."

"What bad things?"

"Shhh. If I hurry, I can sneak past them." She ran out the door, heaving the duffel bag over her shoulder.

"Mama!" Eden screamed. All she'd heard was the slamming of the front door and the start of the car motor, and then silence descended in a blanket of desolation.

That first time Eden cried, afraid of being left alone. She'd never known a father, a subject that would set Gwen off if mentioned. Over time, Eden stopped asking. Gwen was gone nine days and had returned looking dirty and disheveled, emotionally empty, almost robotic. No explanations. No apologies. Life resumed. It happened many times over the years, this leaving. Eden learned to cope. To cut. To endure. But she never cried again.

This was Eden's life with a bipolar mother. Manic-depressive. An illness. A disorder. Lifelong. Life-altering. Not Eden's fault. Except . . . it always *felt* like her fault.

Eden kicked the pile of her mother's clothing deeper into the closet and slammed the door. She crossed to the tiny bathroom, saw that the floor was littered with a colorful array of pills scattered like tiny petals from a bouquet of pharm flowers. When had Gwen stopped taking them this time? She'd been stable at Eden's graduation, two weeks before. But it only took a day or so for her mother's demons to arrive when she stopped her meds. Eden never understood why Gwen would stop the pills that kept the lid on her illness. What was wrong with normal?

On the meds. Off the meds. Sometimes Gwen stayed on the meds for months. Day-to-day life was smoother then. Gwen was never abusive to Eden. She turned inward, neglectful, heard whispers from voices Eden couldn't hear. The voices always told her to stop her meds. Or did she stop taking her meds and then hear the voices? Eden never knew. However, Eden took the blame, telling herself that if she were a better daughter or a different daughter, prettier or more lovable, her mother would have had no reason to run away. During that time, Eden had taken up cutting, and watching the blood seep from the cut gave her release and a sense of control. Over time, the scars multiplied, on her arms, torso, and inside her thighs—relief for a while.

As Eden stared at the scattered pills, she felt the familiar tightening sensation grip her belly. The pressure was building, closing her inside a dark cloud. If she didn't leave now, she wouldn't be able to stop from slicing open her skin. She thought of Tony, of her promise to him made at sixteen to stop her cutting and to come to him instead, to burn away one desire with another—his bed, his body becoming a substitute for her blood sacrifice. She should go to him now before she cut.

Reluctantly she reached for her cell phone and punched in Ciana's number. When her friend answered, she put great effort into sounding breezy. "Bad news, girlfriend. The boss wants me to stay and do an inventory."

"No!"

"'Fraid so. I hate inventories. Takes forever and is *b-o-r-i-n-g*. You and Arie have fun tonight."

"Shouldn't you call her?"

"Please handle it for me, okay? This weekend we'll do something spectacular, just the three of us."

"I'll tell her." Ciana paused. "You all right? You sound out of breath."

"Fine. Just bummed about missing tonight. Please tell her I'm kicked about her remission." She turned off her phone and headed down the stairs, thinking back to the summer before ninth grade when she turned fourteen and everything changed. That was the summer she had first met twenty-one-year-old Tony Cicero. And two years later traded one compulsion for another.

# 4

"What do you mean you can't come with us?" Eden asked Arie.

"We've planned this. It's your celebration," Ciana added.

Arie gestured to the mob scene of relatives and well-wishers in her backyard. "I'm stuck," she said. "I promised Mom I'd stay. They've got some big surprise planned."

Eden looked out onto the patio and lawn, at the crowds around the tables and grill. "Just how many relatives do you have?"

"A bunch," Arie said with a sigh.

"But this dance hall is brand-new and really hot," Eden argued. "Best band in Nashville."

Ciana wasn't thrilled about Eden's plan either. She'd have opted for dinner at Chili's and a movie, but when Eden set her mind to something, it was hard to weasel out of it.

Arie shrugged helplessly. "Can't help it. Plus, Eric is bringing home his latest girlfriend." Arie leaned closer and with an exaggerated lift of her newly regrown eyebrows added, "This is 'the One.'"

"What happened to his other two 'Ones'?" Eden deadpanned.

"Good one!" Ciana said, turning to Eden for a high five.

"That's mean," Arie said with a wry grin. "My brother's had a bad year and you both know it."

*As if you didn't have a worse one*, Ciana thought, but didn't say it. Ciana thought Arie looked tired, not long enough out of chemo to be going with them to Nashville, but Eden seemed oblivious.

A gaggle of running children burst between the three of them, with girls screaming and boys peppering them with water pistols.

"You two go on. No use missing out on fun for the two of you. If you like it, we'll all go next time. Promise," Arie said.

"Oh, I don't think we should—" Ciana started.

"We're going!" Eden said emphatically, looping her arm through Ciana's and dragging her backward. She waved cheerfully to Arie. "Hugs and kisses."

"Call me tomorrow," Arie shouted as they went through the side gate.

"But I don't want—" Ciana started to say.

"Hush up," Eden interrupted her. "It's a forty-five-mile drive to the dance saloon, a chance for us to have a good time, and you're not going to whine about going for the entire drive. Hear me?" She stuffed Ciana into her car.

"I'm not a good dancer," she groused as Eden headed toward the freeway.

"No one will notice. They'll all be drunk. And before you tell me you don't have an ID, look in my purse. I have doctored driver's licenses for both of us."

"How?"

"Tony, of course. I usually only flash it when I'm with him, but I begged him to make one for you, and he did!"

Ciana didn't care much for Tony. She thought he was too old for Eden, too much of an unknown for her. There were rumors about him running in gangs that moved drugs, but he seemed to have some kind of hold on her friend. Eden didn't do much to break his hold either. The one thing Tony had accomplished with Eden was to make her stop cutting herself. Ciana should be pleased, and she was, but she still didn't like the guy.

Knowing that Eden spent every spare minute with the man, Ciana asked, "Where's Tony this weekend?"

"He's in Atlanta, so that's why I planned for us to all go out together."

"Sorry Arie couldn't come."

"Me too. I don't know when I'll be free to do this again."

Ciana bit her tongue to keep from saying something sarcastic. She punched on the radio, aware that the car Eden was driving had been a gift from Tony too. "So I won't be a prisoner every time Mom takes off," Eden had explained when she proudly showed off her wheels to Ciana and Arie for the first time. Ciana was glad the car helped out Eden, but she didn't like thinking about what Eden might have had to trade for it.

The dance saloon, Boot Steppers, was on the southwestern side of Nashville near the banks of a slow-moving creek. Eden parked in an open grassy field because both parking lots were full. So was most of the field. "Told you this place was hot," Eden said, locking the car door.

A bright full moon lit their way to the freestanding

clapboard building that had been designed to look like an old Wild West saloon. Loud music poured from the front doors, and men and women were gathered outside to grab a smoke. Olivia would have pronounced the whole scene "unseemly," her word of choice for anything that went against her standards of good manners. Good thing she'd never caught Ciana and her friends lighting up in high school.

Ciana wore a belly-skimming sleeveless top, a short tight denim skirt, and her sexiest aqua-colored Western boots with long suede fringe. Her thick cinnamon-colored hair was clipped upward at either side of her face and fell into a cascade past her shoulders.

They walked into a giant room where a greeter at the door asked for their IDs, and Eden whipped hers out. Ciana felt guilty about her fake ID—eighteen was a long way from twenty-one, but the bouncer stamped her hand and passed her through.

"Come on!" Eden shouted above the noise. She grabbed Ciana's arm and pulled her to the bar where three bartenders worked frantically to fill orders. "Cold pitcher of beer," she told one of them.

"I don't like beer," Ciana said.

"Don't start with me. You're *going* to have fun! And a little alcohol will loosen up that tight butt of yours." Eden threw down some cash and scooped up the pitcher and two frosty mugs from the bartender. Together, she and Ciana wove their way around the sides of the huge, crammed dance floor in search of an empty table. Ciana found one way back against the wall away from the crush of bodies.

Eden never sat down. She poured Ciana a tall frosty glass and said, "Just for tonight, take some chances. Let go, girlfriend." Eden glanced behind her. "Back in a jiff!"

Ciana watched Eden merge into a line dance out on the floor but lost sight of her as others crowded in. Colored spotlights spun over the dancers in bright red, green, and blue while glittering disco balls rained sparkles across every surface. Cheesy, she decided. No true saloon in the Old West spun disco balls. Ciana envied Eden in a way. She was uninhibited around people and had a good time and few regrets for hard partying.

Ciana, on the other hand, was always aware of who she was—a Beauchamp. Olivia's doing. Her grandmother had drummed certain rules into Ciana's head since she'd been a small child. Her mother never cared about them, but she did. Rule one: A Beauchamp must never sully the family name. Rule two: A Beauchamp lived by the motto *Do unto others as you'd have others do unto you.* Rule three: A Beauchamp never— She halted the recital in her head. *Stop!* What was the matter with her? No one in Nashville knew or cared who she was. Still, she missed Arie. This night was supposed to be about her. Arie was sweet and long-suffering and would have kept her company while Eden played.

She grabbed the filled frosted glass, which was already beginning to sweat and grow warm on the table. Eden was right. It would be easier to get it down cold. She put the oversized mug to her lips and chugged it. She set down the empty glass with a satisfied thud, burped loudly, and wiped foam from her mouth with the back of her hand.

"Dance?"

She looked up to see the most gorgeous guy she'd ever laid eyes on standing in front of her. Had he seen her guzzle the mug of beer? Belch like a redneck? She heard Olivia whisper, *Unseemly*.

The guy grinned, showing off straight white teeth and deep

dimples. He winked, then dabbed her upper lip with his finger. "Missed a spot."

If only the floor would swallow her. "Um . . . thanks."

"Come on." He took her hand and led her to the dance floor. By now the line dance was over and couples were moving to country swing. The man took her hand, pushing her out, pulling her close, twirling her around and under his arm. The movement and the beer hitting her bloodstream began to make her woozy. *Please don't let me fall down.* Just then the band segued into a slower tempo. Piano keys tinkled and her partner pulled Ciana close to him, pressing her against his warm body. She felt every lean, well-muscled cell of him down to the tops of her boots.

His arm felt like a steel band around her waist, and his hands were rough and calloused. She wasn't a serial dater, had considered the boys in high school silly and immature. The few dates she'd had with college guys had disappointed and led nowhere. But in this man's arms, she knew he was no pretender with a fake ID or a frat boy out to get wasted.

"Loosen up," he said. His breath in her ear caused goose bumps along her arms. "I won't bite."

She pulled back and saw his good-natured grin and his amazing green eyes. The beer mellowed her and she leaned into him, resting her head in the crook of his neck. He smelled wonderful, like leather and spice.

Onstage, the lead singer began an old Garth Brooks song that had always been one of Ciana's favorites, "The Dance." The singer sounded eerily like Brooks as he sang, "*Our lives are better left to chance. I could have missed the pain, but I'd have had to miss the dance.*" The song spoke to her heart, to the arms of the man holding her, to her longing.

When the music ended, he pulled back, searched her face

with his incredible green eyes, and said, "Nice. . . . You're a very pretty lady."

Their gazes held, and her pulse pounded. What magic was in those eyes that stirred her so? That made her want to taste his incredibly perfect lips?

He said, "How about some introductions. I'm—"

She quickly pressed her fingers against those lips. "No names. Tonight it's about the dance."

His gaze narrowed, considering her, before he tipped his head to one side in concession. "For now."

She broke the spell of his gaze and turned toward the table, her blood singing. He returned to the table with her. Ciana could tell that Eden had stopped by because the pitcher was low and the other mug was gone.

"Want another?" he asked.

"Um . . . not really."

"You don't like beer, do you?"

"Not so much," she confessed, remembering their meeting.

"Tell you what, why don't I get you a margarita?" He didn't wait for her answer, just headed toward the bar.

She watched him, the way he walked, and could tell he'd ridden his share of horses. His boots were well worn, as were his jeans. He wasn't a weekend cowboy like so many guys in Nashville. When he returned, he set the icy-cold drink in front of her and settled across from her. "Bourbon," he said, raising his glass in a salute to her and taking a swallow.

She sipped the frozen drink in order to keep her hands busy. The cold alcohol immediately shot to her brain, creating a painful brain freeze. Soon, however, the whole room glowed with soft colors that melted together. When her glass was empty, another appeared in front of her.

"You with someone?" he asked at one point.

"A friend." She scoped out the dancers but saw no sign of Eden. She drank another margarita, warning herself to slow down, but it tasted yummy and the man across from her was pulse-rattling handsome. She was at the ball with Prince Charming, and she wanted to be someone other than Ciana Beauchamp, just for tonight.

The band started another slow dance and the man reached for her hand. "Dance with me, pretty lady."

This time when his arms closed around her, Ciana melted into his embrace, rested her head on his shoulder, and ignored how the room was spinning. In his arms, she felt protected and blissful. The band's lead singer ran through another oldie, singing, "Let the devil take tomorrow, tonight I need a friend."

This time when the music ended, Mr. Green Eyes held her at arm's distance. She was swaying and couldn't focus. He caught her upper arms. "I think we should go get fresh air."

"Whatever you say, cowboy." Her smile felt lopsided, her lips numb.

He encircled her waist, led her across the floor, and outside into the night air. People jammed the pavement and cigarette smoke turned the night hazy. "I think I sipped that last drink too fast," she mumbled. She'd only drunk too much once before, but it had been in private when she'd sampled too much gin in order to experience what an alcohol buzz felt like and what its appeal might have to her mother. She'd gotten sick.

He took her hand. "Let's take a walk down by the water, clear our heads."

She hesitated.

"I won't hurt you."

Fear of him wasn't why she hesitated. Her stomach roiled. What if she threw up on him? "You going to toss me in?"

He laughed heartily. "Never crossed my mind."

They walked along a grassy bank above the slow-moving water until the sounds of katydids and tree frogs replaced the sounds of the saloon music. She stopped, still woozy, and plopped cross-legged onto the grass. She patted the ground next to her. He joined her, plucked a long blade of grass, and began chewing on it. Ciana flopped backward, fighting to keep the sky from spinning out of focus. Once she regained her equilibrium, she saw that without the competition from the building and parking area, the sky was studded with countless glimmers of starlight.

"Feel better?" he asked after a few minutes.

"Better." She reached upward as if to catch a handful of stars. "Look at all those stars."

"You can see more of them in Texas."

"Is that where you're from?"

"Long as I can remember. How about you?"

"Born and raised in Tennessee." Moonlight glanced off the planes of his face. "What brings you here?"

"A job. After my folks divorced, my dad took a job near here on a ranch. But a few months ago he had a stroke. Put him in a wheelchair. The man who hired him asked me to take his place."

"What'd he do?"

"Horse trainer." He leaned over her, withdrew the blade of grass, and tossed it aside. "What about you?"

The last thing she wanted to discuss was herself. "Just helping my mother run the family farm. Not very exciting." She chose a blade of grass for herself, tickled his arm with it. "Truth is, I'm comfortable on a tractor."

That made him laugh. "Can't say I've had a woman tell me that before."

Ciana giggled too. "Different strokes, I guess." His mouth looked dangerously close in the moonlight. "How about you? I mean, what do you do in Texas?"

"I ride the rodeo circuit."

"I knew it!" Ciana rose up on her elbows. "You walk like a rider."

"How's that?"

"Just . . ." She lost her nerve to confess she'd been checking out his backside during the evening. "I . . . um . . . can tell."

He looked amused. "I checked you out, too, the minute you walked in the door. I liked what I saw. Still do."

His words sent shivers through her but made her feel self-conscious too. Beauchamp rule number something-or-other: Remain under the radar. She peered over at him. "Rodeo rider, huh? Why, I bet you've left a string of broken hearts all across the Lone Star state."

He tipped his head to one side. "Rodeo circuit doesn't leave much time for breaking hearts. You wrap up one rodeo, load your horse in the trailer, and drive to the next place. Lot of miles in Texas and out west. Roping and cutting. Dropping steers. Racing. I own a great little quarter horse that can do anything."

"No bull riding?"

He touched her nose with a fingertip. "Do I look crazy? Guy could get hurt on those things. I like horses. Horse and a man can work as a team. Bulls are just mean."

She liked the way he talked—his accent, his voice, kind yet seductive. "Broncs can be mean. I've seen the way they buck."

"Man can talk to a horse before he rides him. Find out what he's up against. Horses' eyes tell you everything you need to know."

"You ride year-round?"

"Summer and fall. Hire out as a ranch hand in winter."

She thought his vagabond lifestyle sounded romantic. "And you can earn a living that way?"

"Only need enough money to feed me and my horse."

She lay down, stretched her arms above her head, closed her eyes. "You going to do that forever?"

How wonderful to be with someone whose world was bigger than hers. She'd spent all her life in Windemere being a Beauchamp.

"Just until I save enough to buy me a little spread in Texas and train horses for the ranching life."

She felt that life was predetermined from birth. It started from the time that the first Beauchamps, husband and wife, had moved from the farmlands of France to buy the land and make their fortune. She sucked in the sweet summer night air, the smell of grass and clover and the cowboy's scent of leather and spice, and relished the sounds of the river below. Surely this was heaven.

"Open your eyes," he said.

She did. "Why?"

"Because I want you looking at me when I kiss you."

When his mouth met hers, her arms automatically wound around his neck. Her heart thumped as he held the kiss. When he broke away, he traced the shape of her mouth with his finger. "Tasty," he whispered.

"Again," she said, smiling.

He obliged.

She felt his hand, calloused and warm, on her bare midsection. An ache for him grew hotter. She wanted all their clothes to evaporate like campfire smoke. She wanted him skin to skin.

He pulled back, taking a ragged breath. "You're vibrating," he said hoarsely.

*How could he tell?*

"I think it's your phone."

She gasped, sitting upright. Saved by the buzz. With a shaking hand, she pushed her cell out of her skirt pocket. Eden! Ciana had forgotten about her. "Hi," she said breathlessly.

"Whoa, sounds like you're running a marathon. Where are you? It's time to go."

"I . . . um . . . I'm taking a walk by the river."

"Bored?"

"Not really."

Silence. Then, "You got another way home?"

Ciana's cowboy gave her a pleading look and shook his head: *Don't leave yet.*

Every fiber of her good sense fought against that look. In the end, she said, "I'll catch up with you later, Eden."

"I'll take that as a yes. I'm impressed. You call me first thing tomorrow. I want details." Eden hung up.

Ciana's cowboy grinned and kissed her forehead. "Thank you for staying."

She pocketed the phone. "I guess I'm not through at the ball."

He looked at her quizzically, then lay back and pulled her into the crook of his arm so that her head rested on his broad, muscled chest. "Let's take this slower," he said against her hair.

She cozied up against his body. His heartbeat rumbled in her ear. "Good idea," she said with a yawn. And she promptly fell asleep.

# 5

"I missed you, baby. Miss me too?" Tony bent over the bed and nuzzled Eden awake the next morning.

Sunlight streamed through the bedroom window. "I missed you," she murmured, still half asleep.

"What did you do while I was in Atlanta?"

"Too early to talk," she said, snuggling into the covers.

"Tell me what you did."

She was instantly awake. His voice held a warning that she knew well. She looked up at him standing by the bed, a looseness in his body that flashed a danger signal. Tony had eyes everywhere, even in Nashville, miles from Windemere. "I told you. We went dancing. Took Ciana. Arie was supposed to come but she got jammed up at one of her family gatherings." She saw him tense when she mentioned dancing.

"Have fun?"

The two words were a land mine, so Eden chose her answer carefully. "Much as I could have without you and with Ciana. She's not exactly a party girl."

"Did you like dancing with other guys?"

Her heartbeat quickened anxiously. "You told me to have fun," she said. "I never danced with the same person twice."

Tony wasn't a handsome man, but his looks were striking, dark and moody and dangerous. His eyes were as black as his hair, his body hard, compact, and well muscled. "Yes, I did. But I don't like other guys putting their hands on you."

"Dancers touch each other. Even square dancers."

"But no one do-si-dos at a dance hall." His eyes were marble hard, challenging her.

Eden realized then that someone had seen her and reported back to him. "It was supposed to be Arie's night, but plans fell through and I didn't want to be alone." She shifted, lifted her arms in invitation to join her in the bed. "You know how I hate to be alone," she whispered.

Desire flared in his eyes, and need for him rose in her like fire in a wind. No one could understand her need for him, because she didn't understand it. She just knew it lived inside her like a ravenous wolf.

He got into the bed, fully clothed, cupped her chin, stroked her cheek softly. "You're mine, Eden. You know that, right?"

"Yes."

"You'll never belong to anyone but me."

A tingle of fear shot up her back, igniting every cell in her body. He was respected on the street because to not respect him was bad for a person's well-being. And although she feared him, she wanted him, needed him. "Talk's cheap," she said, her need supplanting the fear.

His mouth came down on hers, hard and hungry.

Eden first met Tony when she was fourteen. She had crashed a street party one summer night, blocks from her house. Her mother was on one of her manic tears as an evening activity and Eden was in no mood to experience it. At the party, she lost herself in the crowd, older kids and frat and sorority kids from summer term at MTSU looking for a good time. Eden eased inside a house with an open front door, found the kitchen and a keg of cold beer. She helped herself and wandered into the trashed living room. She noticed a dark-eyed guy on the sofa staring at her. His unrelenting stare made her shiver, and she decided to take her beer and return to the crowds outside.

She made it to the front door before a hand caught her elbow. She spun to face a tall girl who looked wasted. Eden vaguely remembered her from school. "Hey, let go!" Eden tried to pull away, but the girl was surprisingly strong.

"Tony wants to meet you," the girl said.

"I don't know any Tony."

The girl ignored Eden's words and herded her to the sofa, where the man studying her stood and took Eden's arm. He said, "Thanks, Meghan," and handed the girl a small baggie.

Eden watched Meghan walk away. Her heart thudded. What had she fallen into?

"Sit with me," Tony said affably.

"Um . . . I can't stay."

He grinned and pulled her down next to him. "I'm Tony Cicero. You are . . . ?"

He had not a trace of Southern accent, so she knew that he wasn't from the area. "Eden," she said.

"Just Eden?"

"For now," she said, her anxiety giving way to curiosity. He was an outsider, new blood in a town full of guys she'd grown up with.

"You're very pretty, Eden."

She raised the beer. "Thanks."

"You in school here?"

"Sure. What about you? I don't remember seeing you around."

"I'm out of school."

Somehow that made him more interesting to her. He wasn't the typical high school jock or flake. Jocks and preppie guys bored her, nor was she attracted to rednecks. "You go to MTSU?"

"No. Does it matter?"

"Just asking." He tilted his head but said nothing. Eden squirmed, but emboldened by the beer, she asked, "So what did you give to that girl Meghan? Drugs?"

"You do drugs?"

"I could."

"Well, don't."

His warning surprised her—was he a dealer warning her off of drugs? It didn't fit. "I can do what I want," she answered.

So far she'd stayed away from hard drugs, mostly because of her friendship with Ciana, who just never *would*, and Arie, who'd spent months of her life taking chemo drugs that made her dog-sick and who swore even the idea of recreational drugs made her want to barf. Eden sometimes sneaked a few of her mother's tranquilizers, but the pills made her zone out and she didn't like the feeling. Besides, the pills never satisfied. What she learned to do to herself was cutting. She needed it now. She couldn't help herself.

"So what *do* you want, 'just Eden'?" Tony's soft question scared her. She feared he'd make a move on her. They were in plain view, so she was hopeful he wouldn't force her backward on the sofa and paw her.

"To get out of this town."

"Where would you go?"

"Bigger city."

"I came to a smaller city. Better survival odds." He traced a finger down the side of her cheek, sending a tingle along her skin. He was both dangerous and fascinating, but she was mostly bravado. She had some experience with boys, but none with a guy like Tony.

"I . . . um . . . gotta go," she said, hoping he would let her.

His dark eyes buried into her blue ones, but after a few seconds, he stood and pulled her up in front of him. "I'll walk you home."

She hadn't mentioned going home, but suddenly it seemed like a good idea. "I can go by myself. I got here by myself."

"It wasn't a request," Tony said, taking her elbow.

She wasn't sure she wanted him to know where she lived. He ushered her to the door and down the steps. People parted, staring at them as they passed. This told her Tony was known and also important. At the street corner, he said, "Which way?"

With her heart in her throat, she pointed back the way she'd come. They walked in silence, not touching. When they arrived at her house, she stopped. Every light was ablaze, and for a moment she was relieved that her mother was in one of her hyper moods. "This is it," Eden said.

Tony turned her to face him, then let go of her shoulders. "Someone left the lights on."

"Mom. She hates the dark." Eden's heart flipped like a Ping-Pong ball in her chest. Now what?

"I'll see you around, Eden."

"Maybe," she said belligerently.

He stepped closer and pulled a card from his pocket. She barely made out the words: *Tony Cicero, Security* and a phone number. He flipped it over, wrote down another number, and handed it to her. "This is my personal cell phone number. Never share it."

She took the card, her heart hammering wildly.

"When you call, and you will call one day, I'll come get you."

Dumbstruck, she watched him walk away.

Tony stayed clear of Eden, which baffled and disappointed her. She didn't call him and swore she never would. She caught glimpses of him from time to time—in the school parking lot just sitting and watching kids come in and out, and now and again, playing soccer with men in the city park—but he never approached her. Eden didn't tell either Arie or Ciana about her run-in with Tony; it had been so fleeting yet unsettling. Before the school year ended, though, Eden screwed up her courage to approach Meghan, a senior. "Remember me?" she asked.

Meghan was rifling through her locker and glanced down at Eden, her eyes half closed. "The girl child Tony took notice of. I remember you."

Eden's mouth went dry. "I-I'm wondering about him. Who is he?"

"Someone you should avoid."

"No problem there. He hasn't said a word to me since that night of the party."

Meghan slammed the locker door. "Look, little girl, he's out of your league."

Eden tried again. "Why? Because he deals drugs? I know guys who deal," she said boldly, wanting to wipe the smug look off Meghan's face, wanting to let her know that Eden wasn't "a little girl" who could be dismissed like a bothersome fly.

Meghan snorted. "I'm just trying to do you a favor."

"I don't do anything I don't want to do," Eden snapped.

Meghan rested books on her hip and stepped backward down the hall. "Well, here's a news flash—Tony Cicero *is* a drug. Stay away from him. And his products. You've been warned now."

Ciana awoke with a start, found that the sky was streaking red in the east. She was covered with a blanket. Where was she? What had happened? She sat up and felt a pounding behind her eyes that hurt bad.

"Good morning," a deep male voice said.

She looked over, saw her green-eyed cowboy, and buried her face in her hands as the night before came flooding back to her. He was sitting on the grass beside her, a half smile on his face, which she noted was just as good-looking as it had been the night before beneath the stars when she'd had those margaritas.

"Did I stay out here all night?" Ciana was horrified.

"We did," Cowboy said. "I found an old horse blanket in the back of my truck and covered you. Hope that's all right and that you don't mind smelling like horse hair."

The scent of horse clung to the blanket's fibers. She rubbed her throbbing temples and cut her eyes sideways, a movement that sent pain knifing through her head.

"Headache?"

She closed her eyes, rubbing her temples. "More like a freight train." She shivered, wondering what had pooped in her mouth. She raised her head. "What happened?"

"You fell asleep while we were talking." He grinned broadly, showing dimples through the growth of stubble on his chin and jaw. "I don't usually have that effect on women."

His expression was teasing, but she groaned. "So nothing *happened.*" She emphasized the word.

He leaned forward. "Well, while you were sleeping, I kissed your eyelids."

A knot of anxiety began to unwind inside her.

His expression went serious. "But no, nothing happened that might make you want to slap me. You see, I want a woman to be aware of everything we're doing together."

Ciana's face went hot. "So now what?"

He stood, offered her his hand, and pulled her to her feet when she took it. "We get some breakfast and hot coffee. Then maybe we can pick up where we left off."

They spoke little on the ride to a diner not far from the dance saloon. Ciana hugged the door of his pickup and watched the sun rise through the windshield, her brain dull, her emotions raw. She'd made an idiot of herself the night before. At the diner, she made a beeline for the restroom, pausing just long enough to read a sign for taxi services in the hallway. She pulled out her cell and called the first number, ordering a cab to come pick her up at the diner's clearly posted address.

In the small restroom, she could hardly look at herself in the mirror. She washed her face with the dispenser soap, rubbing off every speck of eye shadow and smudged mascara. It was time her cowboy saw the real her. She tugged her fingers through her tangled nest of cinnamon-colored hair, found a squished scrunchie in her string purse, and made her usual ponytail.

When she settled at the table across from him, she saw mugs of steaming coffee and a plate of warm toast. If her fresh-scrubbed face startled him, he didn't show it. "I thought this might be a good start," he said. "I ordered fried eggs, bacon, grits, biscuits, and a short stack. You can order whatever you like."

Her stomach heaved and she grabbed the coffee, sipping the hot liquid. "Toast and coffee are fine."

His order arrived and she watched him smush the runny eggs into the grits and wished she hadn't. "Want a bite of pancakes?" he asked. "Real maple syrup."

"Don't think so." She glanced out the window, willing the cab to get there.

"Expecting someone?"

She felt her face redden. "I . . . I called a cab."

"I'll take you home." He looked insulted that she might have thought otherwise.

"I . . . um . . . don't live around here. Long drive to my place."

He reached over the top of the table and took her hand. "I want to see you again."

She couldn't imagine why.

After a few seconds of silence, he said, "That would require your name and phone number."

Just then, she saw the cab stop in front of the diner through the large plate glass window. She stood, ambivalent. Why shouldn't she give the information to him? She wanted to see him again too. "Um . . ." Her phone vibrated. "Let me get this," she told him, feeling the pressure of the cabby revving his engine. She took out her phone and saw that she had a text message from her mother. Great. Had Alice Faye called Eden looking for her? That was all she needed. She punched the button. The text read: OLIVIA RUSHED TO HOSPITAL. COME NOW.

Fear seized her. "Oh my God!"

"What's wrong?"

"I . . . I have to go!" She ran for the door, even as he called for her to wait up. Ciana jumped into the cab.

"Where to?" the cabby asked.

"Windemere."

"Whoa. That's a pretty expensive ride, lady."

Ciana dug into her string purse, found the hundred-dollar bill she'd brought to the dance hall but hadn't spent, and waved it under the driver's nose.

He pulled out of the diner's lot. She glanced out the back window to see her cowboy emerge from the diner. The cab gathered speed and he grew smaller and smaller as the distance widened between them. Ciana fought back tears—for Olivia, for the responsibilities resting on her shoulders, for having to leave such a man behind—but the spell was broken. She'd stayed too long at the ball.

# 6

"Where are you and why haven't you called me?" were the first words Ciana heard from Eden on Sunday afternoon when she answered her cell phone.

"I'm at the hospital," Ciana said.

"What? What happened last night after I left you? You said you were fine—"

"Calm down. I'm at the hospital because Olivia was brought in last night with pneumonia. She's really sick, Eden."

"I'll come right over."

"You don't have to—" But Ciana was talking to empty air.

Late afternoon sunlight shone through a window in Olivia's area of the ICU room and onto the overstuffed chair beside the bed. Ciana watched Olivia's chest rise and fall, listened to the rattle of her breath through the oxygen mask across her face. Her eighty-five-year-old grandmother looked frail. Her white hair, usually smooth and bright white, was a tangled yellowish mess, her cheeks were sunken, her hands spidery with blue veins. IV lines ran into the crook of her elbow, which was strapped down to the bed. Tears swam in Ciana's eyes. Olivia couldn't die. She just couldn't!

Ciana's earliest memories were of Olivia telling her family stories, her voice pouring over words like sweet cream, bringing long-dead ancestors to life in Ciana's imagination. She heard about how the great house had burned to the ground in the months following the Civil War, of how in the 1890s it was rebuilt brick by brick, board by board into the Victorian house they lived in today. Ciana learned why Beauchamp women kept the Beauchamp name even if they married. It was done as a pledge to Colonel Beauchamp made by his daughter, Madeline. When he lay in his bed passing from this world into the next, and with no sons to carry on the family name, Madeline swore that she and all future daughters would keep the name as their own whenever there were no male heirs.

Ciana smoothed the pale green sheets on Olivia's bed, folded her arms, and rested her head. She closed her eyes and drifted to the night before, to the cowboy who'd held her, kissed her, covered her with a blanket, to waking to his striking green eyes and to his voice saying, *"I kissed your eyelids."* She didn't even know his name, and yet last night had been magical, a fairy tale. She'd run away and left him, not leaving even a glass slipper behind. Gone without a trace.

"Ciana, wake up." A hand shook her shoulder.

Ciana startled awake and looked up at her mother. She blinked, disoriented, unsure of where she was until the hiss of oxygen brought her back to reality. "Mom."

"If you're that tired, go home. She's unconscious. There's nothing you can do for her. Get some rest and come back later." Alice Faye sounded as cross as the expression on her face. "You look a wreck. What exactly did you and Eden and Arie do last night?"

Ciana ignored her mother's question. "I'm not leaving, Mom. What if Grandmother wakes up and gets scared? She needs to see someone she knows."

Alice Faye wore no makeup except lipstick, and Ciana saw how age was creeping over her mother's face. She also saw Alice Faye's hands trembling. Her mother needed a drink. Ciana straightened. "Eden's on her way here. You go on home," she said quietly.

"You wouldn't mind?"

"I don't mind."

Alice Faye patted Olivia's hand, clouds of sadness forming in her eyes. "When Eden leaves, you come home," she said in a choked voice.

"She's not going to die," Ciana said, her chin trembling.

Alice Faye didn't meet Ciana's eyes as she left the room.

"How's she doing?" Eden asked as she breezed into the room.

Ciana looked up sadly.

Eden put her arm around Ciana's shoulder. "I'm really sorry. Take a break. Let's go down the hall for a minute to talk. I saw a visitor's area when I got off the elevator."

Ciana hesitated.

"We'll be steps away. Come on."

Ciana went, stopping to buy herself a soda before they sat down in padded chairs swimming in sunlight from a bank of windows.

"Tell me what's happened," Eden said. "Is she going to be all right?"

Ciana shrugged. "Don't know yet. It's a viral pneumonia."

Eden crossed her legs. "They'll take good care of her here. I'm betting she'll be fine."

"She'll just have to go back to Evergreen."

"It's a nice place," Eden said.

"It's not her home." Ciana ran her finger around the rim of the soda can. "She's had a hard life, you know."

Eden knew Olivia's history but waited for Ciana to reminisce.

"She had a baby when she was eighteen—Charles Junior—and then two miscarriages. Two! She told me nothing's sadder than burying an unborn baby. But her troubles weren't over."

Eden nodded sympathetically.

"Then when Charles Junior was just twelve, he was killed in a tractor accident. Granddad was out of town. He got home as soon as he could, but Grandmother was inconsolable. That boy was their pride and joy, their only child. And then he was gone in the blink of an eye." Ciana sniffed back tears.

"But next thing she knew, she had your mother," Eden interjected, trying to lift Ciana's spirits. "And your mother had you. So Olivia has lots of joy too. You're the light of her life."

Ciana offered a rueful laugh. "And haven't these last few years been a barrel of fun?"

Eden sure didn't want Ciana wandering down that road of memories. Nothing but feuding and fighting between Ciana and Alice Faye over Olivia's welfare. "Then tell me something fun. Tell me what happened last night. Did you have a good time?"

Ciana's mood lightened, and she smiled shyly. "I met a gorgeous cowboy from Texas. He . . . he was amazing."

"Did you . . . um . . . spend the night with him?"

"Yes, but not in the way you think. We sat out by the river. Talked. Kissed."

"And?"

"And I fell asleep."

Eden pushed back in her chair. "You're kidding."

"Woke up at sunrise covered with a blanket and him sitting next to me. So nothing happened." She shrugged self-consciously. "Seems he wasn't overly excited about having sex with an unconscious lump."

Eden laughed. "That's a good thing! A lot of guys would have. So he didn't jump you. Good for both of you. Then what happened? How did you leave him? How'd you get home?"

"We went to a diner for breakfast."

"Is he going to call you? You going to call him?"

Ciana said nothing.

Eden intuited the truth. "Please tell me you two traded phone numbers. You didn't, did you?" She remembered Ciana's protectiveness of her precious Beauchamp name. "Did you at least tell him your name? Your *whole* name?" Silence. "How did you figure some guy all the way from Texas might have known who you were? Osmosis?"

"It had nothing to do with me being cagey. I was going to tell him, but then I got Mom's text, freaked out, and split."

"How *did* you get home?"

"Taxi."

Eden whistled. "That couldn't have been cheap."

"Didn't matter. I had to get here."

"So you left him in the diner with no way for either of you to contact the other?"

Ciana picked at a hangnail.

Eden studied her. "All's not lost," she said brightly. "Just go back to the dance hall until you run into him again. I mean, if he's interested, that's where he'll go and hang out. Plus we owe Arie a trip."

Ciana felt a glimmer of hope. "Maybe so. Where is she anyway? I sent her a text but haven't heard from her."

"She called me early this morning. Said she'd be out at some ranch looking at horses."

"Why?"

"She wouldn't say. Wanted it to be a surprise."

Ciana rubbed her eyes, sighed, and stood. "I need to go back to Olivia's room."

"You need to let me take you home."

"In a little while."

They returned to the room where Olivia lay. Her eyes were open, and her gaze darted everywhere, looking panicked. Ciana rushed to the bedside and picked up Olivia's hand. "Grandmother! Don't be afraid. You're in the hospital. You're sick, but you're going to get well."

The old woman's eyes fastened on Ciana's face. She recoiled, snatching away her hand. "Who . . . who are you? I don't know you." Her voice was weak but her rebuff strong.

"It's me, Ciana."

Olivia shook her head. "No! My Ciana's just a child. A little child."

Ciana was speechless. Olivia Beauchamp's mind had retreated into the past, having forgotten the present completely, leaving grown-up Ciana and years of their lives together out in the cold.

# 7

It was him. Arie was sure of it. She watched the group of five men pointing and discussing the newly arrived wild horses inside the small corral. The men's backs were to her, but she was certain of the identity of the one in a black T-shirt and brown Stetson hat. It was Jon Mercer, five years older than the first time they'd met, but unmistakable. A girl didn't forget her first serious crush.

"What do you think?" her dad, Swede, asked in her ear. "Think you can choose a horse from this bunch?"

They were at Bill Pickins's cattle ranch, on the north side of town. Pickins owned acres of grazing land and raised some of the best beef cattle in the state. This year he'd experimented with bringing in a few wild mustangs from the Montana plains with the express purpose of training them for ranching work. Wild mustangs, rounded up by the government to be sold, weren't very expensive; plus they were smart and genetically sound because they'd not been overbred. They had what horse people called "good feet"—they were sure-footed and in general could work without being shod. Blacksmiths were scarce and expensive. The downside was that they were fresh off the plains and not used to men, ropes, and corrals. Breaking and training took investment money, but Pickins was betting he'd come out ahead financially in the long run.

Arie's gaze drifted to the untamed horses, their coats hot in the afternoon sun and dusty from the dry earth. "They're beautiful. How can I pick just one?"

"Well, that's why your present includes the trainer too—he'll help you choose a good one. Can't own a horse you can't ride."

Arie's heart swelled. This had been her gift from her family the night of the backyard barbeque days before. All of her family and relatives had chipped in to give Arie her lifetime dream—her own horse, a private trainer, six months of private boarding, feed, and tack. The gift was especially touching because many of her relatives weren't wealthy. Yet still they'd pooled their money toward her surprise. Pickins had agreed to let her have first choice of the mustangs. Her dad had insisted on driving her to check out the herd. She was grateful that all her relatives hadn't shown up for her big day.

"Let's go look at those horses," Swede said.

At the corral, Arie cut her eyes to Jon, wondering if he remembered her. She faced Bill Pickins, a big man in his sixties, his body as hard as rock, his skin leathered by years in the sun. His face lit up when he saw Arie, and he gave her a bear hug. "Hey, little lady! Here to take the pick of the litter from me?" his voice boomed.

She laughed. "I want them all!"

Swede shook Bill's hand. "How do they look after a trip across the country?" He gestured at the snorting horses, clumping in a tight protective circle inside the fenced area.

"Ask my trainer," Pickins said. "Jon, tell your pupil what you think about these horses."

"They look good, especially after the cross-country trip. They're strong. Used to free roaming and avoiding cougars and wolves since birth."

Arie's heart skipped a beat as Jon's gaze honed in on her. He grinned, touching the brim of his hat. She held out her hand and he shook it. "Arie Winslow. I think we met years ago."

His brow furrowed; then his grin widened. "I remember. You were a kid."

She felt heat crawl up her neck and face as she turned beet red. She hoped he didn't remember her mooning over him like a lovesick calf.

"She ain't a kid no more!" one of the men shouted. Pickins and the other men hooted. Her father saluted her.

Jon shook his head at the men, took her elbow, and walked her toward the stables. "Let's lose these guys."

She went happily, leaving her father to talk with the others. Once at the stables, they sat together on a long bench facing the corral. "So you're the trainer," she said.

"Hired for the summer," Jon said.

"You were seventeen when you showed up the last time."

"Visiting my dad. And you were . . . ?"

"Younger," she said quickly. "My dad was doing a carpentry project in the Pickins' house, so I hung around." On the days she didn't go to Ciana's or meet up with their newly acquired friend Eden, she'd come along with her dad to handle any odd job he needed doing. She hoped Jon didn't recall how she'd also haunted the stables just to catch glimpses of him.

"You'd been sick. Wore a baseball cap all the time. How are you now?"

"Better." She had worn the cap because her hair was regrowing and stuck up every which way.

"And so you're buying your own horse. Why a wild mustang?"

"I've been partial to them ever since I saw a TV documentary years ago."

"For riding?"

"Maybe a little competition in barrel racing. For fun and state fair prizes. Mostly for riding."

"So you can ride?"

"My friend Ciana taught me, and she lets me ride anytime I want on one of her family's horses."

"And how can I help?"

"Right this minute I want your advice on picking a good one. Then I need help breaking him to saddle. I love horses, but I need help training one."

He spun his hat in his hands. "Got to win his trust first. You'll have to work with your horse every day once we get started. I'll be by your side, but your horse needs to bond with *you*. It can be a slow process in the beginning, so plan on about an hour and a half every day—Sundays off—to come here and work with me. And plan to work on your own too; your horse needs to know you're the boss."

"Not a problem. I'll be here every day." She had planned to follow her doctor's instructions this summer—rest and rebuild her stamina, but now that a horse and Jon Mercer were in the picture, she was doubly motivated to regain the strength she'd lost during the last school year.

Jon flashed a heart-melting grin and stood. "Let's get started. Come to the corral and look at your choices. Tell me what you like."

At first, Arie saw only a sea of earthy colors, browns, reds, beiges, a streak of black, of manes and tails and head shaking, of hooves working up dust clouds, but slowly the mass took on distinction and differentiation. She watched for a while, then finally pointed toward a couple of the nervous animals. "That roan with the black tail looks good to me. And so does the gray one."

"Why?" Jon asked.

*Great*, she thought. *A quiz*. "I like the way they carry their heads. I think their necks look strong."

"Very good," Jon said. "It's a characteristic of sound mustang horseflesh. They're power horses; we call them 'hot bloods.' They can jump into action, run fast, are quick, and have light feet, making them good for speed events and for working cattle. My horse, Bonanza, is a quarter horse, bred for ranch work, but a well-trained mustang makes a great herd cutter. And barrel racer," he added with a wink.

Jon's knowledge impressed her, and so did his physical proximity. Bill and her dad had walked up to the house, so only she and Jon walked along the fence.

Jon gestured toward the animals. "You want to pick a horse that has a squarish shape, good legs, and a back long enough to hold a saddle. I'm going to cut the gray and the buckskin. When you come tomorrow, I'll do a hands-on check while you watch. I can tell a lot about a horse by going over him with my hands, make sure he's well composed all the way around. The key in choosing horseflesh is balance."

Arie's head was swimming by the time Jon told her goodbye for the day. She watched him walk off, her chest tight and her pulse light as air. She hunted down her dad and said she was ready to go home. On the drive back, he asked, "How'd it go?"

"Great. I should have a horse picked out soon, but Jon

wants me to come every day, early." Jon's time to train with Arie had to be early because he was Pickins's hire and had work to do with the other mustangs the rest of the day. She didn't care. She'd have met with him at midnight if he'd asked.

Arie wasn't like Ciana or Eden. She had to share a car with her mom. Eric had his own truck but acted as if it were a national treasure, so he rarely allowed Arie to drive it. All the way home, she stared out the car window, thinking about the horses but also about Jon Mercer. While years had passed since she'd last seen him, meeting him now and feeling the way she did when she was near him made her realize that her schoolgirl crush had not faded one tiny bit.

On Friday night, Arie met Eden and Ciana at a popular eatery on the outskirts of town, near the expressway. "Sorry I'm late," she said, sliding into the booth across from her two friends. A pitcher of sweet tea—the official drink of the South—sat on the table, already down by two glasses.

Eden poured Arie a glass. "How's the horse training coming along? Pick you a stud yet?"

"Nice backside?" Ciana asked. "Good chest?"

Arie had gone on and on about Jon to her two friends, so she had expected to be teased. She ignored their jibes and said, "Actually, my horse is a filly, and she's beautiful—a buckskin." The gray horse hadn't met Jon's high standards of confirmation. The smaller filly, the color of yellow sunshine with a black mane and tail and four black stockings and intelligent brown eyes, had won him. The idea that Jon had chosen the horse just for her made the animal more special.

"You name her yet?" Ciana asked.

"Caramel."

"Like candy?" Eden asked.

"She looks yummy enough to eat," Arie said.

"Sounds as if her trainer does too," Ciana said, which made Arie blush and her two friends laugh and exchange smug looks.

"Funny," Arie said coolly.

"So, I guess you'll spend the summer training." Ciana scooped a tortilla chip through warm cheese sauce. "What about you?" she asked Eden.

"I'll be staying at the boutique. You?"

"The usual—planting, plowing, and mowing. Horses have to eat, and so do Mom and I."

"What about you?" Arie asked Eden.

"I'm going somewhere. *Anywhere*. Just as long as I can see this town in my rearview mirror."

"You'd leave your friends?" Arie feigned hurt feelings.

"Sacrifices must be made." Eden nibbled on a chip. "And you? If you weren't 'training,' I mean," she asked Arie.

"The art museums of Europe, but that's been my wish for years and you both know it."

"Good thing you have a distraction," Ciana said. "The trainer, not the horse."

Eden giggled.

Arie said, "How did I get two such funny friends?"

"Luck?" Eden ventured.

Arie said, "Well, before you two jokers get too busy, I want you to come out to the Pickins ranch and see my horse. And I want you to meet Jon Mercer. He's so gorgeous you'll both start drooling, but just remember, he's mine. I saw him first." She looked upward dreamily. "I think I'm in love."

"Or in heat," Ciana joked. Eden and she slapped high fives.

Arie shook her head. "Why do I put up with this abuse?"

A waitress stopped to take their order, and Arie opted for

soup. As soon as the waitress left the table, Arie said, "Can you come tomorrow? You don't have to show until nine-thirty. I want you to see Jon and Caramel with your own eyes and become very jealous of my good luck."

Both girls agreed.

"How's Olivia?" Eden asked Ciana.

"She's out of the hospital and back at Evergreen. I never thought I'd be glad to see her there again, but I am. She's alive. That's all that matters."

"Does she recognize you?" Eden asked.

"Sometimes she's her old self, sitting in bed and chatting me up. Other times she thinks I'm an imposter because Ciana is 'a little girl.' I never know what to expect when I visit her. I never know how much time she has left."

Arie identified with Ciana's emotions. Having cancer had often made her feel the finiteness of life. "She's tough. And so are you."

Ciana offered a grateful look.

Arie spent the week in a small corral with Jon by her side and calling to Caramel by name. The horse refused to go near them. "Get her used to her name," Jon told Arie. "Our goal is for her to come to you when you call her out. Working in this small space doesn't give her many options."

At first Caramel turned her backside to them. "When she does that, wave your arms and chase her away. She'll tire of being run off. Eventually she'll move toward you. It's called 'facing up.' I know shooing her away doesn't make sense, but it works. Horses are curious. Soon enough she'll wonder why you don't want to look at her rear end."

They wrapped the Saturday morning session just as Eden

drove up to the stables. Ciana was close behind in her old pickup. "Here they come," Arie told Jon, frustrated over not making much headway with Caramel, who stood in the corral staring at the commotion of vehicles and people. "Now she looks," Arie grumbled.

He laughed. "She's stubborn, but you're going to win the war."

Eden arrived first and Arie hugged her, then pointed excitedly at her horse. Ciana hurried up to the group. At that moment, Jon Mercer turned and looked straight at Ciana, and Ciana felt all the color drain from her face and her breath stop moving in her chest.

# 8

Moments moved like glaciers. For Ciana, time stood still. Arie's love interest was Ciana's cowboy, the man she'd left standing outside a diner after one unforgettable night. Memories rushed her like floodwaters, memories of kisses, of touching and holding on to one another's bodies, of waking with him near her in a cool fresh dawn. Jon's expression went from genial to stunned surprise.

"—my best friends."

Arie's voice broke through the ice of silence and snapped Ciana into the present.

Jon turned to Eden and touched the brim of his hat. When he turned to Ciana, his eyes grew wary, unsure. "Ciana Beauchamp," he said, repeating her name as Arie had introduced her. "It's so nice to have a name to put with a face."

Ciana caught the put-down aimed at her and tried to warn him with a look that begged, *Say nothing! Please, act like you don't know me. Act like we've never met.*

Eden said, "Don't you mean a face to put with a name?"

"Sorry," Jon said. "Us Texas boys sometimes get things bass-ackwards." He must have gotten her silent message because he turned abruptly toward the corral. "What do you two think of Arie's horse?"

Everyone's attention diverted and Ciana could have kissed Jon. Or not. Not ever again.

"Isn't she something else?" Arie asked, apparently oblivious to what had passed between Ciana and Jon.

"She's amazing," Ciana said, careful not to glance at Jon. "Does this mean you're leaving Sonata for another?"

Arie touched Ciana's arm. "Break it to her gently, all right?"

They laughed, Ciana perhaps too hardily for the humor of the joke.

To Jon, Arie said, "Ciana's the friend I told you about who lets me ride one of her horses. She has a huge farm on the other side of town—Bellmeade."

"Horses are better riding than tractors," Jon said with a curt nod.

His comment made no sense to anyone except Ciana. She jogged to the fence and with trembling knees clambered up and honed in on the buckskin filly. The horse turned her rump toward them.

"Not very friendly," Eden said, climbing beside Ciana and leaning over the top fence rail. She wasn't a horse fan like her friends.

"We're working on that," Arie said, joining them on the fence. She whistled and called out to Caramel, but the horse ignored her.

"She's got a mind of her own," Jon said from the ground below them. "Just goes her own way whenever she wants."

Ciana winced at his double meaning and the barb aimed at her. She and Eden fussed over the animal, then jumped down.

Ciana steadied herself and faced Jon with Arie standing close to his side. They made a nice couple, Arie with her white-blond hair and blue eyes, Jon with brown hair, streaked gold by the sun and his bright green eyes. She looked at her watch. "Oops! I have to run. Promised Olivia I'd stop off for a visit."

Eden said, "Ugh! I have to go into the boutique. Our busiest day and Patty, my coworker, called in sick."

"But you two just got here," Arie said, sounding hurt. "I was hoping you could stay longer, watch me work some with Caramel."

"Sorry," Ciana said. "Come over later, all right?"

Jon glanced down at Arie. "Lunch?"

She looked surprised but delighted by the invitation. "Love to."

Ciana turned on her heel, her emotions reeling, and headed to her truck. "See you later," she called, more sociably than she felt.

Behind her, she heard Jon say, "Count on it."

---

Ciana never knew what to expect that afternoon at the Evergreen Assisted Living Center. Would she see lucid Olivia or childlike Olivia? She wasn't sure she could face Olivia's rejection today. Not after what she'd already faced at Pickins's. Seeing Jon had been like seeing a ghost. Except that he was real. And she was real. And Arie was real. And now Ciana faced choices—of desire and loss.

On the drive to Evergreen, she'd kept the truck radio blaring to force away the enduring image of Jon's green eyes appraising her. She had parked, rubbed her temples. After signing in, she gathered her courage and breezed into Olivia's room with a cheerful, "Hello, Grandmother."

Olivia was sitting in a wheelchair in front of a small desk, her laptop in front of her. She looked up, offering a beatific smile. "Ciana, darling. How wonderful to see you. Come kiss me. Why have you stayed away for so ever long?"

Of course, Ciana had been there the day before, and every day since Olivia had been out of the hospital. Relieved by Olivia's greeting, Ciana swept over, bent down, and kissed her papery cheek. "Forgive me," Ciana said, which was easier than reminding Olivia about what she couldn't remember.

"I always forgive you, precious girl," Olivia purred in her honeyed voice. "Barry Boatwright was just here. Perhaps you saw him in the parking lot?"

"Your attorney? But why?"

"The family attorney," Olivia corrected. "I had some family business I wanted him to attend to."

Ciana wasn't sure if Boatwright had actually been visiting or if Olivia had conjured him out of her imagination. "I must have missed him." She settled into a comfy chair beside the desk. She had known the elderly white-haired man since she was a small child. He never seemed to change.

"We discussed paperwork." Boatwright had handled Bellmeade business for many years—bookkeeping, taxes, necessary government subsidy paperwork. Much of the farm's acreage had once successfully been leased to other growers, but now because of the economic hard times, vegetable planting had fallen off, and so had the leases.

"What business?"

"Oh, child, a farm the size of ours doesn't run by itself."

Ciana needed no reminder. She seeded, fertilized, fought weevil infestations, and harvested alfalfa four times a year to feed their horses. The grass had to dry free of mold and dust and then be bundled into manageable bales and stored under tarps in an outbuilding as winter feed. In summer the horses grazed in the pastures, their diets supplemented by alfalfa hay for necessary protein, but the winter months meant a lot more hay and grain—which had to be bought. The back acre garden fed herself and Alice Faye, and Ciana sold any excess to tourists at the summer farmer's market. She kept the property surrounding the house and stables mowed and trimmed and the chicken coop well maintained, and she made any necessary minor repairs to equipment, fencing, and damaged outbuildings. All hard work and long days.

"Mama and I are watching over the land," she assured Olivia.

Olivia dismissed the remark with a hand gesture. "Alice Faye never gave a hoot for the business end of Bellmeade. But when school's over for you . . ." She seemed to lose her train of thought. Alice Faye had brought Olivia to Ciana's high school graduation, but apparently she didn't remember it.

"High school's over," Ciana said quickly to fill the awkward silence. "Got my diploma too."

Olivia nodded, her expression clouding, as if trying to see something that wasn't quite clear enough. *Don't go away.* Ciana hoped Olivia hadn't slipped into another time and place, but Olivia smiled suddenly, returning to the moment. "You'll go to college. Vanderbilt, is it?"

"I've been accepted."

"Of course you have. You're a Beauchamp." Olivia made it sound as if the name were a free pass to all of life.

"Has Mother been by today?" Again Ciana changed the topic quickly, hoping to keep Olivia in the present.

"My daughter only comes out of duty."

"Mother loves you," Ciana said.

"Like a dog loves a master who doesn't kick it."

Friction was a constant between the two women, a subtle undercurrent that ran like a fault line through a piece of property. "Mom works with me in our garden every day. Tomatoes are popping off the vines, squash is ripe, and green beans are climbing up their poles."

"I miss our garden," Olivia said.

Schoolwork never gave Ciana the sense of achievement a vegetable harvest gave her. "Why, Mama's canning tomatoes and squash once a week," Ciana told her grandmother. In the kitchen, making breads and pastry, whipping up meals was as close to happy as Ciana ever saw her mother.

Olivia reached over and took Ciana's hand. "I'm tired, child. Could you help me to my bed?"

Ciana jumped up, rolled the wheelchair to the bed, and locked the brake. She helped Olivia stand and then half lifted her into the bed. She fluffed the pillows and made sure the covers were all smooth and tucked. "Snug as a bug," she said, quoting what her grandmother had often told her at bedtime when she was a child.

Ciana straightened, but Olivia held tightly to her hand. "Don't leave just yet."

Did Olivia sense that these rare moments of lucidity were as precious as gold to both of them? "I won't leave. I know," she added with an inspired smile. "Why don't I snuggle with you and you tell me a story."

The old woman's eyes brightened. "What story would you like to hear?"

Anxious to hold on to the moment, Ciana suggested Olivia's favorite. "Tell me about how you met Grandfather."

Olivia beamed. "A wonderful story. Haven't I told it to you before?"

"Not lately." Ciana got on top of the covers, lying on her

side so she could watch Olivia's face. "Did you always know you loved him?" She knew the answer but still wanted to hear it.

"From the very moment we laid eyes on each other. When he emerged from his car, when our eyes met, the earth moved. And I knew then and there, he was the one."

Caught up in the spell of the story, Ciana hungered to feel such certainty. Perhaps she'd come close one summer night weeks before. *Close only counts in horseshoes*, she thought automatically. Farm people were practical, even Beauchamp girls who met a stranger in a dance hall and fell into a fantasy.

Olivia's creamy voice spilled over words in Ciana's ear. "But the day he rode up Bellmeade's driveway on horseback to claim me . . . well, I can see him still on that sleek chestnut Tennessee walking horse, saddlebags heavy with apples he would lay at my feet, his offering for my hand, his pledge of his undying love."

# 9

"Well, look what the cat dragged in."

Eden rushed through the living room on her way to her upstairs bedroom, scowling but ignoring her mother's put-down. "Not now. I have to change for work." The trip to see Arie's horse had put her off schedule. She usually left Tony's apartment early enough to arrive home before Gwen woke up, although after a year, it was no secret where she spent most Friday nights.

She made it to the staircase when Gwen announced, "Store manager called me in. I'm at the registers until four today."

The grocery store often used Gwen to fill in their schedule when others didn't show up for their shifts. At least she was back on her meds and could handle the job. "Work strong," Eden said, with more sarcasm than necessary.

Gwen exhaled a mouthful of cigarette smoke as Eden crossed to the stairs. "You need to stay away from that guy you're with. He's nothing but bad news."

Eden jerked to a halt. "I said not now." She took the stairs two at a time, ripping off her T-shirt. In her room, she pulled off her jeans and pawed through her closet. Everything was dirty or at Tony's.

"I'll put in a load of wash before I leave," Gwen said from the doorway.

Eden hadn't realized that her mother had followed her up. "Forget it. I lost a good white shirt last time when you stuck it in with a red towel."

"So you want me to do laundry but get mad at me when I do it. Which way do you want it, Eden?"

Over her shoulder, she shot, "Please don't smoke in my room." After a sniff test, one shirt passed and Eden flung it on. She grabbed a long multicolored skirt.

"Well, excuse me, missy. Didn't mean to pollute *your* air." Gwen grabbed a half-finished and forgotten cola bottle from Eden's bedside table and poked her cigarette through the opening in the neck. The cigarette sizzled in the brown liquid and fizzled out. "And stop ignoring me. You prance in and out of here like it's a motel instead of your home. The only time I can talk to you is between your run-throughs!"

Eden, in front of her dresser mirror, smoothed powder blush over her cheeks and gloss on her lips. She bit back a bitter torrent of words about her and Gwen's relationship. "What have we got to talk about? You only gripe at me."

"I'm trying to help you. Warn you. What do I have to say to get through to you? Tony Cicero is a user of people who will eat you alive. Get away from him. Far, far away from him."

"You don't know him! You've talked to him, what, six or seven times over the last two years?"

"I know his type," Gwen said over Eden's voice. "He's a control freak, and he'll keep his thumb on you until he squashes you."

"Stop it! Stop running him down." Eden shook her hair-brush at her mother. "He's good to me. I have a car because of him. I have pretty jewelry."

Gwen crossed her arms and looked at Eden with eyes hard as marbles. "So, then, what does that make you?"

Eden froze. "Did you just call me a slut?"

Gwen's lips pressed into a thin line. "His gifts are just another way of locking you into him. Buy your own car and jewelry. Believe me, it'll be a whole lot cheaper in the long run."

Eden slung the hairbrush across the room, not directly at her mother but near enough to make Gwen flinch. The brush dented the wall over the bed and dropped harmlessly onto the pillows. "You're not exactly mother of the year," she growled. "And you lecture me? You who can't stay on your medications long enough to give me a life? To raise me? You judge *me*?"

Gwen didn't blink, just plowed ahead. "I'm trying to save you. Trying to help you see—"

"Don't!" Eden yelled. She picked up her purse, brushed past Gwen, and clattered down the uncarpeted stairs in her clogs.

Once in her car, Eden screeched out of the driveway backward and onto the road. Brakes squealed from behind and a driver sat on his horn. She was beyond caring. She held the steering wheel in a death grip. The car was unmercifully hot. She cranked up the AC, pushed her curling hair off her forehead, and struggled to calm herself. She was furious at her mother, but not just because of their fight. Eden would rather chew off her arm than admit to Gwen that she was correct. Tony was all the things she'd said and was getting worse. He wanted an accounting of Eden's every move, a timeline for everything she did when she wasn't with him, and he wanted her with him constantly. He wanted more and more of her, while she wanted him less and less, and she didn't know what to do about it.

It hadn't always been this way. Two years before, the first time she'd taken out Tony's card with his cell number handwritten on the back, when Gwen had left her alone and she was struggling not to take out a razor blade and slice a fine thin line across her upper thigh, *that* was all on her. She should never have punched in his number that night, never opened the door and let him in. But she had. As he once promised, he'd driven over immediately and picked her up.

"Would you take me to my friend Ciana's place?" she had asked timidly.

"No. I'm taking you to my place."

A shiver of fear shot through her.

As if he'd felt it, Tony reached over and squeezed her hand in her lap. "Don't worry. No ulterior motives. We'll order in some pizza, watch a DVD. Sound good?"

She nodded, unsure of her voice. At least he wasn't poking at her to spill her guts about what was wrong. She couldn't have told him if he had asked. Panic attacks had no reasons sometimes—they just seized her.

His condominium was on the outskirts of town, in a newly constructed complex that had risen out of the land almost overnight, built to attract an overflow of Murfreesboro and Nashville commuters. The gated community had every amenity—pool, gym, business center, party rooms—and Tony lived on the top floor in one of the five buildings. He'd taken over two condos, where he'd knocked out walls and lived in absolute luxury. At that time, she hadn't thought that his lifestyle was financed by drug deals. She'd just been awed by the sheer grandeur of his world. Now, at almost twenty-six, he was wealthy beyond her imagination, and she was the focus of his undivided attention.

That first night they ordered pizza and watched a DVD. Harmless. Calming. She had no thoughts of cutting. No pressure from Tony for anything except her company. The evening was repeated the second time she called and he picked her up. Also the third. She began to call more often, began to lean on him, depend on him to rescue her from her dark spells. At first Arie and Ciana were happy for her. "A big-time boyfriend at sixteen," Arie had sighed. "I can't get a guy's interest with a flügelhorn."

Eden and Ciana had cracked up. Then Ciana had asked, "He seems a little old for you, don't you think?"

"Princess Diana was twelve years younger than Prince Charles," Eden said defensively.

"And look how that ended," Ciana fired back.

"Now you two stop it," Arie had interjected. "Eden's smart enough to look out for herself. Aren't you, girlfriend?"

Of course, Eden hadn't shared Tony's "business" venture with them; she didn't dare. Ciana would probably call the police, and Arie, the peacemaker, would be horrified. At that time, Eden was starry-eyed over Tony.

These days, Eden missed being with her friends more than she could say, but if she complained, Tony would say, "Aren't I enough for you? Tell me what you want, and it's yours."

What she wanted, he wouldn't give her. Her world grew smaller. Seeing Arie's horse inside the fenced corral made Eden see that she, too, was fenced in by Tony. Her senior year at school had been like walking a tightrope, balancing classes, activities, friendships, and Tony. Along the way, she'd given in and began spending Friday nights at Tony's apartment. It was easier than bucking him.

With a start, Eden realized she had arrived downtown at the boutique. She didn't even remember the drive. She parked quickly, locked her car, and hurried inside the store.

"About time," the manager said. "I'm starving and need to go to lunch."

"Sorry." Eden slipped on her employee tag that read HI! I'M EDEN. "Busy this morning?"

"A little," the manager said, meaning *Not so much.*

"Off to lunch with you. I'll hold back the crowds." Her stomach growled, reminding Eden she'd missed lunch altogether.

The manager huffed her way out the door and Eden stuck out her tongue at the woman's back. Alone in the store, Eden straightened clothing on hangers. She couldn't get the fight with Gwen off her mind. The words reverberated: *"I know his type. He's controlling and demanding."* How did she *know* men like Tony? She never dated or brought men to the house, although Eden had no way of knowing what Gwen did whenever she left town. She could be turning tricks in strange cities for all she knew.

In the silence of the store, she thought back to the night Tony moved on her. She had been barely sixteen. The pizza was eaten, the movie over. He had poured her a glass of wine, something he'd not done previously. "It's a great vintage," he said. "I want to share it with someone special. You."

She sipped the wine, and like Goldilocks, found it just right, not too tart, not too sweet. She felt grown up. "I've never liked wine very much," she told him, not confessing she had never liked any wine she and Ciana had sneaked from Bellmeade's liquor cabinets.

"That's because you've never drunk fine wines. This is a French vintage, one of the best."

He topped her glass and she drank deeply, feeling the silky liquid warm her throat. "Yummy."

The edges of the room turned softer. Tony took the glass, set it on his glass-topped coffee table, and leaned forward. "I want to kiss you."

As warm and pliable as she felt just then, she wanted him to kiss her, had wanted him to kiss her for weeks. His mouth found hers and in seconds the warm places inside her heated by the wine blossomed. His mouth trailed her neck, teased at her throat. Her arms wound around his neck. His hand drifted to her breast. "May I?" he asked, touching the top button of her shirt.

In minutes, her shirt was off and his hands were sliding over her, heating her body on the outside as the wine heated her from within. Her mind gave itself over to feeling, allowing his hands and fingers and mouth full privilege to her bare skin. When his tongue touched her breast, she trembled. She didn't want him to stop. He did. Her eyes flew open. Had she done something wrong?

"Come with me," he said. He rose from the sofa and led her into another room that smelled of sandalwood and was filled with soft music. Banks of candles glowed on every flat surface, dancing flames that filled the darkness of his luxurious bedroom. He laid her on the bed's silk sheets, stood over her, and began to remove his own shirt. "I won't hurt you. If you want me to stop, say so."

She did not want him to stop, would not have been able to utter the words necessary to stop the exquisite pain that exploded into pleasure and sent her spinning into ecstasy and dependency on that night she first melded into Tony Cicero.

In the beginning she felt euphoric. Tony loved her. She loved him. He met her every need. They laughed. They played. They made love. It took over a year before she began to notice subtle changes in his behavior toward her. Possessiveness. Jealousy. Flares of anger she didn't see coming and didn't deserve. Thinking back to that first night in his bedroom, she slowly realized that the candles had been lit before she ever arrived, the sheets smoothed in expectation, music chosen with a purpose. She had gone to him willingly. She had given him all of herself, fallen into his well-planned and beautifully orchestrated seduction that over time became a free fall into a golden cage more binding than an umbilical cord, more tangled than the bonds of years-long friendships.

In the silence of the deserted boutique, Eden remembered her journey with Tony while she toyed with a letter opener. He discovered she was a cutter. He had forbidden her to cut, and she hadn't for a long time. But for weeks now, her long-held need for him, her hunger, had diminished.

Eden studied the silver tip with a detached curiosity. Would it feel the same as it used to? Would it fill the scared places inside her like it had before? With a single strong thrust, she jabbed the dull point into the underside of her arm and cried out, then endured the pain, standing still as her heartbeat slowed. She watched as bright red blood dripped from the wound and ran down her milky skin like swollen crimson tears.

She wanted her freedom.

# 10

"Ciana! I'm here!" Arie hopped down from the cab of her brother's bright red truck. She wove a path through a maze of wooden booths to where Ciana was loading unsold garden produce into the bed of her old farm truck. "Can I help?"

"All done." Ciana slammed the tailgate shut. "How'd you and your horse do today?"

Arie grimaced. "Caramel hates me."

"You're exaggerating."

"Maybe a little. She does fine with the halter and lead rope but will not come when I call her if she's in the main pasture. If Jon starts her off in the small corral, she'll come to us in her own sweet time, but if she's in the big pasture, no way. Stubborn beast."

Ciana laughed. "Horses can be headstrong. You've only been at it a few weeks. You'll eventually win the war of wills."

"Plus," Arie added with a pout, "she likes Jon better than me. Can't blame her for that, I guess."

Ciana opened the driver's door of her beat-up truck. "Hop in. We'll drop off these vegetables at the community kitchen and then go to lunch."

Arie climbed into the passenger seat, still talking. "You know, I've wanted a horse all my life, and now that I have one, I'm finding I want the trainer more."

Ciana's eyes cut sideways. "I can't believe you're picking a summer cowboy over a horse!"

"And you wouldn't? Jon's fantastic!"

Ciana had no answer for that.

As they drove into town, down Windemere's main street, Arie pointed to the banners strung high between traffic lights heralding the town's upcoming Wild West Days and the July rodeo. "Jon says he's going to enter. Calf roping and broncos too."

"Guy could get hurt riding bulls and broncos," Ciana muttered.

"He doesn't seem to mind." Arie turned to Ciana. "I registered to ride in the opening parade, but I'll have to borrow Sonata like I used to."

"Of course you can ride Sonata. I have a new bling jacket and boots, and I'm using Grandfather's fancy Mexican saddle."

"Mom hot-glued rhinestones and fancy emblems on an old denim jacket she bought off the kid racks at Goodwill for me. I can't seem to put on any weight."

"Some of us wouldn't consider that a curse."

Arie sighed. "Some of us do."

After the produce was unloaded at the community kitchen by two men who were somehow related to Arie, Ciana parked on Main Street, which was full of tourists in town for the upcoming rodeo. "It's hot," she said to Arie. "If you don't feel like walking to Southern Fixin's, I can drop you off and come back and park."

"Stop treating me like an invalid." Arie slammed the truck door for emphasis.

"Excuse me," Ciana countered. "Just trying to be nice."

"You worry too much," Arie added, regretting her sharp tone. "I'm fine. Really."

They walked along the sidewalk, dodging tourists, kids, and baby strollers, passing the general store, the hardware store, Johnson's feed store, Bennet's Tractor and Mower, and the boutique where Eden worked. Arie stopped, cupped her hand to the plate-glass window, and peered inside. "I don't see her. Did you invite her to lunch with us?"

"Course. She said she was doing something with Tony," Ciana said, moving on. "I really don't like that guy."

Arie fell into step beside her. "So you've said. Often. He does monopolize every bit of her time. I'm beginning to get a complex."

"I don't get it. She's always acted so independent. Remember meeting her in middle school? How shocked we were when we found out her mother would leave her alone for weeks at a time?"

Arie would never forget. She and Ciana insisted she stay at one of their houses, telling their mothers that Eden's mother traveled for her work and that they didn't want her to be alone. They kept Eden's secret about Gwen's illness and about Eden's tendency to cut herself. Their families didn't need to know everything. "At first," Arie said, "I thought Tony was good for her, but now not so much."

Ciana said, "She's done a total turnaround. Now whatever Tony wants, he gets. I'm telling you, that's not normal."

"She says she loves him."

Ciana snorted. "Doesn't look like love when someone's got you under his thumb. And what's with the guys who hang out with him? They're big enough to eat hay."

It was true that two hulking men followed Tony like menacing guard dogs. They gave Arie the creeps. Suddenly she stopped in front of the window of the town's small travel agency/real estate office. "Look." She pointed to a large vacation placard that read SEE ITALY! STAY IN TUSCANY. VISIT ROME. THE TRIP OF A LIFETIME! "Now, that would be my dream vacation."

Ciana said, "Tuscany—Mom read a book about that place, said it sure made Italy sound wonderful."

"Wouldn't you like to go there?"

"I don't think so. Too far away. Plus, who'd take care of Bellmeade? And who speaks Italian?"

"They speak English too," Arie said with a laugh. "Milan is all about fashion. And Rome," Arie sighed. "Think of the history! And the art! I'd love, love, love to go."

Ciana studied the poster. "Maybe someday."

"Well, it sounds romantic to me." Arie stole a glance at her friend. "If I tell you something, will you promise not to laugh?"

Ciana raised her hand. "Scout's honor."

"Last October, when I turned eighteen, I filled out the forms and paid for a passport."

Despite her pledge, Ciana laughed.

"You promised."

"I'm laughing because I have a passport too. Olivia insisted. Said I should go visit the Beauchamp clan in France someday before real life rolled over me. But I still don't have a notion to go to Europe."

Arie rolled her eyes. "But college, living at home, studying art and history from books instead of up close and personal is in my future."

They walked on, then entered the restaurant where several patrons and waitresses waved to them. They took a small café table for two near the window. "At least you're going away to college," Arie said.

"Nashville. Hardly far."

A waitress came to their table and smiled. "Hey, Arie, Ciana. What can I get ya?"

They placed an order without bothering with a menu, and after the waitress walked off, Arie said, "That's Martha Ellen, one of my cousins."

"Who isn't one of your cousins?" Ciana deadpanned.

"How's Olivia?"

Ciana's good mood darkened. "Weaker, and more and more lost in a world of her own making. Her heart's having a problem too. Docs have her on all kinds of medicine."

Arie understood the mortality factor better than most. "Well, she may have memory and health problems, but she's still kicking, so don't go dwelling on what hasn't happened. One day at a time, remember?"

"I know, but I miss her. I hate seeing her deteriorate."

"You've still got your mama."

Ciana sighed. "But it was Olivia who taught me how to farm, gave me life rules to follow. She taught me how to make sweet tea in the antique glass pitcher when I was eight. When I was nine, Mom taught me how to measure out a jigger of gin and pour it into her glass with tea and lemon and fresh mint. She still likes it that way."

Arie hurt for her friend. Her own mother was guilty of

"smother-love," but Arie had always known that Patricia would storm the gates of hell for Arie's sake. She slapped the edge of the table, making Ciana jump. "You need a boyfriend."

"Are you joking? A guy is going to make my life better? How?"

"Not just any guy. The right guy."

"No such thing."

"You're a cynic. I just know that ever since I've been around Jon Mercer, my outlook's changed. I look forward to starting every day because I'm going to be near him. He makes my heart happy."

"Endorphins," Ciana insisted, biting into the sandwich just placed in front of her.

"It's beyond chemistry, Ciana Beauchamp. I'm crazy for him. And you'll feel different when the right one comes along for you. Wait and see."

Ciana got a look in her eyes that made Arie stop talking. She asked, "What? Have you met someone?"

"Once," Ciana confessed, without meeting Arie's insistent gaze. "One night, one magical night." Her face reddened. She looked contrite, as if she'd said far more than she'd meant to. "But it can never work out for him and me."

"How do you know? Is he with someone else? You need to fight for him." She straightened as a thought occurred to her. "He . . . he isn't married, is he?"

Ciana laughed outright. "No way. But he is off-limits. I never should have said anything. It's over anyway."

Arie was intrigued. As far as Arie knew, her friend had never even had a serious crush. "Tell me about him. And what makes him off-limits?"

"It's history," Ciana told her, with a smile that intrigued Arie all the more.

"But—"

Ciana tossed her napkin onto the table. "Right now, I need to go over to Evergreen for my daily visit. Come on, I'll run you home first." She moved toward the door.

Arie jumped up, scrambled after her, bewildered by Ciana's refusal to talk about the guy she'd met. They'd been friends forever, and Ciana had shared the secrets of her heart many times over the years. Why wasn't she sharing now? When had this happened? Why was this a secret?

"Keys, please," Arie asked, coming into the kitchen, where Eric sat hunched over a bowl of breakfast cereal and the sports section of the newspaper.

"What for?"

"Hello. Art day at the children's hospital in Nashville, same as always. You told me I could take your truck last Monday."

Eric groaned. "You still doing that?"

"Twice a month every summer for the past two years." When she was seventeen, Arie had volunteered to lead drawing and painting classes on the children's oncology floor two Saturdays a month. Even while she was going through chemo herself, sick and frail, she'd held the classes. And if a child was too sick to get out of bed and meet in the recreation area, Arie went to the patient's room and gave a private class, because the real value of the work lay in helping kids express in their art what they might not be able to say with words about having cancer.

"When will you be home?" Eric grumbled. "I have a date with Abbie."

Arie crossed her arms and tapped her toe. "Has Abbie ever seen you first thing in the morning, Grumpy?"

"Don't be so nosy."

Arie paused, studied her brother. "You love that girl, don't you?"

"Whoa!" Eric said. "Where'd that come from? You know I don't use the L-word for any reason except when I'm talking about my truck and Tennessee football."

Arie smirked. Eric had serial dated over the years. Abbie held him spellbound. The whole family was talking about the two of them. "I'm sure Abbie will be thrilled to know you prefer two inanimate objects over her."

Eric dropped the paper onto the table and peered up at his sister. "Is this bashing going someplace, Sis?"

"Not a bashing, Bro. Maybe just a wake-up call. If you love this girl, don't put off telling her."

"You're not the boss of me," he mumbled under his breath, something they used to say to each other as kids. But his face was beet red, so she knew she'd scored points.

She wiggled her fingers. "Keys."

Eric dug into the pocket of his jeans and dangled the truck keys on the end of his forefinger. "You park way in the back lot away from other cars. I don't want some idiot dinging up my paint with his car doors."

Arie snatched the keys, bowing. "Grasshopper will walk a mile to protect precious red paint."

He made a move to grab and tickle her, but she scampered to the side door. He grinned, calling out, "And only put high-octane gas in it too."

"I'll leave it as I got it," she called out. The door slammed behind her, and she dashed to the shiny red truck.

As Arie drove the fifty-two miles to the hospital in Nashville, she engaged in her favorite pastime—daydreaming about Jon Mercer and how much she liked him and wanted to be with him. She'd been infatuated before, but what she felt for Jon was different. She hadn't exaggerated when she'd told Ciana that being with him had given her life an amazing jolt. Jon was physical perfection, but he was also kind and gentle to his core. The way he handled horses, with both firmness and affection, gave her insights into his nature. She knew that she was falling hopelessly in love with him. Before, she had been some crush-addled preteen. Now she was a grown woman living her life on the edge of eternity, and Jon was the embodiment of all she wanted in a man.

The choke hold of having cancer had created deep insecurities in Arie. With each relapse had come new fears, escalating from *Who will be my friends?* to *What guy will ever kiss me?* to *What man will ever want me?* She already knew she could easily love Jon Mercer for the rest of her life. The unknown was, could he love her? She didn't ever think about how long she'd live.

A horn honked and Arie startled, realizing that she'd been so deep in thought that she was drifting into the other lane on the expressway. She snapped upright and pushed the gas pedal, and the truck's powerful engine shot the vehicle forward and back into her lane. Lordy, if she wrecked Eric's precious truck, she'd be banished to Alaska!

At the hospital, she found a parking space way back in a corner of the lot. Inside she rode the elevator up to Pediatric Oncology and stepped out in front of the nurses' station, where the busy RNs warmly greeted her. Ruth said, "Your budding artists are waiting in the rec room."

"Any new faces?"

"Cory's back."

Arie's heart squeezed. She'd first met Cory a year before, when he'd been five, a beautiful little boy with a rare form of leukemia. His mother was a famous country singer, using the code name of "Lotty Jones" to help protect her identity from a prying press. The media hounded her constantly, and she wanted Cory to escape them and any lurid tabloid headlines they would create. Cory had taken to Arie immediately because she liked to draw and paint and so did he. He drew well for such a young child, especially fanciful creatures from outer space.

The pediatric floor was clean and bright with colorful walls and white and yellow floor tiles, laid out like the yellow brick road to Oz. Every room door was painted a different and vibrant shade. Arie breezed into the rec room, which was flanked with glass walls on two sides that looked out into the corridors. Her little artists were waiting, some in wheelchairs with IV poles and fluid drips, others in chairs at the low long tables. Each wore a protective apron over their hospital issue pj's. Cory and Lotty sat to one side, but he perked up when Arie entered. At the end of each table stood a stack of ceiling tiles.

"Bet you're wondering what we're going to do with these," she said, holding up a plain white twelve-inch square tile. "We're going to decorate them with special markers. And once the tiles are finished, the janitors are going to take out some of the old boring ceiling tiles in our halls and put your wonderful decorated ones in its place."

"Will they stay up forever?" one small girl asked.

"I think so. So do your very best work and don't forget to

put your names on your tile. We're going to make this ceiling gorgeous!" She passed out the tiles.

Lotty asked, "Can I help?"

"Thanks." Arie handed her boxes of fresh markers.

"It's a great idea," Lotty said. "I know they try to make this place cheerful, but . . ." She let the sentence trail.

"But it's still a cancer ward," Arie finished the thought.

Lotty shrugged.

"How's Cory?" Arie asked.

Lotty's eyes filled with tears. "Not so good. Doc says he'll have to go back on chemo. I haven't told him yet."

Arie recalled when she'd been dragged back into treatment, how angry she'd been. She'd felt cheated and deceived. "He'll get through it. He's a great kid and a fighter."

"Like you."

Arie smiled kindly at the beautiful petite woman whose rich, husky voice could sing with a fire and intensity that earned her awards on almost every CD she recorded. She had tons of money and could buy anything she wanted. Except her son's health. Cancer was no respecter of age, race, or money.

# 11

The county fairground was decked out with flags, banners, and streamers. A carnival stood at one end, and at the other was a football-field-sized arena surrounded by stands and packed with sunburned tourists. Ciana sat tall in her saddle as the long parade of horses and riders cantered through the arena gates and wove in concentric circles to cheering spectators. In the center of the arena wearing baggy pants and painted faces, rodeo clowns performed tumbling routines. Following the mounted riders came the men and women competing for cash prizes and the glory of winning a coveted belt buckle.

Earlier Ciana had caught sight of Jon Mercer as she saddled her horse for the grand entrance, and for a brief moment they made eye contact. His green eyes appraised her, unnerving her. She quickly mounted Firecracker and rode away.

After the parade, she locked up her grandfather's prized saddle, brushed the dust from her horse's lustrous coat, and put the roan into a holding pen. She hurried to the bleachers and searched for Eden, finally spotting her sandwiched between Tony and two hulking giants who looked more like pro wrestlers than cowboys. She grimaced but made her way up the steps to where they were sitting. She looked directly at Eden and, ignoring Tony and his "boys," said, "You hungry? I'm starved."

Eden stood to give Ciana a hug. "You were gorgeous in the parade. That jacket sparkled so hot it almost blinded me!"

Ciana had removed the jacket but still wore the studded boots.

Beside Eden, Tony grunted, "Must have cost a bundle."

"It's vintage. I bought it from a former rodeo queen on eBay." She turned to Eden. "Come to the concession stand with me."

Eden sidled Tony a glance. "You mind?"

The fact that Eden had to ask Tony's permission irked Ciana. "Do you have to get approval to go to the bathroom?" she asked testily.

Tony lifted his sunglasses and gave Ciana a glare that would curdle milk. "You going to hold her hand while she pees?"

Ciana smiled sweetly. "Cowgirls do it by themselves."

Eden inserted herself between Ciana and Tony. "I'll be back soon," she said to Tony. She took Ciana's hand and started down the bleachers. "Do you have to aggravate him?"

"I do. It makes my day."

"Well, it complicates mine."

Once off the bleachers, Ciana turned and asked, "Does he threaten you? Because if he does—"

"Give it a rest."

Ciana felt the presence of a man-mountain and saw that one of the beefy men had come down with them. "What? We need a bodyguard to buy fries?" She glared at him, but he ignored her.

Eden tugged her to the concession stand where they got in line. "Tony doesn't like being challenged."

"What's happened to you, Eden? You used to be ferocious. No one pushed you around. How did this man get such a hold on you?"

Eden glanced over her shoulder. "It's complicated and we're in a food line surrounded by a hundred people. Please don't dig around in my private life in front of the whole world."

Ciana felt stonewalled, but she understood Eden's point. "Can we talk about it sometime?"

"Sometime," Eden said with a shrug.

"Sometime *very* soon!" Ciana insisted. "Listen, I miss my friends. You're always corralled by Tony, and Arie's head over heels over her horse trainer."

"He *is* hunky."

Ciana scuffed the ground with the toe of her boot. She was well aware of that.

"Look, I promise to come over one night next week. We can order pizza, hang out, talk. Okay?"

"I'd really like that," Ciana said, mollified by Eden's assurance.

They bought their food, but before Ciana could figure out a place for her and Eden to sit and eat, the Hulk moved in, took Eden's cup and fries, and said, "Let's go."

Shocked, Ciana was about to tell him to buzz off when Eden gave her a pleading look that warned her to say nothing. Ciana stood and watched her friend and the man walk away. She seethed but didn't follow.

An hour later, Arie found Ciana by her horse trailer in the parking area. "Thought I'd find you here. Come on. Jon's event is coming up. Let's go cheer him on."

Watching Jon maybe break his neck trying to stay seated bareback on a bucking bronc wasn't anything Ciana wanted to do, but she had no graceful way out. They returned to the arena and shouldered their way into the spectators standing along the corral near the chutes that contained the horses and bulls. The animals were forced into the chutes so that a rider could lower himself onto the animal's back. When the chute opened, the animal would charge out bucking and whipping its body sideways to dislodge the rider—a contest of athletes. These broncs were chosen for their bucking abilities and could sell for as much as fifty thousand dollars.

In Jon's event, a rider had to stay on the horse for eight seconds while holding on to a leather strap around the horse's girth with one gloved hand. His other hand had to be held high in the air without touching the animal or the girth strap. In the stadium box, a panel of judges would grade each rider for time and form. One slip and the rider was disqualified, even if the rider wasn't thrown. Highest score won.

The announcer called the event and minutes later an angry bucking horse shot out of a chute. The rider was tossed before the buzzer sounded, and clowns rushed in to distract the horse while the cowboy rolled out of the way of the deadly driving hooves. Another rider made it the full eight seconds, but Ciana didn't think his form was great. The announcer called out, "Next is Jon Mercer from Amarillo, Texas, on Blacksnake." A cheer went up from the stands.

Ciana's heart lodged in her throat, and Arie seized her arm in a death grip. The chute opened and the horse was out like a gunshot, bucking and twisting like a corkscrew, but Jon held on for the full ride. When the buzzer sounded, he threw a leg over the horse's back and dropped to the ground, rolled, and sprang upright. The crowd went wild and Arie hugged Ciana hard. "He did it! Isn't he amazing?"

"Amazing," Ciana verified, watching the clowns corner the horse and a rider herd the animal into a pen. Jon picked up his hat from the dirt, held it high, and waved at the cheering audience.

"Let's go congratulate him," Arie said.

"You go on. I promised a few girls from the old flag corps days that I'd meet them on the midway."

Arie darted off, and Ciana left, struggling not to feel envious of her best friend.

Ciana met her friends and together they went on every ride and played every game, ate funnel cakes and corn dogs and cotton candy, and when the midway shut down at eleven o'clock, they hugged goodbye and promised to do it all again next year. Ciana returned to the corral area near the horse trailer parking lot and saw that only Firecracker was left in the enclosure.

"Sorry, sorry," Ciana said when she saw her horse's head drooping, half asleep. Firecracker raised her head and Ciana was certain the horse gave her an accusatory stare. Ciana muttered, "Don't look at me like that." Yet she did feel guilty. She should have taken the animal home hours ago.

"How about an extra bucket of oats before we load?"

Firecracker's ears pricked forward, seeming to understand that she was going to be rewarded with food. Ciana laughed and poured a few cups of oats into a wooden trough. While

Firecracker ate, she opened the cab door of her truck and turned the radio on to her favorite country station. She leaned back to savor the summer night sky, where the moon was a half circle with wispy clouds scuttling across it. Rain was coming. While Firecracker crunched oats to the guitar music of a country song, she closed her eyes. The scents of cotton candy and popcorn mingled with the smells of horseflesh and leather.

"Hello, Ciana."

Her eyes flew open. Jon Mercer was standing a few feet in front of her. She straightened slowly from the truck seat. "I . . . I didn't hear you come up."

"You looked to be in another time and place."

"Just waiting for my horse to finish up some oats. Why are you here so late?" His proximity rattled her, and yet her eyes feasted on him.

"Went out for a few beers with some of the other riders. Came back for my truck."

"By the way, great ride today. How'd you do overall?"

He reached into his jeans pocket and pulled out a belt buckle. It flashed silver in the moonlight. "Won this and a hundred sixty bucks."

"You deserved it, although it doesn't seem like enough money to have your brains rattled by a wild horse." She scooted from the truck to stand in front of him.

"Bragging rights," he said, sliding the buckle back into his pocket. He was silent for a minute, and she knew he wanted to say something to her. Her heart raced nervously. Finally he said, "I'm a plain man, Ciana. Words don't come easy for me." His gaze settled on her eyes. "There's something I want to ask you. Something I need to know."

She took a deep breath. "All right. Ask me."

"What happened that night between us? Was it just a game to you? Did any of it matter?"

She did owe him an explanation, but how honest could she be? "It mattered. I was going to tell you everything about me at breakfast. Then that text came." She blew out a breath. "My grandmother was in the hospital. We're very close. I had to leave."

"And you didn't trust me to understand? You couldn't have jotted down your phone number before running off?"

"I freaked out. I-I'm sorry. I handled it badly."

He looked thoughtful, as if weighing how to say what else was on his mind. "You called the cab before the text message came. Did you think I'd leave you stranded at the diner?"

She stared down at the toes of their boots, only inches apart. How could she say, *I'm a Beauchamp. We don't act the way I did.* "Things looked different in the clear light of day. I was a little ashamed about . . . about spending a whole night with a man I didn't know."

He shook his head. "Nothing hinky happened. I respected you."

She touched his arm. "I believe you, but we were strangers. I-I'd never done anything like that before. I swear that's the honest truth. And I . . . um . . . let's be honest, I had thrown myself at you—an offer you politely declined. And thank you for that. I was embarrassed. And I haven't had a margarita since," she added quickly, bringing a half smile to his face.

He moved a strand of hair that had fallen across her cheek and tucked it behind her ear. "I ride the rodeo, Ciana. I go from one town to the next with my horse and saddle. Sometimes I have to buy a newspaper to remember where I am.

There are girls. Rodeo groupies who think it's cool to bed a cowboy in every town."

Instantly she disliked every one of the unknown females, but she nodded, understanding because she'd heard such stories before. Girls threw themselves at him. Who could blame them?

"I won't tell you I've never had a one-night stand on the road. I have. But I don't want that for myself. It's no way for a man to live, bedding every woman who crosses his path just because he can."

Ciana was acquainted with the kind of guy he spoke of—high school jocks who took a girl's starry-eyed dreams, used her, and left her. College frat guys who hung hearts out to dry with no concern for their owners. She had seen the pitfalls clearly and avoided them. It hadn't always been easy, but she'd never regretted her choices. Until now. Until that one perfect night under the stars with Jon. "What do you want?"

Jon searched her face. "To tell you that night with you . . . it was . . . different. From the minute you walked in the door, I was . . . taken. I can't explain it, and I'm not feeding you a line. I want another chance with you."

His words should have flattered her, should have made her melt into his arms. Under normal circumstances, she might have, but what he did not know was that someone stood between them.

"You didn't seem happy to see me that day at Pickins's place," he added.

"I was blindsided that day. I went back to that dance saloon a few times, but you never showed. Then I look up one day weeks later, and there you were. I was blown away, then mad when you almost shot daggers at me. I got your message loud and clear: 'Back off.'"

"It was because of Arie."

He looked confused. "She's my student. She's paying me to help train her horse. I don't think about her in any other way."

Could he not see how crazy Arie was over him? "Maybe she wants more with you."

He dug a trench in the ground with the heel of his boot, keeping silent. When he spoke, he asked, "What about what I want? Does that count?"

Ciana fidgeted, shoving her hands into the back pockets of her jeans, wanting to dodge his question. "Of course, but she's my best friend. She's had some rough breaks in her life."

"I know. I think she's brave and tough, and I think the world of her, but that's all I feel for her."

Ciana wanted nothing more than to throw herself into his arms. Why didn't he understand the situation she was caught up in? "I won't do anything to hurt her. Absolutely nothing. No matter what." She squared her shoulders.

He stepped closer, made a move to hold her.

She ducked. "Don't." If he touched her, she might fracture.

He searched her face, then finally said, "Good night, Ciana," and walked off.

She forced herself to turn away, hot tears pricking her eyes. If he only knew how much she wanted a second chance with him.

Firecracker neighed. Ciana swiped at her tears. She quickly loaded her horse, climbed into her truck, and turned the key in the ignition. When the engine coughed to life, she backed the truck and horse trailer away from the area and aimed toward the main road.

The radio began playing the Garth Brooks song she'd

danced to with Jon. "*Our lives are better left to chance, I could have missed the pain*," Garth sang. She turned off the radio with a violent twist of the knob and pushed the accelerator harder, forcing the old truck to groan in protest on the empty night road.

Stupid song.

# 12

Eden arrived home one evening to see Ciana's truck in her driveway, and when she went inside, Ciana was stirring pots on the stove in Eden's kitchen. Pans simmered on all burners and the microwave hummed in the background.

"What's this?" Eden asked, the screen door slamming behind her. "Has the Food Network come to shoot a video?"

"Hush up, sit down, and eat a meal made with my hands out of vegetables grown from my garden." Ciana waggled her fingers.

"Where's my mom?"

"Work. She gave me free rein over the kitchen. Now sit."

"Why not? Very little happens in this room except coffee and breakfast cereal."

Eden slid into a chair and Ciana set bowls of fresh green beans, corn, beets, and salad greens with ripe tomatoes onto the table. "And why are you cooking for me?"

"I felt domestic today. And I considered it my good friend

duty. Look at you. I'll bet you've lost ten pounds since we graduated. And you didn't have it to lose." Ciana sat across from Eden and draped a pretty linen napkin over her lap. She had to bring the cloth napkins. Gwen didn't own any.

"You made biscuits too?" Eden grabbed one from the bread basket, fragrant and hot from the oven, ignoring the truth of Ciana's weight-loss remark.

"I have many talents," Ciana said, sliding a glass butter dish toward Eden. "That's fresh-churned too. Stopped by Fred Owens's dairy farm and bought it."

"That's one way to fatten me up." Everything was done to perfection. Savory food, cloth napkins, crisp matching tablecloth. The taste of the food perked her up considerably, and gratitude came with it. She ate until she finally pushed away from the table, stretched out her legs, and said, "Wow, that was great. I'm as full as a tick on a dog."

Ciana grinned. "Glad you liked it."

Eden waited a few beats, then asked, "So aside from rescuing me from an evening of fast food and showing off your cooking skills, why else are you here?"

Ciana's brow furrowed. "Because I'm worried about you."

"Don't be silly. I'm just fine." Eden's lie was so transparent even she choked on the words.

"How can you be fine when Tony controls your life? And don't bother to deny it. I've seen it with my own eyes. What's happened, Eden? Used to be no one could push you around."

Eden stared up at the ceiling. She was exhausted from carrying the burden of her and Tony alone. She was in over her head and she knew it. And she was scared. "Sometimes love has a dark side."

"Are you really in love with him?"

"I am . . . was . . . for a while. Now I just don't know."

"Well, I'm no expert, but he doesn't act like someone in love. He acts like someone in control."

Of course, Ciana had zeroed in on the crux of Eden's problem. Often she felt as if Tony wanted to crawl inside her head, her skin, and bend her totally to his will, and the deeper in she went with him, the more tangled she became in his web. "I don't know what to do," she confessed quietly.

Ciana looked incredulous. "You drop him, walk away. Tell him to get lost."

*How naive.* "It doesn't work that way with Tony. If it did, I'd be gone."

"What do you mean? Are you a hostage?"

"In a way, yes."

Ciana shoved the empty plates aside. "Explain how this works to me."

Eden wasn't sure she could explain it to herself. She was ensnared by him sexually, but certainly it would have been simple for him to replace her in that role. "He . . . he thinks I'm some kind of 'perfect' female. Me. Can you imagine? I'm some kind of object of desire, his 'angel,' his lucky charm. I don't get it, but so long as he thinks that, I can't break away from him. He won't let me go."

Ciana blinked, trying to grasp hold of such a concept. "Would he hurt you?"

"Maybe."

"My God! That's awful. Can you run away somewhere?"

Eden laughed bitterly. "And where would I go? It's not like I have a family anywhere. Mom's cut off everything from her past. Which I might add is my past too. She never told me anything about anyone. For all I know, someone left me in a basket on her doorstep."

"Can you skip the country? All you need is a passport—"

"I have a passport. Tony insisted. He keeps it in a locked desk in his condo. I live in fear that he'll want to leave the country and drag me with him. And then what would I do? In a foreign country, I'd be completely dependent on him. I'd never get away. No one could find me."

"Your mom's worried about you too. She told me so."

Eden rolled her eyes. "I know she hates Tony, but all she does is gripe to me about him. She's offered me nothing about how to change what's happening." In truth, Gwen was acting more responsibly than Eden could ever remember. She took her meds faithfully. She worked often, covering all shifts that the grocery store offered. She cleaned the house, did laundry, even rented a lawn mower every couple of weeks and cut the grass when it reached shin height. *Too little, too late*, she thought. "I don't have any family except for a messed-up mother."

"I get that," Ciana said. "I'm not exactly drowning in relatives myself—my mother, and Olivia in a rest home. Any others are MIA—either dead or nonexistent. But," she added decisively, "you do have friends. And you have a job."

"Had a job. Tony made me quit a week ago so we could spend more time together." She shivered, remembering the finality of his demand, couched in pleading language about how much he wanted and needed her with him, then haunting her with constant shadowing by his intimidating bodyguards until the boutique owner had asked her to leave.

Ciana's jaw dropped. "So now you have no money and no job?"

"He buys me anything I want. Except a ticket out."

The room went silent as Ciana pondered all that Eden had said. Finally she asked, "Doesn't he work? You've never told me what he does."

A chill shot up Eden's spine. Tony was becoming more powerful and secure in his drug business, and she was no longer able to pretend that his business was a casual occasional thing. But to tell Ciana about it could put her in danger. Best to keep some things a secret. "He works at home. Just my luck. Now he wants me to move in with him."

"No way! You can't do that!"

Eden shrugged. "So far, I've given him the excuse of having to stay with mom. I've told him I can't leave her alone. That she's unstable. I've said, 'How can I live with myself if she hurts herself?' Which, as you and I both know, isn't exactly a lie. But he won't let me keep using that excuse much longer. I can feel it."

"Can you talk to the police or social services? Ask them for help?"

Eden reached across the table and grasped Ciana's hand. "They can't babysit me. Not round the clock. Tony has too many eyes. Too many friends. I'm stuck, Ciana. Like a rabbit in a trap, I'm stuck."

Eden drove back to Tony's to spend the night, as she had told him she would. If she'd defied him, he'd have sent Billy Jim to fetch her like a bag of laundry. Plus she really didn't want to be at the house when Gwen returned. Sometimes it was better when Gwen wasn't on her meds and didn't concern herself with Eden. She shook off the thought. Hadn't she wanted a sane mother all her life? Hadn't she longed for a mother who was "normal"? And yet, she couldn't deny that talking to Ciana had lifted her spirits. Nothing was resolved, nothing had changed, but she'd shared her fears and felt better. She'd asked Ciana not to tell Arie, to keep her secrets, and Ciana had said she would. No need to get Arie tied up in knots with Eden's problems. She had plenty of her own. She begged Ciana not to do anything and thanked her for listening.

Eden parked, entered the glassed-in foyer of Tony's building, and walked to the elevator that would take her up to his suites. She reached to punch the up button when a hand grabbed her wrist. Fright almost made her wet her pants. A voice from behind her rasped, "Please, don't scream. Please."

Eden turned, pressing her back against the cold metal doors, and looked into the desperate eyes of a girl who looked vaguely familiar. Eden tried to pry her wrist from the girl's hand, but her grip was viselike.

"Just let me talk to you for a minute. Around the corner. Where no one can see us."

Eden was terrified but couldn't make her voice work.

The girl took it for compliance and pulled her around the corner, where they couldn't be seen. There she stepped closer. "Don't be afraid. I . . . I won't hurt you. I need you to help me." Desperation never left the girl's eyes. "Don't you recognize me, Eden?"

Eden saw a girl with scraggly, unkempt hair, skin with a gray pallor, and facial lesions. Dark circles ringed her eyes, and her body looked impossibly thin. The brief smile she'd offered revealed stained teeth. Eden swallowed hard as recognition dawned. "M-Meghan?"

"Yes," she answered. "It's me."

Eden was stunned into another stretch of speechlessness. She hadn't seen the girl for several years, and now she was almost unrecognizable.

Meghan released Eden's arm. "I didn't mean to scare you. It's just that, well . . . I need a favor."

"What?" Eden felt queasy.

"I . . . I need some stuff. Tony's cut me off. I owe him money. I told him I'll pay him, but he said no more until I catch up. I can't catch up unless I get a hit. You're his girlfriend. If you ask him, he'll let you have something for me. Please."

Eden stiffened. Meghan's voice sounded as if it were coming through a tunnel. How could this frail, pathetic girl be the attractive person she'd first met at a street party? "I . . . I can't," Eden whispered. "I'm so sorry."

From around the corner, Eden heard the elevator bell ding, meaning that someone was either coming down or going up. She broke for the corner and stepped into the elevator just as the door closed. She shook violently, afraid she might hurl. Meghan was a hard-core addict. A benefactor of Tony's business.

When the doors opened, she was on Tony's floor, unaware that she'd even pushed the button to his suite. She stepped out and saw Billy standing at the penthouse door. He nodded at Eden, said, "Tony's out doing business, but he said for you to go in and wait for him."

She obeyed meekly, still so shaken that she could hardly think straight. Inside the elegant and expensively decorated condo, she crossed to the balcony doors, opened them, and took deep ragged breaths. What was she going to do? How was she going to get away from this horror called her life and this demon of a man?

# 13

The old woman dreamed.

*She stood on the veranda of a grand Victorian looking down a long tree-lined driveway that stretched to a dirt road fronting the property.*

*October had begun to edge the leaves with the colors of autumn. The woman felt featherlight. No aching bones. No throbbing muscles. Her mind was as clear as a bell . . . no muddled thoughts. She turned to the window behind her and saw her reflection in the old-time glass. Why, she was so young! Just a girl. Her long blond hair was tied with a length of blue satin ribbon and her dress was a Sunday best, white linen edged with eyelet lace. Why was she dressed so finely?*

*She pinched her cheeks to make them glow, nibbled on her bottom lip to redden it. Growing anticipation filled every cell in her body. Turning back toward the lawn, she saw a rider on horseback turn into the property from the road. A man sat ramrod straight in the saddle. The horse, dark as sooty wood, stepped high, approaching in a fluid graceful motion that defined it as a Tennessee walking horse, bred and trained to perform this perfect gait.*

*She squinted, unable to see the man's face, partially covered by a fedora low on his forehead. Her heartbeat accelerated, knowing the man was coming to meet her. She stepped down off the porch, onto the ground in anticipation. Then they were towering over her. "May I help you?" she asked.*

*The rider said nothing but lowered a saddlebag into her arms. It was heavy, and when she rested it on the step, bright red apples rolled from the overstuffed pouch. "Oh!" she cried, delighted. "For me?"*

*The horse stood absolutely statue still. The man reached down his hand, inviting her to join him on the horse. She hesitated. What if Papa saw her with a stranger? Still, the man's offer was irresistible. She smiled, placing her youthful palm into his. In one smooth and impossible motion, she floated onto the horse's rounded rump behind the man. Only in a dreamscape could she have moved so effortlessly. The horse snorted. She settled her arms around the man's waist. This felt so right. She tightened her grip and rested her cheek against the man's broad, well-muscled and absolutely familiar back. She sighed with contentment.*

*"I love you," she whispered into the rough fabric of his shirt, which caught her warm breath. "With all my heart, I love you."*

Arie punched in Jon's cell number with shaking fingers.

"Hey," he answered.

Arie's voice clogged with tears, and for a moment, she couldn't speak.

"Arie? Is that you? What's wrong?"

She cleared her throat. "I won't be coming this morning.

Ciana's grandmother died in the night, and I have to be with my friend today."

Jon was quiet. "Ciana was real attached to her, wasn't she?"

Arie wasn't sure how he knew this, but she said, "Yes. Olivia was more a mother to her than her own."

"Look, don't worry about training until you feel like it. We'll start again when the timing's right."

"I have to go."

Just before she punched off, Jon said, "Wait! Tell Ciana how sorry I am, okay?"

"I'll tell her."

For Ciana, the best thing about having good long-term friends was the sense of history they brought with them. She thought back to the first time Arie came to spend the day with her when they'd been kids. Ciana had been nervous—friends never came to Bellmeade on the outskirts of town. She wondered what Arie really thought of her. Did she think Ciana was stuck-up because she was a Beauchamp? Her concerns had been ungrounded. No one could be a better friend to her than Arie.

Ciana hadn't wanted to include Eden in their twosome friendship until Arie had insisted, recognizing quickly that Eden was "a fellow wounded soul." But once Ciana learned about Eden's life with a mental-case mother, Ciana's defenses buckled. She knew what it was like to live with a broken mother. Eden brought a sense of adventure to her and Arie's mix of personalities. She was daring, a risk taker, and fun to be around. Now these two sat with Ciana and cried with her over losing her beloved grandmother.

During the visitation at the funeral home, it seemed as if the whole town turned out to pay respects to Miz Olivia, matriarch of the Beauchamp family. Especially when the town had not been able to pay respects after Ciana's grandfather and father had perished in the plane wreckage, leaving nothing of themselves to bury.

Ciana recognized most of the mourners, farmers in their best jeans, their faces sun weathered and worn by years of outdoor work, and tradesmen who sold goods and products, often on unconditional credit, in a town down on its luck. She greeted them, thanked them for coming. What she couldn't do was bring herself to view Olivia's body lying in the satin-lined casket surrounded by flowers, plants, and numberless baskets at the front of the funeral parlor.

"You may regret not saying goodbye," Alice Faye told her. The visitors were gone. Only Ciana, her friends, and her mother remained.

"I don't think I can." Ciana had held herself together all evening.

"Funeral's tomorrow and the casket will be closed. This is your last chance to see her. She looks wonderful," Alice Faye said, encouraging Ciana.

"Your mama's right. Say goodbye proper. We'll go with you," Arie offered.

Eden nodded, although she also looked reluctant.

"This is about *you*, not her," Alice Faye added, squeezing Ciana's hand. "Go on."

And so, banked on either side by her two friends, Ciana walked to the casket and looked down on Olivia Beauchamp. She lay in a royal blue dress and wore her favorite pearl necklace, looking serene, better in death than she had in the last year of her life. Ciana felt numb. As a farm girl, she'd come to see death early with animals, but when she had realized that one day Olivia would die, she'd panicked. Grandmother knew all things and told wonderful stories. How was it possible that she, too, would die?

Olivia had wiped Ciana's cheeks, saying, "Death will come one day, but that means I'll see Charles once again. We'll be so happy together."

"She looks asleep," Arie whispered in Ciana's ear, dragging her into the present.

"And pretty," Eden said.

"And gone forever," Ciana added before turning and walking away.

Rain fell on the August afternoon Ciana and her mother went to the attorney's office to review Olivia's will. Barry Boatwright practiced law a block off Main Street, in a stately refurbished Victorian painted yellow with dark brown trim. His front office assistant, one of Arie's aunts, greeted them warmly. "I'm so sorry for your loss."

"Thank you," Alice Faye said.

The woman ushered them into Boatwright's office, which had once served as the home's dining room. Boatwright's desk faced a worn leather sofa nestled under a bay window. Large purple-headed hydrangea bushes drooped outside the window, shielding the room from passersby.

"Welcome," Boatwright said. He kissed Alice Faye's cheeks and clasped Ciana's hand warmly. "Do sit," he said, motioning to the sofa, issuing condolences and praising Olivia's life. "Sweet tea?" he asked as they settled in.

"No thank you," Alice Faye and Ciana said.

He lowered himself into his squeaky desk chair and picked

up a large file. "The terms of the will are mostly unchanged from your great-grandfather Jacob's. The land is always passed to the family first." He peered over the tops of his glasses. "You are joint heirs and required to pass it along to your heirs. It cannot be sold without each other's express consent."

Ciana grimaced, knowing that supplying future heirs was her responsibility and knowing that while the will may be simple, the "if/whens" and "wherefores" of no additional heirs filled most of the file Boatwright was holding. But Ciana silently swore that as long as she lived, Bellmeade would not be sold, even if she died a dried-up old prune without heirs.

"Miz Olivia did make one change, however," the attorney said, rustling pieces of paper.

Beside her, Ciana felt her mother sit straighter.

"A change?" Alice Faye asked. "What kind of change?"

"A thoughtful change," Boatwright said with a smile. "She set up a savings account for you, Ciana. Money for you to attend a college or university of your choice. Although she underestimated the cost of attending college, it's a nice amount of money, enough that if you're prudent, you can stretch it to cover tuition and books at a good institution."

Ciana simply stared at him, stunned by his news.

"And," Boatwright continued, "you have total control and discretion over it. She wanted you to have it because she said you were a girl of extraordinary good sense and therefore should never be dependent on the whim of any other person to choose your way in life."

"It was a smack at me," Alice Faye said, fuming, as Ciana drove her mother's old Lincoln Town Car home through the rain.

"How do you figure that?"

"I wanted to attend college, but Old Man Jacob thought spending money on educating a woman was foolish, a waste. What was left for me? Nothing. I was trapped. So when Jackson came along, I married him." Alice Faye offered a derisive laugh. "Neither Olivia nor your great-grandfather cared much for Jackson. Thought he was more attracted to my family name and money than to me. Jackson discovered afterward there was no vast fortune. But he stayed. They were surprised—as though no man could care for me for myself."

Alice Faye grabbed a tissue, swiped her eyes.

"How about your daddy, Charles? Didn't he have any say-so about his daughter going to college?"

"He stood up for me, but trust me when I say that Jacob and Olivia were formidable forces. Daddy gave up quickly."

Did Ciana want to hear this? "I don't remember Granddad or Daddy very much."

"My grandfather scared the starch out of me, but your granddad, my daddy, was my guardian angel. He loved me and was good to me," Alice Faye said. "But Olivia made me feel like I never measured up to my dead brother. Charles Junior was perfect. I was not."

Ciana didn't interrupt, keeping her eyes on the road through the downpour. She hadn't heard this story before, not from Grandmother, not from her mother.

"Anyway, after Jackson and I were married, Daddy took Jackson into the business, even though he was never into farming like Daddy and Jacob. After Jacob died, Jackson seemed less pressured and more at ease in the business. Daddy loved to fly that plane of his. He and Jackson went all over the country selling our farm goods to small grocers. When supermarkets began to change the grocer business, they went after contracts with them. According to Mother, when Charles

Junior died, it took four days for Charles to get home because of bad weather. Mother Nature played a mean trick on Olivia when she got pregnant with me," Alice Faye muttered, sighing heavily. "Years later, he was piloting the plane when it went down forever with him and my dear Jackson."

The catch in her mother's voice left no doubt in Ciana's mind about that crash being the worst day in her mother's life. The day was stamped in her memory because the sight and sound of her mother and grandmother crying uncontrollably had terrified her. And at age six, the idea that her father and grandfather were never coming home didn't make sense. They went away lots of times, but they *always* came home.

Alice Faye gazed out the car window. "I redeemed us both when I had you," she said softly, moving back in time to before her husband and father had died. "You were my saving grace, even though you became more hers than mine."

Ciana glanced over at her mother's somber profile, cast in gray by the rain against the windshield. "I . . . I don't think—"

"She named you, you know." Alice Faye was tuning Ciana out, lost now in memories. "I wanted to call you Sara Elizabeth. A pretty name. But I didn't get a choice about your name."

Ciana hadn't known this. She tried on Sara in her head, but it didn't feel right. "I like Ciana."

Alice Faye didn't seem to hear her. "She came into my hospital room, lifted you up, saw your full head of reddish hair, and said, 'Look, Charles. She looks like a sweet little cinnamon bun.' And so she christened you Ciana."

Ciana wondered if she was supposed to feel guilty about the way she looked.

"You were so much like her as you grew up. A take-charge personality. Loved hard work. Loved the land, the horses, the garden. You were all the things I wasn't and never would be."

The car's wipers and pounding rain almost drowned out Alice Faye's softly spoken words. "Then the plane crashed and we both lost our men. And you became even more important. I had no other children, but then neither did she. Yet here she is, reaching up from the grave to control our lives once again." Her last words sounded peckish.

"Are you saying you don't want me to have the college-fund money?" Ciana didn't see the savings account as vengeful. Did her mother?

Her mother scoffed. "Don't be foolish. Of course I do. You're my daughter, and I love you. Truth is, the money's your ticket out, Ciana. You have a door open for you I never had."

Ciana blinked in amazement. "You would have left Bellmeade?"

"Far away. But where would I have gone, Ciana? Where does a woman go when she has no education, no husband, no money of her own, and no real purpose in life?"

*Echoes of Eden*, Ciana thought. "You had Bellmeade," she said. She'd never heard her mother express such deep regrets about her life. She'd figured every Beauchamp woman wanted to cling to the land, to hold on to her birthright and destiny.

"I didn't especially want the place." Still deep in her own musings, Alice Faye smiled enigmatically. "But I guess I did leave in a manner of speaking. I have found both escape and great pleasure in sweet tea and gin."

After leaving Alice Faye at the doorstep, Ciana parked the car, slipped on a slicker, and ran to the stables, her mind reeling from her mother's words. Olivia had always preached that being a Beauchamp was a gift from the Almighty, clearly a responsibility and duty that only a privileged few had been granted. There had been times when Ciana sometimes felt overwhelmed by it all, but never had she wanted to be someone other than who she was. Now she had learned that her mother had wanted to be anyone *except* who she was. Disturbing.

Deep in thought, she entered the barn. Firecracker and Sonata whinnied. "I haven't forgotten you," she said, but then stopped, staring. Both horses were in their stalls, dry and eating a trough full of hay. She'd left them out before going into town. "How did you—"

"I did it," Jon Mercer said from behind her.

# 14

Ciana whirled to see him leaning against the open doorway of the tack room and stamped her foot. "You scared me half to death."

He held up his hands in surrender. "Just wanted to help. Saw the horses out in the rain, so I brought them in and toweled them off, gave them something to munch."

"Just driving past?" His story wasn't quite believable. She lived miles from Pickins's ranch.

"Okay. Driving by on purpose. I wanted to apologize for not coming to your grandmother's funeral. I wanted to say I'm sorry she died because I know what she meant to you."

She had looked for him covertly in the crowd of mourners but didn't want to admit it to his face. "Not a problem. No one likes to go to funerals."

"Plus, I wanted to surprise you." He held out his hand. "Come inside."

The old desk had been pulled away from the wall and

covered with a tablecloth. Cartons of fried chicken, potato salad, and baked beans along with paper plates and plastic forks sat on the checkered cloth.

"Supper," he said, pulling out a chair and guiding her into it. "Bought it at the Chicken Palace downtown." He took a seat across from her on the other side of the narrow old desk. His knees hit the solid wood backside, so he twisted sideways.

Caught off guard, thoroughly surprised, and touched by his effort, she confessed, "I don't know what to say."

"No need to talk. Just eat."

She dug into the cardboard box until she found a crispy fried chicken leg. "What if I hadn't come home?"

"I figured you'd come back eventually for the sake of the horses. And if you hadn't come home, the horses were dry and fed and I'd have a lot of leftover chicken."

She smiled. "I appreciate you caring for my horses. A little surprised, though, that Firecracker came to you. She can be ornery."

He found a crispy thigh and bit into it. "I specialize in ornery."

She blushed, knowing he was referring to her. After a few minutes of silence, she said, "Arie says you're a good trainer. That you have a gift for connecting with horses."

"Don't know about being gifted. Just know I like being around them. I train them gentle-like. No need to be mean to a horse. I've seen trainers who are. Takes them twice as long to gentle an animal with meanness. I don't teach a horse anything. I just bring out the things that come natural to them."

Ciana watched his hands gesture expressively while he talked about horses. To her his hands were beautiful, squarish and capable, calloused and marked with faint white lines from old leather strap and rope burns, working hands that were as gentle as cotton on a woman's skin. Remembering, she shivered. "Pickins must be happy with your work."

He grinned. "Bill thinks he's a genius for bringing in the mustangs. The work's gone fast because the horses are smart."

"How about your father? Wasn't this supposed to be his job?" She remembered Jon telling her that.

"It was, but his healing from the stroke isn't going well. His fault, though. He won't go to rehab like he's supposed to. He still has paralysis on his left side. His arm's useless, and his foot drags when he walks."

Ciana felt instant sympathy for the man. "Where is he?"

"In a dump of a trailer on a half acre out west of here. Pickins said he could offer Dad a room in the bunkhouse, and that way I could keep an eye on him, but Dad's stubborn. He won't budge. And we've never been on the best of terms."

"You going back to Texas when the job's finished?"

"Would it matter?" His question caught her off guard.

"Not many rodeos around here."

"True. And I still want my own spread and my own horses. But Bill's saying he'd welcome me back next summer. If I want to come."

Her heartbeat accelerated, then dropped like a stone. Could she face another summer with or without him? Could she maintain her distance and her resolve for Arie's sake? "Good man is hard to find," Ciana mumbled.

By now the meal was finished and their conversation had no place to go. Jon stood, scraped the leftovers into their cartons, and put the scraps into a bag. "I'll throw this away at my place."

Ciana stood, too, wanting him to stay but knowing she couldn't allow it. "Thanks for the meal and for caring for my horses. I really appreciate both. It's been a hard few days."

"Happy to do it." He turned at the doorway of the tack room and repeated, "Would it matter to you? If I returned next year?"

That set her adrenaline flowing through her body in a rush. "It . . . it would mean the world to Arie," she said carefully. Not a lie, but not the truth either.

He put on his Stetson, bent over, and blew out the candles. "But not to you."

He left the barn and Ciana felt as if the light and air had gone with him.

Arie cleaned the art tables hurriedly, already late for her appointment with Dr. Austin in the adult oncology wing. Three months had passed since her last appointment, meaning her "status was "unchanged." *Good enough.* A nurse passing the rec room said, "Hey, Arie, the janitor just finished installing the first of the ceiling tiles. Come see."

Arie followed the nurse into the hall to where a handyman was folding up a ladder. She looked up. Every third tile was emblazoned with a hand-drawn image a child created during her art classes. "Oh my gosh! They're gorgeous."

Seeing the tiles gave Arie a feeling of great satisfaction. Something from a child who fought cancer would be seen for years to come. Some tiles would memorialize its creator; others would herald a child who beat the Big C. All were signed, colorful reminders of a child who passed through this hospital on a life journey not to be forgotten.

"Have to run," she said, and broke for the stairwell, where she climbed to the adult oncology floor and went into Dr. Austin's office. The receptionist directed her into an exam room where she saw Dr. Austin looking at CT scans hanging on the light board on the wall. "I know I'm late. The art class ran long and the tables were a wreck. Ever seen what a group of kids can do with acrylic paint?"

Austin, with his wire-rim glasses and balding head, waved away her stream of words. "Have a seat."

She didn't want to sit. Her eyes cut to the light board. "Mine?"

"Yours."

"What's the word?"

"Come here. I'll show you."

Arie bravely stepped to the glowing scans and stared at the pictures of her torso's midsection and saw three small dark spots in the area she knew to be her liver. "It's back?" she asked, forcing out the words, tamping down panic.

"Yes," Dr. Austin said. "I'm afraid so."

"But the area was clear just months ago. No spots at all. How could they come back? And so fast?"

"I'd never have predicted this."

"Short remission." The words tasted bitter.

"I'm sorry, Arie." He put his big hand on her shoulder. "It's a setback, but not a defeat."

"So now what?"

"More treatment, a new direction."

"What new direction? Haven't I tried them all?" Chemo. Radiation. Drugs. Diet. Holistic, at her mother's request. And pain. Always pain. "I'm supposed to start college in September."

"I'm reviewing options now. In the meantime, we'll put you back on some meds. Chemo for sure."

His words sent shivers through her. She felt defeated. And afraid.

"Arie? Are you listening? We need to get you into a protocol quickly."

She turned away from the light board that held the brutal truth and looked up at her doctor. "Not now," she said softly. "Soon. I just want to go home now."

"Of course. Talk it over with your family and call me." She turned to leave. He added, "Don't wait too long. We need to get right on it."

Arie didn't remember the two-hour drive to Windemere from the hospital, nor when the rain began to fall, but somehow the car was on the edge of town. She didn't go home, though. Instead she drove out to Pickins's place, turned off the engine, and stared into the pasture, numb all over. On the far side, several horses huddled in a group, their heads down, their rumps toward the driving rain. She picked out Caramel in the small herd and realized the horse should be in her stall. She couldn't even manage her horse; how was she going to manage another cycle of cancer treatment?

Ignoring the pelting rain, Arie left the car, climbed over the fence, and called out to her horse. The animal's head lifted and her ears pricked forward, but she didn't budge. Arie shouted until her voice gave out, realizing she had no control over the animal just as she had no control over her life. She buried her face in her hands, sank to her knees, and began to sob. Cold wet mud oozed through her slacks and her shirt stuck to her back.

"Hey! What's going on?" Jon Mercer came jogging across the muddy pasture, soaked to the skin like Arie. He stopped as Arie, weighted down with water and mud, struggled to right herself. "Arie? What are you doing out here?" He bent, lifted her up, and turned her to face him.

"I came to see my horse."

"Did you notice it was raining?" Water dripped off the sides of his hat. "I was busy in another pasture. I didn't see you drive up. I thought you were in Nashville, at the hospital."

He bent his head, looked her full in the face. "Are you crying? What's wrong? Tell me what's wrong?"

Unable to keep her grief away from him, Arie released an anguished sob and began to shake all over. "Life isn't fair," she screamed, clenching her fists, turning her face into the needle-sharp rain.

"Nashville. The doctor." He looked into her eyes, into her soul, and she allowed him to see the truth. "I'm sorry, baby," he said, pulling her close and holding her tight. "Real sorry." She should have known that the man who read and gentled horses could read people too. He said, "I'd do it for you if I could."

"You can't," she told Jon. "Nobody can."

"Come inside the barn and get dry."

She went with him into the barn where it was warmer. He sat her on a bale of straw, found a stack of towels, and wrapped several around her; then he began to rub the terry cloth on her skin to encourage circulation and stop her shivering. "Just got these from the dryer, so they're clean," he said. "Pickins keeps a washer and dryer in his tack room for us ranch hands' laundry."

"Th-the horses," she said through chattering teeth.

"Horses are fine. I'll bring them in soon." He began to towel-dry her hair.

She imagined it falling out in clumps into the towel. She gagged. *Not again.*

"Hey, take it easy." He stepped in front of her, lifting her chin with his forefinger. "How bad is it?"

"Bad enough. I can't talk about it now."

He returned to towel-drying her hair, wisely offering no

platitudes of how she was a winner and could beat this thing, this monster inside her body.

"You need to get those clothes off. I'll wash them."

She was cold to her core but unable to move. Her teeth wouldn't stop chattering.

Jon guided her into the tack room, pulled a load from the dryer, and offered her one of his denim work shirts. She took it and held it close. The fresh scent of his clothes and the scent of fresh straw and leather helped calm her. "Just put this on, wrap up in the towels, and hand me everything. And I mean everything."

He left the room and she did as he'd asked, dropping the soggy clothing into a heap. She wrapped herself in his shirt, holding on to the warmth and the comfort of knowing it was his. Barefoot, and with shirt and towels cocooning her, Arie stepped into the barn. "Okay."

He nodded and walked past her. Soon she heard the washer going and soon after that, a teakettle whistling. He emerged with two cups. "Hope you like tea. Wallace, one of the wranglers, drinks the stuff. I'm going with coffee." He paused. "But if you'd rather have the coffee—"

"Tea's fine." She eased onto the bale of straw and Jon pulled up a stool to settle in front of her. She grew acutely aware that she was naked beneath the shirt and towels. She took a sip of tea and closed her eyes as the warm liquid spread through her. "Thanks for rescuing me."

"One of my hobbies is rescuing pretty girls. Now what can I do to help?"

"You've helped me get through this afternoon. Where's my cell? I better call home before they call out the National Guard to search for me."

"I'll get it." Jon returned in seconds with her phone from her car.

She dialed home and her mother answered on the first ring. "Hi, Mom," she said brightly.

"Where are you? We're getting worried," Patricia said.

"Calm down. It's raining really hard, so I pulled over to the side of the road to wait until it slacks off a bit." Arie gave Jon a pleading look that asked him to forgive her lie. He shrugged.

"Oh. Yes. That's good thinking," Patricia answered. "Just wait it out. A good idea. We . . . we're wondering what your doctor said."

Arie stared Jon straight in the eyes, bolstering herself to tell the ultimate lie. "He said I was doing just fine. The scans look clean and clear."

Patricia squealed and passed the word to others apparently waiting in the room for this news. Arie's hand went numb from holding the phone so tightly, and her conscience tingled with shame. Jon's gaze never left hers, but it held no reprimand.

Arie promised to be home as soon as possible and punched off the phone. She ducked her head, staring down at the floor. Jon had heard her lie, straight-faced. She was naked before him in many ways. "Will you keep my secret?"

"It's not my story to tell," he said gently.

At this moment, she felt futureless. Three remissions. Three failures. And now, dark ominous spots on her liver yet again. She cleared her throat. "Actually I need to think this out. Decide with my doctor." Tears brimmed in her eyes.

Jon's large hands covered hers. "They're your family. Maybe—"

"I get to make my own choices now," she interrupted him. "I have jurisdiction over my body. And just now I don't know what I want to do. There are so many other things for me to think about. Other things I want. I'm tired of being sick." She wanted college, travel, horse shows, a place of her own. She wanted him. At the moment, dreams lay at her feet like broken glass.

In the stillness, the washer buzzed, signaling the wash cycle was over. "I'll get your stuff into the dryer," he said.

She watched him head toward the tack room, her longing for him as tangible as his shirt on her body.

# 15

Eden painted her toenails meticulously with a Day-Glo shade of polish called Pink-a-licious 911. She disliked the color but considered it an area of her life she still controlled. *Pathetic*, she thought. *Nail polish as a statement*. She sat in Tony's living room, on his huge white sofa, the massive 3-D TV tuned to the evening news. Tony was out, but he'd be in soon, and she'd been instructed to "stay put."

She heaved a forlorn sigh. She felt like a fly caught in a spider's web. On one side of the web stood Tony, weaving silky strands around her, while on the other side was the life she once led. Returning to the ordinary was one thing she'd never expected to want, yet she did. Her mother kept begging Eden to leave Tony and come home to live. If only she could. Compared to the life she was living with a drug lord, her old life seemed infinitely superior, crazy mother and all. Ever since she'd run into Meghan, she had ceased to defend Tony to her mother, yet she still lacked the courage to tell Gwen about Tony's business. Fear, not pride, kept her quiet.

". . . female body found at Miller Lake."

Eden's head snapped to attention at the announcer's words. The video was unremarkable, just pictures of cops and yellow crime scene tape marking off a lakeside area at dusk. The announcer continued: "The body has already been identified as that of Meghan Oden, twenty."

Eden shot upright as a photo of the victim filled the screen, a photo obviously from a high school yearbook. Eden's heart hammered. Meghan! Only a week had passed since Meghan had cornered Eden in the lobby. Now she was dead.

". . . picked up for solicitation numerous times by the police," the announcer intoned. Another photo flashed onto the TV screen, this time a mug shot of the girl who hardly resembled the one in the first photo. This was the ruined, emaciated girl who had confronted Eden—disheveled hair, blotched face, bloodshot eyes, and bruises along one side of her mouth.

". . . suspected drug overdose."

Meghan had gotten the drugs she had wanted so desperately from somewhere. *Oh God.* Eden felt tears well behind her eyes. Dead. There was no coming back from dead. She'd not been friends with Meghan, but she had known her, talked to her, been warned by her to stay away from Tony. News of celebrities overdosing on drugs was something abstract, something she read about or heard about. Meghan was real. Had been real. She hadn't helped her, but what could she really have done? Now she was no more. ". . . exact cause of death will be known following an autopsy," the announcer said.

Eden grabbed the TV remote and pushed the Off button, as if that might turn back time, erase the story she'd just heard on the news. She sat numbly and was still sitting there staring into space when Tony arrived.

"Hey, babe. Why's it so dark in here?" He flipped on two lamps.

Eden couldn't bring herself to look at him.

He lowered himself to the sofa and turned her to face him. "What's wrong?"

Still she couldn't look at him. "Meghan Oden's dead."

"Who?"

The single word seared into her heart and mind. "Meghan! One of your clients."

Tony leaned away. "Are you thinking this is my fault? I cut her off weeks ago."

No remorse in his voice. Cold and indifferent.

"I knew her," Eden cried. "She's dead."

"Shit happens."

"Don't you feel *anything*?"

"She was a big girl. She knew what she was doing." He sounded irritated. "She chose to be an addict."

"You made her one."

Tony grabbed Eden's shoulders and shook her hard. "She made herself one. She had a crappy life and drugs made it easier for her to live it."

He was blaming Meghan, as if he'd done nothing wrong. It hit Eden that his inability to assume any blame was arrogant, and the fire in his eyes told her she should keep quiet. He let go of her arms and smoothed his hand along her cheek. She flinched, wanting to scream, *Don't touch me!* but she stifled the impulse. Tony was explosive and without a conscience. She'd seen him be cruel to others.

He stood, lifting her chin to stare into her eyes. "Go to the bedroom. I'll be in after a few phone calls."

Did he expect her to make love to him after all that had

happened? Did he expect her to whisper words of love when she felt only revulsion toward him? Icy cold fear crept up her spine, and because she knew how volatile he could become, she thought it best to cooperate. She knew she was pathetic. How sad. There was a time when making love with Tony had been the center of her world. She got up and turned toward the bedroom. He caught her arm. "One more thing. I hate the color you've put on your toes. Take it off tomorrow. Paint on something red. I like you in red."

She lay awake in the dark shaking, waiting for him, her stomach sick and her brain in turmoil. She couldn't live this way anymore. She had to get away.

Or die trying.

Ciana shut down the house for the night. Alice Faye had gone to bed long before, weaving up the stairs to her bedroom on the upper floor. Ciana's bedroom was on the ground floor, in what had once been the maid's quarters, renovated to her liking years before. She was undressing when the house phone rang. Who in the world? Her friends called her cell. She snatched up the receiver. "Beauchamp residence."

"Miz Ciana? This is Bill Pickins. Hate to bother you, but I don't know who else to call."

"It's all right. What's wrong?"

"It's my trainer, Jon Mercer. He's in a bad way."

Her heart seized. "What happened? Is he hurt? Sick?"

"He had to put his horse down today. Animal stepped in a gopher hole at a full gallop. Broke its leg so bad that Mercer had to put the horse out of its misery."

"He . . . he loved that horse." Tears stung her eyes. "How can I help?

"He's holed up in the bunkhouse, drunk. His heart's broke clean in two and I'm right worried about him." Bill cleared his throat. "I'm thinking the situation needs a woman's touch. My Essie's visiting her sister this week, or she'd handle it. I'm no good at talking a man down from this kind of hurt. I tried calling Miz Arie first, but her mama says she's back over in Nashville 'cause one of her little patients is dying and was asking for her."

Ciana felt bruised, petrified. If Arie went to Nashville to be with a dying child, she didn't need to know this about Jon right now. "It's okay, Mr. Pickins. I'm on my way."

# 16

By the time she arrived at the ranch, Ciana was tied in knots. What could she say? What words did she have to help him? She got out of the truck and walked to the bunkhouse, where each hired hand had a small private room. Jon was in unit six—Arie had told her and Ciana hadn't forgotten the number. She rapped on the wood door.

From inside, a gruff voice shouted, "Go away!"

She took a deep breath. "It's me, Jon. It's Ciana."

No response. She tried the doorknob and found it was unlocked. She opened the door and stepped inside to a room lit by a small lamp on a bedside table. Jon sat propped on the bed, wearing jeans but bare-chested and barefoot. A fan circulated warm, stuffy air from the foot of the bed. He held a jelly jar of amber liquid. A half-filled whiskey bottle rested on the floor. Pain, unmasked and raw, shadowed his face.

Her heart ached for him. "Hey, cowboy."

He tipped his head to one side, raised his glass to her.

"Well, well, looks like Bill's called in the cavalry. Have you come to save me?"

She walked to the bed and stood looking down at him. "I'm right sorry about your horse—"

"Bonanza," Jon interrupted. "He had a name."

She felt stupid for not being more sensitive. "Will you tell me about it?"

"What's a man say when he's killed his best friend?"

"He recognizes that it was an act of mercy."

Jon took a gulp from his jelly jar. "I raised that horse from a colt. His dam rejected him, and I hand-fed him until he could make it on his own. He followed me everywhere if I didn't tie him up. He was a great horse."

Pity for Jon, for Bonanza and for the loss swarmed Ciana's heart. She stood woodenly by the bed, still looking for words to comfort him but not finding them.

Jon cocked his head. "Sit down. Have a drink." He scooted over, patted the rumpled sheets next to him, and poured more liquor into the jar. She hesitated. He said, "Can't give comfort looking down on someone, Ciana."

She sat, facing him sideways, watching beads of his sweat trickle downward, where they got caught in his chest hair. Heat rose to her cheeks. He had been wearing more clothes on the summer night they'd first met. Now, in spite of the circumstances, their proximity, his bare skin and hardened abdomen, felt more intimate than when she'd lain in his arms.

He held out the jar to her. "I'm sharing."

"No thanks." She felt the fan ruffle her hair from behind. "Want to tell me what happened?"

"We were chasing a spooked cow. Bonanza hit a hole, went down. He was in a world of hurt, thrashing on the ground and screaming. Ever hear a horse scream, Ciana? Bad sound." He paused, sipped from the jar.

"You couldn't let him suffer." She glanced across him to the far side of the slim mattress. She saw a long-nosed revolver, a Colt .45. Her stomach clenched. Deep down she knew this was the gun he'd used to put down his horse. Just how depressed was he? Could he be trusted with the gun tonight? He was in pain and drunk too. Drunk people did stupid things. She braced her arm on the far side of the bed, leaning across his hips as casually as possibly when he raised the jar to his mouth. Her palm inched over the sheet until her fingers closed over the cold metal.

With a quickness that stunned her, Jon's hand clamped around his wrist. "What are you doing?"

She startled. "Um . . . thought I'd move your gun."

"You thinking I might shoot myself?"

She felt color drain from her face. "Thought I'd just move it out of harm's way."

"Let go of it."

She didn't. "Just a precaution."

Her words stopped when he flipped her over as if she were a calf he'd roped. His agility amazed her, and in one fluid motion she found herself stretched out on the bed, with Jon straddling her and holding her wrists over her head with one hand. The gun was lost with the movement. She bucked her body but couldn't budge him. "Let go! I'm not your enemy."

"You were stealing my gun."

"Don't be silly. I'm just going to take it with me. I'll return it in the clear light of day." She attempted to scoot from under him but couldn't.

The bedside lamp threw light on his features, etching his

anger in clear, clean lines. "Know what I'm thinking?" he asked.

Her heart hammered, alarmed at the way he was staring down at her. "That you'd like to shoot *me?*"

A half smile turned up one side of his mouth. He leaned lower, hunger filling his green eyes. "I'm thinking I'd like to finish what we started at the beginning of the summer."

His mouth came down on hers. She struggled, tried to twist away, but soon found herself as lost in his kiss as the first time. She stopped fighting and tasted the heady, smoky flavor of the whiskey on his tongue, felt his hard body as he stretched out along the length of her. She thrust herself upward, this time not to remove him but to mold into him. He released her wrist and she flung her arms around him, worked her fingers down his broad back, felt gooseflesh rise on his taut skin. His mouth traveled down the side of her neck, and his tongue darted into the rise of her cleavage. Ciana gasped.

He broke off and rose up, his expression burning into her. She couldn't control the pounding of her heart, the roughness of her breath. She didn't want him to stop touching her. She let him unbutton her shirt, peel it away.

In his soft Texas drawl, he whispered, "I want you, Ciana. I love you. God help me. I've never said those words to another woman, and that's the truth."

Her heart believed him. "Not even your mama?"

His half smile appeared, and he nuzzled her neck. "Not since I was ten."

"Long time passing." She could hardly swallow.

He searched her face like a man taking a long, slow drink of water, studying every feature as if memorizing each one. He tangled his fingers into her hair and drew his thumbs down her temples and onto her cheeks. He bent lower, whispered, "Close your eyes."

She did as he asked and seconds later felt his lips on her eyelids in a kiss as soft as a flower petal.

His lips trailed downward to caress her mouth, draw in her tongue.

An aching tenderness bled through her. Her chin trembled and tears gathered in her eyes. There was no firestorm now, only a slow, delicious sense of belonging. This time, when their kiss broke, he traced the path of her tears with his mouth, drinking in each drop. Her arms tightened around him. She loved him too. But when she gazed upward, a face formed in the shifting shadows of the ceiling—Arie's face. Ciana sobbed aloud and pushed Jon away. Her voice broke as she whispered, "No."

Looking confused, he watched her weep as she tugged her unbuttoned shirt together and closed her arms across her chest. Jon flipped himself onto his back in the bed, taking long, ragged breaths.

"I . . . I can't. I'm sorry . . . ," she said, tears running freely.

"Don't say that, because I don't want you to be sorry. *I'm* not sorry."

She rose up on her elbow to peer down at him, wiping her cheeks, feeling coolness from the fan where only his warmth had covered her moments before.

His arm was thrown across his face, hiding his eyes in the crook of his elbow. "Just go," he said.

Shakily, Ciana eased off the bed and stood on rubbery legs. "Jon—"

"Go!"

"I didn't mean for this to happen. I only came to . . . to help."

He said nothing.

At the door, she looked over her shoulder to where he lay unmoving. He was beautiful to her, a temptation too strong for her to resist forever. "Why is it that we end up this way when one of us is drunk?"

"I'm stone-cold sober now," he mumbled.

She had no comeback for him.

Ciana slipped through the doorway and hurried to her truck. She drove home fast along dark country roads, without regard for traffic rules, pushing the old truck hard, ignoring the engine needle pointing hot on the temperature gauge. Her teeth chattered, not from cold, because the night air was sticky, but from what had almost happened between her and Jon Mercer. He'd said he loved her. She knew she loved him, but so did Arie, her friend, and friends didn't betray friends. An impossible situation. Crying hard, she pressed her boot harder onto the gas pedal, racing temptation and memories that chased her like screaming banshees.

# 17

"How's Cory?" Arie asked at the nurses' station, still breathless from the breakneck drive to Nashville and the footrace from the parking lot to the pediatric floor.

"Arie! Thank heaven you're here. He's so scared and he keeps asking for his mother. And also you. Thank you for coming."

Arie nodded. "Where's Lotty?"

"She's in Idaho on a concert tour, but she's chartered a private jet and is flying home now. Cory became sick at home, and his au pair brought him into the ER this afternoon. His doctor checked him in a little while ago. He's having a terrible reaction to his chemo."

"And his daddy?" Arie knew that Lotty and her movie-star husband had split two years before, but certainly he'd be wanting to be with his son.

"In Poland shooting a movie. We haven't been able to reach him yet."

Arie's nerves tightened. "Is he aware of what's going on?"

"It's touch and go."

Arie rubbed her eyes, weary to the bone. She didn't want to be the person with Cory if he died. She didn't have the strength, the fortitude to be his pillar if he slipped away in the night before his mama arrived. Still she knew she couldn't abandon him either. No one should have to face death alone, least of all a child.

The nurse walked Arie to Cory's private room, where a woman in her midtwenties sat beside the hospital bed. The girl, looking panicked, jumped up when Arie entered the room. She turned out to be Maria, the au pair, a Columbian girl hired to watch Cory during Lotty's short tour. Maria was not faring well under the circumstances. Arie took her hand. No one expected this to happen now. "If you want to go back to the house, I'll stay here until Lotty arrives."

Maria looked conflicted. Her job was to stay with Cory. "I . . . I don't know."

Just then, Cory opened his eyes. When he saw Arie, his pale face struggled to make a smile. "Arie, you're here," he said through cracked lips.

She snapped on latex gloves from a nearby box, knowing that his immune system was compromised because of his chemo and the gloves guarded against germs. "I'm right here, sweetie." She took the child's hand.

"Where's Mama?"

"She's flying home right now."

"Will you stay with me?"

"Of course I will." Arie saw relief in Maria's expression.

"I'm thirsty."

Arie grabbed a cup of ice chips from the bedside table and

fished out a small wedge, placing it on Cory's tongue. "You know these will make your mouth feel better." Arie picked up a sterile cotton-tipped stick and rolled it in a jar of lemon-flavored petroleum jelly and smoothed it over his lips. "Don't lick it off," she said when his tongue darted out of his mouth.

"Tastes yucky." Cory screwed up his face.

"Pretend it's a greasy French fry," she urged with a smile.

Cory's eyelids half closed and pain racked his little body. Arie pressed the button on his morphine drip to bring him relief. As a child, she'd learned to press the button for herself, and she knew the drip was set to ease pain quickly.

Soon his face relaxed. His eyes opened but held the glaze of the drug. "You'll hold my hand till Mama comes?"

"Absolutely." She looked to Maria, who turned over her bedside chair to Arie. Tears had flooded the girl's eyes, and Arie gestured that she didn't have to stay. Maria nodded and mimed that she'd be down the hall in the waiting room. Arie watched her go, wishing she could do the same.

Cory asked, "You won't let go?"

"Course not." She smoothed his damp hair off his forehead, curling tendrils with her fingers.

"Even if the angels come for me?"

A lump rose in Arie's throat. Lotty must have told him as much, not realizing that he might be afraid of leaving this earth before he could say goodbye to her. "I'll shoo them away," Arie told him.

She watched him drift into sleep and thought about how her family had sat diligently by her bed when she'd been younger. She'd never been alone. Someone was always beside her bed to pat her, talk to her, give her ice chips, calm her fears. Chemo had come a long way since those earlier days—she'd done well through the last round during her senior year.

Mercifully she'd kept her hair, but now the murderous cancer had returned, this time so fast. At least previous treatments had allowed her a few years of normalcy in between.

Dr. Austin had called her several times since her CT scan results, pushing her to come in and get into a treatment protocol. She still had not told anyone, not her friends, not her family. Jon knew because he'd caught her that day crying in the rain. She wasn't sure why she was holding out. What difference did it make if another treatment program ruined her freshman year of college as it had her last year of high school? Maybe it was the sense of pity she'd invoke from everyone. The pity party had gotten old. *Been there. Done that.*

Cory groaned and Arie patted his arm. "I'm right here, honey. You rest." The child settled down and her thoughts drifted to Jon. She melted inside every time she saw him. She loved him so much! A one-sided love, she realized, but it hardly mattered. Just being near him made her heart sing. Yet in the beginning when she'd dared to hope he would want her, one-sided love hadn't mattered to her. Now it was beginning to matter because he was kind to her, but there was no passion for her in his eyes. She knew it but lived with hope.

His job with Pickins would last until October. She'd asked him if he might stay on, as she knew about his father's stroke and the old man's refusal to leave his run-down trailer out in the boonies for an assisted-living facility. Jon had told her, "He's a stubborn old cuss, but I can't force him to move. So I'll head to Texas when this job's finished."

Crestfallen, she'd forced herself to smile all the while realizing that she wasn't a strong enough attraction to keep him in Tennessee. And once she went back into treatment, she'd be less of one. Her first college classes started soon. Ciana's too. Except Ciana would move to the Vanderbilt Nashville campus. And with Eden focused 100 percent on Tony—well, life as she'd known it was changing forever. And facing another round of radiation and chemo wasn't something she wanted to do.

Her eyelids grew heavy. Keeping hold of Cory's hand, she laid her cheek across her outstretched arm on the bed. In minutes, she fell asleep.

The bustle of activity awakened Arie.

"Sorry to wake you," Lotty said in a whispery voice.

Arie bolted upright, stiff and groggy with her arm numb. She yawned, shook her arms as pinpricks of feeling returned. "You're here . . . He'll be so happy. He's been asking for you."

"Got here as soon as I could. I never should have left him, but he'd seemed okay." Lotty was wearing jeans and an oversized shirt but was still in stage makeup. Face glitter caught in the dim light and the hair piled on her head was studded with glimmers of sparkling jewels. She looked every bit the star that she was. "How can I ever thank you for staying with my son?"

Arie stood on wobbly legs. "He wanted you. He substituted me." She stretched. "What time is it?"

"Four in the morning." Lotty leaned over the bed to trail kisses down Cory's cheeks. "Hey big boy, Mama's here."

His eyes flickered open and he grinned. "Arie said you'd come."

"And so I have."

"She kept the angels away so I could hug you." He lifted one arm; the other, laced with IV lines, was strapped to the bed. She leaned into his embrace. "Your hair's all scratchy."

"Hairspray. I'll wash it out after we eat breakfast together."

Arie backed out of the room. Watching the tender reunion

from the doorway, she saw the electronic lines on Cory's monitor strengthen. Love could do that, bring someone back from the brink of the precipice.

A nurse touched Arie's elbow. "I've made up a cot for you in a private room. Get some sleep."

"I should go home—"

"After you've slept awhile. No need to leave in the dark."

Arie agreed and followed the nurse to a small quiet room where she lay in the dark, still in a quandary about further treatment for a cancer that hunted her like a merciless enemy.

# 18

Once she returned home, Ciana walked the floor, stretched out on her bed, stared at the ceiling, got up, paced the floor again, and trembled with memories of what she'd almost allowed to happen between her and Jon Mercer. She'd been on fire for him, was still on fire. But passion alone couldn't explain away all the things she'd felt in his arms. The connection, the bond she'd experienced with him went much deeper than simple passion.

She kept remembering her reaction to his gaze, to how his eyes had swept her face, to how his heat had soaked into her skin, and to his voice whispering, "I want you. I love you." She wanted him too. All of him.

Only the sudden shock of guilt had saved her from taking what she'd wanted. Hours later, guilt stalked her still. She'd come dangerously close to betraying her best friend. The code of honor stated that friends don't betray friends. Arie loved Jon. How could Ciana take someone so precious from Arie? Hadn't her friend been through medical hell most of her life?

And now that Arie was finally healthy, what kind of a person took away another's hope for happiness?

Ciana would give anything to talk to her grandmother. Once during the long night, she'd closed her eyes and saw herself sitting at Olivia's feet, resting her head in Olivia's lap. "*What can I do, Grandmother?*" In the vision, Olivia stroked her tangled cinnamon-colored hair, making soothing sounds with her honeyed voice. "*It will be all right, child. Don't fret. Doing the right thing is always the best thing. It's the Beauchamp way.*"

For the first time in her life, Ciana didn't want to be a Beauchamp, bound by rules of duty and honor. She wanted to be wild and carefree. She wanted to have what she wanted and damn the consequences. But she couldn't and wouldn't.

She forced her exhausted thoughts onto Eden. A text message earlier had told her about the death of a girl they both knew from high school—Meghan Oden. Was Eden afraid of dying too? Tony's possessive form of "love" was insane. Would Tony be the one to destroy Eden while no one did anything to help her? How could Ciana live with that on her conscience?

When the long night ended, she went to the stables, saddled Firecracker, and rode the fields of the Beauchamp property. In the breaking light, a low mist clung to the dirt. In every direction the land looked desolate. There was a time when crops had been plentiful and a fall harvest awaited machinery and workers. Not now. Between Olivia's illnesses and confinement to an assisted living center, Alice Faye's alcoholic indifference, and Ciana's youth, the fields of thriving crops had vanished. What a sad commentary on the Beauchamps' once-grand homestead.

Ciana reined in her horse and watched the sun rise over the haze. The sky glowed with yellow and blue streaks—

autumn was knocking at the door. By mid-October, the whole countryside would be ablaze with color. Then winter would come and the land would turn frosty, and after that spring and summer. A farmer chased the seasons, a slave to sun and rainfall, a victim of hail and wind. Attending college meant that planting season for her would supply only enough alfalfa to feed her two horses. Without time and money, most of the land would remain dormant. Once, she'd had direction, a purpose, commitment to the certainty of her life. Now her heart felt like an empty cup. If only she'd never met Jon Mercer. He had awakened things inside her she didn't know were there, never suspected she wanted.

She watched the sun climb higher, watched it melt away the morning shadows. She had things to do back at the barn. She should take Sonata out for a ride too. She needed to check on Arie and see how the little boy she'd sat with throughout the night before was doing. She'd already decided she would only give the barest mention of going to see Jon after Pickens's call. *I went because you couldn't*, was what she'd say. She should think about packing up for college. In truth, she didn't want to go, but she didn't want to stay either. A conundrum.

Firecracker stepped sideways, restless and hungry. Ciana lifted her face to the sun. It shone down on everything. *Everything*. Even on the far side of the world. And that was when a half-remembered conversation returned to her. She and Arie standing on a hot July sidewalk staring at a poster of Italy. And in the same instant, she thought of her college fund. Hers alone. She, Ciana Beauchamp, had the power; she had the means to change her life and the lives of her friends. Simple. Why had she not thought of it before now, when she was punch-drunk with fatigue?

With the plan still taking shape in her head, she jabbed Firecracker in the flanks, shouted, "Yah!" and gave her full rein. At a gallop, the horse carried her across the fields toward the barn. Looking up, she shouted, "Thank you, Grandmother!" Olivia Beauchamp had given her the perfect answer from beyond the grave.

"Italy? You want us to go with you to Italy?" Eden sat across the restaurant table staring at Ciana, wide-eyed. "Are you kidding?"

"Is this the face of someone who is kidding?"

Eden's heart lurched into jackhammer speed. This was it. This was her way of escaping Tony, and Ciana was offering it on a silver platter. "And you're paying for it? You've got the money and you'd use it for us?"

"Olivia left me some money and this is the way I want to spend it—the three of us having a good time. A big send-off into the rest of our lives." She saw no reason to tell them anything more. "Listen, I've already put a deposit on a small private villa outside Cortona in Tuscany. If we don't go, I'll lose my money. You two don't want that to happen, do you?" She opened a file folder she'd brought with her. "It's ours for three months—September through November. Here are photos of the place from the Web." She spread out color prints of a lovely two-story stucco house boasting three bedrooms, each with a private bath, a stone courtyard, and a modern kitchen. "And it's only a ten-minute ride into Cortona, one of the oldest walled cities in Italy. Thought you'd like that part, Arie. I've already talked to the travel agent on Main Street, and she says all she needs is a firm set of dates and then she'll book our flight to Rome. She'll get us a rental car and we'll drive to the villa from the airport. I say we get out of here as quick as possible." She glanced between the faces of her stunned friends.

"Three months?" Eden asked. She imagined that Ciana's inheritance was more than "a little money."

"Sure. Why go for less? We'll be home by December first. In time for Christmas. And think of the presents we can buy."

Eden sidled a sideways look at Arie, who had yet to react. Eden would have expected an explosion of whoops from the girl who'd always wanted to visit European art museums. Instead Arie sat in silence. Frankly Eden was glad Arie wasn't jumping up and down. It would have brought unwanted attention from the goon near the door Tony had sent to accompany her to the lunch with her friends.

"Arie? What do you think? You haven't said a word." Ciana wanted this trip for all of them. "Are you in?"

Arie blinked, numb from Ciana's announcement. Her dream of a lifetime lay at her feet. She'd come today to tell them about her relapse—first telling her friends, then her family—a much more difficult task. She cleared her throat. "What about college? Are you giving up Vanderbilt?"

Ciana shrugged. "Plenty of time for college. What's wrong with starting in the January term? Would that be so terrible? I thought you'd jump all over going to Italy."

"Italy's a lifelong dream, and you know it. I'm just thinking about what Mom and Dad might say," Arie said. Her brain was traveling a mile a minute, delving into options and strategies. "What's your mother saying about you changing the game plan?"

Ciana had been surprised by Alice Faye's reaction. Ciana told her about the trip, ready for a fight if she objected. But her mother had simply looked her in the eye and said, "Go and have a good time. I'm sure Bellmeade will still be standing when you return." She'd added, "You're lucky to be able to have such freedom and the money to make it happen. It was something I never had."

Now Ciana told Arie, "Mom's okay with it. She says she'll hire help to bring in the alfalfa and get it bundled and stored. What do you say? Want to come with me?"

"I'm in," Eden said too eagerly.

"Good. Don't we all have passports?"

Eden knew she'd have to steal hers from Tony's locked desk drawer and pack stealthily, maybe a piece at a time, but she would do it, positive that Ciana would help her. They'd plan her escape together and confess everything to Arie when they were safely over the Atlantic.

"Arie? What do you say?"

Arie weighed her options. Go to Italy or go back into treatment for a disease that kept dashing her hopes. Her horse was broken to saddle. Jon Mercer would be leaving. She had only to keep her silence about her relapse. Dr. Austin would honor it, too, what with the Hippocratic oath and patient confidentiality laws. He might even be able to help her find medical care in Italy, not for treatment but for pain management if or when she needed it. And who knew—maybe the spots would remain small and she could begin treatments once she returned. December wasn't such a long way off.

"You can count me in," she said, flashing a radiant smile.

The girls bumped fists over the top of the table.

# 19

Eden plotted her getaway carefully, deciding to buy new clothes for the trip rather than attempting to sneak any she owned out of Tony's condo. Since one of Tony's men always accompanied her, she took Ciana with her on shopping expeditions to shield her purpose. Men recognized that women shopped together, so it would raise no questions when the two of them took off to buy "a new college wardrobe for Ciana." When the girls went into Nashville, Tony's man waited outside of smaller boutiques. The dressing rooms were private, so Eden and Ciana gathered armloads of clothing and in the privacy of the room chose what Eden wanted. She paid using the credit card Tony had given her, then shifted the bags to Ciana, who took the purchases to Bellmeade. Once there, Ciana packed Eden's new items in a new suitcase. Within ten days, she was completely outfitted for Italy. Eden knew she'd be long gone by the time the credit bill arrived. Sticking it to Tony in that way pleased her.

"What have you told your mother?" Ciana asked.

They were in Eden's car with the goon following in another. "I told her the truth, that we were going to Italy. And I asked her to stick around until after we left."

"She's been around all summer," Ciana noted.

"Yeah, and taking her meds, but that's how she is. I'll begin thinking everything's going swell and then boom! She runs off. I need her to keep up the routine until we leave."

"I hope she does."

"She said she would."

"What about your passport?"

"Have to wait until the last minute to snag it." Stealing it had Eden on edge. She would have to break the lock on the desk, and if Tony saw it, he'd know she was up to something.

"We're leaving this Friday. How will you get away?"

"Arie's farewell party. I'm going to go and somehow lose my bodyguard. Just have my suitcase with you."

Ciana reached across the seat and squeezed Eden's shoulder. "Arie's hundred-plus relatives will be a good smoke screen. We'll get you away."

Eden smiled thinly. "Who knew her family would figure into our escape? Must be nice to have a huge family."

"She called me all frustrated," Ciana said with a smile. "She tells me, 'You'd think I was going to the moon by the fuss they're making.' I told her they only want her to be happy. Arie will be the first to go out of the country since her relatives came over from Sweden."

"Well, for the record, you're making both of us happy." Eden made a left turn, checked her rearview mirror, and watched the dark SUV follow. She shook her head in disgust, wishing he'd have a wreck. "And speaking of happy," she said, "how's she feeling about leaving Jon behind?"

"She told me that he's returning to Texas in October

anyway, so I'm hoping the offer of going to Italy will take out the sting of telling him goodbye." *For both of us*, Ciana thought.

"Too bad. I know she's crazy about him. I was hoping he'd stick around for her sake."

Ciana drummed her fingers on the dashboard to the beat of a song, trying to distract herself from thoughts of Jon.

Eden continued. "I guess he'll have to find another horse."

"She's letting him use Caramel while she's gone. She really felt bad about not being available when he lost Bonanza." Ciana had listened to Arie cry over the phone when she learned she'd not been there for him, and she'd squirmed uncomfortably while Arie thanked Ciana profusely for consoling him in her place. On the upside, the little boy she'd sat with all night at the hospital had rallied and gone home.

"That's Arie, kindhearted to the bone," Eden said, turning onto Bellmeade's tree-lined driveway. The muscleman stopped outside the fence and waited on the shoulder of the road.

At the crest of the drive, Ciana exited the car, opened the back door, and scooped out packages. She leaned through the window and said, "See you on Friday."

"Count on it."

"Please be careful, girlfriend."

For Eden, the most difficult part was behaving as if nothing were out of the ordinary in day-to-day life with Tony. On Thursday before the party, she broke into the desk drawer, found the passport, and stuffed it under the desk blotter.

"What are you doing?" Tony's voice from behind her frightened a year's growth out of her.

She straightened and turned with a smile. "Just straightening up the piles."

"Stay away from my desk."

She draped her arms around his neck. "Now don't get crabby. Not when you're leaving me tomorrow afternoon." Earlier he had told her that he had an important meeting lined up in Memphis and wouldn't be home until very late Friday night. Her heart leaped, but she kept her cool. "I was going to ask you if I could go over to Arie's Friday. It's her birthday," Eden lied, "and her family's throwing a barbeque bash for her in the afternoon. I'll be home before dark. In fact, I'll beat you here." She grew serious. "She's my friend, Tony. I really want to go."

Tony considered her request while she simmered inside over how degrading it felt to ask for his permission to go out. "I guess I could send Tim-o with you."

"Please don't let Arie's family see him skulking around after me. They'd never understand and I can't explain he's just protecting me." That was the line Tony had fed her when she'd wanted free of surveillance. But she knew the goons weren't protecting her—they were watching her, making sure she didn't split. That was what Gwen had insisted was happening with Tony's around-the-clock "guard." "Wouldn't he be better off protecting you?" Eden asked.

Tony studied her face with his dark eyes. "I don't want anything happening to you."

She smiled coyly, even though she felt revulsion. "At Arie's party? No way. I'll be surrounded by scores of her relatives."

"I'd like to have Tim-o with me," he mused thoughtfully. "Maybe just this once."

Her heart raced. She rose on tiptoes to gently kiss his mouth. "I'll bring you a cupcake."

He cradled her face. "I love you, Eden. I wanted you since the first minute I laid eyes on you. I still want you."

*Obsession isn't love,* she thought. Slowly she began to unbutton her blouse. He watched her fingers, following the slow process, desire rising in his eyes. She removed the garment and with a practiced toss, threw it atop Tony's desk, making sure that the blouse draped over the lock of the drawer. She spun in a circle to further distract him, took a few steps backward, and, holding out her hand, whispered, "Prove it."

Ciana arrived at Arie's in her mother's borrowed Lincoln. The party was already in full swing. She thought it would be more comfortable riding to the Atlanta airport than in her rattletrap of a pickup truck. Alice Faye said she'd figure a way to get the car home later.

Ciana parked the tank-sized car, and once in the crowded backyard, she searched for Arie's brother, Eric, so that he could put Arie's luggage into the car's trunk already packed with hers and Eden's gear. They were on a tight schedule. Their flight left Hartsfield-Jackson Atlanta International Airport at ten-thirty p.m., but they had to be checked in at least two hours before their international flight left. The drive took two hours, another forty minutes for parking and baggage check-in, and who knew how long to get through security? To be safe, she wanted to leave the party in less than an hour.

Eden caught up with Ciana while she was searching for Eric. They hugged quickly. "You made it," Ciana said.

"Goon-free," Eden said with satisfaction. "Tony won't begin to miss me until he returns tonight. Last thing I'm doing before we get on the plane is tossing my cell phone in the trash. I'll be free."

Arie joined them, bubbling over with excitement and dragging along her brother and his girlfriend, Abbie. Ciana handed over her keys to Eric, who had agreed to put his sister's bags into the car.

Once the couple left, Arie searched the crowd. "I'm looking for Jon. He said he'd come."

Ciana's heart lurched. The last person she needed to see was Jon. The excitement of the past several days had eased the memory of him from her head and heart. Almost.

"I see him," Arie cried, dodging through a group of people.

Ciana turned her back and asked Eden, "Want anything to eat or drink?"

"I'd throw it up. Too nervous to swallow. I'll eat when that plane's high in the air."

Ciana nodded. "Think I'll get a hamburger." She walked to the grills, which were set up in the far corner of the yard. After waiting briefly in line, she stopped at the condiments table beside washtubs filled with iced soft drinks and beer. She grabbed a soda and was deciding where to sit when a hand reached out and took her plate.

"Let me help," Jon Mercer said.

Her knees went weak, but her back stiffened. "I can carry my own food."

He ignored her. "Why are you taking Arie to Italy?"

His question confused her. "Because she wants to go, and always has."

"But why now?"

Her voice stuck in her throat. Had his heart turned toward Arie? "The timing was good for all of us. What's wrong with her going?"

"And Beauchamp money gets you whatever you want," he said acidly, without answering her question.

Little did he know of the truth of the dwindling Beauchamp money. "I don't think it's any of your business," she said, her temper rising. "Who are you to judge a gift I want to give to my best friends?"

"'Scuse me." Eric stepped between Ciana and Jon, fished for a beer in the tubs, and straightened, separating the two of them. "Didn't mean to interrupt anything."

"You're interrupting nothing. I was just going to find a place to sit and eat." She couldn't understand why Jon was acting oddly about the Italy trip.

Jon glanced at Eric, handed back Ciana's plate, tipped his head, and walked off.

"What's his beef?" Eric asked.

"No idea."

Eric fidgeted, then finally asked, "This trip . . . it isn't all about my sister, is it?"

His question startled her. "Why are you asking?"

"You're nervous, twitching around like a cornered cat. Abbie noticed."

Ciana blew out a breath, hoping Eric would drop his grilling. When he refused to move, she said, "No. The trip's for all of us."

"It's Eden, isn't it?"

Her gaze darted to his face. "Yes, but I can't say anything. Arie doesn't know yet. We'll tell her when we're in the air."

Eric held up his key ring, removed one key, and handed it over to Ciana. "I switched all the luggage to my truck. I'm afraid that old Lincoln is burning oil. It may not make it to the airport."

"*Your* truck?" Ciana knew how special it was to him.

"I want my sister to arrive safe and sound. It's best to take my truck."

Gratitude filled her heart. "Are you sure?"

"Text me its location and Abbie and I'll go over and get it tomorrow. We'll pick you up when you return."

She clutched the key. "Thank you. I'll be very careful with your truck."

"Just be careful with my sister," he said, and walked away.

On the other side of the yard, Jon cut Arie away from a group of chattering cousins as smoothly as a calf from a herd. She wanted to throw her arms around him, kiss him, but such a display would start everyone gossiping, plus he didn't look especially happy.

"You didn't tell them, did you?" His tone sounded accusing.

Her face flamed hot. No use dancing around. "If I had, I couldn't have gone to Italy. Mom and Dad would have hog-tied me, and Ciana and Eden might not have gone without me. Or they might have gone, but come back early. My news would have ruined everything for everyone."

"Don't you think they deserve to know before they take you halfway round the world?"

"Yes," she said ruefully. "But I'm not saying a word until I have to. And neither are you. You promised."

"You're putting your life on the line for a *vacation*." He sounded baffled.

"Not a vacation. A dream fulfilled. Dreams die hard, Jon Mercer. And when one is offered to me like a magic carpet ride, I'm jumping on. It's what I want. It's what I'm doing." She wanted him, too, but the trip was within reach. He wasn't. Still, his concern for her was touching.

"It doesn't seem fair to Ciana and Eden. What if you get sick over there?"

"Cancer's not fair either," she said stubbornly. "My doctor's given me the name of some oncologist in Rome. They went to med school together, so I'll go to him if I have to. Plus I'm taking meds on the trip. I think I'll be fine till I can come home."

"You may be betting your life."

She forced a smile. "Don't be so dramatic."

He hooked his thumbs into the belt loops of his jeans. "I hope you know what you're doing."

She offered a wan smile. "Me too. But it's a chance I'm willing to take. I've been tethered to this illness all my life, so now I'm calling the shots for a while. I'm going to Italy."

"Take care," he said.

"You take care of my horse," she said lightly. "Show her my picture occasionally and remind her who really owns her."

He nodded, his expression troubled. "I won't let her forget."

An hour later, amid cries of "Goodbye, good luck, have fun, write us, we'll miss you, we love you," the three girls piled into Eric's truck and started for Atlanta. When morning broke, they'd be in Italy.

# 20

Gwen sat alone in her darkened living room knowing he would come. His kind always did. She lit a cigarette, and the glowing red tip penetrated the dark. Her nerves felt raw. She wished she'd taken a second tranquilizer before coming downstairs to wait. She was scared, afraid she'd blow it. And she was afraid of him. She'd faced down such a man once before, but she was out of practice. She hoped she could do it one more time.

A car screeched to a stop in front of her house. Doors slammed. She snuffed out her cigarette. Her front door was kicked open and Tony and two other men came inside. "It's customary to knock first," she said, her voice steadier than she'd expected.

Tony crossed the floor and jerked her up from her chair, his fingers digging into her upper arms with a vengeance. "Where is she, old woman? And don't lie to me."

One of the muscle boys turned on the table lamp beside the chair. Although the light was dim, she saw her adversaries clearly. Tony and his menacing henchmen, as large as brick walls and about as solid. Their two faces wore no expressions. Tony's blazed with wicked fury.

Tony shook her.

Gwen cowered, partly an act, mostly real. It had been a long time since she'd been on the receiving end of a man's wrath. "I . . . I don't know—"

Tony slapped her hard across her face. She yelped. "Stop wasting my time! Tell me where she went."

"Please, don't hit me. Please." She tried to buy time by begging. Abusers liked to hear a woman beg.

He gave her a second jaw-rattling slap on the other side of her face. "I'll do worse than hit you if you don't tell me what I want to know."

She sagged, went limp. Her face stung like fire and she tasted blood from a cut on her lip. "Sh-she said you were going to hurt her. She's my child! I have to protect her."

Tony's eyes were cruel, heartless. "I don't give a shit. You tell me or I'll have one of my boys beat it out of you." To prove his point, one of his men grabbed her arm and twisted it so severely that she screamed. How many years had passed since she'd been hit, punched, and kicked?

"No one walks out on Tony Cicero. No one." He emphasized each word with a painful jab to her chest.

"If . . . if I tell you, you won't hurt her, will you?"

"I'll decide that when I catch her."

Gwen's interior defiance hardened. She'd played this game before with Eden's abomination of a father, and she knew all the right evasive moves to prolong the expected beating. "She left with Ciana and Arie."

Tony bared his teeth. "And where did she go with Ciana and Arie? I know she took her passport. Stop stalling."

"A long trip. Ciana planned it. She paid for it too."

Tony squeezed the arm he still held until she winced. "Where?"

"Greece."

The lone word stunned him into silence. Gwen bided her time, dragging out the silence. Just as she anticipated his upcoming eruption, she added, "They've been planning the trip. She wanted to go away. She wanted her freedom."

"Her *freedom*? I gave her anything she wanted." Tony's voice turned into a snaky hiss. "The lying bitch." He shook Gwen hard, rattling her brain. "She said it was her friend's birthday. I let her go out alone and this is how she repays me?"

"There was a party for Arie," Gwen cried out. "That was true."

"When did they leave?"

"Less than an hour ago," Gwen lied. She hadn't attended the party, but expecting the worst from Tony, Gwen figured he'd leave more quickly if she made him think he could catch her fleeing daughter. "For the airport."

"Which airport?"

Gwen trembled, adrenaline pumping through her body. International flights went out of Atlanta and Nashville, so this was the tricky part. She had to make him believe her. Should she lie or tell the truth? If he didn't believe her, he might kill her on the spot. "Nashville," she whispered, dropping her head and shoulders to show he'd broken her resolve.

"What vehicle did they take?"

"Ciana's old farm truck. The banged-up blue one. I think it's a Ford." She added the unsolicited detail to underscore her willingness to cooperate. To an abuser, it sounded as if she'd been broken.

Tony looked to his boys. "We still have time to catch her."

He slapped Gwen hard again. "That's for wasting my time. I'd better catch her, or I'll be back to settle with you." He shoved her backward and Gwen collapsed into the chair where she'd been sitting when Tony had first walked in the door. She kept her head down, gushed tears, stared at her hands in her lap, waited for the sound of car doors to slam shut and the powerful engine of Tony's chase car to start up and roar away.

Alone again, she continued to shake all over. She wiped her eyes, reached for her pack of cigs on the table, and turned off the lamp. Her hands shook so badly she barely got the cigarette lit, but when she did, she inhaled deeply, pulling the smoke deep into her lungs, held it, released it and waited for her nerves to settle. She took several drags, snuffed out the cigarette, then went upstairs. In her bathroom, she turned on the light and saw bruises already rising on her cheeks and upper arms. She raked fingers through her wrecked hair, bent down, and splashed cold water on her face. She rinsed out her mouth, spit blood into the sink.

She went into her bedroom closet, dragged down the blue duffel bag, tossed it onto the bed, opened drawers, and tried to figure out what to pack. Crazy. She never took this kind of time when she was on a manic tear. Everything was crystal clear with the whispering voices to guide her. She threw clothes haphazardly into the bag, remembering the night she'd left Oregon and Eden's father, another no-good piece of human waste. He'd gone to the liquor store and she'd frantically grabbed up a few of her and her month-old baby's belongings. She had squirreled away money for months, hiding it in a Bible, knowing he'd never look there. In a matter of minutes, she broke for the door, clutching a grocery bag of stuff and her baby. Her escape had to be fast and clean because he'd sworn he'd kill her if she ever tried to leave him.

That night she boarded a cross-country bus under an assumed name and rode it to Nashville. She had an aunt there, an old woman who'd told her to come if she ever got away from her situation. Gwen nursed Eden, ate peanut butter crackers and raisins cross-country, and counted every penny, hoping her money would last her on the long bus ride.

Once inside the Nashville bus terminal, she clutched baby Eden and called Aunt Myrtle, then waited under a garish streetlight until the gray-haired woman arrived in a rust bucket of a car. They arrived at Myrtle's house—this house—miles from the city, a safe haven. Gwen's parents had disowned her, unable to accept a daughter who was a "bad seed," but Myrtle liked her and would help her with the baby. Gwen's affliction, her bipolar disorder, was growing worse. It was the thing that Eden's father hated most about her. The thing he'd tried to beat out of Gwen with his fists but couldn't.

When Eden was two, Myrtle died, leaving the house to Gwen, where she lived as a neighborhood built up around the old house. She raised Eden and struggled against the rising tide of her illness, taking meds and abandoning them because none of them were ever quite right. None made her feel "normal." Eden had suffered because of it, but it had also helped make the girl stronger and self-reliant. Until Tony came along. No matter. Eden was far away from him for now.

Gwen opened the top drawer of her dresser and pulled out an old tin box, her only keepsake from her hellish childhood. She opened it and removed a roll of money wrapped in a rubber band. Her habit of secretly hiding money had never changed. A little here, a little there. Piggly Wiggly job to her rescue. In the bathroom, she grabbed a toothbrush, toothpaste, and a few cosmetics. Her hand skimmed over the row of medicine bottles that kept her illness at bay. She disliked taking them, but she had taken them faithfully for months, sensing that Eden would need her well enough to handle breaking away from Tony. Without the meds, she'd feel like her old self in a few days. She'd hook up with others in Florida, a collection of homeless misfits she'd met over the years with mental problems bigger than hers. They were her friends. They understood her, accepted her "as is."

Gwen hurried downstairs. Outside she threw her bag into the car. Only one more thing to do. She took out her cell phone, made two calls, spoke briefly to the recipients, then placed the cell under the right rear tire of the car in the driveway.

She got into the car and took deep breaths. She looked out, staring at the place that had been her home for almost twenty years. Tony would return to an empty house. Maybe he'd burn it to the ground. So be it. "This one's for you, baby girl," she said, for all the times through the years she'd left her child to manage on her own.

Gwen started the car and backed over the phone, turning it into a tangle of crushed circuits and plastic dust, then drove off into the night.

# PART II

# 21

"Look! It's Rome." Arie pressed her nose to the plane's window, watching the clouds part and shred like paper as the plane descended over a great sprawling city.

"Where? I can't see a thing with your head in the way," Eden grumbled.

Arie leaned back, tears misting her eyes. She glanced across the aisle at Ciana, who was straining against her seat belt to catch sight of the Eternal City.

"Big city," Eden said, awestruck.

"Almost three million people," Arie said, dabbing her eyes.

"Are you crying?" Eden turned from the window toward Arie.

"Just a little overwhelmed. I never thought I'd actually come here."

"We all needed a vacation. Think of it as the senior trip we never got," Ciana offered.

Arie's gaze connected with Ciana's and she mouthed, "*Thank you.*"

Ciana waved off the gratitude. She was cross-eyed from lack of sleep. Who wouldn't be after chasing the sun across the Atlantic for over nine hours? They'd left Atlanta on time and were arriving in Rome midmorning. She'd attempted to sleep, but her head was too full of the drama of leaving and the excitement of the upcoming months. All the travel info the agency had given her urged them to hit the ground running, stay awake, and go to bed at a regular time. Get on Italy's time schedule as soon as possible. She yawned, hoping she could.

The plane landed. The girls disembarked into the chaos of the crowded airport, the sound of foreign languages, and the long lines leading through customs. Once their passports were stamped and they gathered their luggage, they emerged into the bustle of the outer area of the terminal, where other crowds waited to greet family and friends.

Ciana was heartened to see a woman holding a sign with the word *Beauchamp* written on it. "Over there," she told her friends. "Our greeter."

The Tennessee agent had said they'd have a go-between in Rome to help them navigate and negotiate the rental car, money exchange, and any other hurdles. The woman was warm and friendly and spoke perfect English with a distinctive Italian accent that Arie thought charming. In no time they were in their rental car armed with tourist brochures, maps, and a GPS navigator in the car's dashboard. "The hardest part is getting out of the city," the woman told them.

Eden elected to drive and bravely thrust the car into the snarl of noonday traffic, dodging cars, buses, scooters, bicycles, and pedestrians; managing city roundabouts; and waving at motorists' blasting horns when she veered in front of them.

"Don't kill us," Ciana warned, her knuckles white on the car's armrest.

"If I'm too nice, they'll plow me down."

Eden kept glancing in the rearview mirror, looking for a tail, some goon of Tony's who couldn't possibly be there.

Arie stared out the windows dreamily, unaffected by the traffic congestion. "We are going to spend some time in Rome, aren't we?" she asked as the car passed ancient ruins in the heart of the city.

"We are," Ciana assured her. "There's just so much to see and do, but that's why we're staying three months—so we'll have time to do it all."

The drive up to the Tuscany region and their villa was less than a hundred miles, and once they left Rome, traffic fell off significantly. The two-lane road passed fields of grazing animals and a line of cypress trees, olive trees, and a vineyard. A blazing sun shone down through air pure and sweet.

By late afternoon, the car was at last winding up the narrow road to their villa. When they crested a hill, they saw a lovely two-story house and heard the GPS announce that they had arrived at their destination.

"Wow," Eden said, turning off the engine. "Not too shabby."

Ciana felt a wave of relief. The place looked as charming as it had on the rental website, with cream-colored stucco, a red barrel tile roof, and dark wood trim under the eaves and around the door and window frames. "Let's check it out."

The front door had a lockbox hanging on the doorknob, and Ciana punched in the code the rental agency had given her. She removed the door key and unlocked the door, then stepped inside with Arie and Eden tight on her heels. They took a breath in unison. The foyer was open to a great room that soared two stories. A dark wood staircase off to one side led up to a second floor with a walk-around interior balcony and doors standing open. "Bedrooms," Ciana said, motioning to the upstairs area.

Downstairs, built-in sofas lined two walls, a modern kitchen claimed another wall, and a bank of windows and French doors led outside to a bricked patio on the fourth wall. On a rustic table beside the kitchen sat an enormous plastic-wrapped welcome basket heaped with food, fresh fruit, and two bottles of wine.

Eden headed straight to the basket, untied the ribbon, and rescued one of the wine bottles. "We don't have to be old ladies to drink in Italy."

Ciana scoffed. "Age requirements never stopped us before."

Eden found wineglasses in the kitchen, uncorked the wine, and poured three glasses. She passed them to her friends. "To us," she said, raising her glass for the others to tap.

"To the best three months of our lives," Arie added.

"And to fun, fun, fun," Ciana said. She said it as if a burden had been lifted from her. Tennessee and Bellmeade were far away, and so was her day-to-day grind and constant concern for Eden. She'd been at loose ends ever since Olivia's death and needed the break.

They flopped onto a sofa, passed around crackers and cheese, prosciutto slices, and several varieties of olives from the basket, and sipped their wine. After a minute of contented silence, Arie put her glass down on a coffee table, looked at her two friends, and asked, "Okay. Will one of you please tell me what's going on between you? What secret are you two keeping from me?"

Ciana and Eden exchanged guilty glances. Eden said, "Why do you think—"

Arie interrupted, "You have been acting paranoid ever since we left my party. Don't tell me otherwise. I watched you throw your cell phone away in Atlanta, and you acted as nervous as a squirrel in a taxidermist shop for most of the flight."

Eden shrugged. "Can't use our old cells over here anyway. No reason to hang on to it."

"And the villa has a phone if we need to call anyone. Plus I have calling cards," Ciana added. In truth, she and Eden had opted out of rental cell phones. Wasn't their whole purpose to get away from everything? "And I lugged my laptop to send email to make everybody at home sick with envy."

Arie ignored Ciana's devilish grin. "You're not telling me what the two of you are hiding. I'm in this group, too, you know."

Ciana said, "It's your story, Eden. Tell her."

Eden blew out a long-held breath. "I was always going to tell you, Arie, but not until we arrived in Italy."

"I believe we're here."

"We are." Eden took a gulp from her wineglass and launched into her story about her years with Tony, of her naiveté, of his slow but steady takeover of her life, of his obsession with her, of how she'd been ensnared beyond escape. And she told them both of his involvement in drug trafficking, of how he hooked kids at their very own middle and high schools, and of Meghan's plunge into prostitution and death by overdose. It took a while for her to get it all out. Arie and Ciana sat spellbound and were horrified about Meghan's death.

"But he . . . he never hooked you? With the drugs, I mean." Fear from concern creased Arie's brow.

"He said he'd hurt me if I did drugs. I believed him. For some reason he saw me as this pure, flawless woman. A symbol of some kind. Totally unrealistic. He could defile me, but no one else could." She shivered. "I was his prisoner, and I couldn't escape. He had eyes on me all the time."

"Why didn't you say something to somebody?"

"I was afraid. I knew too much about his drug business." Eden's voice grew small. "And I was ashamed of who I'd become."

Ciana had known the relationship had been difficult, but hearing details was truly terrifying. Soon all three of them were crying and wiping their tears on napkins from the basket. By the time her story was over, the wine bottle was empty and the napkins were wadded in a soggy heap.

"I wish you'd told me this back home," Arie said in a quivery voice.

"I felt that I couldn't tell anyone because of the drugs. What if I was sent to jail? Besides, you had enough on your plate," Eden said. "I only told Ciana what I had to. This trip was my get-out-of-jail free card."

Arie picked at a napkin still in her hands. "So this wasn't all about me, then? You figured out how coming here could be for both of us."

Ciana nodded, unable to admit that coming had been about her too. She had planned the trip to flee from the temptation of Jon Mercer, from her desire for him and his for her. She had run from her fear that she might betray Arie if she stayed. And of knowing that even if she'd fled to Nashville and college classes, it wouldn't have changed anything between them. She would have given in if she found herself alone with him again. She felt weak and pathetic. Coming to Italy was her fail-safe.

"And the money was from an inheritance?" Arie asked skeptically. "Ciana, I know how your grandmother was. She would have earmarked the money to be used for something other than just a good time. Olivia was practical and Bellmeade was everything to her."

Ciana fidgeted, self-conscious under the questioning gazes of her two best friends.

"You might as well tell us everything," Eden said. "I told my secrets."

Arie asked, "What was the money for?"

"College."

Arie's mouth dropped open. "You're spending your college fund? Your education from Vanderbilt?"

"Highly overrated. I didn't want to go there anyway. Besides, there's always MTSU and online college."

"Oh, Ciana." Arie shook her head in disbelief.

"The deed's done. We're here, and we're going to have a good time. End of story," Ciana said. "Unless, of course, *you* have a story or a secret we haven't heard."

Arie had a secret all right, one she wouldn't share until she must. She raised her glass in an attempt to hide the lie already on her lips. "With me, what you see is what you get. A very grateful girl who's going to examine every work of art in Italy. Now let's unload the car and find our bedrooms. And supper? Who's up for some Italian food?"

# 22

As it happened, none of them made it to supper. Each chose a bedroom and unpacked, and when Eden went to see what was keeping Ciana and Arie from joining her, she found them both sound asleep on their respective beds. Eden didn't have the heart to roust either. She was still wound up, so she ate more food from the basket and relived her escape, shuddering to think about what might have happened back home when Tony discovered she had fled. The only people who knew their exact destination were Arie's parents.

Over time, Eden had watched Tony turn cold and indifferent as his drug business grew. *No mercy.* The code of the streets. He had told her, "If you let down your guard, there's a line of dealers waiting to pick off your spot." She had been his only soft spot, but she couldn't have counted on that forever. According to Gwen, Tony would tire of Eden and she, too, would be disposable. Eden had no idea how Gwen was so confident of this, but every one of her warnings had come true.

Luxuriating in her solitude, she went into her private bathroom, drew herself a fragrant bubble bath, and soaked. She toweled off and snuggled naked under the heavy bedcovers, feeling safe and secure in the knowledge that she was half a world away from Tennessee and that Tony Cicero would not come to her in the dark.

The scent of coffee lured Eden downstairs and onto the patio, where Ciana sat with a carafe of coffee and an assortment of cookies. Brochures were fanned out on the glass tabletop.

Groggily, Eden reached for the carafe, but Ciana reached it first and poured a cup for her. "Let me before you hurt yourself."

"You the only one up?"

"So far."

"How long?"

"Since five."

Eden rolled her eyes. "Oh, you farm girls. This is vacation." She sipped the coffee, which was so rich she could have chewed it.

"Old habit. Remember I was up feeding horses and chickens before going off to school every day. You didn't wake up until second period."

Eden glanced around at clay pots and urns full of brilliant red geraniums and climbing bougainvillea. The hills looked rugged, and on one hill a town nestled, surrounded by a stone wall. "Cortona?"

"Yep. Hope you're rested. Arie's making plans for day trips."

"Did I hear my name?" Arie stepped through the open patio doors.

"Ciana says you're the tour guide."

Arie grinned. "Guilty. And today is the city on the hill." She gestured toward Cortona.

"Let's get started," Eden said.

They drove a few miles to the ancient city while Arie provided historical tidbits. They parked outside the walls because no motor vehicles were allowed on the old stone and brick roads inside the wall. They walked into a place that seemed to have been untouched for centuries. "Whoa," Eden said. "Did we fall through the looking glass?"

"I feel like I'm in the Middle Ages," Ciana said.

"You are," Arie said. "Older, really. Goes back to the Etruscans—the first settlers."

"Enough with the history lesson," Eden said. "Let's just find a grocery store."

The main street through the stone arch entrance turned out to be the only flat street in the town. A fountain stood in the town square, the heart of any town according to Arie. Shops surrounded the cobblestone square, and on one side was an old theater. Side streets jutted off, all with stacks of worn stone steps that led upward through neighborhoods of stone and concrete buildings consisting of homes, small eateries, and shops. Pretty window boxes filled with flowers hung from windows and interior courtyard gardens could be seen through wrought-iron gates.

They found a store, bought supplies, and started back toward the main street. Once there, Eden spied a coffee bar with picturesque café tables. The aroma drifting from the shop was heavenly. "Sit," she told her friends.

Inside, the tiny store held a bar with an amazing gleaming copper coffee machine. Behind the bar stood a grinning young man with an outrageous crop of blond curls, tan skin, and electric blue eyes. He asked a question in Italian. She looked blank. He laughed and repeated his question in English. "G'day. Help you, miss?"

"You're Italian?" Eden blurted, shocked by the unexpected non-Italian accent.

"Aussie. From down under. Name's Garret Locklin. You're American, right? From across the pond?"

"Yes." Until he had asked the question, it hadn't occurred to Eden that she was a foreigner too. "Um . . . three coffees."

"Sit with your mates. I'll bring your espressos. I make the best in all of Cortona."

She ignored his boast and returned to the outside table where her friends had settled. "We're not in Kansas anymore."

Garret soon brought out their coffees and Eden introduced her friends. He asked, "Staying nearby?"

"A villa a few miles out."

"Just clicks away," he said.

"Clicks?" Ciana asked.

"Kilometers. We say *click* in Sydney. You new here?"

"Does it show?"

Garret's easy smile lit up his face. "Most locals greet you with *buon giorno*, 'good morning.' When they depart, they say *ciao*, which also means 'hello'—economy of words. *Grazie* is 'thanks.' Manage those phrases and you'll never be identified as a newbie."

Eden realized that she'd been so focused on making an escape that she hadn't really been aware of much else. She was woefully ignorant of all things Italian.

"Are the stores closing?" Ciana asked, pitching forward, watching women locking up shops along the street. "I'm not finished looking."

Arie shook her head. "People go home for lunch. They eat, rest, play with their families. I told you all that on the plane trip. Weren't you two listening?"

Eden drew a blank. She had barely heard Arie's discourse about Italy on the long plane ride.

Garret bent over the table and in a conspiratorial voice said, "Yes, but everything reopens about four. Come back about five and have antipasto and meet my mates. We all eat dinner about nine, then come back to the square for whatever's happening."

"We?" Eden asked.

"There's a group of us. We work here and play when the work's done." His mischievous gaze flirted with Eden's. "If you come, I promise you'll have a good time."

Eden rolled her eyes at his less-than-subtle innuendo. "Puh-leze."

"Won't know unless you join us." He bounded back into the bar, where he shut and locked the door before she could react.

"I think the Aussie has plans for you," Ciana teased.

"He's cute," Arie added.

"Not interested. And he talks too fast. I can hardly understand him."

"I'm sure he has other ways of communicating," Arie offered in a sweet singsong voice.

Eden growled at her.

Ciana stood. "Let's get the food home and have some lunch. I'm starving."

Arie yawned, stretched, and stood. "I love Italy. We need to soak up the culture."

"I need to spend the afternoon with an Italian dictionary," Eden groused. "And you"—she pointed at Arie—"are going to tell me everything you know about this country all over again. I won't be upstaged by some hairy, smart-aleck Aussie."

Eden returned to the square with her friends around five o'clock, going over Italian vocabulary words in her mind. True to his word, Garret was waiting along with a small group of twentysomethings. "The American sheilas," he said. He pointed to individuals in his group and rattled off names. "Tom, my best mate from Sydney, his girl, Lorna."

And after that Eden sort of lost track because the names were strange to her. She was amazed by the variety of countries they represented—South Africa, Denmark, France, Ireland. "Are you on a tour?" she asked.

"A walkabout," Garret said.

Ciana shrugged, saving Eden the trouble.

"A long trip," the girl from Denmark offered.

Garret added, "Tom and Lorna and I took off five months ago. Met several of these blokes in Cape Town, South Africa. We traveled up the east coast of Africa, took a ship from Morocco, and hopped over to Gibraltar, worked our way over to Italy and decided to spend summer and fall here in Tuscany. Good wine, you know." He waggled his eyebrows and his friends laughed.

"Five months?" Eden said. "Where do you stay?"

"Here we have apartments, but when we travel, we stay in youth hostels. Places are cheap. We get a night's sleep and sometimes a meal."

The girl from Denmark said, "Communal bathrooms inside if we're lucky. Otherwise outside. Not always hot water, though." She shivered and hugged her arms to illustrate her point.

Eden was intrigued. "All of you? Together?"

"Sure," Garret said. "All for one and one for all. Cozy. Safety in numbers. We sort of agree on a travel course. Some peel off, others join up. You meet a lot of people, travel the world, have a lot of fun, make mates for life."

"And you work along the way?"

"When we need the money. Which is often."

Everyone laughed at that.

"Can we talk over wine and olives?" the guy from France asked. "Come with us. Tell us about your travels."

Eden hated to admit that this was her first real trip.

Arie said, "We live near Nashville, in Tennessee," then launched into an account of the state.

As the group trudged up the street and the stacks of stone steps, Garret fell in with Eden, whose head was buzzing with questions. "How do you land jobs in different countries?"

"It helps to speak two or three languages. English is preferred for shop work. I man the coffee shop, Tom's working as a bellman in the only hotel in town with a few of the others, and Lorna's selling tours for a Cortona travel business."

"And then you quit and move on?"

"That's right. Going to France next. Jacques says we can crash at his family farm."

"How do you travel?"

"Trains, mostly. And we walk."

Eden was astounded. Who just took off months at a time to travel? Maybe retired people with money, but kids in their twenties? "When do you plan to go home?"

"When I feel like it. Look, my mum and dad are good people, but I look at them, working hard to pay for a mortgage and cars and furniture. They take one vacation a year." A grin split his face. "Not for me. Not yet. World's a big place and I want to see all of it before I settle in." He spread his arms. "I keep a journal. Take photos. Try to sell an article to a magazine now and then."

"You dream big."

"I do! But I also act on my dreams. And that makes a difference. Dream or act. Safety, like my folks, or adventure. No contest for Garret Locklin. None at all."

# 23

"Hey, look. Here's a brochure for a winery that's not too far away. We can take a tour, then do a tasting." Ciana brandished her find in the air while having breakfast on the patio.

"That should be fun," Eden said over her mug of steaming coffee.

"Most people in my family drink beer, so I have the palate of a gerbil," Arie offered.

Eden snickered. "My one benefit of hanging with Tony was drinking good wine. He loved the stuff, so he only drank the best, although he preferred French wines. I think we should give Italian wines equal opportunity."

After lunch and while Cortona rested, Ciana drove the three of them up into the hills on a serpentine road to the Bertinalli Vineyards, a long-established vineyard fronted by long-abandoned stone watchtowers that stood like silent sentries. Beyond the walls lay fields of well-tended grapevines, heavy with leaves and clusters of hanging grapes ready for harvest.

After parking, they gathered with a group of tourists signed up for a tour of the winery on a tiled loggia. Conducted by a young woman, the tour led them into large stone buildings heady with the scents of wine tinged with fruit and chocolate. Ciana saw stacks and rows of oak barrels—harvests from years before, awaiting their time of perfect maturity.

Drawn to the outdoor sunlight, she slipped out the door and headed for the verdant fields. She tucked herself between the rows, away from the buildings, and leaned over the grapes, closing her eyes and sniffing the velvety clusters, swollen and heavy with juice. She crouched, dug her fingers into the soil, and examined it closely. She held a fistful in her palm, balancing the weight.

She was lost in the process when a man's voice said, "*Signorina! Cosa stai facendo?*"

Startled and with heart pounding, Ciana leaped to her feet. She thrust her hands behind her back like a child caught stealing cookies. "Oh! I . . . I'm sorry. I didn't mean—"

"English?" he asked.

"*Si* . . . I mean, yes. American."

The man was ruggedly handsome, with black hair and dark brown eyes, but he looked angry. "Do you know it is a crime to steal vine cuttings from Italian vineyards?" he said in excellent but accented English.

"But I'm not stealing anything. Honest." She was petrified. What had she been thinking?

"And behind your back? What are you hiding from me, *signorina?*"

Guiltily she brought her hand around and opened her fist to show him. "Dirt," she confessed. "I . . . I was studying your dirt."

He looked incredulous.

She hurtled ahead with her explanation with one long rambling sentence. "I'm a farmer from Tennessee, really . . . your crop is amazing and I was looking at the soil . . . you know, what it's made of . . . and what makes the grapes so wonderful . . . I'm on a winery tour, actually, but the fields are so beautiful I came over to study them and the soil and . . . and . . ."

He crossed his arms, holding her eye while she sputtered to a halt. His brown eyes narrowed. "And what does my soil say to you?"

Ciana shifted from foot to foot, realizing he was serious. She brought the clump to her nose, sniffed. "Rich in iron." She squeezed the dirt in her palm into a clump. "Clay too. I have clay on my farm. Heavy, solid stuff. Thicker than this."

He was nodding. "Perfect soil for growing wine grapes."

"I grow vegetables, no grapes." She let the soil drop back to the ground, then dusted her hand on the seat of her jeans. She held out her hand and blasted a smile at him. "Ciana Beauchamp."

He took her hand and held on to it. "Enzo Bertinalli. My family has owned these vineyards for many generations." He did not release her hand. "Beauchamp—French. They have always envied our vineyards."

*Just my luck.* She had to meet the owner, not some worker bee. She backed off on her smile. "I'm not a thief. My ancestors raised cotton and soybeans."

His brown eyes had lost their hostility, and he seemed amused by her obvious discomfort. "That is good. Stealing grapevines from Italy is worthy of prison."

Her heart bumped. "Dirt too?"

A wry smile broke across his face. "That is free." He tucked her arm through his and began to walk toward the winery with her in tow. "Perhaps we should return to your tour. Tell me, why are you in Italy?"

"I have two friends with me. We came because . . . well . . . because it's Italy." She saw that the tour had gathered back on the loggia and a man was behind a wooden bar pouring tastes of wine for the group. "There they are," she said, relieved to see Arie and Eden in a line at the bar.

When Ciana walked to her friends on the arm of the man, both simply stared. She introduced her escort. Enzo offered each a courtly nod. "Are you farmers also?"

Arie and Eden shook their heads. "Just friends," Arie said while Eden mouthed, "*What did you do?*" when Enzo wasn't looking.

Totally embarrassed, Ciana ignored her.

Eden said brightly, "Glad to meet you. You have an amazing place. Gee, Ciana, you got a man. All I got today was this wineglass." She twirled it by its stem.

Enzo laughed heartily. Ciana shot daggers at Eden.

"Come, *bella* Ciana, and her friends. I will let you taste some of the best wines my vineyard has to offer."

"Oh, but we shouldn't," Ciana said, begging off his offer. "I've already imposed—"

"Speak for yourself," Eden said, and smiled flirtatiously at Enzo.

"Come to my private cellar." He led the girls inside the modern building behind the loggia designed for commerce. Crates of wine bottles stood along the walls, and in the center of the room were tables attractively arranged with Italian pottery, dishes, and seemingly every wine accoutrement known. "I will offer you some of my best vintages."

Ciana balked. He smiled, showing his straight white teeth. Hard to resist him. He led them down a staircase and into a large chilly room lined with wooden stacks reaching the ceiling. Inside every cubbyhole, a bottle of wine rested on its side. He pulled out chairs for each around a circular wood table, all the while talking about the history of his vineyard.

He pulled out bottles, examined labels, and placed some on the table or returned others to their slots. "You know not every year is perfect for the grapes. So much depends on the benevolence of Mother Nature. Too much rain, not so good. Too little, not so good."

Ciana understood what he was saying. It was the same on her farm.

Enzo had a collection on the table, which he uncorked and poured gently into bowl-shaped glasses. "We let it breathe." He picked up a phone receiver on the wall and said something in Italian. In less than fifteen minutes, a man appeared with a tray of bread and an assortment of cheeses. "To complement the wines and cleanse the palate."

The four of them spent the afternoon savoring red wines, and Enzo talked of the Bertinallis' storied past, of how the Greeks came through Tuscany after the Trojan War and how one general fell in love with the area. By the time they had sipped from every bottle, each attached to a story, all of them were laughing and giddy. When Enzo led them back upstairs, Ciana was surprised to see the sun was sinking behind a rise of distant hills.

"You must have dinner with me," Enzo said. "I cannot send my lovely guests away without good food too. You are excellent company and a lovely surprise."

They stayed, treated to his gracious hospitality and a dinner upstairs in his private apartment. They ate fish, pasta, salad, and fresh crusty bread, each course accompanied with a special wine, served by a woman and the man who'd brought the cheese platter to the wine cellar. The meal took several hours and ended with espresso and gelato, rich Italian ice cream. When Enzo walked them to their car in the moonlight, he held Ciana back slightly and said, "I would like to see you again, *bella* Ciana."

She was grateful for his hospitality and that he hadn't called the Italian police for her trespassing, so she told him how to reach her at the villa. He kissed both her cheeks. "Until the next time. *Ciao, bella.*"

She slipped into the backseat, and Eden drove away with Arie humming some Americanized Italian song lyric. Ciana glanced through the back window and saw the tall, slim Enzo standing in the moonlight. With a heart-wrenching jolt, she suddenly had a vision of another man watching her leave. Jon Mercer. She took a deep breath. The wonderful afternoon at the winery faded. The memory of Jon had followed her across an ocean, all the way to Italy. She wondered if she would ever break free—or would she always be haunted by a man she could not have?

# 24

Arie liked coming into Cortona to write her emails to her family while Eden and Ciana languished in the sun at the villa. The coffee café had Internet access, and Garret always had a cheery word for her. Her chatty emails helped relieve some of her terrible guilt over not having been honest with them about her failed remission and true condition. Perhaps if they read how happy she was in Italy, they'd forgive her when it came time to confess.

Truth was, she felt good. Whatever the tumor was busy doing inside her, it wasn't affecting her daily life so far. A blessing. As long as she felt fine, she pushed her health out of her mind. If only she could put it out of her body as easily.

The other reason she came was to contemplate the town's various art treasures. She loved staring at Fra Angelico's seminal work, *The Annunciation*, one of the most revered paintings in Italy. She never tired of touring the small museum with its Etruscan treasures or visiting the church of Santa Margherita, built in the fourteenth century to hold the tomb of Margaret of Cortona, the city's patron saint.

She sat in the warm sunlight, chuckling as she read her mother's latest email, filled with gossipy tidbits. It ended with *Don't faint, but Eric popped the question and Abbie said yes. We're looking toward the spring for them to get married, so don't you be having such a good time in Italy that you decide to stay. We miss you! Love, Mom and Dad.*

She missed home too. And she missed Jon Mercer. She'd grown accustomed to seeing him every day while they worked on training her horse. She missed the sight of him, the sound of his voice, his nearness as he whispered directions on how to get Caramel to execute a certain move. Arie had written him two chatty postcards in the month they'd been in Italy but lacked the courage to pour out her heart to him in a letter.

"Some tea?" Garret interrupted Arie's thoughts.

She smiled up at him and nodded, and he placed a small pot of tea on the table. "Thanks."

"You're smiling. Good news?"

"My brother's getting married next spring."

"Love makes the world go round." He lingered, then asked, "Mind if I sit with you a bit? No customers at the moment."

"I'd love the company."

He pulled out a chair. "Where are your mates?"

Sensing his disappointment over not seeing Eden, Arie said, "Don't worry. We'll all be here tonight."

Garret's grin was quick. "I'm obvious, right?"

"In a cute way."

"Can I ask you a few things?" She agreed and he said, "What can you tell me about Eden?"

"She's a great person."

"We're in agreement there, but what else? Why is she so"—he searched for a word—"skittish? She's friendly and talkative, likes to party and dance and have fun, but she won't talk much about herself. I want to know more about *her*."

Arie scooped her hand through her too-long bangs. She thought about all of Eden's baggage, so she chose her words carefully. "Garret, you'll need to dig answers out of her."

His brow furrowed. "I've tried, but she turns questions away." The shops around the perimeter of the square began their locking up routine. Garret drummed his fingers on the tabletop. "Will you answer yes or no to a few questions? Maybe it can give me some hope. I don't want to tumble and then get shot down."

Arie figured he'd already tumbled but felt sorry for him. She knew what it felt like to be nuts about someone and not have the feeling returned. She wanted Eden to be happy, because Tony had burned her badly. "Try a question out on me. I'll see if it's answerable without me blabbing too much."

"Does she have a bloke back home?" The question leaped from his mouth.

Easy one. "No."

His face brightened. "That's good. It's what I was hoping."

"Next question."

"Does she have a fear of falling? You know . . . falling in love. Some girls do."

Harder. "Maybe."

"Did some bloke break her heart?"

His question was too complex for a simple yes or no. Tony had used Eden, turned whatever feelings she had for him into fear. Arie reached out and placed her hand on Garret's. "You've wandered into quicksand. You have to keep pressing her for answers. She'll need to trust you first. Please understand."

He smiled, his blue eyes shot through with understanding. "You answered the most important question. She's unattached. I'll just keep pouring on my Aussie charm until I break her down."

Arie laughed and squeezed his arm. "She hasn't a chance against genuine Aussie charm."

He waggled his eyebrows. "That's what I was thinking."

Still laughing, Arie scooped up the laptop. "See you all tonight."

Eden looked forward to the time she spent with Garret and his friends in the town square. Each evening after a late supper, they all settled around the fountain, talking, laughing, playing guitars, and dancing. No one drifted away until after midnight, in spite of having early job check-ins. She listened avidly to spirited debates between the kids from different countries and cultures. They spoke about politics, about hunger in Africa, about jobs a few had taken with world relief organizations. They talked about home and friends and music and about where they wanted to go on their walkabout and their plans for the future.

She was beginning to grasp how big and diverse the world was, and how small her world had been back home. Hearing of the magnitude of world problems, hers seemed like a soap opera with a shallow plot. Ciana spoke of farming, and its difficulties, costs, rules, and regulations. Arie talked about medical issues and drug research, and discussed pros and cons with two kids who'd grown up under socialized medicine. Arie never divulged a thing about her own cancer battles, but her knowledge about medicine astounded Eden. What had she to share except stories of the sordid underbelly of drugs and addiction?

So she said little, unwilling to confess to her past, ashamed of it and how she hadn't followed any world issues, only her own small life.

She often felt Garret's eyes on her, watching her. She was attracted to him. Who wouldn't be? He was likable, funny, cute—all the things Tony had never been. And yet she'd been drawn to Tony at sixteen and had become addicted to him, even though now, under the Tuscan stars, she couldn't remember why. Even with an ocean between them, she was afraid of Tony. An email to her mother was never answered. She wasn't surprised, certain that Gwen had fled home the minute Eden was gone. She hoped Tony hadn't hurt her mom. She realized he'd probably tried to scare her and she fled. The safety of Italy would evaporate in two months, and Eden would have to return home and face him. She kept pushing it out of her mind, focusing instead on the here and now.

The first time Ciana and Arie wanted to head back to the villa early, Eden protested. "I'm a night owl," she said.

"Not me," Ciana said, yawning.

"Ditto," said Arie.

"But you've got the car. If you both leave, I'll have to go with you."

"Sorry," Ciana said, fetching the keys from her jeans pocket.

"I can run you, Eden," Garret said. "That is, if you don't mind doubling on my scooter."

Eden was hesitant. She'd love the scooter ride, but being too close to Garret made her nervous. She really didn't want to become involved again, and it would be too easy with a guy like Garret.

"It's settled," Arie chirped. "We're off."

Eden watched her friends desert the square.

"I won't bite," Garret said. "And I won't run out of petrol like in the movies."

Seeing that she had no choice unless she chased after Ciana and Eden, she agreed. When the evening broke up, she walked with Garret to the parking area outside the city wall and to a lone scooter under the light of the moon. He handed her his helmet. "Take this."

"What will you wear?"

"The wind in my hair."

She suppressed a smile. "What if we crash and you fall on your head?"

"It's only a ride up the road. I think I can dodge disaster for a few clicks this late at night."

So she threw her leg over the scooter behind him and tentatively embraced him.

Over his shoulder, he said, "You'll have to hold on tighter than that. Think of me as a last bit of toothpaste in a tube and squeeze."

She chuckled and squeezed him tightly.

The moon turned the road into a silver ribbon on the ride to the villa in the cool October night. When Garret approached the villa, he cut the motor and coasted into the driveway. "Don't want to wake your mates."

"Impossible," Eden said, slipping off the helmet and resting it on the scooter's seat. "They sleep like rocks."

"Nice place," he said, looking upward at the villa.

"Ciana chose it. Arie and I love it." She pulled back from further explanation, realizing her only contribution to the Italy trip had been desperation.

"What's around back?" Garret asked as he began to move along the side of the house.

"Patio," she said, jogging after him, torn between wanting him to stay and wanting him to go.

On the patio, he settled on a lounge chair, put up his feet, and lay back, turning his face toward the moon. "This is the life. Now, don't let me get burned."

Cautiously she sat on the edge of the chair, just out of arm's reach. "I think you're safe."

"Seems I'm safe from getting a good-night thank-you kiss too."

Her heart lurched as she recalled nights with Tony. She recoiled. "I . . . I didn't know the ride had strings."

He leaned forward, his expression serious. "Hey, hey. Don't panic. There are never any strings with me, Eden. I was teasing."

Her heartbeat slowed and she felt foolish. Impulsively she dipped forward, kissed him lightly on the mouth, pulled away. "Thank you."

His grin was as bright as the moonlight. "I like bringing you home. Maybe we can do it again."

"Maybe," she said. "Now go away. I need my sleep."

He stood, still with the silly smile on his face. He backed to the edge of the patio, saluted her, and said, "G'night, Eden."

She heard him whistling as he started up his scooter. She remained on the patio, listening until the sound of the motor faded into the night. She turned her face skyward and lifted her arms, offering herself to the moon, letting it wash over her, as if to cleanse her mind and heart from a past that she couldn't change and that still frightened her.

# 25

"I've got the dish on the Bertinalli clan." Eden looked up from the laptop as she spoke.

Ciana sat in front of her makeup mirror, smoothing on mascara. "I hate mascara. I look like a raccoon after a couple of hours."

Arie, lying on her belly across Ciana's bed, was leafing through a travel book about the art treasures in Rome and offered, "My lashes are the color of sand—when I have eyelashes."

"Are you listening to me?" Eden snapped. "I've done some major research and Web hunting on Enzo and his family."

"Did I ask you to research him?" Ciana was uptight about the upcoming date but refused to let her friends know. This was a new avenue for her, dating a man like Enzo, a native Italian, who looked as if he belonged on the cover of GQ magazine. He was way out of her comfort zone. As if she had one when it came to men. Except for one man, the one she couldn't have. But it was time to move on, and why not here in Italy?

"Listen, missy, we're not sending you out on a date with him without knowing more about him than what he told us last week. Maybe he's a liar."

Ciana turned to Eden, sitting cross-legged on the floor beside the dressing table. "I'm going out with him in broad daylight. I think I can handle it."

"Humor me."

"Yeah, humor her," Arie echoed.

Ciana returned to her makeup mirror chores. "Is he a liar?"

"No. But you need to know some things. Stuff he didn't tell us. He's twenty-nine, the youngest sibling of three. Kind of old, don't you think?"

"Ten years. That's not so much of a gap." She'd had a birthday in late July.

"His brother, Gino, is thirty-six and a real playboy. Sleeps with movie stars and models and other men's wives. Had some party on his yacht last year and three people fell overboard and almost drowned."

"I'm not going out with his brother."

"And his sister just married some prince in Austria. She's thirty-two, and this is her third marriage."

"And Enzo? What do the tabloids write about him?"

Eden sniffed. "Actually, he appears to be the only heir who's serious about the family wine business."

"Fascinating," Ciana said drolly. "And after all that hard surfing work you did. Turns out he's just what he says he is."

"Not so fast. He's a serial dater. He's with a different woman in every photo."

"So what?" But a glance at the computer screen told Ciana she wasn't approaching the glamour level of Enzo's typical arm candy. And yet when he'd called and asked her to spend the afternoon with him, she'd been flattered and had agreed. Now she was anxious.

The sound of a car engine made all three girls jump. Arie made it to the bedroom window first and looked out at the front driveway. "Wow. He's driving a Ferrari."

"Seriously?" Eden pushed Arie aside and looked down.

A sleek jet-black convertible with red upholstery came to a stop directly below.

"Eric had a poster of one on his bedroom wall when he was a kid."

Ciana craned her head over those of her friends. The car *was* impressive. She watched Enzo as he walked to the front door. Seconds later, the chime rang. Her palms were sweaty and she took deep breaths to slow her pulse.

"Wait," Arie called. "I'll grab my camera. Eric will eat his heart out."

Ciana groaned. "Don't embarrass me."

Arie and Eden exchanged mischievous glances. Arie turned to Ciana and with wide-eyed innocence said, "Please, we're your friends. Are we going to embarrass her, Eden?"

"Of course we are," Eden said. "It's our duty."

They clambered down the stairs, jockeying for position, jerked open the front door, and ran into the bright sunlight to pose with a laughing Enzo and his gorgeous F430 Spider.

Enzo had asked Ciana to dress casually, and he took her to his family estate that adjoined the acreage of the rolling vineyards. The sprawling house was set back on a manicured lawn that stretched between flowering gardens and bubbling fountains. He drove past the house, took a winding road, and braked at an outbuilding, a pristine stable where horses poked heads over stall half-doors. In the courtyard, grooms were walking, washing, and brushing horses tethered to poles.

Ciana was out of the car before it came to a complete halt. "Oh, Enzo! They're beautiful."

He came quickly to her side, his expression pleased over her reaction. "You told me you owned horses. Come. I will show you mine."

She approached a horse in a stall and held out her hand, curling her fingers under so that the animal could sniff the back of her hand. Its warm, soft muzzle examined her, then turned toward Enzo, ears pricked forward. "You never said a word about owning horses when we were together, but you told us everything about the winery."

He scratched the horse behind its ears. "Wine is my business. Horses are my passion. A man does not discuss his passion with just anyone."

"How many do you own?"

"Twelve here. I breed them for dressage competition. For the Olympics. But they also are fine for leisure riding." He tipped his head toward her. "Would you care to ride?"

"Would I ever!" Until this moment, she hadn't realized how much she missed Firecracker and the feel of leather over the broad back of a horse.

"Wait here," Enzo said. He walked over to one of the grooms and spoke rapid Italian. In no time, the groom appeared, leading two horses, one a dark chestnut, the other a bay. Both horses were big, a few hands taller than either Firecracker or Sonata, both saddled with English saddles—no horn. She'd never ridden in this type of saddle before.

"I usually ride Western," she told Enzo, nibbling at her bottom lip.

"Only minor adjustments to make. You will have no trouble." Enzo led the horse to a mounting block, where Ciana stepped up and threw her leg over the big bay's back. She was used to mounting from the ground, but she needed the extra height with this horse. "Her informal name is Venus because she is so beautiful," Enzo said while making adjustments to Ciana's stirrups. "Oh, and she only understands Italian." He primed Ciana with necessary phrases to speak to the horse.

The saddle felt odd at first, but as the horse cantered around the courtyard, Ciana got the hang of it. She communicated with the animal in her sketchy Italian and with her knees, heels, and reins, and the horse settled into a long, smooth gait. It reminded her of Olivia's stories of Grandfather Charles's famed Tennessee walking horse. The memory made Ciana smile.

"See? What did I tell you?" Enzo said, bringing his horse up alongside hers. "You are a natural. And Venus clearly recognizes your authority."

They rode through a field on a simple dirt trail lined with tall browning grass. Cyprus trees flanked the field, acting as a natural fence. Ciana was in her element with the heat of the sun on her face and the power of the horse beneath her, yet twinges of homesickness nipped at her heart. By now the trees would be bright with fall colors. Pumpkins and winter squash and rhubarb would be selling in the farmer's market, and bundled straw would be rolled up in fields and looking like giant sausages.

"Where are you, *bella* Ciana?" Enzo asked.

"Oh, sorry. Just thinking of home."

"Tell me."

She told him about Bellmeade and then about Olivia and their shared love for their land. She told of her grandfather's and father's sudden deaths and of how Olivia ran Bellmeade until she died, omitting the difficulties of Olivia's final years.

"Your nana sounds like a special woman."

"She was. I miss her and always will."

As they rode and talked, Ciana lost track of time. When Enzo wove a trail through the grass and a clump of whispering trees, she was surprised to see a lake as the tree wall thinned. "What's this?" she asked as they emerged from the woods.

"A place of beauty." Soon they came upon a grassy area beneath shade trees near the water's edge. A blanket had been spread and on it rested a large basket and a small cooler.

"A picnic? For us? Did you do this?"

"I thought we might enjoy some food and wine together. And the horses can use the rest." He dismounted.

Ciana's surprise gave way to suspicion. She stayed seated on her horse.

"A little surprise," Enzo said, flashing his smile and offering up his hand to her. "I have pure motives—hunger and thirst."

She swung her leg over the horse's withers, slid down, and found herself pressed between the solid side of the horse and Enzo's hard, lean body. Gazing up into his dark eyes made her pulse race. He was devilishly handsome, but she shoved her back hard against the horse, making Venus move to one side.

Enzo bowed graciously and motioned for her to move forward in front of him.

She went to the blanket and sat cross-legged, recalling Eden's warning about him being a serial dater and being way older than her. "So what's for a snack?"

"An Italian feast." He opened the basket and removed china plates, polished silver utensils, linen napkins, and fragile wineglasses.

"Elegant," she said.

He uncorked a wine and handed her a glassful. She drank a gulp, allowing it to relax her while he took out food. This reminded her of eating with Jon by candlelight in her stable. The memory unnerved her. Why couldn't she wipe thoughts of that man from her brain? Why did he always surface when she least expected or wanted it?

While the horses grazed, she and Enzo talked, him telling of arduous hours of training Olympic dressage champions. She was enthralled. He was easy to talk to; Olivia would have described him as *charming*. Ciana heard her grandmother's voice: *Be careful of the charming boys, child. Before you know what's happening, they'll talk you right out of your underpants.*

Enzo leaned on his elbow to clink his wineglass to Ciana's. "To other long afternoons together."

"We leave for Rome in ten days."

"Ah, Roma, our eternal city. I would show you our city, but I have to oversee the harvest a while longer. How long will you be gone?"

"A week."

"Only a week? This is not enough time to see Roma."

"I wish it could be longer." Truthfully her money was going fast, much faster than she had anticipated when she'd planned the trip.

"Where will you be staying?"

She named the hotel. "Arie's birthday is October twenty-fourth, and going to Rome, seeing the art treasures, has been a wish of hers for many years."

He raised his wineglass to her. "May you have the best of times. I will make a list of wonderful places to eat." He kissed his fingertips. "Until you leave, I shall take you riding and beg you to spend as much time with me as the vineyard harvest permits."

Again, she was flattered that he wanted her company, and the chance to ride was a genuine gift.

He stared out at the lake, at the sun sliding low on the horizon. "We must go," he said with a regretful sigh.

Together Ciana and Enzo packed the basket and rode the horses to the stables where a groom took them. It felt odd to Ciana not to groom the horse herself—she thought she owed it to the big bay. Still Enzo issued orders and ushered her to the car. The wind made it impossible to talk in the convertible as they returned to the villa. By the time they arrived, dark had fallen. The outside light was on, but Eden and Arie were gone.

"We have friends in town," she told Enzo. "We all meet most nights for late suppers."

"Shall I drive you to Cortona?" Enzo asked.

"No, I think I'll just crash." At the doorstep, Ciana's case of nerves attacked again. She wasn't sure what he was expecting from her—a hug, a kiss, an invitation inside? The good feelings from the wine had worn off, and she reminded herself of her lack of sophistication, of their differences—over ten years and two cultures. "Thank you for a wonderful day. The horseback ride, the food, the scenery, and most of all, your company."

He smiled, more reserved than he'd been all afternoon. "I will call you." He leaned forward and brushed his lips across her forehead.

Her knees went a little weak. "*Ciao*," she said. Ciana watched him drive away and unexpectedly felt a void when he was gone.

A chirping sound kept nagging at Ciana. The sound was annoying. In a Herculean effort, she struggled to rise through darkness, finally opening her eyes and realizing that she had been sound asleep and the chirping noise was really the phone beside her bed. Groggily she fumbled to turn on a lamp and grope for the receiver. "Hello."

"Darling! How's Italy?"

Ciana sat up. "Mother?"

"Yes, it's me."

Alice Faye sounded so cheerful that Ciana hardly recognized her voice. "What time is it?"

"Four in the afternoon. I've been waiting all day to call you."

Eleven o'clock in Italy. "Is everything all right?" She shook her head to clear the cobwebs and the vestiges of the wine from her picnic with Enzo.

"Everything is wonderful," her mother said with uncharacteristic liveliness. "I have the most wonderful news."

"I give up," Ciana said tentatively.

"Our money problems can be over forever."

"How so?"

"An investor from Chicago named Gerald Hastings wants to buy Bellmeade. Isn't that marvelous? All we have to do is agree to sell it to him."

# 26

Arie and Eden patiently watched Ciana pace the floor, listening to her rant about Alice Faye's phone call.

"Sell Bellmeade! Can you believe it? She wants me to sign off on paperwork to sell our land. Our heritage! What's wrong with her?"

"Calm down," Eden said. Twice the two girls had tried to rein in Ciana and failed. "She can't sell anything without your approval and signature. You told me that years ago."

"Did you ask any questions?" Arie ventured.

Ciana stopped and turned toward her friends, seething with fury. "I hung up on her." Ciana twisted around and started pacing again. "Maybe I should fly back home."

Arie shook her head and Eden stood up. "Do we need to throw cold water on you? Stop shouting and talking crazy and sit down." She dragged a chair over and pushed Ciana into it.

Ciana buried her face in her hands. "She'd never have suggested selling out if Olivia were alive."

Arie crouched by the chair. "Please don't drop out on us,

Ciana. I owe this trip to you and I want us to see Rome together. We can't celebrate without you."

"Or wade barefoot in some fountain," Eden added. "We're tourists. I want to do all the tourist things we've read about—the Colosseum, the Spanish Steps, Gucci, Prada, Fendi—"

Arie shot Eden an impatient look and jumped in with, "St. Peter's Basilica, the Sistine Chapel, the works of Michelangelo—"

"Sure," Eden said. "And all that old pretty stuff too."

Ciana sniffed, leaning her head against the back of the chair, staring up at the ceiling and feeling like a deflated balloon. "I'm just mad. I won't leave Italy without the two of you."

"That's more like it," Arie said, knowing how important Bellmeade was to Ciana. The land was sacred ground, despite hard work, bad weather, even crop failure.

"Well, shame on her for dropping this bomb on you when you're so far away," Eden said. "She can't make a move without you. Forget about her for now."

Ciana had grown up with a baffling relationship with her mother. She had sometimes felt like a chess piece, moved on an invisible board by Alice Faye and Olivia, her loyalties divided. When a checkmate occurred, she felt like taffy, pulled between their opposing wills. Her mother's retreat into alcohol had made Ciana feel guilty for years. As if she lacked something, as if she sported some flaw that drove Alice Faye into a place governed by gin and sweet tea, where maternal love faded to black. Only Olivia's love had saved Ciana from self-loathing. If Olivia loved her, then she must be all right. If Olivia considered her worthy to shepherd Bellmeade, then she was honor-bound to do so. Yet beyond honor was her pure, clear sense of purpose to hold on to her family's land. She loved the land. It was part of her DNA. Perhaps that was why she got on so well with Enzo. They both found purpose in their land. She sighed, telling her friends, "All right, my tantrum's over. Let's go conquer Rome."

Arie cheered. "We're the Three Musketeers." And yet even as she said the words, Arie felt the weight of her secret—actually, her *two* secrets. The health disclosure would keep for a while longer; her other admission would have to come in a matter of days. She hoped they'd be as happy for her as she was for herself.

Ciana and her friends were getting ready to go into Cortona for their meet-up with Garret and his fellow travelers when Ciana heard the front door chime. *Now what?*

Eden called up to her, "Enzo to see you."

He hadn't said he'd come the day before they left for Rome. She hurried downstairs to find him leaning against the front doorjamb, holding a bottle of wine and wearing a beguiling smile. "I apologize for not calling before coming. Is my popping up—how do you say—acceptable?"

She felt flattered and a little off balance. "A nice surprise."

"I will not take much of your time. Can we sit on the patio to speak?"

She walked with him to the patio where a cool breeze was sending fallen leaves dancing across the tiles. They pulled out chairs at the table, and he set down the wine bottle. "A gift," he said. "One of our best reserve wines. For Arie's birthday."

The way his voice flowed over the words in his sexy accent charmed her. "We'll drink it on her birthday in Rome."

He removed a piece of paper from his jacket pocket. "This is a list of all the best places to dine in Roma. Many are near your hotel. There's no reason for you and your friends to eat with tourists. There is much fine food in Roma the tourists do not taste."

His thoughtfulness touched her. Of course, he had no way of knowing they wouldn't be dining elegantly most evenings—too expensive. "You're so sweet."

"Sweet?" His brow puckered. "Like candy?"

She realized she'd used an idiom he probably didn't grasp. "Kind and nice," she clarified.

He laughed. "You say funny things, Ciana."

She tucked the list he'd prepared into the pocket of her slacks. "*Grazie* for the recommendations."

He reached over, pulled her to her feet, and gazed at her, grinning. "I leave now. But one thing more. Yes?" His face grew serious. "An idea for you to think upon."

"All right." Looking up into his dark eyes quickened her pulse.

"When you return, I wish to take you to Portofino. This is a town on the sea where I own a villa and a boat. I would be pleased to have you spend a few days there with me."

His request struck her like an electric shock. *A few days*. This was no offer for a boat ride and dinner. No day picnic after which each of them went home to their own beds. And what would she tell her friends? *Oh, by the way, Enzo and I will be going off for a little bump and tickle. Go do some sightseeing on your own*. Ciana couldn't imagine—but then, she could. Enzo was a gorgeous man. He had been considerate and kind to her. Except for Jon Mercer, she'd never felt the desire to give herself to someone. And that, she knew, was the problem. This decision to go off with Enzo was one of her head, not her heart. She cleared her throat. "I . . . I'm not sure—"

"Say nothing now." Enzo stopped her words with a knowing

smile. "Think upon it. Give me an answer once you return from Roma. I am patient." He squeezed her hands, pivoted. "*Ti penso sempre, bella* Ciana," he said. "This means 'I think of you always, pretty Ciana.' "

He left and she stood rooted to the patio, his invitation swirling in her head like a tempest.

The evenings had become a routine—dinner with a mix of local kids and Garret's friends, of Ciana and Arie returning to the villa early, and Garret giving Eden a ride there much later. The good times made Eden begin to relax her guard. She felt affection for Garret, who was talkative, full of fun and jokes, devilishly adorable, and easy to be around. And he liked her. Tony had wanted to own her. Garret seemed to just be happy when they were together. No demands. No strings.

Unknowingly, he also had awakened a wanderlust in her. The idea of travel, of seeing foreign lands, wondrous sights—at least the sights seemed wondrous when Garret described them—left her hungry to experience the world for herself. She never wanted to return to Windemere and had said as much.

The night before Eden was to leave for Rome, Garret asked, "Before I take you to your villa, I'd like to take you someplace else. You game?" He cocked his head. "Instead of winging back to your villa, would you like to see a special place I've found?"

"Where?"

"A surprise."

Intrigued, she snapped on her helmet, a new one he'd bought especially for her, and straddled his scooter. "Let's go."

"Button up," he said. "It'll be a bit cool on the ride."

Eden zipped up her leather jacket, a fashion find from a

three-day visit to Florence in late September. She hooked her arms around Garret and snuggled against his back.

They took a road that went north, and after about forty-five minutes, Garret drove off-road, across a pitted rocky field where Eden thought her internal organs would dislodge. When they finally stopped, the silence was sudden, unearthly. "Check my kidneys," Eden groaned. "I think I lost one."

Garret dismounted and unsnapped his helmet. "Come along, then. You'll be glad."

She followed him up a rise and in the moonlight saw a body of water, steam curling off its surface. "A lake?"

"A hot spring." He beamed a smile and began to strip off his clothes.

"What are you *doing*?"

"Going for a swim."

"Are you crazy?"

"Probably."

In no time, all his clothing lay in a heap on the ground. She watched his snowy white bum dart to the water where he dove under, then popped up, water streaming off his thick curly hair. "It's warm. Really. Come in with me."

Her teeth were chattering and she shivered from the chilly night air. She wanted to throw herself into the water too. "Turn around," she ordered.

He obeyed and she quickly undressed. When she was nude and a mass of goose bumps, she rushed into the water and ducked beneath the surface. It was as warm as bathwater. She came up a good distance from Garret, keeping just her head above the surface.

"What did I tell you?" he asked cheerily.

She touched the bottom with her toes. "How deep is it?"

"Over your head in the middle." He came closer and she thrust backward. "Aw, what's this? I won't bite, you know."

"It isn't your teeth I'm worried about."

He laughed, and the sound bounced off the sky. He disappeared under the water, making Eden turn in every direction to see where he'd emerge. He was under so long she began to worry. Without warning, she felt his hand grip her ankle. She shrieked, and he bobbed up next to her, laughing breathlessly. She pushed his shoulders down and forced him underwater again. This time he came up sputtering. "Truce! I promise to be a good bloke."

"You'd better." He was so close that she could see the water droplets on his face. His eyes stared straight into hers.

"I'd like to kiss you," he said. "Really, really kiss you."

She stiffened. So far she'd only allowed him to put his arm around her or kiss her lightly, no more than a brush across the mouth. She'd revealed some of her past, her years of growing up with a bipolar mother, but she'd held on to other secrets, namely her past with Tony. "I'd rather wait until we both have clothes on." She shoved off, but he caught her arm before she got very far.

"Why are you afraid of me?"

"I'm not." That was true. She wanted very much to be in his arms. "I think you're pretty amazing."

"But not amazing enough to fall for?"

"Now you're fishing for compliments."

He shook his head. "No, still just fishing for a real kiss."

The tone of his voice was light, but he looked frustrated. She knew she couldn't put him off forever with quips and teasing. "I'm not trying to be mean, Garret. I know there's lots you want to know, and when I come back from Rome, we'll sit down and have a real long talk. How's that sound?"

He considered her words. "I'll miss you while you're gone. Getting sort of used to seeing you every day."

She was getting used to seeing him every day too. He was filling a hole inside her, one she'd known since childhood and had been unable to fill, not through cutting, not through sex with Tony.

She reached out and ran her palm down Garret's cheek. "I'll miss you too." She dipped lower into the water. "Now, did you bring towels? Or are we going to freeze to death when we get out of this water?"

"In the saddlebag on the scooter. I'll get them." He started to the water's edge.

"Allow me," she said. Pulling his arm and then locking her eyes on his, Eden rose out of the water like a nymph. She turned, walked toward the shore unashamed while he watched her nude body shimmer in the pale moonlight.

# 27

From the moment the bellman opened the door of the hotel room and ushered them inside, Ciana realized there had been some kind of mistake. The room was actually a two-bedroom suite with a sitting room and a balcony overlooking Rome. The travel agent had told Ciana that although this hotel was one of the most beautiful in the city, it was also expensive, yet she'd been able to reserve a small room for them.

"Awesome," Arie said, circling the spacious gilded room. "This is gorgeous."

"I'll say," Eden added, stepping out onto the balcony.

Ciana turned to the bellman. "Are you sure we're in the right room?"

He glanced at the passkey and smiled at her. "*Si, signorina.* This is correct."

She knew she'd have to deal with this quickly. She told her friends, "I'm going down to the front desk. Don't get comfortable." She bolted from the room and rode the elevator down to the luxurious lobby with marble floors and crystal chandeliers.

The desk clerk who had checked them in looked up. "May I help you?"

"I . . . um . . . I think there's been a mistake in our room assignment."

His eyebrows shot up. "Is the suite not to your liking?"

"Oh no. The room's beautiful. I just don't think it's what my travel agent said she reserved for us."

He looked puzzled, went to his computer and typed. A minute later he smiled and said, "You were upgraded."

"But why?"

"Ah. I did not give you the note. *Scusi.*" He opened a drawer and extracted a long envelope with her name written in a florid, graceful swirl of black ink. He handed it to her.

She sat in a crimson velvet chair, opened the envelope, extracted a single handwritten sheet of heavy linen paper, and read:

*Bella Ciana,*

*Please forgive me for my intrusion, but I took the liberty of upgrading you to my favorite suite at my expense for your enjoyment and pleasure. I have been a frequent client of this lovely hotel for many years. Arie's birthday should be celebrated in Roma style of the highest order, and you should be pampered as you deserve. This is my gift to you both. Please accept it with my best wishes. I look forward to your return.*

*Ciao,*
*Enzo*

Ciana read the letter twice. Heat slithered up her body, some from embarrassment, some from anxiety. She'd not said a word to her friends yet about Enzo's request to take her to Portofino. She'd simply proffered the bottle of wine when they'd asked why he'd shown up at the villa. The letter was undated, so she had no idea as to when he'd written it. Was it simply hospitality? Was it his way of nudging her toward the trip? The room must cost hundreds of dollars per night. Would Enzo be so hospitable? She didn't like indebtedness, and although he'd said it was a gift, accepting the suite would make her feel obligated to him. She batted around the idea of days with him in his villa, of his total attention, of his hands and lips on her body. She exhaled, stirred by the images. *And why shouldn't I?* she asked herself. It wasn't as if she had anyone in her life. Neither was she some silly, starry-eyed schoolgirl. So what if she didn't love him? He was urbane and attractive. And there was no one back home waiting for her. No one at all.

Arie lived on adrenaline during the week, anticipating her birthday. She spent hours absorbed in visiting Rome's museums and staring transfixed at the great sculptures, statues, and paintings, each one more stunning than the last. She was especially attracted to the depictions of Madonna and child. She thought them glorious, a woman clutching a beautiful baby, a beatific look on the mother's face, the child's face ethereal, seeing beyond the moment and into an unknown future. Arie would stand so long in front of a particular depiction that Ciana and Eden would ask, "Can we move along?" or "I think I've memorized this one, Arie. Let's look at some others."

She didn't hold their restlessness against them. They would one day marry, have babies, grow old, and greet grandchildren, but she would never give birth to a child of her own. Even if, by some miracle, she survived this latest setback, all the treatments she'd experienced had closed the door to childbearing. Barrenness, a chemo side effect. *No.* A runny nose with a cold was a side effect. Barrenness was a sentence. So every Madonna painting made her stop and silently mourn for what would never be.

She insisted on spending a day at the Vatican, a city unto itself, where the greatest artwork of all time was housed. Within the halls of the Pope's realm was the Sistine Chapel, its ceiling and walls adorned with art of such magnificence that Arie could scarcely breathe in its presence. Benches along the sides of the walls offered a place to sit and contemplate the beauty of Michelangelo's frescos, commissioned in 1508. The magnitude of the work shook Arie to her core. How could one man have created such a wonder?

"Wow," Eden whispered softly, for to talk loudly in the chapel seemed a sacrilege. Words had no power here.

Ciana mumbled, "This makes the whole trip worthwhile."

Moved by their reverence, Arie whispered, "I'm going to be here awhile, so let's pick a time and place to meet."

When they had gone, she sat and gazed up at *The Creation of Adam*, located in the foremost area at the top center panel of the chapel, with the finger of God reaching out to bestow life on the first human. She stared until she had a crick in her neck, yet still could not look away. In a desperate moment, she wondered how she might climb to the ceiling's center and touch her finger to God's, for surely if he could create Adam, one touch from him could cure her. A tear trickled down her cheek and she whisked it away.

She consoled herself with knowing that in two days, another wonderful thing would come her way. She knew the time had come to tell her friends her plans. It hadn't been right to keep the secret so long to herself, yet every time she thought of telling them, she'd chickened out. But now they were in Rome and she'd seen Ciana and Eden plotting some birthday surprise for her that she had to forestall. She'd have to suck it up and tell them tonight.

"What's up with you?" Eden asked Arie back in the suite before bed that night. "You were all jumpy during dinner."

Ciana flopped onto the sofa beside Eden, saying, "Eden's right. You haven't been yourself today."

Arie nibbled on the quick of her thumb. "Nothing's wrong." Her voice lacked conviction, but she realized this was her opening to confess. "I've done something. Something I have to tell you." Her friends looked bewildered. She squirmed. "I should have told you sooner. But didn't."

Eden asked, "You didn't take one of those paintings off the Pope's walls, did you?"

Arie shook her head. "Nothing criminal." She took a deep breath. "I . . . um . . . made special plans for my birthday."

"You did? But so have we." Ciana sounded disappointed.

"I figured you might have."

"Spit it out," Eden said. "The suspense is nerve-racking."

Arie bounced her gaze between them, her pulse racing with pent-up tension. "I've invited Jon Mercer for a visit. And he'll be here tomorrow."

# 28

Ciana felt as if the wind had been knocked out of her. *Jon's coming!* She went cold, then hot; her spine went rigid and she was rendered speechless. Fortunately, Eden spoke up.

"He's coming to Italy? Tomorrow? And now you're just mentioning it?"

"I said I was sorry about that part." Arie's face reddened.

"How did this come about?"

"You both know I email home once a week."

"Your *family*."

"Well, a couple of times, I emailed Jon. To ask about my horse. I told him what a good time we were having. And . . . and . . . one time I wrote that I wished he could come visit us—well, me, really, for my birthday. And he said he would." She grew animated. "I never dreamed he'd actually agree to come. But now that he is . . ." Her sentence trailed off. "Please don't be mad at me."

A knot filled Ciana's throat. She wanted to see him. She

didn't want to see him. His last words had been off-putting when he'd made some crack about "Beauchamp money." She dredged up the anger and vowed to hold it and use it to steel her emotions against him when she saw him.

Eden asked, "How long is he staying?"

"Just three days in Rome."

"Long way to travel for three days." Ciana finally spoke. "It's eight to nine hours each way."

"I know. But don't you see? That's what makes it all the more special." Arie's eyes lit up. "There's nothing in the world I want more than to see him and to be with him on my birthday."

"What makes this birthday so special?" Eden asked. "We'll be home for Christmas. Can't you celebrate then?"

"He's leaving before we come home."

"When?" Ciana asked before she could stop it.

"Not exactly sure, but he's going back to Texas. Says that Pickins has nothing else for him to do."

Ciana's heart skipped a beat. *Leaving*. This would be her last chance to see him too. She knew she'd be better off never seeing him again. "Part of coming to Italy was to whoop it up on your birthday."

Arie looked contrite. Of course, her friends had no way of knowing that she might not see another birthday. She was beginning to feel the effects of her illness—pain in her lower back, in the area near her kidneys. "I'm really sorry I didn't tell you sooner. Coming here, to Italy, is the best present anyone could ever give me. And once Jon's gone and we go back to the villa, well, things will be just like before. Back to Cortona and our friends there. Back to day trips to other cities. Nothing will change."

Ciana doubted that, but she couldn't say it. She needed to

act indifferent about Jon's arrival. Eden was already eying her curiously. Ciana needed to play this better. She forced a tight smile. "I'm happy for you. Have a good time with him."

"You're not mad? I didn't mean to spoil any plans you two made for my big nineteenth. I really need you to be happy for me. I love Jon with all my heart." Ciana knew of Arie's feelings for Jon, but Eden looked befuddled.

"What? Why didn't I know this?" Eden asked.

"You had enough troubles. And Tony kept you isolated," Arie said. "And it wasn't as if Jon acted all that interested." A smile lit her face. "But now that he's coming, well, now I have hope that he's missed me."

"He must have," Eden said. "Lot of money for only three days. Why would he spend it if he didn't care?"

Abruptly, Ciana stood up. "I hate to break up the gabfest, but this girl is going to bed."

"It's early," Eden said, glancing at the ornate golden clock resting atop the fireplace mantel. "Even for you."

"I'm reading a good book, and I'm close to finishing it."

"You forgive me for inviting Jon?" Arie asked, unconvinced.

*Furious*, Ciana thought. "Course I forgive you," she said, turning her back to them, afraid her friends might see the truth on her face.

"You aren't coming with us to the airport?" Arie asked Ciana the next morning when preparing to leave.

"It's a little car." Ciana was drinking coffee on the balcony and scanning the Web on her laptop, feigning interest in the pages that flew onto the laptop screen.

"We can squish," Eden said, who was driving and paying

way too much attention to Ciana's refusal to go with her and Arie to pick up Jon.

"Don't wish to squish," she said with a tight smile. "Go on."

Once they left, Ciana slammed her laptop shut. She'd hardly slept the night before and her eyes felt like sandpaper. Maybe she wouldn't care a bit about Jon when she saw him. She had Enzo now. Or she could have Enzo. She should call him, agree to Portofino. She glanced over at the telephone on the antique Italian desk just inside the French doors. She gazed at it for a long time but never went to make the call.

Arie was a jangle of nerves in the airport waiting area with Eden. "He should be here by now."

"Give it rest or you'll combust. You know it takes a while to get through customs."

Arie asked, "Haven't you ever wanted anything so bad that it hurt?"

"I have," Eden confessed, knowing that Arie's adoration of Jon should have been expected. The girl had longed for a boyfriend all through high school. What didn't make sense was Eden's suspicion that something was going on with Ciana, an undercurrent she felt after Arie's bombshell about Jon coming for her birthday. Ciana wasn't the kind of person to begrudge Arie—especially Arie—anything. *Puzzling.*

Just then the doors from the inner terminal slid open and arriving passengers poured into the waiting area. Arie stood on tiptoe, searching the crowds for Jon, her heart pounding with anticipation. When she saw him emerge, she rushed forward, wanting to throw her arms around him, but suddenly she became self-conscious. Maybe he didn't want her to hug him.

Jon grinned down at her and hugged her first. Relieved, she returned his hug enthusiastically.

"Nice to see you," Eden said from behind Arie.

Jon gave Eden a friendly squeeze too. He glanced around. "Didn't three of you come to Italy?"

"Ciana's waiting at our hotel," Arie said. "Come on, we'll take you there."

"I didn't get reservations at your hotel," Jon said.

"We'll take you to your place afterward," Eden said. Her sharp eyes hadn't missed his momentary disappointment over Ciana's absence. "I know Ciana's anxious to see you."

"Let's go." His voice and expression were noncommittal.

Arie hooked her arm through Jon's. His other hand gripped a worn leather duffel. Eden followed, watching the two of them carefully. Arie was obviously in heaven. Jon was a question mark.

Ciana had showered and applied makeup. She was standing on the suite's balcony when she heard the door open and Arie call, "Hey, girlfriend, guess who's here?"

Ciana took a deep breath and reminded herself to smile and stay calm. She turned just as the threesome walked onto the balcony. With an ease that shook her, Jon's gaze found hers. Her breath caught as his green eyes lit up her heart.

He came forward, hands in his jean pockets, and looked her up and down. "Howdy."

"*Buon giorno*," she returned in her best Italian.

"That the way people say 'howdy' over here?"

Ciana nodded. "And 'good day.' I think the language is pretty. Don't you?"

His green eyes held hers. "Italy looks good on you, Ciana." He slid his arms around her, pulled her close.

He smelled of leather and spice and Tennessee. Home. She closed her eyes and forced down a lump in her throat and pushed away. "You must be tired."

"I slept on the plane."

"No one sleeps on the plane," she said, rolling her eyes.

"I did." He flashed Ciana a heart-melting smile. "I just slid my hat over my eyes and zoned out. Next thing I knew, the pilot was talking about landing in Rome."

Just then the doorbell rang. "I'll get it," Eden said.

"It's room service," Ciana said. "I ordered up some goodies, coffee and sodas."

"Thoughtful of you," Eden said, scoping out Ciana's body language. Then she felt the undercurrent once again.

Arie breezed in from her bedroom, where she'd brushed her blond hair and applied fresh lipstick. Her face glowed whenever she looked at Jon. Having him at arm's length was intoxicating.

Room service set up the delivery on a small table on the balcony, which overlooked the busy street below and the hills surrounding Rome far in the distance. Ciana had ordered olives, prosciutto-wrapped melon balls, bruschetta and marinara sauce, and hot espresso that Arie rejected. "Too strong for me."

Jon looked over the food tray. "No salsa and chips?"

They laughed. "Try it," Ciana said. "It's good."

"So what's going on in the boonies?" Eden asked, skittish about asking yet anxious to know whether Tony was hunting her. If he was, she wouldn't go home again, an option she hadn't discussed with her friends. She could take a job in Italy. Somehow she'd manage to get one, perhaps here in Rome.

Jon sipped his espresso, then set down the cup. "That's part of the reason I came over. To talk to you and tell you some things that went on after you left."

Arie's sense of exclusiveness over his visit dulled. "What things? I email my folks all the time and they never mentioned anything unusual."

"It was agreed that nothing would be said until you all came home, but now that I'm here, I can tell you face to face."

Eden's stomach went queasy. "What's happened?"

"Tony didn't take to your running off. Mean bastard, you know."

"I know."

Jon leveled a look at Eden. "The night you left, he paid a visit to your mother."

Eden's heart seized. She and her mother had a prickly relationship, but she'd never have wished Tony on Gwen. "Is . . . is she all right?"

"She left town."

"Not surprised."

"But not before she sent him down a rabbit trail. Told him you'd gone to Greece via Nashville International and only had a short head start." Jon chewed an olive. "That took guts, lying to him with a straight face. He knocked her around but took off after you all, thinking he was only miles behind you and you were driving Ciana's blue truck."

"And my mother? Was she hurt?" Eden's voice quivered.

"We don't think so. Before leaving, she called your mother and yours"—his gaze bounced between Arie and Ciana—"and warned them. It gave them time to prepare."

Ciana dug her nails into her palms. "But they're all right?"

"It was ugly for a while." Jon grimaced. "Tony came back when he realized your mother had pulled a fast one and was gone. He trashed your house, Eden."

Tears brimmed in Eden's eyes. She'd never loved the place, but it had been her home all her life. "But Mom got away?"

Jon nodded.

"What about *our* families?" Arie asked, feeling betrayed that her parents hadn't mentioned a single thing about what had happened. She wasn't a child! They should have told her.

The corners of Jon's mouth lifted in a smile. He looked at Arie. "Your family really stepped up to the plate. Round-the-clock guards on your property. Someone on your front porch all night long. Tony made the mistake of driving by late one night, stuck a gun out his car window. Guy on your porch took out two tires in the dark. The car went away and didn't come back."

Arie nodded. "That'd be my uncle Cecil. He was once an army sniper, and he hunts every season. Why, he can shoot the eye out of a wild turkey at two hundred yards."

Jon, looking respectful, said, "I'm thinking Tony and his goons figured that out."

"What about my mother?" Ciana asked. Alice Faye was no match for Tony. "What about Bellmeade?"

"She's a Beauchamp," Jon said matter-of-factly. "Cops protected her and your farm."

Intuiting there was more to the story than he wasn't telling her, Ciana asked, "And you?"

"He stopped by one night with his posse for a short visit. Knocked me around."

"Why you?" Ciana asked, feeling queasy.

"I guess he thought I knew something about your leaving because I trained Arie's horse. Guy was crazy."

"Did he hurt you?" Arie asked, her voice trembling.

"I ride broncs. I can take a few licks. That and Pickins showed up with a shotgun to persuade them to leave," Jon said with another wry smile.

Ciana sagged with relief. Jon and their families were guiltless and hadn't deserved Tony's wrath for something she had engineered.

"So Mom and I have no house to come back to?" Eden's heart filled with hate for Tony.

"But you do. Arie's kin fixed the place up." He looked at Arie. "Your dad and brother mostly. They didn't want Eden coming home to a mess."

An act of kindness. Except for Ciana, no one ever had treated her with pure kindness. She closed her eyes as tears swelled. "And Tony? Did he leave all of you alone after that?"

"That's another reason I came to talk to you face to face. You don't have to worry about Tony anymore. He's dead."

# 29

*Dead.* Jon's last word hung in the air. No one moved. *Dead.* Ciana and Arie cut their eyes to Eden, who looked ghostly white. Jon asked, "You okay?"

Eden's mind spun backward in time, to days less chilling, to when she'd loved Tony and had walked on clouds feeling safe and secure, loved and wanted. He had been her first love, her first and only lover. And he'd morphed into a stranger, a possessive, controlling, demanding, and selfish tyrant who dealt drugs and hurt people, perhaps even had some killed. She let go of the finer memories, let them tatter and tear in the wind of regret that blew through her head in the fine bright sunlight of Italy. "I'm sorry he's dead," she said in a soft voice. "But I'm glad everybody back home is safe."

Fearful one of her relatives had taken him out and gotten caught, Arie asked, "How did he die?"

"Drug deal gone bad. In Memphis. And his goons with him. A cartel from Mexico, according to the cops. Didn't like him pushing into their territory. There was a big shoot-out. By the time the Memphis cops arrived, six men were dead, including Tony. Story made all the papers and national television news."

Jon's soft Southern drawl smoothed over the words, the ugliness of the images planted in Eden's mind. Tony had died as he'd lived—on the edge. And from the scene inside her head, Garret's face emerged, his unruly head of curly hair, blue eyes, and charming smile. Another chance. "So now Windemere is safe for all," Eden said under her breath.

"It is from Tony."

"I'm sorry you got roughed up, Jon." She stood. "Think I'll hang in the bedroom for a while."

Filled with concern, Arie watched her leave.

Ciana announced, "I'm glad he's gone. Tony took part of her life."

Arie shot Ciana a disapproving look, then rose from her chair. "I'll be right back," she said, and headed off to be with Eden.

Arie knocked lightly on Eden's closed door. Not waiting for an invitation to enter, she eased inside. Eden sat on the bed, shoulders drooping, staring at the wall. She was dry-eyed. Arie eased onto the bed beside her. "Talk to me."

"I'm okay," Eden said. "You don't have to stay with me. Go out there and be with Jon."

"I will in a minute. Tell me what you're thinking."

What Eden was thinking was how the shoot-out might have gone down. She heard phantom explosions and saw Tony's body ripped by bullets. "I'm thinking that I've seen too many Hollywood movies about how people die." Eden patted Arie's hand. "Don't worry about me." Without warning, Eden broke down and began to cry.

Arie slipped her arm around her friend and held her tight while her tears flowed.

Alone with Jon, Ciana shrugged. "Guess I'm not being sensitive, huh?"

"His dying didn't upset me that much either. He hurt people."

She crossed to the rail of the balcony, and Jon followed. He braced his forearms on the railing, leaned outward, his face toward the distant hills. "What do you think of Italy?" she asked, changing the topic.

"Too much city for this country boy."

She stole a glance at him, his rugged profile, his work-worn hands. Hands that tamed horses. Hands that had once stroked her body and lit her on fire. She compared them to Enzo's hands, which were long-fingered and manicured. Enzo worked in the vineyard, she knew, but mostly he gave orders to workers. "Arie says you're heading home to Texas in a couple of weeks."

"That's my plan."

"What about your dad? How's he getting along?"

"Stubborn as ever. He's still messed up from the stroke, but he won't go to rehab. It's dangerous for him living alone in that old trailer. When I tell him that, he explodes. We're better off not seeing much of each other."

"He probably hates to lose his independence, a scary thing to somebody who's always valued it." Watching Olivia's downhill slide and eventual death had taught her as much. Ciana took a deep breath, said, "Thoughtful of you to come all this way for Arie's birthday."

"I didn't come just for her birthday. Or to tell you all about Tony." He straightened, turning toward her. "I wanted to see you too."

What could she say to that? *I've missed you.* What would it accomplish to dredge up old feelings and memories? Sadness stole over her for what would be gone when she returned home. She needed to talk about something else before she broke out sobbing, or worse, threw herself into his arms. She thought of her mother and their last conversation. "Something's going on with Bellmeade. Do you know what it is?"

Jon leaned again into the rail, the spell of intimacy between them broken. "Some developer's in town. Talking about building a housing subdivision on your end of the county. Lot of the smaller farmers want to sell out, but Bellmeade's the linchpin. Without it, he can't build."

Ciana shook her head in disgust. "When Mom called and told me, I lost it. I'll never sell our land."

"You'll have a fight on your hands. It's dividing the town."

Arie breezed out onto the balcony, interrupting their conversation.

"She doing better?" Ciana asked.

"She's getting there. She's torn about his death and still relieved about her new life." Arie hooked her arm through Jon's. "How about I take you sightseeing?"

"Now?"

"You're only here a few days. Have to make the most of them. And tomorrow's my birthday, so we have to do whatever I want," she told him with a wink.

Jon raked his hand through his hair and gave Ciana a lingering look. Then he turned his full attention to Arie. "No arguing with a determined woman about her birthday, I reckon. But first let's find my hotel so I can wash the smell of travel off me."

"Sure. We'll catch a cab. Got an address?"

"In my bag." He started for the front door, where he'd dropped his duffel.

Arie said to Ciana, "Catch you later. Make Eden go out with you. Don't let her stay locked in that room by herself."

Ciana said she would, then turned toward the streetscape below, unable to watch Arie and Jon go out the door together.

They found his small hotel, which was nothing like the palatial Old World building where Arie was staying. She waited for Jon in the lobby, and when he emerged, hair still damp from the shower, she considered kissing him senseless. She tamped down the urge.

"Where to?"

"The Colosseum. It's amazing. It can seat up to fifty thousand people. That's bigger than some U.S. sports arenas."

They had no car, and cabs were expensive, so Arie negotiated the transit system using the Italian she'd learned over the past weeks. Jon told her he was mighty impressed, making her laugh. "You should hear Eden's Italian. She really picked up the language fast. Has a natural ear, I think."

The Colosseum was crowded with tourists, but Arie couldn't have cared less. In her heart, she was alone with Jon. He stared up at the stone walls, once soaring a hundred sixty-five feet but now broken and pockmarked by time and war and invaders. Inside they walked the solid perimeter, Arie pointing out certain features and reciting statistics. When they went down into the catacombs below, Jon let out a low whistle, looking into the small catacomb cells. "This where they kept prisoners?"

"Yes, for public executions, also wild animals that they raised up on platforms and hunted inside the arena."

"Doesn't sound very fair to the animals."

"They held reenactments of plays, too, so it wasn't all blood and gore. But this is also where the gladiators fought."

"To the death?"

"Unless the emperor or the spectators gave a thumbs-up, the mercy sign, to let the defeated live."

"And if not?"

"Thumbs-down. Death."

"Mean crowd."

Arie took his hand, lifted it high. "Hail Caesar."

He grinned. "I'd rather watch football."

After thoroughly checking out the huge stadium, they walked along several streets, Jon fascinated with the contrast between the ancient and modern buildings.

"Looks can fool you. Some of these 'newer' places go back to the seventeenth and eighteenth centuries. The Italians never abandon real estate."

She took him through the Arch of Titus, where soldiers once returned to present their bounty and captives to the emperor while cheering people lined the streets. Arie told him of other ruins, of the Roman Forum, where laws were enacted, and promised to show him wonders. "Tomorrow I'm taking you to see my two favorite places, the Sistine Chapel and St. Peter's Basilica. Both are so beautiful I cried when I first saw them." She glanced at him quickly. "Probably a girl thing."

"Well, right now, this man would like to see the inside of a restaurant. The olive snack didn't hold me."

Arie laughed. "Way too early for dinner. Most Italians don't eat until nine."

"I won't make it."

"I won't let you starve. Lots of cute cafés with yummy appetizers down every street."

Soon they were seated outside at a small eatery with an antipasto tray on the table. Jon ordered an Italian beer and Arie a soda. She didn't want alcohol. She wanted to be clear-headed, wanted to savor every moment with Jon in sharp relief, like the images on the stone friezes atop ancient buildings.

Jon took a swallow of beer and leaned back in the chair. "Your mother came to see me at Pickins's place when she heard I was coming over for your birthday."

Arie gave him a cautious look. "What did she want? To come with you?"

"She misses you. Your whole family misses you." He set down his glass. "And she's worried about you."

Arie waved her hand in dismissal. "She's always worried about me."

"Why shouldn't she be? You didn't tell her about your checkup."

"My life. My decision."

Jon bit into a crispy toast round dipped in olive oil. "Have you told your friends yet?"

Her face warmed and she didn't meet his eyes.

"You haven't, have you?" Jon shook his head. "You should, you know."

"Did you come all this way to crab at me?"

"I told you, I came for a lot of reasons."

"Well, I got the message. Now tell me what my mother wanted. Please," she added in a less grouchy voice.

"What do mothers ever want? She wanted me to evaluate you, tell her how you're *really* doing. If you're eating right." He grinned. "Bet you haven't had a decent burger in a month."

Arie rolled her eyes. "Tell her I'm just fine." She didn't dare confess about her bad days when her lower back ached horribly and she was forced to swallow a narcotic to dull the pain. "So what will you tell her?"

"That I think you look thin."

"I eat plenty. Walking and sightseeing takes tons of energy."

Jon drained his beer. "Then let's ride to wherever we're going next."

The tourist places and museums were closed, so she took him to a street with rows of small shops. The sidewalks teemed with people coming out for a long evening. The air was chilly, but Arie was prepared with a jacket stuffed into her large purse. Jon bought a beautifully cut leather jacket that emphasized his broad shoulders and narrow waist. With his boots and Stetson, he looked like a cowboy from a spaghetti Western, and absolutely delicious.

He bought his mother a silk scarf and Essie Pickins a pair of silver earrings. "She's been like a second mother to me," Jon said.

They went to dinner closer to nine, in an intimate trattoria not far from his hotel. The place held only twelve tables, all lit by candles, and their waiter doted over them. Jon ordered two glasses of champagne. "To toast your birthday," he said, clinking his glass to hers.

Because he had bought it for them, Arie sipped the sparkling bubbly, felt it tickle her nose and spread warmth down her throat.

Jon finished off his champagne and had the waiter bring him a beer. He raised the drink to Arie, then said, "So tell me about Eden and Ciana. How are they liking Italy? What are they up to?"

"Eden doesn't get out of bed until noon and Ciana's up with the chickens. Says it's country living in her blood. Some days we take day trips into nearby towns." She did a brief countdown of the cities they'd visited. "Every place is old. Medieval. Craftsmen still make copper pots, stained-glass windows, leather goods, gold jewelry like their ancestors before them. Pretty amazing."

"What about nights?"

"We meet up with a group of kids doing a walkabout—that's a travel group that hangs, works, and travels together." She warmed to telling him stories. "The leader of the group is an Aussie named Garret, and he's taken a shine to Eden. She likes him, but she's gun-shy after Tony. Can't blame her. Shame too. Garret's got it bad for her."

"And Ciana?" Jon rolled his finger around the top of his beer glass.

Arie giggled, leaned forward. "Best story of all. We were touring a local winery and Ciana caught the eye of the owner, Enzo. He's older but has some aristocratic heritage that goes way back, according to a Web search Eden did on him. He's richer than all get-out. He has horses and he and Ciana go riding on his estate. Secretly I think she likes him but won't say so to either me or Eden." Arie rolled her eyes dramatically.

Jon stared into his beer glass, where the liquid glowed in the candlelight.

For a moment, Arie thought she'd lost him.

He tossed the remainder of the beer down in one swallow, then reconnected with her. "Sounds like you're all having a real good time."

A note of sarcasm in his voice made the moment feel awkward. "We are," she said lamely. "But that's why we came."

He raised his empty glass at her, offered a conciliatory smile. "I think I'm running out of steam. Guess the trip's catching up to me."

"No problem," she said, trying for cheerful and failing. He was ending their evening and Arie wasn't ready. Time was going by too quickly. If she could have stopped the clock, she would have gladly, because time had never been on her side. Now she had even less of it.

"Before I forget, your brother gave me a present to give you for your birthday. I'll bring it tomorrow when I come and pick you up."

"Can't we get my gift now?" she asked eagerly. "We're not too far from your room . . . so close we can walk. I'm so full I could pop, so a walk would do me good."

"You sure?"

She nodded and he paid for the meal, and together they went out into the night. Although it was almost eleven, the sidewalks and streets were full.

"These people ever go home?" Jon asked.

"Not until very late. Getting on their schedule takes some getting used to."

As they walked, she wanted him to take her hand, but he didn't. When they were at his hotel, she followed him into the elevator. "You don't have to come up. I'll bring it down," he said.

"I want to see your room." *Any excuse to linger.*

"Very ordinary."

"Enzo upgraded our room to his favorite suite, as a surprise, so that's why we're in the best place," she explained, realizing she was babbling useless information.

"Thoughtful guy," Jon said, sliding his old-fashioned key into the lock of his third-floor-room door.

The room wasn't large, but there was a curtain separating the space into two sections. A table and two chairs stood in one half. Arie surmised the sleeping area was behind the curtain, where Jon disappeared, reemerging a minute later with a small wrapped box. She took it, smiled. "Thanks."

"I'll take you down and put you in a cab to your hotel and call you in the morning. We'll spend the whole day going wherever you like, birthday girl."

Arie's heart raced. Jon had been kind to her, but she wanted more than his kindness. She stood with her head bowed like a marble statue, her voice as frozen as her body. Seconds passed. Using the back of the table chair for support, she eased into the seat, staring down at her trembling hands.

He crouched beside the chair, peering at her anxiously. "Is something wrong, Arie?"

She lifted her head, connecting with his green eyes, his look of concern. "I . . . I don't want to leave you." Her voice quivered slightly over the words. "I want to stay with you tonight."

A look of confusion crossed his face. "Here?"

She nodded.

Then his expression changed from one of confusion to one of understanding as to what she was asking of him. He searched her face. "Look, Arie, I don't think—"

She stopped his words with her fingertips. "I've practiced this speech in my head for weeks. Please hear me out." She took a deep breath to calm her jitters, then began pulling out the words from the depths of her soul. "I know you don't love me, Jon, but that's okay. I have enough love inside me for both of us. I know you'll be gone when I get home, so there aren't any strings or conditions on tonight. I . . . I just want to stay.

Tonight. In your bed. With you." She fell silent, afraid to look him in the eye.

He reached out, lifted her chin. "Look at me."

She did so slowly, feeling tears swimming in her eyes. *Don't cry*, she commanded herself. *Do. Not. Cry.* His face was tanned with crinkles at the corners of his eyes, his sensuous mouth serious.

"Have you ever—"

"No."

"I shouldn't be the one. Not the first—"

*Not only the first, but the only*, her heart cried. She said, "I want you to be the one. Don't you see? I love you. I trust you." Jon blew out a breath and stood, still holding her hand in silence. He smoothed her silky hair.

Whatever courage she'd had fled. What had she been *thinking*? That he would magically want her just because she wanted him? That he'd take all the facts about her relapse into consideration and feel obligated? Humiliation seeped through her. Haltingly she said, "Look, I understand. I should . . . should never have asked." Bravely, she looked up at him. His expression was pensive, his thoughts unreadable.

After a long minute, he asked, "Are you sure about this?"

Her heart sped up. Her nerves steadied. No need to mince words now. "I'm sure. But please, not out of pity," she whispered. "And if you . . . don't want to . . . if you want to send me back in a cab, it's all right. We'll chalk it up to the champagne and birthday euphoria."

Without a word, he bent, scooped her into his arms, and lifted her as if she weighed nothing.

She clung to him, nestling her face into the crook of his neck, hoping his shirt would soak up the wetness on her cheeks. She loved him so much. As he carried her behind the curtain and gently laid her on the bed, she whispered, "She's very lucky."

"Who's lucky?" he asked.

"The girl you'll one day truly love," she said.

# 30

Something was going on, and Eden was determined to get to the bottom of it if it took all night. Ciana lay on the sofa, her arm across her eyes, jumping every time she heard a horn honk on the street below or a noise in the hallway outside their room. She was strung as tight as a hunter's bow. Eden's stomach growled. "I'm hungry. Time for antipasto."

"I'm not hungry. Go get yourself something."

"I don't want to go by myself."

"So order room service."

Eden said, "Look, I've been hammered with some bad news. I could use some support here."

Ciana raised her arm just high enough to see Eden sitting on the floor hugging her knees. She recalled her promise to not let Eden be alone. However, at the moment her own emotional ocean was swallowing her alive. Seeing Jon, watching him walk out the door with Arie, felt like a knife in her gut. She was nauseated with jealousy. She lowered her arm, covered her eyes. "Tony's dead. You're free of him. I don't see the problem."

She heard Eden stand up, felt a small sofa pillow slap her in the head.

"Well, aren't you just the friend of the year!"

Ciana righted herself, angry, but also stricken by her own insensitivity. *Unforgivable*. "All right, we'll eat antipasto," she said, as if that would make up for her hateful remark.

Eden glared. "Not here. I want to go out. I feel like I'm going to crawl out of my skin."

"What if Arie comes back?"

"We'll leave her a note."

Irritated at Eden and anxious to see Arie come in, Ciana agreed.

Eden, looking relieved, said, "I'll be back in a flash. First, I want to speak to the concierge."

Ciana waved her off, lay back down, and gave in to her feelings of self-pity. She had not expected Jon's physical presence to hold such power over her. Arie loved Jon and Arie was her best friend. Always. Ever since fifth grade they'd been inseparable. Yet today, from the moment Jon had walked out the door, Ciana had been gripped by unrelenting, gut-gnawing jealousy. Now she was sick with it.

Her grandmother had once warned Ciana about jealousy, the green-eyed monster—a vicious emotion that only corrodes from the inside out. But even knowing that, even applying the Beauchamp rule that such an emotion must be controlled, Ciana was facing a monster that threatened to consume her. And she also wondered if she was partly to blame for Jon's visit. Hadn't she asked him to be nice to Arie? He'd said he had come to see Ciana too. Had he meant it? She wanted to believe him but knew she shouldn't. It only made the monster inside her bigger.

The door flew open and Eden entered, looking all mysterious and self-satisfied. "Grab your purse and come down to the lobby. I have a surprise."

"What?"

"It wouldn't be a surprise if I told you, would it?" Eden was determined to get inside Ciana's head and pull out her secrets. The girl was in pain, and it had everything to do with Jon Mercer. Ciana had helped her escape Tony; now it was her turn to help Ciana.

"A scooter! Seriously, Eden?"

"Seriously," Eden told Ciana, pointing to the bright red scooter parked in front of the bell captain's station. "I've been wanting to try one for ages, but we can't do that with three of us. Tonight, we can."

"We have a rental car," Ciana countered.

Eden handed Ciana a helmet and mounted the scooter. "Too much traffic. This will be more fun."

"Says who? Do you even know how to drive the thing?"

"Garret lets me drive his all the time. So, yes, I know how. Now get on or I'll start yelling."

Ciana scowled but jammed on the helmet and took the narrow seat behind Eden. In truth, she didn't want to be alone with her thoughts, so a traffic accident seemed preferable.

"Hold on," Eden said.

"To what?"

"To me. If you don't, you'll fall off and break your butt." Eden started the machine and gunned the engine. Eden drove slowly at first, as she hadn't been entirely truthful about driving Garret's scooter "all the time," but it didn't take long to get the feel of it, and soon she was weaving in and out of traffic and around slow-moving cars at will.

"You'll kill us!" Ciana called out.

Eden stopped and parked at a trattoria on a narrow cobblestone street miles away.

Ciana followed her inside.

"A bottle of wine. And an antipasto platter," Eden told the waiter in flawless Italian.

"You speak like a native," Ciana said grudgingly, dropping into a chair at a table beside a window.

"Yeah, who knew I could pick up languages so easily? Should have taken one in high school instead of faking my way through math."

As soon as the waiter set the wine bottle on the table, Eden poured Ciana and herself generous glasses. She figured some alcohol would soften Ciana's stubborn Beauchamp resistance to talk about herself. Realizing it might take a few glasses, she started her story first. "Just for the record, it did hurt when I heard that Tony was dead."

Ciana hung her head. "Sorry about the cheap shot in the room."

Eden heaved a sigh. "You know why I'm reluctant to get involved with Garret?"

"Because Tony was a control freak?"

"Because I stopped developing my emotions and dating skills when I was fourteen. Think about it. I've never had another boyfriend."

Ciana emptied her wineglass and Eden quickly poured her another. "Arie and I sure didn't date much. The few college guys I dated only wanted one thing, which I wouldn't give them. And poor Arie had her heart broken all through school. So we didn't have much experience either."

"Maybe, but you both had variety. I didn't. Tony consumed

me. And by the time I wanted to move on, he had me all tangled up with him. What if that happens with Garret?"

Ciana drank more wine and thought about it. "Garret's a different guy. He's nice. He's kind. He hovers over you in a good way. He's nothing like Tony, so don't use that as an excuse."

"Scares me, though." Eden nibbled on a piece of prosciutto and cheese. "I let him see some of my scars from my days of cutting."

"What did he say?"

Her mind revisited her skinny-dip in the warm spring water with Garret. On land, as they both shivered and dressed, he couldn't take his eyes off her. It wasn't just her nakedness he was seeing. It was the scarring on her body, usually covered by clothing. When they were clothed, he gathered her in his arms and held her. He didn't question her. He seemed to know and understand and accept her as she was, marred skin and all. He'd turned her arm and brought it to his lips, planting soft kisses on every self-inflicted mark. "Said he wished he could kiss them and make them go away."

"He sounds like a keeper to me."

Eden snapped back to the present with Ciana's comment. She topped off Ciana's wineglass. "Tony did cure me of cutting. Cold comfort."

Ciana reached for a slice of olive bread. "I'm getting dizzy."

Eden caught the waiter's eye and he strolled over, whisked away the antipasto plate, and handed them two menus. They ordered, and once the waiter left, Eden determined that her friend was sufficiently softened. She rested her forearms on the table and leaned forward. "So now you know my fears and secrets. It's your turn, Ciana. Tell me what's going on between you and Jon Mercer."

Ciana stiffened, then turned to stare out the window. "Nothing. Why do you ask?"

Eden gritted her teeth. Ciana wasn't going to make this easy. "At the suite, when he came in, the tension between you two was thick enough to cut with a knife. I'm not making it up."

Ciana wanted to tell her, get it out in the open, yet she'd kept it to herself for so long, it was difficult. Where would she start? How would she start? "You're imagining—"

Eden smacked the table, and Ciana jumped. "Stop denying it! I have eyes to see. So far Arie doesn't. She's head over heels for Jon, but her ignorance won't last forever. Soon she'll see that you are too. And you are, aren't you? Tell me the truth."

Ciana's heart lurched. Her composure stripped away. She pressed the heels of her palms into her eyes, grinding back tears. "It's a long story."

"I've got time." Eden reached out and stroked Ciana's hand. "Maybe I can help."

Their waiter set their food in front of them, poured more wine into each glass, and slipped away from the table. The distraction gave Ciana time to regroup as she struggled to put her story into words. "Think back to June. To the night you dragged me to that dance saloon in Nashville."

"Okay," Eden said, attempting to fix the night in her memory. "I danced and drank too much. You met someone and stayed out all night." Suddenly Eden straightened. "Oh my God! You met *Jon* that night?"

Ciana nodded. "He was my mystery man. I might have been blitzed at first, but some kind of magic happened between us. We connected in every way. I fell asleep in his arms, woke up to his smile. Everything else I told you was just the way it happened. I was so rattled after Mom's text about Grandmother that I bolted without giving him any personal stats. That day we went out to see Arie's horse, well, you could have blown me over with a sneeze when I saw the man she'd been raving about. It was him. My cowboy."

"Why didn't you *say* something?" Eden looked incredulous.

"I couldn't. She wanted him so much she was loopy. She crushed on him when she was twelve, hanging around on a job site at Pickins's ranch. Seems as if Jon was visiting his dad that summer from Texas. When she saw him again, all grown up, well, she tumbled hard."

"And you just stepped aside." Eden shook her head.

"She's my friend. She's struggled all her life with cancer. She was in remission. She was happy. What would you have done?"

"I'd have *said* something to her! She would have understood."

Ciana pressed her lips together. "But I didn't. I couldn't break her heart."

"What about Jon? What did he say?"

Ciana toyed with her food—fish. She hated fish. "I begged him to keep it a secret, to not ever tell her about us meeting."

"So it wasn't just that one night with him?"

Ciana had said more than she'd wanted to. The wine had loosened her tongue too much, but there was no turning back, not with Eden. The girl had read between the lines. "Every time . . . whenever we were alone, whenever he held me, it was like being inside a bottle rocket."

"Sex?" Eden asked outright.

"No!" Ciana said hotly. She shuffled self-consciously,

dropped her voice. "Not that I didn't want to. But then Arie's face would float in front of me and . . ." She sat on her hands while tears gathered in her eyes. "If it had been any other female on planet Earth . . ."

"Jeez. You've got to be kidding me! And he went along with you?"

"It's just hormones between us. Chemistry," Ciana said, dismissing Eden's question.

"Hormones? You just used the word *magic*. Don't make me ask Jon."

Ciana's eyes widened. "Don't!" She shoved her half-eaten meal aside. "Please. This is a pinkie-swear confidence."

"So it isn't all about Arie's birthday, is it? Jon came to Italy to see you."

Amazed that Eden had come to that conclusion so effortlessly, Ciana reminded her, "And to tell us what happened with Tony."

The waiter reappeared to offer them dessert menus, but Ciana waved him off. The lump in her throat was huge, and she was afraid she'd toss her meal if one more morsel crossed her lips. She asked for the bill, but when it came, Eden snatched it out of her hand.

"This is on me. I still have one of Mom's credit cards and the company hasn't cut it off yet."

Outside, the air was crisp and cool. Ciana shivered in spite of her sweater. "We should go back to our room," she said, putting on her helmet.

"Why?"

"It's after eleven. What if Arie comes back and we're not there? I know we left her a note, but maybe we should check in, just in case."

Eden turned to face Ciana. She put her hands on her

friend's shoulders, squeezed. "Ciana, girlfriend, get a grip. Reality check. Arie's not coming back tonight."

Ciana searched Eden's face and saw the truth she couldn't bear written in Eden's blue eyes.

Eden pulled Ciana close and hugged her sympathetically. She knew what she was going to say would wound Ciana, and yet she knew she had to say it, because in the end, the truth was kinder than a lie. "Here's the situation, honey: Jon wanted you and you gave him to Arie. He's a guy. And tonight with Arie, he's going to do what guys do. And she's not going to turn him away, trust me." She felt Ciana's shoulders shake and her breath heave. "But the good news is guys don't have to be in love to do it." Experience with Tony's moods and appetites had shown Eden that much. "Please, don't hold it against either of them."

Ciana sobbed.

Eden held her, letting her cry herself out. Somewhere, Eden found a wad of napkins, and when Ciana's sobs had turned to hitching breaths, Eden made her blow her nose and wipe her eyes.

"I guess I don't want to go to our hotel either." Ciana's voice was thick and hoarse. "Where should we go? Two lost girls and their scooter."

Eden smiled wanly. "I'm thinking we should check out the Spanish Steps and the piazza where everyone gathers. I think we need a crowd around us tonight. Maybe even a nightclub or two."

Ciana was running on empty. She didn't care where they went or what they did. Not tonight. "Sounds like a plan." She straddled the scooter, wrapped her arms around Eden, and asked, "How'd you learn so much about love?"

Eden snapped on her helmet. "That's what I've been trying

to tell you. I don't know squat about love. But I know a lot about sex, and how a man thinks about sex. For men, the two don't have to go together. And sometimes that's all right."

The motor chugged to life and the scooter headed out. Ciana raised her head and silently begged the wind rushing past to blow images of Jon and Arie out of her mind and heart.

# 31

Arie was gone for two nights and only returned to the hotel suite after leaving Jon at the airport on the final day of his visit. Even after spending so much time together, their goodbye had been stilted, and they did not behave like parting lovers. What had she expected? That he would fall madly in love with her? While the days and nights had been the happiest ones of her life, she'd have to accept that although he'd been attentive and kind to her, she'd seen no spark of love for her in his eyes. She didn't know what she'd report to her friends. She didn't want to share the intimacies with anyone. Arie wanted to hold on to her memories. And her fantasies.

Standing at the suite's door, she fished out her key. Unsure of the reception she'd receive from Ciana and Eden, she took a few deep breaths to calm her nerves. Pasting a smile on her face, she marched into the room.

Eden tossed aside her fashion magazine and shot off the sofa. "Look who's home!" She hugged Arie. "We've missed you."

Ciana was on the balcony drinking coffee, soaking up the morning sunlight, and didn't appear to have especially missed her. Not that Arie blamed Ciana. She had brought Arie to Italy in part to celebrate her nineteenth birthday and Arie had blown her off to be with Jon. And although she'd hoped Ciana would forgive her and cut her some slack, Arie realized that Ciana's acceptance wouldn't come quickly. Arie had never planned to hurt her best friend, but her chance to be alone with Jon had been too perfect to pass up. For once all the stars and planets in the universe had lined up in her favor.

Arm in arm, Arie and Eden strolled to the balcony. Arie said, "The wayward friend has returned."

Without looking at Arie, Ciana said, "Have fun?"

Eden encircled Arie's waist with her arm. "Now, now, we agreed not to bombard Arie with questions. Her story to tell in her own time, right?"

"Sorry, forgot the rules," Ciana said coolly.

Arie felt the sting. "I . . . I'm not holding back. I just need some time."

Ciana chewed her bottom lip. Whatever had happened between Arie and Jon had not left Arie in the state of ecstasy Ciana had expected. And feared. "Fair enough," she said.

"What have you all done, seen, since I've been out?"

"The Spanish steps," Eden answered. "Awesome crowd of people. We went with a group of locals to a nightclub and danced our booties off." She wiggled her backside for emphasis.

"You too?" Arie asked Ciana.

"I mostly watched."

"Look, I'm sorry about bailing on my birthday—ruining any plans you all made."

"We accept your apology," Eden said quickly.

Too quickly, Arie thought, and without Ciana's agreement.

The slight stabbed Arie's heart. "We only have two more days in Rome. Shouldn't we be out sightseeing?" she asked brightly.

"I've made reservations for us to tour the Villa Borghese gardens tomorrow," Ciana said, adding, "If you haven't made other plans."

Eden glared at Ciana, but Arie let the catty comment pass.

"Really? I'd love to go there. It's supposed to be one of the most beautiful places in all of Rome." The Borghese family legacy stretched back to the sixteen hundreds when the great estate once boasted a vineyard. But one of the family members, a cardinal, had begun turning the wine-making fields into lush gardens and began a collection of Roman art from antiquity. The gardens were now a public park in the heart of the city, the museum still open for the price of admission.

Ciana said, "The next day we pack up and return to Cortona."

"Where we have another month before we have to go home," Arie said, hoping to disperse Ciana's bad mood.

Eden could hardly wait to return to Tuscany and Cortona. She was eager to see Garret. Still unsure of her place in his life, she'd decided to tell him everything about her past. If that ruined things between them, so be it. She wasn't about to take a chance on another relationship that wasn't honest.

Ciana was eager to return too. She had a man to see about a side trip to Portofino. She still wasn't sure what she was going to do about Enzo's offer. With Jon out of the picture, the offer was more tempting than ever, because once she left Italy, she'd return to her former life and a fight with her mother over Bellmeade's future. And, according to Jon, with several of her neighbors too.

"So nothing planned for today?" Arie asked.

"Nope," Eden said cheerfully. "Unless you want to take a

ride on our rental scooter." She quickly told Arie of her impulse to rent the thing and of how she and Ciana had been driving and riding all over the city.

"Sounds like fun," Arie said, without meaning it. Her back hurt, her head ached, and at the moment, she wanted to take a pill and lie down. "Maybe later today after the sun's not so warm."

Eden eyeballed Arie. "You do look like you should stay out of the sun. Your skin's kind of yellowish."

Arie filled with dread, knowing that her yellow cast came not from the Italian sun but from the beginnings of liver failure. "Well, we all know I don't tan, but with so much sun, yellow is better than ghost white, don't you think?"

Ciana took a hard look at Arie. Realizing she didn't look a hundred percent, her hardness softened. "You hungry? We discovered a Hard Rock Café a few blocks away. What say I take that scooter and bring us back burgers and good old American French fries? I, for one, am over spaghetti."

"You're not going without me," Eden announced. "I'll carry the food. How about three milk shakes to wash it all down? Chocolate for me," she called, raising her hand.

"Me too," Ciana said.

"Vanilla," Arie added, not wanting either food or drink. As soon as Ciana and Eden left, Arie took two pain pills and went to bed. There she lay clutching the sheets and gritting her teeth until the pills kicked in and dulled the pain. She couldn't put off telling her friends about her relapse. Jon had been correct about that. She had withheld the truth too long.

The drive to the Cortona villa from Rome was quiet, with none of the girls talking much, and once there, Arie pleaded a headache. She insisted Eden and Ciana to go meet Garret and his friends without her. The moment the girls appeared in the square, Garret launched himself toward Eden and caught her in a bear hug, lifting her off her feet. "You're cutting off my air supply," she said with a laugh as he twirled her in circles.

"Let me perform mouth-to-mouth," he said.

"Don't encourage him," said Colleen, a fellow traveler from Ireland. "Poor lad's been moping around like a sad sack since you went away."

The words pleased Eden immensely. She winked at him. "Is that so?" She slid down his body until her feet touched the ground.

"Not true. I haven't moped. I've been totally depressed," Garret said without taking his eyes off Eden. "It's just that it's time to move on because the tourists are leaving."

"Move on? You're going?"

He pulled Eden close and locked his fingers behind her back. "End of the week."

Two days. That was all the time she had left with him. Not the news she'd wanted to hear.

"I need a beer," one of the guys called out. "Can you two share giggles in a bar?"

The group set off on its familiar evening route. Garret held Eden back until the others were out of earshot. "Like to talk to you later," he said.

"About what?"

"An idea of mine. A serious idea."

"Not too serious, I hope."

Garret said, "Later," grabbed her hand, and hurried to catch up with the others.

Ciana returned to the villa early, unable to get into the camaraderie of the evening. As usual, Eden chose to stay with Garret. Ciana parked and came inside, hoping that Arie had gone to bed earlier, but that wasn't the case.

Arie sat on the low sofa bench, wrapped in her pink fuzzy bathrobe and painting her toenails. "Hey," she said to Ciana. "Want a cup of hot tea with me?"

Ciana felt awkward alone with Arie, still unable to manage her unresolved feelings toward both Arie and Jon. "No tea," she said. "Think I'll just head upstairs."

She'd only taken a few steps when Arie said, "Wait. Please. Sit down and talk to me. I . . . I know something's wrong between us, Ciana, and it's eating me up."

Ciana halted, Arie's plea ice-picking its way through her feelings. In all their years of friendship, they'd never had such a chasm between them. Ciana knew that the current rabbit hole was all hers. Self-consciously she sat, propping her boots on the cocktail table. "Sorry, I just have a lot of things on my mind."

"Tell me. I can't shake the feeling that I've done something to upset you. You're my best friend." Arie screwed the top back on the nail polish bottle, taking her time, wanting to say what was in her heart. "Before you came along, no one wanted to befriend the 'sick girl.' You held that fund-raiser in fifth grade and . . . and helped my family. And then you became my friend. So now I . . . I hate thinking we're not in harmony. Please tell me how I can fix things."

This was Ciana's moment to come clean, to tell Arie the truth about her and Jon. Ciana watched Arie's face, saw the dark circles under her eyes, the planes and angles that made her skin look too tightly stretched over her cheekbones. Emotion clogged Ciana's throat. She realized she couldn't tell Arie the truth. She simply couldn't. So she dredged up a lesser matter, certainly a true one, but not nearly so paramount. "Jon told me that some developer was looking to build a subdivision in my end of the county. That's why Mom wants to sell Bellmeade. Some adjoining farmers have already agreed."

"And that's what's been troubling you?" Arie sounded as if she wanted to believe Ciana but wasn't quite convinced. "I thought you were mad at me."

"No," Ciana lied.

Arie heaved a sigh of relief. "I thought you weren't going to let this problem get the better of you when there's nothing you can do about it while you're in Italy."

"Guess I have, though. Plus I'm homesick," Ciana added in a flash of inspiration. "I miss home. My land, my horse. Stupid, huh? I'm all grown up. You'd think I'd have gotten over homesickness. But it's a fact."

Arie smiled. "Not stupid. Honestly, I've missed home too. Mom, Dad, Eric—"

"Your three hundred closest relatives," Ciana interrupted, flashing a wry grin and with it, a peace offering.

Arie laughed and relaxed, looking as if a weight had been lifted off her.

"Let's think about where we should go next. Milan? Naples?"

"Cities at opposite ends of Italy. We should wait for Eden." Ciana rose from her chair. "I think I'll have that cup of tea now." She went into the kitchen, realizing that if she went off to Portofino with Enzo, she wouldn't be going anywhere with Arie and Eden. Enzo would want her answer about the trip when she saw him, and Ciana still wasn't sure what she was going to tell him. A few days of being pampered and loved by Enzo might flush Jon Mercer out of her heart for good.

"Thank you for talking to me," Arie called out as Ciana found a cup and a tea bag and turned on the burner under the kettle. "I'm glad you're not angry at me, because our friendship truly means the world to me."

Ciana answered, "Me too." It was true. She couldn't allow anything to break up her and Arie's lifelong friendship. The kettle screeched, and as an afterthought she added, "As for your birthday, sure, I was disappointed, but you'll have another one next year."

Arie didn't answer, so Ciana chalked it up to not having said it loud enough for Arie to hear over the whistling kettle.

After the group broke up for the evening, Garret took Eden to his closet-sized room over the coffee shop.

Eden balked when she saw the unmade bed that seemed to dominate the space. "Maybe we shouldn't come here."

"No place else to talk where it's warm. And while I'd like to jump your bones, I promise I won't." Garret waggled his eyebrows comically. He motioned her toward one of two straight-back chairs. "Some wine?" He opened a tiny cupboard.

"No more wine," she told him.

Garret dragged his chair so that he was facing Eden and straddled it backward. "I want to ask you something important. And I want to see your face when you answer."

"No pressure," she said, feeling her pulse rate shoot up.

"I care for you, Eden. A lot." He searched her face. "Join us on our walkabout."

Her heart beat faster. "An interesting idea."

"More than that. You see, the others will eventually peel off and move on to other things. Tom and Lorna are already talking about going home. But not me. I want to see the world. All of it. I want to go to India, see the Taj Mahal. I want to go to China and walk along the Great Wall. I want to sign on to a sailing boat and go to Bali. I'd like to walk in the rain forests of the Amazon."

"Wow. Ambitious." In truth, his idea appealed to her.

"These are no small journeys. It costs to travel, but I have an employer. An Aussie travel magazine. I write a column called 'Travel on the Cheap.' I email the pieces and photographs every few weeks and they pay me. Not a lot, but some to help on expenses. There's talk of syndicating my pieces, which will mean more money."

Her mouth dropped open. "You sneaky bloke!"

He shrugged, laughing. "I told you when we met that I was keeping journals."

"But you kept your job in the café."

"Work in my travels helps me write better articles. You know, get under the surface of everyday life. It's what the editors want. It's what sets my articles apart." He took a deep breath, skewered her with his gaze. "I want you to see the world with me."

"Me?" He was asking for more than a walkabout.

"I don't want to leave you behind, Eden. I don't want you returning to the States. I want you with me because if you don't come now, our chance will be gone. You'll fly back to your world and I'll be here in mine. We'll be two voyagers with an ocean between us. If you're with me, I have a chance of you falling for me. If you decide you want to dump me, you can fly straight home at any time. It will break my heart, but I'll let you go. At the very least you'll have some adventures and see some great places."

Unexpected tears filled her eyes. All of her past mistakes tumbled through her head. "There's stuff you don't know about me, Garret."

"Not sure I care. Person can't change the past, you know. It's over. Move on."

She reached out to touch his arm resting along the back of the chair. "Seeing the world could take a lifetime."

"I know. But I love you. And I want you to love me too."

She blinked through the mist gathered in her eyes. "And you think constant togetherness will make a difference?" Tony had made her feel claustrophobic, smothered. She never wanted to be so trapped again.

"Well, I expect it might take some time—charming as I am."

The word *love* scared her. "I . . . I have my friends. They expect—"

"They're good eggs. They'll send you my way with a smile and a shove."

Eden thought he was correct with his assumption. Ciana and Arie both would be happy for her. "Let me talk to them. I have nothing for camping or clothes—"

He beamed her a room-brightening smile. "No problem. Sigrid wants to go home to Sweden. I'll get her gear for you. We'll pick up clothing along the way."

"This is going so fast." Eden's head was swimming.

"We're all supposed to meet at noon by the fountain day after tomorrow. I'll wait for you there. And please want to come with me, Eden. It'll be a lonely road without you."

She studied his blue eyes, her decision already made. "I'll be there."

"You will?"

"Don't look so surprised. I want to see the world too."

He kissed her deeply, then pulled away. "Now let's get you home, before I beg you to stay."

She followed him into the cold, moonless night, where overhead a million stars spread out against the sky like unfulfilled promises yet to keep.

# 32

Autumn rain in Tuscany kept Ciana and her friends inside their villa all the next day. Ciana rattled around the place, knowing that Enzo was coming for a visit later that evening. Her nerves were bowstring tight, because she'd have to answer his invitation and her head and heart were at war about her answer. One minute, she wanted to go. The next, she didn't.

At lunch, over platters of pasta, Eden dropped her bombshell about joining Garret.

"You won't come home with us?" Arie asked, incredulous. "What about seeing your mother?"

"What about it? I've never had a mother like yours, Arie, and you know it."

With a trace of sarcasm, Ciana asked, "So what will you do? Send her a farewell postcard?"

Eden had weighed her options all night long. Now she asked, "What's waiting for me in Tennessee? Memories of living with a dead drug dealer? A bipolar mother? Some dead-end job?"

"You have us," Arie said.

"And you'll both start college in January. New lives. Why should I go back? Makes perfect sense to stay in Europe and tag along with Garret. I like it over here. Traveling and seeing the world sounds like a blast to me."

Arie asked, "Do you love him?"

"Why should that matter? The journey is about travel, not about love." Eden dodged discussing her feelings for Garret. She'd been fooled before by love, or rather, the illusion of love.

Arie shrugged. "Call me old-fashioned, but I think you should be in love with him before trotting off around the world with him."

"Why? Can't we just have a good time with each other?"

Ciana kept her silence.

"I'll be fine."

Ciana, ever the practical one, asked, "What about money? You haven't got any."

"I'll work. I've held a job before. Garret says businesses like to hire English-speaking workers."

"What if you don't like the travel?"

"Ciana, part of the fun of this trip is not knowing what will happen. It's called an adventure. I don't have any other plans for my life. I'm going."

"But . . . but . . ." Arie looked troubled. "I—we—might not see you again."

"I'll come home eventually. Maybe." Eden took Arie's hand and squeezed it. "And I'll send you postcards from the ends of the earth and keep in touch on Facebook."

Arie didn't seem mollified. She seemed pensive.

"Aren't you happy for me, Arie?" Eden asked.

Arie looked up quickly, offering a half smile. "I'm happy for you. It's just that I'll miss you. Back home."

"We've been together almost three months. Aren't you sick of my company yet?"

Ciana began clearing the table, too antsy to remain sitting. "What about your stuff? Your clothes and souvenirs?"

"I'll pack up a bag for you to haul onto the plane for me. If you'll be so kind. I'll pack some things to take with me. The leftovers I'll leave here. I'm not attached to any of it."

Arie looked especially sad, and Eden couldn't figure why, but her mind was made up. By tomorrow afternoon, she would be with Garret and heading into the rest of her life. Rain or shine.

Enzo arrived bearing wine and sweets. "I would have liked to take you out," he told Ciana, shaking off his umbrella. "I wanted to be alone with you."

"We'll be plenty alone. And dry. My friends are confined to their rooms."

Eden was up separating her things into piles and packing for her travels, while Arie was more worrisome to Ciana. The girl had claimed a sinus headache. Ever since their return from Rome, Arie had complained of minor ailments and retreated to her room. Plus her art hunger had diminished and caused Ciana to wonder about her. Which led to thinking about Arie and Jon, a subject she didn't want to remember because it hurt too much. Arie had kept mum about the time they'd spent together, acting as if it had never happened.

"But where have you gone, *bella* Ciana?" Enzo's voice and the touch of his hand to her cheek pulled Ciana into the here and now.

"I'm right here with you," Ciana insisted with a quick smile, and took the dessert box from him.

They went into the kitchen, and while Enzo uncorked the wine, Ciana spread delicate morsels of pastry and candy on a plate. "Are you trying to make me fat?"

He handed her a glass of rich dark wine while his eyes moved up the length of her. "You are just right, *cara mia*."

*My love*. Her heart tripped with his endearment. He oozed charm. "Let's sit." She walked him to the sofas and set the pastry plate on the coffee table aglow with candles. The flickering flames danced across Enzo's skin and reflected in his dark eyes. *He's gorgeous. And he wants me*.

He took her glass and parked it on the table with his, eased her back into the cushions, and trailed kisses down her neck. Her breath caught when his lips took hers. She waited for an explosion of passion. It never came, replaced instead by a slow warmth that made her sigh but not ignite. She felt like what she was—a barely nineteen-year-old country girl playing in the big leagues, inexperienced, unsophisticated, unprepared for what he was offering her.

She pushed away, righted herself. Enzo looked puzzled, confused.

"I haven't said thank you for the room upgrade in Rome. The suite was fantastic, and it made our whole visit that much better." Ciana took a drink of her wine, wishing to calm her nerves.

"*Mi piacere*. My pleasure." He drank deeply from his glass, then picked up a small pastry and brought it tantalizingly close to her lips. "*Crema*." He brushed the creamy confectionary over her mouth, then bent and kissed the traces away. "Now you try."

He was moving much too quickly. She was stuck in ambivalence. Without giving her words conscious thought, she asked, "Do you believe in love, Enzo?"

He pulled back. "But of course. I am Italian. Italians know much about love."

"Forever love?"

"Forever is a long time." He shifted away, still searching her face, like a chess player reading a baffling arrangement of pieces.

"My grandmother Olivia—remember me speaking about her?" He nodded. "She loved my grandfather from the first time she laid eyes on him. She told me the story of how he rode his horse onto our farm one day and lay a bag of autumn apples at her feet. It was all he had to give her at the time. She was just seventeen, but she knew then and there that they were going to be together for always. I listened to her story many times but thought that knowing instantly about being in love was an exaggeration. What do you say?"

He leaned into the cushions, stretching his arms across the plush tops. "Love is like good wine. To be savored and enjoyed for the different seasons of life."

"But not necessarily with the same person," she said, defining aloud his subtle message.

He shrugged. "When wine is young, it is bright and exciting. As it ages, it grows in depth and beauty. The flavor intensifies, turns transcendent. That is the way with love. It is a very rare person who can span all the seasons of another's life. That is not a bad thing. Different vintages bring appreciation for what was once savored before."

A romanticized way for him to say one woman would never be enough for him. She picked up her wineglass and spun the stem, studying the dark ruby color. "We come from different worlds, Enzo."

"I agree. I also must be honest, *cara*. The idea of one lover for all of life is not my way."

She smiled at him. "Honestly, I'm not sure if it's my way either. I can't say yet. Like good wine, though, to use your analogy, the mix must be just right. Isn't that what great wine is all about, just the right mix of the best grapes?"

He returned her smile, held her gaze. "You are not going to Portofino with me, are you?"

Until that moment, she hadn't been sure. Suddenly she was. "No." Perhaps someday she would wish she had gone, but not this day, not at this time.

He leaned in, kissed her lightly. "It will forever be my deep regret."

His courtly manners astounded her. She'd rejected guys before, but never one like Enzo. Yes, he was older and way more experienced than she, but he was also pragmatic. As was Ciana. The cat-and-mouse game they'd played over the past weeks had been good fun for both of them. She'd learned a lot about herself, and about what she wanted. She wanted the right mix.

Enzo got to his feet slowly, pulled her up beside him, and smoothed her curly hair. She slid easily into his arms. "You are amazing," she said, resting her head on his chest, listening to the steady sound of his heart.

"I would have enjoyed making love to you," he said. "And I promise, you would have enjoyed it too."

No doubt. "Thank you for everything. I'll miss our rides and our talks. And I'll miss you."

Moments later, Ciana closed the door behind Enzo and watched him drive away in the rain. Her life was full of goodbyes. To her father and grandfather, to Olivia, to Eden, to Enzo, to Jon Mercer. Through all of the leavings, the one constant was Bellmeade. Her land. *Hers*. Ciana jogged upstairs, feeling lighter than she had in weeks.

Ciana woke to sunlight pouring through her bedroom window. She knew it was late morning by the brightness swimming across the duvet. Unlike her to sleep in, but she felt rested. She stretched, listening for sounds from downstairs. The house was church-mouse quiet. Odd. She figured Eden might still be bedded down, but Arie was usually up. Ciana sniffed but couldn't smell fresh coffee brewing.

She tossed off her covers and went into the hallway. More quiet met her. She rapped on Arie's door. "You awake?" No answer. "How's your headache?" Silence.

Ciana twisted the doorknob, then inched open the door. The bed was rumpled and awash in pillows. Arie loved sleeping with piles of pillows, yet the bed held only pillows—no Arie. The bathroom door was closed, but there was no sound of running water. Ciana knocked on the door. "You in there? Want some coffee? I'll run down and make us some."

No answer.

Something wasn't right. Arie should have responded. Ciana tried to open this door, felt resistance. The door felt wedged, as if something were holding it back. She shoved her shoulder into it and forced the door against the blockage. She peered inside and saw Arie lying on the floor, the limestone tile stained with pools of bright red blood.

And Ciana screamed.

# 33

"What are we going to do?" Eden asked in a panic.

"We need a doctor. An ambulance. Oh my God. Help me get her up." Ciana felt Eden's panic. What was the emergency procedure in Italy? Was 911 even valid over here? Was there another number for emergencies?

"Maybe we shouldn't move her," Eden said.

"Well, we can't leave her lying in her own blood on the bathroom floor!" *Think!* Ciana pounded her forehead with the heel of her hand. The travel agent had given her paperwork filled with information. Where had she stashed it?

Arie groaned. Both girls fell to their knees beside her. "Pills," she whispered. "Drawer by bed."

Ciana ripped open the bedside drawer, gasped. It held an array of pill bottles. Why were there so many? "Which bottle?" she yelled.

"The Vicodin," Eden relayed, because Arie's voice wasn't loud enough to carry. "Two."

Ciana's hands shook, but she found the correct bottle and

dumped out the pills, then hurried into the bathroom and fed them to Arie. In a little while, she was able to stand. Eden and Ciana got her into the shower, held her upright, rinsed her off, dressed her in clean nightclothes, and tucked her back into bed. Ciana said, "You need a doctor."

Arie's breathing was shallow. "I have a doctor. In Rome."

"Rome!"

"His name's in the packet in the drawer."

Eden found the packet, removed the paperwork and the information from Arie's doctor in Nashville. "This says . . . it says . . . in case you need treatment." Eden looked up. "Treatment for what?"

In a much-labored voice, Arie said, "I have to get to Rome."

Ciana's cold fear turned colder. Arie's skin was tinged yellowish gray and looked papery thin. "You've been sick for quite a while, haven't you?"

"Rome," Arie said again, closing her eyes.

Eden grabbed Ciana's arm. "It'll take us hours to drive her to Rome. How do we get an ambulance in this country?"

"I don't know," Ciana said. "But I know someone who does." She clambered down the stairs to the house phone and called Enzo.

Arie woke surrounded by a thin curtain, on a bed she knew only by its design—hospital. IVs ran into her arms, and leads from her heart were attached to a monitor beside the bed. Machines must be alike the world over. The hardware, the sounds, the antiseptic smells fed her the information—she was in a hospital for certain. *Same song, second verse.* Cancer had found her in Italy. She remembered little of getting to the hospital—the sound of a siren blasting, a sense of being moved and placed into a vehicle on a stretcher, the voices of Ciana and Eden, of people in scrubs speaking in bursts of Italian as she floated in and out of darkness. Her throat was bone dry, her brain fuzzy with drugs. Still she needed some answers. Arie moaned.

The curtain flew aside and Ciana and Eden rushed to her bedside. Behind them, she saw Enzo. "Thirsty," Arie croaked.

"Oh, Arie! We've been so scared." Ciana speaking, as if not hearing Arie's words.

Eden asked, "What happened?"

Just then, another man came to her bedside. He was her doctor, a man she'd visited once before in Rome.

The physician took her hand. "Dr. Rozelli. Remember me?"

Jon had insisted he take her in to meet the physician once he saw that she was in pain when they'd been together and learned that she had not done so. That was how they'd spent most of the second day of his visit, running a gauntlet of tests and having X-rays taken in the hospital before going sightseeing. Now she had returned, or more accurately, been returned.

She nodded. "Thirsty."

The doctor gave her ice chips. "I tried to reach you with results of your lab work but could not." His rich, accented voice seemed to be coming through a tunnel. "You are heavily sedated and have a fever. You have a greatly elevated white blood cell count, and your liver function is degraded. Why did you not call me back?"

"Sorry," she whispered.

"Someone please tell us what's going on," Ciana pleaded.

The physician asked, "May I have your permission to speak freely to your friends? They have waited patiently for many hours."

Arie nodded, then closed her eyes. She didn't want to see,

couldn't bear to see their faces while he talked, revealing her duplicity. His assessment was thorough, tumors in her liver and pancreas. He ended his explanation by saying, "I have sent all information to my fellow physician in Nashville. I understand Dr. Austin has tended your case for years. And that he advised you against coming on this trip."

"True."

"Whoa!" Arie heard Ciana say. "You knew before we left that you had relapsed?"

"Not now," Arie said in an anguished voice.

Dr. Rozelli addressed both Arie and Ciana: "We will move you to a ward for more comfort, but it will be best for you to make arrangements to take Signorina Winslow home as soon as she can travel. She is very ill."

Hot tears burned behind Arie's eyes, and in more years than she could remember, she longed for her mother.

"Why didn't you say something before we left?" Ciana asked Arie later when she was sitting up in the bed on the ward and feeling stronger after a unit of blood had been pumped into her.

"Because we would never have come to Italy. It was the trip of a lifetime for me."

"Worth risking your life for?"

Arie stared into Ciana's cinnamon-colored eyes. "Yes."

"Well, not to me!" Ciana snapped.

"Or me," Eden chimed in.

Arie leaned her head into the pillow. "I would have been sick whether I stayed at home or if I came. Coming was better."

"And so you didn't tell anyone?"

Arie cut her eyes to Eden, thinking she must have some special psychic gift for ferreting out truth. Why deny it? "Jon knew."

An electric current shot through Ciana. "And he said *nothing* to us?"

Arie said, "Don't blame him. I made him swear to keep my secret."

"How could you tell him and not us?"

Eden touched Ciana's arm, flashed her a look that said, *Back off*.

"He found out by accident. On the day I got the news, I went to see my horse and it was raining and I fell apart in the pasture and Jon found me crying my eyes out. He figured out the truth. He begged me to tell you both. But I didn't."

Ciana shook her head. "Bad choice on his part."

"Don't." Arie's voice strengthened. "Not. His. Fault."

Ciana wasn't convinced. "Well, we can't stay here."

Arie knew Ciana was right. Their final month would have to be canceled. "Don't think it doesn't break my heart," Arie said, closing her eyes.

"I should call your family," Ciana said.

"No, I'll call. It's my mess."

"Not until we have some plan," Eden cautioned.

"I think I need to sleep now," Arie said, weariness slamming her. In truth, she wanted to fall asleep and not wake up. Returning home, facing weeping family members, going back into treatment, was going to be hell.

Ciana stretched across two chairs in the hospital waiting room, desperate to grab some sleep. Two days had passed, and Arie was stronger, but they were no closer to getting home.

"Coffee?" Eden stood over her, offering yet another paper cup of machine coffee that tasted like dirty water.

"Thanks. I think." She sat up, took the cup.

"Any news?"

"Enzo's fighting with the airlines to get us rebooked into Nashville instead of Atlanta. Everything's booked solid this time of year." Arie had talked to her family and they were frantic. They'd told the girls to fly first-class because it would be more comfortable. So had Alice Faye.

"So we won't be returning to Cortona?"

"Don't see how we can."

"What about our stuff?"

"Enzo's sent the couple who work for him to go pack everything up. They're bringing some necessary personal items just to get us home and will ship the rest."

Eden sipped her coffee. "That's good. A big help."

Ciana stroked Eden's mass of tangled dark hair. "Of course you were already packed. I wish you and Garret—"

Eden shook her head, interrupting with, "I wish it too. But he's gone by now."

Just then Enzo came into the waiting area, a triumphant expression on his face. "*Avere successo!*" he said. "I have your reservations. First-class."

"When?"

"Tomorrow."

Ciana put her arms around Enzo. The weather had turned much cooler in Rome overnight, and his scent was of very fine cologne and his cashmere coat. "Thank you."

He held her close. "Ah, *mia bella*," he said, his lips against her hair. "How is it that you have stolen into my heart so completely?" He lifted her chin. "Next time, I will not give up so easily to take you to Portofino." He smiled, kissed her forehead, stepped away. "I will find her doctor and let him know."

When he was gone, Eden asked, "Portofino? Forget to mention something to me?"

Ciana rubbed her temples, nodded, and told Eden about Enzo's offer. "It was nice to be asked. And as it's turned out, I couldn't have gone anyway."

Eden took Ciana's hand. "Let's go tell Arie we're going home."

They were on a jumbo jet high over the Atlantic. The aisles were spacious and the seats folded flat to become a real bed with fresh linen. Arie could recline and rest all the way home. Her condition was stable, and once they landed in Nashville, an ambulance and a customs agent would meet the plane on the tarmac and whisk her to the hospital, where her parents would be waiting for her. Ciana and Eden would have to go through customs in the normal way before going to the hospital.

Eden stared out the plane's window, at the banks of clouds below. An hour before, she had watched Italy slip away. And she brooded.

From across the aisle, in a small soft voice, Arie said, "I messed up your plans to go with Garret, didn't I?"

Eden startled, looking over at Arie's pale face. "It's okay."

"No, it isn't. I hope you got a message to him before we left."

Eden didn't want Arie to fret. She reached across the aisle and squeezed Arie's hand. "I'd probably have been a terrible camper. And staying in a cheap hotel? Can you imagine?"

Arie didn't smile. She clung to Eden's hand, but once she drifted off to sleep, Eden slowly let go, returning to her vigil at the window. Images of Garret slid through her mind's eye—his smile, his crazy hair, her arms around him riding on the scooter. She imagined him, too, standing in front of the fountain in Cortona, waiting for her. Tears trickled down her cheeks. She brushed them away, her heart aching, and wondered how long he'd waited before he'd given up, before he'd left the plaza, before he'd realized that she wouldn't be coming at all.

# PART III

# 34

Arie's homecoming and entering the local hospital was everything she had dreaded. Relatives, chastisement for having taken her trip in lieu of getting treatment, and lots of weeping. She didn't need it, and sure as anything, she didn't want it. Everyone was shocked. Everyone was sorry and sad. And everyone was asking, "Now what?"

Ciana and Eden were lost in the shuffle of foot traffic and a waiting room full of people, and they had to explain why nothing had been said before the treasured trip to Italy. It fell to Dr. Austin to clear Arie's room of any except her parents, Eric, and Abbie.

Arie explained her reasons as simply as she could, imploring Eric to look after her friends, to get them home safely, and to make sure they weren't the targets of rumors and accusations.

Patricia's face was drawn and her eyes red-rimmed with exhaustion. Arie felt guilty and responsible for bringing pain to her mother. "Oh, Arie, why didn't you tell us before you left for Italy?"

"Because I wanted to go to Italy. Because it's my life. Simple as that."

Swede shook his head. Eric scowled at her. Only Abbie offered the sympathetic look Arie needed. "*Thank you,*" Arie mouthed to her soon-to-be sister-in-law.

Dr. Austin intervened before any grueling interrogation could proceed. "Right now, I'm throwing all of you out. My patient needs rest."

She called to Eric, "See to Eden and Ciana."

She saw a film of moisture in his eyes that twisted her heart. "And don't say one nasty word to either of them. They didn't know either."

When the room was cleared, Dr. Austin dragged a chair to her bedside. "Is it your turn to smack me around?" Arie asked. "Because if it is . . ."

He shook his head. "Not at all. Can't unring a bell."

"So you want to tell me how you're planning on torturing me? On what my next treatments are going to be?"

"Not yet." He steepled his fingers. "First I want you to tell me about Italy."

His request surprised her but opened the floodgates. As Arie talked, as she told him about the sights, the old cities, the art, the culture, her enthusiasm built. Merely talking about Italy and the places she'd been, the things she'd seen, buoyed her spirit. Dr. Austin let her talk uninterrupted until her voice was hoarse and her eyelids were heavy. Finally he stood, checked her vitals, gave her some water, and told her to rest.

Arie's verbal revisit had brought on an emotional purging of her guilt over messing up the last few weeks of the trip for her friends and the scoldings of family. As she watched Dr.

Austin cross to the door, she said, "I'm not sorry I went, and if I could turn back time, I'd do the same thing again."

Once she was alone, her memories turned to her birthday and to her time with Jon Mercer. She fell asleep remembering his hands and lips on her skin with moonlight coming through a window in his room, knowing that that first night was the real treasure of her heart.

Eric drove Ciana and Eden home to Windemere in his truck. Abbie peppered them with questions about Italy as he dropped off first Eden, then Ciana, before returning to Nashville and the hospital. Once Eric drove away, Eden stood on her front lawn surveying the home she'd fled months before. The yard was brown with winter dead grass, and the potted plants were dried and wilted. The carport held only her old car from Tony. She wondered if the battery was dead. And she wondered why he'd spared it.

She had no idea whether her mother was home or still on one of her escapes. It didn't matter. Eden needed a place to regroup, somewhere free until she found a job and made a plan for the months ahead. She sighed, picked up her bags, and dragged them through the carport door and into the kitchen. Stepping inside, she could hardly believe her eyes. New flooring, cabinets, countertops, kitchen hardware, and appliances made the space shine. Eden left her bags and went to the living room, also redecorated with new carpeting and freshly painted walls and shelves. The sofa and chairs looked gently used, much nicer than the former pieces. Jon had said Arie's family had spruced up the place, but she'd had no idea how perfectly they'd done their job.

Eden heard the kitchen door open and Gwen came inside. "Well, well, look who's home."

"I might say the same thing," Eden said, turning toward her mother.

"Since October. Got my old job back at Piggly Wiggly." Gwen set down her purse, lunch bag, and athletic shoes. "You look good."

"You too." It was more of a courtesy than the truth. Gwen's hair needed coloring and her lined face sagged. She was calm and controlled, though, so Eden assumed she was taking her meds once more.

"You staying for a while?"

"I thought I would. That okay with you?"

"This is your home, Eden. You're always welcome."

Eden glanced around. "Place looks nice."

"Arie's folks. Tony really did a number on it, but Arie's dad and brother and more helpers than I could count showed up and worked for five days fixing the place up. All family, they said."

"I thought you left town the same night we did."

"I did. But the shoot-out made the news all the way to Florida. Must have been some firefight," she mused. "Anyway, I figured I'd need to make sure the house was still standing for you when came home."

"For me?"

"And for me too. And Aunt Myrtle. Place looked pretty bad. Ugly things written on walls in red paint, not a piece of furniture that wasn't broken or cushion that wasn't slashed. Got the new stuff at the Goodwill store. Couldn't have done it without all the help."

Eden plopped onto the sofa and rubbed her eyes, stinging from lack of sleep.

Gwen asked, "Aren't you home sooner than you said you'd be?"

"Arie got sick. We had to come back."

"What kind of sick?"

"Cancer. She's in the hospital in Nashville."

Gwen eased into a lounge chair. "That's too bad about Arie. Hers are good people. Shame she has to suffer."

"Jon said you faced Tony down and gave us a head start."

Gwen fished a cigarette from the pocket of her jacket. "That's why he wrecked the place. To get even. Dirtbag."

Eden peered at her mother, at the woman she'd lived with all her life but didn't feel she really knew at all. "Did he . . . did Tony hurt you?"

Gwen sucked on the cigarette and blew out the smoke without meeting Eden's eyes. "He got physical, but all he got in return was lies that sent him off in the wrong direction." Her eyes glittered like hard marbles when she spoke. "I can take a few jabs."

Eden went cold all over, hating Tony and wondering all the more about her mother's murky past, which was also her own past. Without the anchor of family history or stories, Eden had been adrift all her life. "I'm sorry about all the trouble Tony caused. You were right about him all along."

Gwen said nothing and Eden appreciated her mother not giving her an "I told you so" lecture. Gwen turned on a lamp, as the house was growing dark in the gathering gloom of the shorter daylight hours. "You want some dinner?"

Eden shook her head. "I'm still on Italy time, so all I want right now is to go to bed." She stood and started for the stairs.

Just as she made the first step, Gwen said, "I'm glad you're home, baby."

Eden couldn't recall the last time her mother had called

her "baby." The endearment caused a lump in her throat. In these last few minutes, Gwen had sounded and acted like a sane, well-grounded person, the mother Eden had always coveted. But she knew better than to count on Gwen's lucidity. Eden had hoped too many times before that Gwen would finally be well and remain on her meds and in therapy. But after so many years of watching the good tranquil times collapse, She knew better. "Happy to be here," she said.

"I'd like to hear all about Italy and your trip."

"I'll tell you tomorrow."

In her room, she saw that the walls had been repainted and the furniture repaired or replaced, and that all her bed linen was different. Her book collection was gone, her stuffed animals from childhood missing. She shook with anger, realizing that Tony had paid special attention to the destruction of her personal belongings. Eden undressed quickly, peeled back the covers, and crawled between the clean sheets. Once there, she quietly cried—for Arie, for her mother, for herself, for all the past that was now destroyed and gone. And she cried for Garret, wondering where under the skies of Europe he was sleeping this night, and if he was longing for her the way she was longing for him.

Eric's truck pulled away and Ciana sucked in the scent of home, of ground and trees and horses, of pastureland and old house. This was Bellmeade, and all that she loved. Tuscany was beautiful, but this was home. She was glad to be here.

Instead of going into the house, she heaped her suitcases onto the wraparound veranda of the house and walked to the barn, excited about seeing her horses. She entered the barn and stopped cold. The place was immaculate. Ciana hadn't known what to expect after leaving her mother in charge for over two months, but cleanliness and order hadn't been on her radar.

She heard Firecracker neigh as the horse caught her scent. Ciana hurried over to the stall and stroked the bay's soft nose. "Hey, girl. Miss me?" Firecracker shook her head up and down just as if she'd understood the words. Ciana laughed and hugged the horse's neck over the stall door. The stall was stacked with fresh straw and looked as cushy as a bed. Sonata stuck her head out of the next stall and whinnied, so Ciana gave her nose a rub too. "Wow, look at you." Both horses had been brushed until their shaggy winter coats shone.

From the next stall down, another horse snorted. "Who are you?" Ciana asked. This one was a buckskin. "Caramel?" Ciana asked, recognizing Arie's horse. "How'd you get here?" How could Alice Faye have managed such a pleasant homecoming for Ciana? Especially when her mother didn't yet know she was home.

"Welcome home, Ciana," a man said from behind her.

She whipped around and saw Jon Mercer standing in the tack room doorway, holding bridles in one hand. Shocked, she blurted, "What are you doing here?"

"Working," he said. "Your mother hired me weeks ago."

# 35

Fresh hurt and anger stormed Ciana's heart. She didn't want to see Jon, not after what had happened in Italy. "Why?"

"To keep this place running while you were away."

"No one told me."

His eyes held a wary look. "Now you know."

"Well, I'm home. We have no further need of your services." She glared at him and heard the horses stir behind her, seeming to sense the tension in the air between their caretakers.

"Your mother hired me. She'll have to fire me."

Ciana realized she was too tired, too off-balance from his physical presence to face this dogfight right now. "We'll talk about it later." She stalked toward the outside door, but he intercepted her.

"Let's talk now," he said. "Let's start with why you've come home three weeks early."

She thought about how to best hurl the truth at him for maximum impact but couldn't do it at Arie's expense. "Arie's sick," she simply said.

Jon frowned. "Tell me."

She did, ending with, "She's in the hospital. If you're not too busy, maybe you could check in on her." The last came out more hatefully than Ciana intended. "She's pretty sick," she added, less angrily. "She told us you knew she had relapsed before we even left for Italy."

Jon tossed the bridles toward the tack room. "True."

Ciana's anger mushroomed. "And you didn't think it was important to tell me and Eden?" Although Arie had explained her reasons, Ciana couldn't stop herself from striking out at Jon, because it was Jon she wanted to wound.

"She asked me not to."

"And you went along with her? You should have said something. If not before we left, at least when we were all together in Italy. After you left, she went straight downhill—"

Jon grabbed Ciana's shoulders, startling her. "She told me she would tell you. She promised me."

"Well, she didn't!" Ciana twisted to break his grasp. "Let go of me."

Jon dropped his hands, but his gaze went hot. "I kept her confidence just like I kept yours when you asked me not to tell her about us."

Ciana felt as if he'd knocked the breath out of her with his well-chosen words. She straightened and with all the frostiness she could muster said, "My mother and I are co-owners of this farm, and that means you work for *me*, mister. We'll talk again tomorrow."

His eyes blazed, but he kept his temper in, nodding in a gentlemanly way. "Good evening, Miss Beauchamp. I'll just keep to my chores."

Her bottom lip quivered, and she shoved past him. Outside, darkness had fallen, and so had the temperature. She shivered uncontrollably as she jogged to the house and up onto the veranda, forcing back tears. *I won't cry.* She pushed open the front door, tumbling into the warmth.

"Mama?" she called.

No answer.

Still upset about Jon, Ciana went upstairs, pausing at her mother's bedroom door, struggling to calm herself. "Mom? You in there? Surprise. I'm home."

No answer.

Ciana touched the doorknob, then hesitated, remembering the last time she'd gone into a closed room, when she'd seen Arie's body and blood on the floor. She pushed her mother's door open and, surprised, saw that the room was freshly decorated—paint, bedding, pillows—all new, and unexpected.

Ciana closed the door. Her mother must have been out for the evening. *A good thing,* she decided. One shouting match for the day had been enough. She really wasn't up to butting heads with Alice Faye tonight about selling off Bellmeade.

On the way to her own bedroom on the first floor, Ciana saw that her bags sat just inside the front door. Jon, doing one of his chores. Irritated, she stepped over them, and once she was inside her room, her spirit quieted. Ciana pulled off her boots and jeans and wrapped herself in the quilt that covered her bed, a wedding present to Olivia and Charles. Bone weary from the long trip, she closed her eyes. If only her grandmother were still here. Ciana could tell her anything and she would understand and help her decide what to do. Remembering Italy, grieving for Arie, angry at Jon, and facing uncertainty about the future, she let go and allowed herself, finally, to cry.

The rattle of someone in the kitchen woke Ciana in the morning. It was almost eight o'clock; she'd grossly overslept. Tossing off covers, she quickly splashed cold water on her face, dressed, and hurried down the hall into the large farmhouse kitchen. She saw her mother busy stirring pots on the stove and rolling out dough. "Hey, Mom."

"Ciana!" Alice Faye hurried over, hugging Ciana enthusiastically. "What a lovely surprise. I knew you must be home because I saw your suitcases inside the door. Coffee's fresh brewed. Help yourself."

"I haven't seen you up this early in years." The comment was more a dig than an observation. Ciana poured herself a big mug of hot coffee. "I'll deal with my luggage later."

"No hurry," her mother said, ignoring Ciana's tone of voice, picking up the biscuit cutter, and deftly slicing the dough into perfect circles. "Take all morning. Sit down and eat a good breakfast first."

During Ciana's childhood, Alice Faye had fixed breakfast every morning once the early chores were done and before Ciana went off to school. That had ceased when Ciana was in high school. She recalled a shouting match between her mother and grandmother about "hungover incompetence" but shook her head to dispel the ugly scene.

"I want to hear all about your trip." Alice Faye popped the biscuits into the oven and set the timer. She turned toward Ciana. "Aren't you home early? Weren't you staying through November?"

Briefly Ciana told her about Arie.

"Oh, that poor girl. Is there no end to her suffering?" Her mother stirred a pot of grits on the back burner. "I'd have been here last night if I'd known you were coming."

Despite the hit of caffeine, Ciana realized she hadn't talked to her mother since their blowup on the phone about selling Bellmeade, but no need to mention it now. "We left in a hurry from an Italian hospital. We called her family so they could arrange for an ambulance to meet our plane and take Arie to the hospital. Eric drove me and Eden home late yesterday."

"I'm very sorry about Arie. Her parents must be beside themselves." Alice Faye dried her hands on a dish towel.

Just then a rap sounded on the outside kitchen door. "There's our company."

"Company?"

"I can't eat all this food. I'd weigh a ton." Alice Faye went to the door, opened it, and invited Jon inside.

Smiling, he handed her a basket of fresh eggs from the chicken coop. His eyes snagged Ciana's, and his smile faded. "Morning."

Ciana turned her back to him and poured herself more coffee.

"Sit," Alice Faye commanded. "This is my daughter, Ciana, fresh home from Italy. And this is Jon Mercer, the man I've hired to help us out."

"We met last night," Ciana said. "When I went to check on my horse."

"Oh, of course," Alice Faye said, turning on the flame under her cast-iron skillet. "I should have known the horse would get top billing." There was no rancor in her voice, just amusement.

Jon still stood at the door. "I can eat in the barn. Don't want to spoil your homecoming."

"Sit!" Alice Faye said a second time. "Breakfast is part of our deal. So sit down and let me scoop up some grits and gravy for you. You want those eggs sunny-side up, right?"

Ciana already knew how he liked his eggs. Alice Faye

didn't know hers and Jon's history, nor did she want her to know. Ciana motioned toward the table, giving him her permission to sit and eat.

Jon sat and offered a servile smile, infuriating her, just as the timer went off for the biscuits.

"Honey, pour Jon some coffee."

Ciana gritted her teeth but complied. She slammed the mug in front of him, sloshing the coffee.

"Eat with us?" Alice Faye questioned Ciana's show of temper.

"I'm going to tend the horses." Ciana's back was stiff as she turned to walk away.

"The horses are fed and the stalls mucked," Jon said casually.

"Thank you, Jon," Alice Faye said, a hint of chastisement in her tone, aimed at Ciana.

"I'm going for a long ride," Ciana said, irritated. "I'll be back when I get back."

As Ciana stalked down the hall to her room, she heard her mother say, "Don't know what's gotten into that girl. Maybe she's just overwrought about a sick friend. You'll forgive her, won't you?"

"I forgive her," Jon said, loudly enough for Ciana to hear all the way down the hall.

Ciana slammed her bedroom door behind her.

# 36

Arie was in Tuscany, in the villa. Sunlight warmed her and from the kitchen, she heard the sounds of Ciana making coffee, and then the scent of the rich brew filled the air.

She woke with a start, saw the walls of the hospital room, daylight streaming through the window, and heard the sound of breakfast trays clattering in the halls. Both of her parents came alongside her bed.

Swede kissed her forehead.

"Your color is so much better," Patricia said, stroking Arie's cheek.

"Did you two spend the night here?"

They glanced at one another guiltily. One of the rules she'd laid down years before was *no sleepovers*.

"Oh, now, don't fuss." Patricia straightened the bedcovers. "We haven't seen you in over two months. We wanted to be with you."

"You should be at work—both of you."

"And tomorrow is another day," Patricia said, closing the subject.

An orderly brought a breakfast tray. "Morning. Here you go."

He swept out and Arie cautiously lifted the metal lid over the plate. "Oatmeal?" Arie said. "Seriously? Do you know how well we ate in Italy? Oatmeal never passed my lips."

"As soon as you come home, I'll fix anything you want."

"Did Dr. Austin say I could go home soon?"

"He thought it might be a possibility now that you're stable."

Her future stretched in front of her like a well-traveled road—back and forth for chemo treatments, blood work, endless tests; physical side effects of barfing, mouth sores, skin lesions, exhaustion, maybe hair loss. She figured treatments would be harsh, because the devil inside her had grown stronger. "Mom, do me a favor? Ask everyone to stay away until I go home?"

"Dr. Austin's already banned everyone but immediate family from visiting."

"Not Ciana and Eden," Arie said. "I want to see them."

"All right. I'll see that they get on the list as family."

"Do you know how my horse is doing?"

"Your trainer . . . Jon, is it? He's watching over your horse for you."

The news surprised Arie. "I thought he was going back to Texas."

"No," Patricia told Arie. "He took a job at Bellmeade. Alice Faye needed some help while you all were gone."

"Really?" Arie's heart leaped. Knowing he was at Ciana's made her feel better than she had since her birthday, because if Jon was at Ciana's, she could see him whenever she wished.

And although she held no illusions that he loved her, she would forever love him. Her mood brightened. Arie picked up the spoon from her tray. "Okay. Bring on the oatmeal."

Her parents flashed her tender smiles.

Over the next weeks, Ciana ignored her mother's breakfast invitations and spent the time instead on long morning rides across Bellmeade land. Too much of the once-fertile fields lay dormant. How would she manage? She was just one person, and there was a lot of acreage to cultivate come spring. She needed people to sign leases, pay leasing fees, and work the land in order to keep Bellmeade going. The fields she kept under cultivation for personal use wouldn't pay the bills. How had Olivia done it for so many years?

There was also the issue of Jon Mercer. Not only was he doing work she could do, but also Alice Faye had promised to pay him, and Ciana knew from maintaining the checkbooks that they didn't have the money. Neither did she want him around her—not the aggravation or the temptation. She often saw him watching her from a distance, cool and guarded. He still made her heart beat fast and her blood run hot, and yet beneath the surface of her attraction, her feelings simmered with unchecked anger. She told herself that anger was her ally because it created a wall of separation between the two emotions.

And then there was her mother, who was acting totally weird. Cooking breakfast? Often preparing supper? Going out almost every evening? What was going on with her? Ciana was baffled. What had happened to the Alice Faye who used to pour herself glasses of sweet tea and gin until she weaved upstairs to her bedroom and passed out? Ciana shook her head. Too much to think about.

By now, the morning sun was high and Ciana felt the heat through her jacket. Her horse was restless, and Ciana headed back to the barn. She was relieved to see that Jon was nowhere around. She quickly unsaddled her horse, brushed her out, then put her into the pasture with Sonata and Caramel. In the house, Ciana found leftover biscuits and ham and made herself two sandwiches. She was washing them down with cold milk when her mother came into the kitchen.

"Have a nice ride?"

"I haven't got time to talk. Have to shower now." Ciana dashed into her bathroom, not wanting a conversation that might turn into an argument, but when she came back out, her mother was sitting on her bed, waiting.

"I need to say some things, and you need to listen," Alice Faye said forcefully. "Jon told me you asked him to leave."

Ciana drew up short. This was one fight she could take on. "He said you hired him while I was gone. Now I'm home. We don't need him."

"Much happened while you were away. Too much for us to discuss right now, but I do want to tell you why I hired Jon."

"You couldn't handle the horses and chores by yourself. I get it."

Alice Faye leaned back on her elbows. "When you and your friends scampered off to Italy, I and your friends' families had to face a maniac all by ourselves."

Ciana shivered. "I thought you had police protection."

"I had some, but they couldn't be here twenty-four seven. Things started happening . . . strange things. Our horses were let out of the pasture and were roaming the roads. I had to call neighbors to help round them up. The horses could have been struck by cars. They could have been maimed or worse. The henhouse was vandalized. Three of our best layers had their necks wrung, and our rooster was stabbed to death. No wild animal did that. Only the two-legged variety could have been so cruel."

Ciana stood in shocked silence, unable to move.

"I was scared, Ciana. I slept with Daddy's revolver under my pillow and our shotgun by my bed. I ran into Essie Pickens at the grocery one day, and she suggested that I hire Jon to help, swore he was a good man and would protect our farm. I promised him wages and breakfast and any other meal he wanted. He has repaired the henhouse and replaced the hens and rooster. He's kept up with the horses and he's handled many an odd chore that needed doing. Perhaps it's escaped your notice, but this place is falling down around our ears."

Jon hadn't said a thing about working at Bellmeade when he'd come to Italy. He should have. One more thing to hold against him. "Why didn't you hire one of the men Olivia used?"

"Those men are all gone, and the state's clamped down on illegals. Not enough legit laborers to go around these days."

"Why didn't you lease the land to other farmers?" Leases would have turned the insufficient labor issue into another farmer's problem.

"At the time Olivia wouldn't hear of it. Beauchamp pride. These past eight years, Mother almost killed herself trying to keep things going. If you hadn't planted the few fields you did last spring, the horses would have starved this winter."

The words sent new shock waves over Ciana. "Why didn't someone tell me? I . . . I could have helped more—"

"You were a teenager, in school. We both wanted to protect you."

"Why didn't you stop me from going to Italy? That money—"

"I wanted you to go to Italy. You needed to get out from under this place. See that the world is bigger than Bellmeade. I'd have given anything for such an opportunity when I was your age. But for now, back to Jon Mercer. He's staying as long as he wants, and don't you dare drive him away. A week ago, he went to see his father and found the man on the floor of his trailer, unconscious and dehydrated. He might have died."

Her mother's revelations were almost too much for Ciana to process. "How . . . how is his daddy now?"

"He's in a county care home in Murfreesboro. He's a sick, crippled fifty-six-year-old man with no one to care for him except Jon. I am not firing that young man just because you're back and don't like him working here. He can stay as long as he wants if it takes every last penny we have."

Alice Faye rose from the bed. In the open doorway, she squared her chin and leveled blazing eyes at her daughter. "And one more quick item. Although it may have escaped your attention, for the first time in many years, I am sober. This has not been easy. I struggle every day, but I am determined not to fail. I have an AA meeting tonight, same as last night, and I'm not missing it."

The next morning, Ciana left the safety of her bedroom and the old house when she heard Jon come into the kitchen for breakfast. She hadn't slept much. Her mother's admission to being an alcoholic had rattled her. She thought of all the years Alice Faye had drifted in a gin haze, all the years Ciana had been ashamed of her mother when her friends visited. Only Arie and Eden had understood Ciana's protective shell, and that was because Arie had a sensitive soul and Eden also had a dysfunctional mother. Olivia had berated her daughter or ignored her. Ciana had clung to her grandmother, the woman she loved and trusted most in the world. She should be happy for Alice Faye, Ciana told herself. But she felt stonewalled. What to do with this new mother who had emerged from nowhere, issuing edicts and demanding changes to both their lives? The woman who wanted to keep Jon on staff? The woman who wanted to sell Bellmeade and abandon their ancestral past?

# 37

"I want you to be my maid of honor." Abbie beamed Arie a sunny smile as she made her statement.

The three of them were having lunch at the family dining table. Eric had brought in Chinese food and Arie was making an effort to eat it, but nausea was making it difficult. "That's very nice of you to offer," Arie said. Spring seemed far away, further than she wanted to think about at the moment. "I'm sure you have a best friend who deserves such an honor."

"Oh, I have a slew of friends for bridesmaids, but you're the person I want to be my special maid of honor."

"Abbie, honestly—"

"Come on, Sis. We both want you."

Arie jabbed something brown on her plate with a chopstick, taking her time, attempting to think of a way to decline politely. She didn't want to hurt their feelings, but shuffling up to the front of a church maybe looking like death warmed over was more than she wanted to think about, even for Eric and Abbie. How was she to know what kind of shape she'd be in come March? "Look, by March—"

"March!" Abbie cried. "We've moved the wedding to New Year's Eve."

Arie blinked. "When did you do that?"

Abbie shrugged. "While you were gone." She and Eric squeezed hands. "We didn't want to wait until March."

Arie glanced between Eric and Abbie. "It's almost Christmas. What about invitations? Your dress? Your caterer, florist, your venue?"

"Now, don't get all wadded up," Eric said. "We've taken care of everything. Reserved a nice church in Nashville with a big old basement for the reception. Got a hotel to give us good rates where people can stay the night after the reception." He grinned at Abbie. "Course, we'll be on our way to New Orleans for a real nice honeymoon."

Abbie flashed him a flirty look, then turned back to persuading Arie. "My aunt Kay is doing the flowers; your aunt Ruth is handling the food. We have a band, a huge cake, and champagne at midnight. Oh, and the bridesmaids already have their dresses. I want you to be my maid of honor. You can't say no." Big tears filled Abbie's eyes.

"Oh, man," Eric said. "Don't let her start the waterworks, Sis. You'll drown."

Arie sighed. "I don't have a dress. Mine won't match the others. Unless you ordered mine in advance too," she added pointedly.

Abbie wiped her eyes on napkin. "Every dress is different in the wedding party. I mean, who wants to get stuck with an ole dress bought for one wedding? All I've asked is that dresses be knee length and midnight blue. Same goes for yours. We'll go shopping for it."

Arie's chemo protocol would be over at the end of the week. She would be out of treatment for the holidays, then begin again after the first of the year. The monthlong hiatus offered her the best chance of feeling good physically during the upcoming holidays. Abbie and Eric knew this and she realized they'd quietly changed their wedding plans for her sake. They were so clever, so transparent.

Eric turned from his fiancée to Arie. "See? Logic. Can't fight it. Go with the flow."

Arie was deeply moved, and for all Abbie's soft Southern charm, the girl had a will of steel. "Guess I can't say no, then. I will take on the mantle of maid of honor." She raised her right hand in a pledge.

Abbie's smile lit up her pretty face. "Now, that wasn't so hard, was it?" She picked up one of the food cartons, held it out. "Kung pao chicken, anyone?"

"What are you going to do now that you're back?" Gwen stood in the doorway of Eden's room, asking a question Eden couldn't answer completely.

"In the short term, work. I need money. My old boss at the boutique hired me for the holidays." Eden was finally sorting through the things she'd brought back from Italy. The things she'd set aside for the walkabout would get jettisoned. She could hardly stand to look at the bag she'd packed for the trip; it made her sad.

"And in the long term?"

"Don't know yet. What about you?"

"Piggly Wiggly, for now."

But Eden could tell her mother was restless. The signs were there that she wasn't fully engaged with day-to-day life, that she was becoming an onlooker rather than a participant, classic signs that her bipolar condition was taking center stage. Eden recognized the signs more easily now that she was older and more attuned to Gwen's moods.

"Isn't Arie getting married?" Gwen jumped to a totally unrelated topic from the current stream of conversation.

*Another sign*. "Not Arie, Mom. Her brother Eric is marrying Abbie on New Year's Eve." Her mother's confusion pained Eden. Just a week before, Gwen had been "normal," talkative and in control, but a few days off her meds was all it took. Eden had hoped she'd have made it through Christmas. "Ciana's invited us for Christmas dinner," Eden said, changing the subject. "She wants you to join us."

Gwen's eyes took on that deer-in-the-headlights look she got when she felt cornered. "I . . . I don't know."

Eden sighed. Happily-ever-after was not going to happen between her and her mother. She expected Gwen to bolt from the room, but instead she stood staring. "You need anything?"

"I'm trying to remember something I meant to tell you."

Eden continued to unpack.

Suddenly, Gwen snapped her fingers. "I know! I'm selling the house. Right after the first of the year, the real estate lady is putting up a sign in our front yard. I think it's a good time to sell since the place is all fixed up. Don't you?"

Eden spun to stare at Gwen. "What? You're selling out? But . . . but where will we live?"

"I'm moving to Tampa. My friends are there. You should come with me. It's always warm in Tampa. You'll like it."

Eden stood speechless, feeling as if the ground had shifted under her. "You should have told me sooner," she managed to say.

"I'm telling you now." Gwen's guileless, childlike demeanor was infuriating but without malice. Eden didn't know how to respond. She was losing her mother once more, watching her slip away in mind and, soon, in body too. And she was losing her home, the house she'd always lived in, and the only home she'd ever known.

In spite of the cold, Arie's palms were sweaty. She stood in front of Ciana's barn, her heart thumping in anticipation of seeing Jon. With Ciana's truck gone, Arie knew they'd be alone for a bit. Her time with him in Italy seemed like a dream, a fabrication her mind had knit together from desire and longing. Still, she held tightly to the images and the feelings. Both were hers alone.

She had taken time and patience with her appearance using the tricks of makeup and clothing she'd learned over the years to maximize her best features and minimize the effects of chemo treatments. She wiped her palms on her jeans, screwed up her courage, and went into the barn.

Jon emerged from behind a stack of bundled straw, a rake in his hands. "Arie! How are you?"

He offered the heart-grabbing smile that always melted her. "I'm doing better. Thought I'd visit Caramel while I'm waiting on Ciana." *And see you,* she added silently.

"Third stall." Jon walked with her to the open half-door. The horse hung her head over and eyed Arie but turned her attention to Jon.

Disappointed, Arie said, "I don't think she remembers me." All the hard work she'd done with the horse over the summer seemed to have been for nothing.

"She'll come around once you start to feed and ride her."

"Maybe later." Arie wasn't sure when she'd be strong enough. She reached to scratch Caramel's forehead, but the horse laid her ears back and moved toward the rear of the stall.

Jon issued a sharp command, and the horse came forward and allowed Arie to rub the soft muzzle. "She always liked you better than me," Arie said with a sigh. "Thanks for taking care of her."

Jon laid his hand across Arie's hand now resting on Caramel's head, stroking the forelock. "She's just been around me more."

"I think she's just a one-person horse. Like Bonanza was." Arie's gaze drifted up to Jon's. She saw kindness there, little else. "Will you come to Eric's wedding with me on New Year's Eve?" she asked softly. "I'm a hostage to their wedding party. And I'm honored," she added quickly. "I don't want to go alone, so I . . . I was just hoping you'd come with me."

Jon looked taken aback. "I'm not much of a black-tie kind of guy."

"Neither are Eric and his friends. A lot of the guests will wear jeans and sports coats to the ceremony, and the groomsmen will be in jeans just as soon as the formal pictures are over." She wasn't sure she could deal with Jon's rejection, not at this juncture of her downhill life. "I'd really appreciate it. And I promise not to ask you for any more favors. Ever."

His expression softened.

Just then, the barn door opened and Ciana came in, followed by a gust of wind. Her gaze bounced between Jon and Arie. She settled on Arie and broadcast a bright smile. "Hey! You wait long?"

Nervously, Arie backed away from the horse and Jon. It had taken time to get back in Ciana's good graces in Italy after

Jon left, and Arie didn't want to go through any awkwardness again. "Not long."

"I buzzed to the store, grabbed up chocolate and chips and popcorn. And a movie too." Ciana never even glanced at Jon.

"Which one?"

"*Gone with the Wind*, of course. Is there any better Southern chick flick on the planet?"

Arie laughed, although she was baffled as to why Ciana hadn't so much as acknowledged Jon, who was standing patiently to the side of the stall. "Is Eden coming?"

"On her way. So how does Caramel look to you? Has our hired help kept her up to your liking?" Ciana recognized Jon's presence but not in a nice way. Arie hoped there wasn't trouble between them.

"Jon's done a wonderful job. I may never regain her affection, though," Arie said, baffled by Ciana's rudeness. *Hired help. Get real!*

"He's a wonder, all right," Ciana said coolly.

Jon stood steely and wordless.

"I've asked him to go with me to Eric's wedding."

Ciana flashed Jon an unreadable look. "You should go with Arie."

"I am," Jon said.

His sudden acceptance caught Arie off guard. Minutes before, she'd doubted he would have come. "Well, okay, then. Details to come."

He nodded and began to retreat, but Ciana said, "Oh, and I have our Christmas tree in the back of my pickup. Bring it into the house and set it up in the front parlor and my friends and I will decorate it later tonight."

"Yes, ma'am," Jon said with a tip of his head.

Arie was shocked and puzzled by Ciana's tone and

demeanor. Once outside, Arie took Ciana's elbow as cold wind whipped fine pellets of stinging snow into their faces. "What was *that* all about? Did Jon do something to make you mad?"

"What?" Ciana asked innocently, hustling them into the house and out of the cold before answering. "I need the tree brought in."

"You were *rude* to him."

"Sorry," she said, sounding only slightly remorseful while she brushed snow off herself. "My bad."

"What's going on between you two?"

Ciana shrugged. "He's taken over my life. My jobs."

"And he's done them better?"

"Not better," Ciana groused. "Neater. Maybe."

Arie shook her head, not wanting to let it go. This wasn't the Ciana she'd grown up with. "How can you possibly be jealous of somebody working hard to make your life easier? I don't get it."

Ciana sighed. "Neither do I." She headed toward the kitchen.

Arie padded after her. "And aren't you violating one of those Beauchamp rules Olivia was always telling you?"

"Probably."

"Well, please stop it. I want us to all have a good time together at the wedding."

"We will."

"That didn't sound convincing." Arie pushed Ciana playfully. "Don't be so bossy."

"As you wish." Ciana curtsied. "Let's start the hot chocolate so it'll be ready when Eden gets here," she said, shivering. "Weather's a far cry from Italy, isn't it?"

"A far cry," Arie echoed. A *world of happiness away*.

# 38

"Ciana, put on your coat and let's go. I don't want to keep Mr. Hastings waiting." Alice Faye stood in the doorway of Ciana's room already bundled up for the drive into town.

Ciana looked up from the book she was reading. "I already told you, I don't want to meet with Mr. Hastings."

"Stop that. This meeting's been set up since before Christmas. Gerald will be leaving tomorrow for Chicago, and I promised him the two of us would meet with him today."

Ciana arched an eyebrow. "Gerald, is it? How nice that the two of you are on a first-name basis."

Alice Faye smoldered. "I've seen the plans and drawings many times. Now it's time for you to see them."

"I don't care about the plans. I'm not selling Bellmeade."

Her mother marched to Ciana's closet and whipped a red coat off a hanger. She tossed it to Ciana. "Put it on."

Ciana exploded. "Stop treating me like a five-year-old child!"

"Well, stop acting like one. Get your coat on and come out to the car. I'll be warming the engine. And put on some lipstick. Hurry. Alice Faye turned and Ciana listened to the clicking retreat of her boots until the door slammed.

Ciana fumed, but she picked up her coat. She had liked her mother better when she was drinking, when she had been compliant and more easily ignored. This sober version was bossy, busy, and intrusive. And although she'd pulled off a delicious and festive Christmas dinner, Ciana had been in a funk. Eden and Gwen had come to dine with them, and so had Essie and Bill Pickins. Gwen had been distracted, staring out windows and only speaking if spoken to. Ciana had seen the strain on Eden's face. She and Ciana both knew Gwen was spiraling downward into depression. Ciana felt sorry for Eden, but there was nothing she could do.

Jon Mercer had been invited to the feast, but thankfully he'd gone to Arie's house and the "feeding of the five thousand," as Arie referred to her family's Christmas dinner. Ciana's case of the blues hung around, and now, three days before the wedding, making a visit to Gerald Hastings to hear about his plans to gut Bellmeade farmland and build a housing project was doing nothing to improve her mood.

Alice Faye parked the car in front of an old Victorian house that had been turned into office suites. A sign out front on the brown winter grass read HASTINGS HAND DEVELOPING, CHICAGO.

Inside, the house was divided into individual offices, all belonging to Hastings. Alice Faye announced herself and Ciana to the receptionist. Moments later, a casually dressed man stepped from an office, offering a smile and a handshake. "Alice Faye." He turned to Ciana. "And you must be the daughter."

"Ciana," she said, with less than a smile for him.

Hastings was middle-aged, of medium height, trim and fit, with a thick head of salt-and-pepper hair and trendy rimless eyeglasses. "Good to meet you. Your mother said you were amazing, but I think she might have underplayed it."

Ciana fought against rolling her eyes at his obvious attempt to flatter. "Mothers can be zealous."

"How was your trip to Italy? Astounding place, huh?"

"Astounding," Ciana confirmed, wishing she were anywhere else.

"Can I get the two of you something? Sodas, coffee, some hot apple cider?"

Ciana wanted nothing from this man.

"All right," Hastings said, "let me cut to the chase and show you what my firm has in mind for your property." He walked them across the hall and into a large room that held a massive table where a three-dimensional model had been constructed. "This is Bellmeade Estates, a rolling, rambling suburb of luxury homes, some set on acre lots, others on higher-density lots. Over here"—he pointed to a cluster of houses—"are garden homes, single level, for retirees and people who want to downsize. We'll have bike trails, walking trails, riding trails, a stable, pastureland, and a golf course. This place will be built as green as possible, with two acres set aside for community farming. There's nothing else like it in the country today."

Ciana didn't find that comforting. She looked over the model and grudgingly admitted that the project was impressive. She thought of the dollhouse her father had made for her when she'd been five. Larger than the table model in front of her, it was built to scale and completely detailed. Once her father and grandfather had died in the plane crash, she hadn't been able to look at it, so Olivia had put it up in the attic for safekeeping.

"Model building is a hobby of mine," Hastings said proudly.

"It's nice," Ciana said. She could admire the work if she separated it emotionally from its purpose.

"Of course, we'll be doing a lot of excavating at first. We'll lay in underground utilities, sewers, streets, streetlights, so it'll take a while before we actually start homes. We'll build it in phases. On this table"—he walked Ciana and Alice Faye across the room—"are the plans for phase one: Bellmeade Acres." He flipped pages of giant architectural drawings of an overall view, then to views of model houses. "The homes will have every amenity of modern life, but as you can see, the facades will look Victorian. Sort of a return to yesteryear with the future in mind. In homage to your beautiful home."

So the man had actually come to their house. It rubbed Ciana the wrong way that her mother had ever invited him.

"Impressive," Alice Faye said. "Don't you think so, Ciana?"

"Why our farmland?" Ciana asked, irritated by her mother's obvious prodding.

"Not just your land. We'll also be buying out a few of the smaller farms that adjoin your property. And these parcels were selected because you're all closest to the interstate. I have to go before a few committees to get permission for a new off-ramp, but once we clear that hurdle, we can break ground on Bellmeade Estates."

Ciana knew the farms he spoke of. The owners were elderly and had no heirs either able or willing to take on the hard life of farming. "Have the others agreed to sell?"

"Several have." He smiled, as if to put her at ease.

"Mr. Hastings, perhaps you know that I don't want to sell Bellmeade."

"Yes, your mother's told me. I'm hoping to change your

mind. Bellmeade Estates is not some haphazard, poorly imagined place. It's designed to attract high-income people from the Nashville area—government officials, entertainers, educators, doctors, lawyers—as well as retirees and young professionals with families."

"It was designed to be farmland by my ancestors. Good farmland, surrounded by other good farmland, some of the best in the state."

"And we want to keep that tradition. That's why we're setting aside community garden acreage."

Ciana wanted to bolt out of the office. It must have shown on her face, because her mother interceded by saying, "Gerald, today is only Ciana's first time seeing your vision. I don't think it's necessary to pin down an answer right now. Do you?"

Hastings's expression, bordering on irritation with Ciana's balkiness, relaxed. "Certainly not. Perhaps when I return in January, we can meet again over lunch and discuss your misgivings at length." He reached into a nearby desk and fished out a folder, which he extended to Alice Faye. "In the meantime, look over this information. If this is going to happen, I'll need some positive feedback by early spring.

"Miss Beauchamp," he said as Ciana started toward the door, "I'm offering a great deal of money to you and your mother. You'll walk away millionaires. The project is immensely expensive, but it will open up this entire end of the county to growth and business, move this area out of an agrarian past and into a progressive future. Open your mind to the possibilities."

She left without another word.

In the car driving home, Alice Faye said, "Stop sulking. Talk to me."

"I'm not sulking. The project is impressive."

"I'm glad you see it as such." Alice Faye sounded surprised. "Tell me what you're thinking."

"I'm thinking I'm not ready to sell our land."

"You're going to college next month. I can't run the place alone. Let me rephrase: I don't want to run the place."

Ciana's college fund from Olivia was almost gone, spent in Italy. The villa's owner had returned the final month's rent once he heard how Arie had become ill. Thankfully, Enzo's two hirelings had returned the house to pristine condition after the girls had scrambled to leave. The refund plus what was still in the bank might pay for a year at Vandy, and only if she commuted. The schedule would be grueling and leave her little time for resurrecting the farm.

Her mother sighed. "It will take both of us to agree to the sale."

"It's not what Olivia wanted. She worked hard to keep the land producing."

"She's dead, Ciana. We're in charge now."

The words sounded cold and final. And they stung. "I . . . I need to think."

"Well, think about the money and being able to do anything you want for the rest of your life."

"How do I look?" Arie sat in the bridal prep staging room of the old church with Eden fussing over her hair.

"Beautiful," Ciana said.

"Stop wiggling," Eden said through a mouthful of hairpins. She reached for the can of hair spray in Ciana's hand and squirted a slipping curl into place.

Around them, girls giggled and talked, all of them Abbie's friends and a few of Arie and Eric's cousins. Abbie was in a separate room being photographed.

"You two look gorgeous," Arie grumbled. "I'm so skinny, my chest looks concave."

"No way," Ciana said, although it was a halfhearted denial. Arie's lovely dark blue velvet dress was long sleeved and covered her thin shoulders, but the front of the dress hung loosely.

"I told you to buy a padded bra," Eden mumbled.

"Padded with basketballs wouldn't help," Arie wailed. "The two of you look like models."

Eden wore a short black dress with sequins and Ciana had chosen a dress the color of champagne. "We're just bystanders," Ciana said. "Abbie is the main attraction, so that's who everyone will be watching."

"Wish I were sitting with you all," Arie said, looking scared and pale.

"You have a date," Eden reminded her. "We're manless."

"A date I asked. Jon's only here because I dragged him."

Ciana shook her head. "All the men are here because their wives or girlfriends dragged them."

"And because of the free food," Eden inserted.

The door from the next room opened and Abbie glided in, her mother quickly following and poufing the gown's train. The bride was a vision in white lace. All the girls clapped when they saw her.

"There," Eden said, putting a final misting of spray on Arie's hair.

Arie coughed, fanned away the excess spray in the air, and walked over to Abbie. "Eric's so lucky to be marrying you."

Abbie leaned forward and gave Arie air kisses on both

cheeks. "He told me I reminded him of you and your great personality. That's why he dated me in the first place. I'm so glad you're going to be my sister-in-law."

The wedding planner stepped inside. "Ready, ladies? The groomsmen are all lined up."

The bridesmaids flurried together in clouds of perfume and nervous twitters, lining up like birds on a wire. Ciana and Eden slipped out the door, down the hall, and into a pew of the candlelit church.

The sanctuary reminded Ciana of the many elaborate churches Arie had dragged them through in Italy. Abundant white garlands of fragrant flowers embraced the altar. Music played softly. From her place in the back, she saw Jon's head and shoulders in the second row on the groom's side of the church. He was there for Arie. She closed her eyes. Arie needed him. He would take care of her and make her happy once she was well.

The organist turned up the volume and struck the beginning chords of the wedding march. Everyone seated in the pews stood. The bridesmaids filed down the aisle, each with a young man at her side. Arie came, her smile trembling, but at the front, she turned, stared straight at Jon, and reinforced her smile with the sight of him. Finally Abbie entered on her father's arm. Ciana forced back tears for the beauty of the moment and for the loss of the man who could not be hers.

# 39

The party had been in full swing for three hours in the church's reception hall as the clock inched ever closer to midnight. Abbie had put on cowboy boots and, holding up the hem of her bridal gown, danced with Eric to every tune the band played. Eden was tucked somewhere out in the dancing melee, while at their table, Ciana took a breather from the crowded dance floor. Arie sat alone at the wedding party table in self-imposed isolation, watching, wishing she had the energy to join the dancers. Jon had asked, but she'd refused.

As the crowd dispersed and the band started a slow tune, Jon walked Eden to her chair, where she flopped and pushed her hair off her forehead. "I'm pooped!"

Jon held out his hand to Ciana. "Dance with me."

"I . . . I'm resting."

Eden rattled Ciana's chair, almost dumping her onto the floor. "*Dance* with the man."

Eden ignored the murderous look Ciana gave her.

On the dance floor, Jon pulled Ciana close, causing the old

familiar uptick in her heartbeat. She refused to move her feet. "You know how to dance with me, Ciana."

She did. "That's all in the past," she insisted.

His expression turned pensive. "What's wrong between us? For a while there, at least we were friends. Now you snap at me every time I come near."

Over time, her anger had morphed into confusion. Having him around her often made her heart ache. She couldn't afford to care about him. "There's Arie."

"I haven't forgotten about her, but do you need her permission to dance with me? To be kind to me?"

Of course, he had a valid point. She'd treated him horribly ever since the return from Italy. At first her anger protected her, but lately she hadn't liked herself very much for being hateful to him. Her chin trembled, and slowly she fell into step within his embrace. Why was life so complicated? "You're right, and I'm sorry. I'll start minding my manners," she said with genuine contriteness.

"Truce?" he asked, peering at her with a dip of his head and a tentative smile.

She wanted his friendship if she couldn't have anything else. "Truce," she whispered. "Now, don't make me cry. My mascara will run."

"You're pretty no matter what," he said.

"And you're delusional," she said, a catch in her voice.

He stopped swaying to the music and held her eyes with his. Time stopped, cradling the two of them as voices in the room began a ten-second countdown to the new year. Jon raised her chin with his forefinger and brushed his lips across hers. "Happy New Year, boss lady."

He stepped away and the world once again began to move. He walked Ciana to her table, where glasses of champagne waited. She watched him return to the bridal table and to Arie's side. A new year, a new beginning. The band played "Auld Lang Syne."

After the toasts and cheers, hugs and kisses, Ciana took Eden's elbow. "Let's split."

"First, look what I captured." Eden brandished an unopened bottle of bubbly.

"How—"

Eden wagged her hand at a young waiter standing in a corner and smiled flirtatiously. "Raoul. Cute, isn't he?"

"What did you promise him? Because I want out of here. Our hotel room is calling me."

"Don't panic. They're promises I won't keep." Eden blew kisses toward the eager-looking Raoul.

"You are so wicked," Ciana said with a shake of her head.

"Ain't I, though." She grabbed her coat from the back of the chair. "I want to go to our room too. I want to talk to you."

"About?"

"The future."

Eden and Ciana snuggled in chairs outside on the balcony of their Nashville hotel room, bundled in flannel pj's, thick socks, and blankets, with an open champagne bottle on the floor between them. They watched the night sky still erupting from time to time with fireworks. "That was a pretty one," Eden noted as golden sparkles shimmered above.

They watched a few minutes longer for the next explosion, until Ciana asked, "What do you want to talk about?"

"Whoa. We can't discuss the future until we celebrate the old year—the good, the bad, and the ugly."

"You first."

Eden said, "The good—we graduated." She took a sip from the bottle and passed it to Ciana.

"Seems like a million years ago, though . . . The bad—Olivia died."

"Take two sips," Eden said. "One for her memory. One just because we can."

Another burst of fireworks popped into a mushroom of red, blue, and gold rain. Ciana oohed in the dark.

Eden said, "And the ugly."

In unison, both girls raised their fists and shouted, "Tony!"

"The good," Ciana said, after sipping from the bottle and passing it to Eden. "Arie's remission."

"And the ugly—her relapse." Eden passed the bottle back, adding, "The very good—going to Italy."

"True," Ciana sighed. Her head was spinning from the champagne, and she was glad she only had to stumble inside and fall into bed. "The art was pretty. Arie was right about that."

"Enzo was pretty too," Eden said, realizing she had no feeling in her lower lip. "Question. Do you wish you'd have gone with him to Portofino? I mean, if Arie hadn't gotten sick?"

"Sometimes." Ciana brooded. "He was gorgeous. And he did promise me a real good time."

Eden giggled. "I'll bet. I saw him on one of the celebrity TV channels. He was rolling out of a limo with some starlet, or maybe it was a countess, hanging on to him."

Ciana shook her head. The patio whirled. "Men are fickle. Imagine choosing some glamorous starlet over a farm girl like me. I'm crushed." She raised the bottle. "A toast to Enzo, both good and bad."

Eden took the bottle, turned it up, but only one lone

drop trickled out. She set it on the cement floor and glanced around. "Where's Raoul when I need him?"

The question sent both her and Ciana off into gales of laughter. "I know a really good thing that happened to all of us last year," Eden said when she regained her composure. "All of us, Arie, you, and me, we fell in love."

Ciana hugged her blanket tightly. "Not me."

"Liar, liar, pants on fire."

Ciana made a face. "Well, this is a new year and I'm going to fall *out* of love. Mind over matter." She conjured up Jon's green eyes, the brush of his lips across her skin. She shivered, but not from the cold.

"And since you bring up the new year and the future, my mom announced that she's selling our house and moving to Tampa."

"What?" Ciana's chair clunked onto the cement. "What about you? Are you going with her?"

"Fat chance."

Ciana shook her finger at Eden. "Good! You can come live with me. Our old house has tons of space. In fact, I insist that you move in with me and my now-sober mother." She hiccupped. "Seriously."

"That's a nice offer, but I have another plan."

"Like what?"

"I want to go back to Europe. I want to find Garret."

Ciana saw Eden's determined expression. "*Can* you find him?"

"No luck so far. I tried reaching him through that travel magazine he was working for, but it's defunct." She snapped her fingers. "Just like that. After the expansion talk, it folded. I've emailed the company, but everything bounces back. I've done a Web search on his name. He's not listed on any social website. His byline comes up and I can read his articles, but the man himself has vanished." She slumped. "I don't even know if he wants to see me again. All I want is a chance to explain what happened and why I didn't meet up with him."

"And until you find him?"

"Work. Save money. Keep looking. And if I do locate him, ask if he still wants me to come on his walkabout. If he does, I'll spend every dime I have getting to wherever he is."

Ciana gently touched Eden's shoulder. "Same offer. If your house sells and your mother moves, you have a home with me until you have enough money to go meet him."

Under her breath, Eden grumbled, "If I'm not too old to travel by then. And if he wants me."

"He'll want you," Ciana said. "Arie and I both agree that the guy was head over heels for you. The crazy Aussie."

A nostalgic half smile shadowed Eden's mouth. "He's crazy, all right. And maybe I am too. But I hope you're both right. I hope he misses me as much as I miss him."

# 40

Ciana lay on the ground under her truck, banging on the universal joint with a wrench and cussing. She'd pulled the pickup into the barn in order to stay warm while she worked, or tried to work. She was out of her element and she knew it. Nothing she'd downloaded from the Web was helping her deal with the truck's leaking problem.

She felt a boot kick her foot. "That you swearing like a sailor, Miz Beauchamp?"

She scooted out from beneath the truck and glared at Jon. He sat on a bale of straw carving a small piece of wood with a pocketknife. "I didn't know you whittled," she said.

"I'm no artist, but I like doing it," he said. Ever since the wedding, tensions had lessened between them. A good thing. They could talk now, banter, joke, and occasionally tease each other. She'd even taken up eating breakfast with Jon and her mother.

He slid off the bale, tucked the knife into his jeans pocket and the lump of wood into his shirt pocket, and pulled her to her feet. "I think you'd better call in backup."

"You?" she asked hopefully.

He threw up his hands. "I work with four-legged creatures, never anything with four wheels."

"You have a truck." She motioned with the heavy wrench. "How do you keep it running?"

"I hire a mechanic."

She growled at him. "Big help you are."

"I can help you tow it into town."

"Not today," she grumbled. "I'm supposed to go to MTSU and see the registrar about late registration. I went online, but all the classes I need or want are full. Thought I'd plead my case in person. Mom's got the Lincoln, or I'd borrow it."

Jon picked straw out of her hair. "I can take you, if you don't mind stopping off at the county home so I can visit my dad."

She was curious about his dad, had wondered what sort of man had fathered Jon. "Seems like a fair trade. Let me clean up a bit."

---

Jon first drove to the campus. "Thought you were going to Vandy."

She was surprised he remembered. "MTSU is closer. I can live at home and drive to the campus with Arie. Thought it would be more fun than both of us going our separate ways." Ciana didn't mention she couldn't afford Vandy anymore.

In Murfreesboro, on the MTSU campus, every parking lot was filled to capacity. "Do you think all these cars have come to see the registrar?"

"Beats me. But it looks like we have to park out here and

either hike in or take one of those buses." He pointed at a bus just leaving one of the parking lots.

Ciana groaned and hung her head. "I'm so screwed."

Jon looked amused. "What do you want to do?"

She nibbled pensively on her lower lip. "I want to take you up on your offer to tow my truck to Ted's Auto Shop tomorrow. After he fixes it, I'll drive out here and camp. No need for you to waste your day. Let's go see your dad."

The facility where Wade Mercer was housed was a far cry from the beautifully maintained Evergreen, where Olivia had lived for three years. This place looked every bit the institutional building it was, with narrow halls, small windows that admitted little light, and paint so faded that the walls seemed colorless. Ciana wrinkled her nose over smells of stale food and people needing showers.

"I don't like him being here either." Jon was apologetic. "It's where he has to be right now. I'll take him back to Texas eventually. Unfortunately someone has to die before he can be moved up on the waiting list back home." Jon signed in at a reception desk, told Ciana, "You can wait here. I won't stay long."

"No . . . if it's okay, I'll tag along."

He hesitated. "Fair warning—my dad's raw around the edges. Just blurts out anything he wants to say. And he's got a lot of damage on his left side from the stroke. His face isn't pretty."

"I get it. My grandmother wasn't in good shape either toward the end." She followed Jon down a narrow hall, dodging wheelchairs and food carts.

Jon entered a room with two beds divided by a limp curtain. One bed was empty, and in the other a man lay watching an old TV hanging on the wall. "Hey, Dad," Jon said.

Wade Mercer turned toward the voice. "Look who's come

to call." His body was twisted on one side, his mouth quirked in a permanent scowl. "You brought a pretty filly with you." The eye on his stroke side stared fixedly.

"Hello," Ciana said, smiling, ignoring the physical wreckage.

"She's a looker, son." Wade's unblinking gaze pored over Ciana's body. "Got a real nice build on her."

Ciana flushed. Jon barked, "Be nice, old man!"

Wade said something else, but between his thick Texan accent and the stroke, Ciana couldn't understand his garbled speech.

She squared her shoulders and held out her hand. "I'm Ciana Beauchamp. Glad to meet you."

Wade's expression hardened. "The hell you say. You a *Beauchamp*?" He made her name sound like a swearword.

Stung by his reception, she stepped away. "Um, yes, I'm a Beauchamp."

"I see it now . . . yeah . . . I see it clear," Wade muttered.

"That's enough, Dad," Jon growled.

"No mistakin' them devil eyes."

"What the hell's gotten into you?" Jon demanded.

"Boy, I'm tellin' you a truth for your own sake. Ain't nothin' good ever come out of a Beauchamp."

"I . . . I don't—" Ciana said, shocked by his words.

Jon took Ciana's elbow. "Let's get out of here." He hustled her out of the room, but Wade's raised voice chased them down the hall.

"You stay away from them Beauchamp women, son!" he yelled. "Stay far, far away. Ain't *nothin'* good in a Beauchamp woman."

In the truck, before he could start the engine, Ciana said, "Wait. Please. Calm down."

Jon was shaking and furious, but he didn't turn the key. "I'm real sorry about that. I told you he was crazy."

Still reeling, Ciana said, "I swear I never saw him before today. Can't imagine why my name caused him to freak out."

Jon struck the steering wheel hard with the palm of his hand. "I don't know either. I grew up in Texas with Mom's people, who helped raise me while she held down two jobs. The Farleys are a whole better class of folks than my granddaddy and Wade."

Ciana heard the affection in his voice for his mother and her kin. Ciana's short history with Jon stretched back only to the previous summer, so she really didn't know much about him. "How did he treat you when you were growing up?"

Jon shrugged. "He was a hard man and I was hardheaded. But Mom says he was raised by a hard man. My granddaddy died when I was about four, so I barely remember him."

"Maybe it's something to do with the stroke. Or his medications. Olivia could get real turned around sometimes and say things that made no sense."

"No need to make excuses for him. It's not the stroke. It's him. He's just mean as a junkyard dog."

"Nice of you to take care of him."

Jon shrugged. "My duty. Mom divorced him, but he'll always be my father."

Jon started the engine and backed the truck out of its parking space. "All I know is that I've got to figure out what to do with him if I'm ever going home to Texas."

Reality hit Ciana. His presence had become such a fixture in her daily life that she'd begun to think of always having him around. Not true. He would disappear from her life the minute he could. What did that say about Jon and Arie's future? "Let's go home. I need a long horseback ride."

"Wish I could join you."

She almost asked him to but realized she needed to step back and keep him at arm's length for many reasons. Beauchamp rule number something-or-other: Never get so close to someone that you can't afford to let them go.

Arie saw the truth on Dr. Austin's face the moment he walked into the room. Her heart seized, but her voice held steady when she spoke. "So much for your poker face."

Austin's eyes narrowed even as he attempted a smile. "That's why I don't play poker. Anyone can tell the cards I hold by my expression."

"And you're out of aces," she said quietly. "Or rather, I'm out of aces."

He shuffled through sheets of paper, her lab work she guessed. "I have no good news," he confessed.

The words she'd always feared and dreaded. Before, when a treatment failure came, Austin had given pep talks, laid out new ideas, new drug programs. Tears welled in her eyes. "I told myself I wouldn't cry," she said, wiping fiercely at the tears.

"Why not? I did."

"There's nothing else you can throw at it?"

"Over time we've tried everything medical science allowed. I thought we had it licked last spring. Really. The tumor had shrunk to nothing, the size of a grape seed. Then it multiplied, seed begetting seed. We can't stop the spread. It's in your bones now."

"*Ask not for whom the bell tolls,*" John Donne wrote. "*It tolls for thee.*" Arie knew she was dying.

They sat in silence for a while in the exam room. Arie sniffed, and Austin handed her tissues from a nearby box. "So what should I expect?" she asked.

"I can help you remain as pain-free as possible. I want to send hospice people to your home. You and your family will need their support. And it will allow you to remain at home until the end."

Having once signed a do-not-resuscitate order, she was grateful not to spend the end of her life hooked up to machines in the hospital. "Do I have a timetable?"

"Perhaps a couple of months."

"No need to start classes, I guess."

"Do whatever makes you happy."

"Well, what more can a girl ask?" She scooted off the table, glancing at her watch. "I have to run. Art classes down in Pedi."

"You could cancel. Go home, talk to your family."

That part was going to be harder than hearing the news herself. They would be devastated. "Mom and Dad are both working. Eric and Abbie are still on their honeymoon. The bad news can wait."

"Don't wait too long. The news will be around the hospital in no time despite patient confidentiality rules. You're a favorite with the staff, you know."

She reached for the door and suddenly turned and hugged Dr. Austin hard. "Thank you for being honest with me."

His face crumpled as she left the room.

# 41

Arie had asked Ciana and Eden to come to her house, and they were on their way. She knew the visit would be difficult. She knew they wouldn't like hearing what she was going to say. Still, she had to say it, hoped they'd understand, if not today, then eventually.

Outside the kitchen window, February rain sheeted down the glass, and the skies looked as dull as gunmetal. She disliked this shortest of months for its dreariness, loved the coming spring for its riot of color, knowing that this spring would certainly be her last. Arie pushed away from the kitchen counter, grumbling for allowing herself to fall into such a morose state of mind. She wanted to greet her friends with smiles, not tears.

She'd put on makeup, styled her hair, and dressed in ice pink, her favorite color. The sweater's high neck hid her jutting collarbones and frail arms. She needed the camouflage after the ongoing chemo treatments, which had been stopped. Through the rain-streaked window, she watched Ciana's old truck turn into the driveway, and Eden's small car arrived from the opposite direction. Arie took a few deep breaths, went to the front door, and opened it wide.

The girls rushed inside in a spray of rainwater, laughing, shaking umbrellas, and slipping off rain boots in the tiled foyer. "Nasty day," Ciana said.

"Glad you came in spite of the weather," Arie said.

"A little rain can't stop us from making a command appearance before the queen." Eden placed her forefinger beneath her chin and curtsied.

"You may kiss my ring," Arie said, holding out her hand.

"When pigs fly."

They laughed together and Arie hugged each one. Ciana felt Arie's thinness through the pink sweater.

"Living room fireplace is fired up and I've laid out coffee and homemade chocolate chip cookies on the coffee table." Arie turned toward the formal room her mother kept pristine and used "only for company."

The room was cozy, warm from the fire burning in the hearth, the scent of coffee and chocolate mingling with that of the crackling wood. Ciana and Eden sank into the thick cushions of the like-new sofa, and Arie took a comfy side chair pulled across from the sofa and coffee table. Eden picked up a cookie, bit into it. "Skipped lunch," she said. She still worked at the boutique, where she had been made the manager.

Ciana said nothing, but she felt the weight of the meeting on her heart. Something was up. Why else would Arie insist she and Eden come together in the middle of the day?

Arie leaned forward, her gaze tenderly lingering on their faces. "I have something to tell you both," she said. "Something you're not going to want to hear."

Ciana drove to a screeching halt in front of the barn, ripping up grass and throwing debris with the truck's tires. She leaped out and as the cold rain pelted her, she hurdled through the side door and slammed it shut. "Jon!" she yelled. "Jon, where are you?"

He was filing Caramel's hooves while the horse stood tied between two posts. Startled by Ciana's shout and sudden entry, the mustang tried to rear. "Whoa, whoa, girl!" Jon steadied the horse, calming her. Caramel settled, and Jon turned to Ciana. "What's going on?"

"You've got to stop her! You've got to make Arie go back into treatment."

He calmly moved away from the spooked horse and toward the stack of straw bales, where he tossed the file and smoothed antibacterial gel on his hands. "She told you."

Arie had confessed she'd told her parents, Eric, and Abbie, and asked that they not tell the rest of the relatives yet, but she hadn't mentioned that she'd told Jon. She drew up short. "When did she tell you?"

"When she dropped by to see her horse a few days ago."

Somehow the revelation offended Ciana. She and Eden should have been told before Jon! Yet she accepted the fact, turned it to suit her argument. "You can stop her. You can *make* her go back into treatment. She'll listen to you. She'll do it if you ask her." Ciana was shaking hard, her teeth chattering, in spite of the portable heaters blasting hot air through the barn.

Jon measured Ciana with somber eyes. "I can't, Ciana. The cancer's too far advanced. There are no more treatments. Her doctors can't turn her around. I'm sure she told you as much."

Of course that was what Arie had said. But white-hot anger swelled inside Ciana, blinding her, fracturing all logic.

She bolted across the barn and hurled herself at him, screaming, "I hate you, Jon Mercer! I hate you!"

Caramel whinnied, stretched the ropes tight, but Jon ignored the horse. Ciana slammed into Jon again, striking him with her fists. He took it for a few seconds before grabbing her wrists with both hands. "Knock it off!"

Ciana kicked at him, landing the toes of her boots against his shins, all the while yelling that she hated him.

In a swift move, he turned her and pulled her against his chest. She shouted, "Let me go!" He didn't. She shoved backward, throwing him off balance and they both went down to the floor. She tried to scramble away, but he caught her, pulled her again so that her back was pressed tightly against him. He put his back against the stack of straw bales, crossed her arms over her chest, and held them in an iron grip; then he wrapped his legs around hers, sprawled out from the fall. In seconds, she was completely immobilized.

Ciana screamed in frustration, bucked, tried to twist out of his body lock but couldn't. Behind her, Jon said, "Stop fighting me, Ciana. Stop it!"

She ignored him, but after minutes of fruitless struggling, she gave up. Breathing hard and crying, she demanded, "Let go of me."

"Not until you listen."

Her hair was pulled back on one side, exposing the side of her neck and ear. She felt his warm breath on her skin, heard his drawl soft and husky in her ear. "I'd give anything if I could stop what's happening to Arie. I can't change her mind, because she's out of options."

Ciana jerked, but his grip held. She didn't want to hear what he had to say.

"I can't change what's happening to her," he insisted. He

took a ragged breath and softly added, "No more than I can change what happened between us in Italy."

Ciana went still and became deathly quiet. His words had pierced her heart, and along with it came real-life images of him and Arie leaving the hotel suite together, of her own seemingly endless wait for Arie to return to the hotel, of crying until she thought she'd turn inside out, of Arie returning and telling her and Eden nothing at all. And she saw imagined images, too, of Jon and Arie entwined, of moonlight spilling across bedsheets and . . . and . . .

"The dumbest thing I ever did," Jon continued into her ear, "was to agree not to tell her about us. About you and me and what I felt for you. Not telling her was wrong, Ciana. It was wrong. And it wasn't fair to any of us."

Fresh tears ran down Ciana's cheeks, but they were no longer tears of fury. Her anger was gone. What remained was pain and the cold hard truth of his words. Her effort to protect Arie had wounded all of them. "Please let me go."

He released her slowly, ready to imprison her again if she bolted.

But the fight was gone out of her. Only bitter tears remained. She wiped her face on her shirttail, ripped from her jeans during the tussle. "You . . . hurt . . . me," she said hoarsely, each of them understanding she wasn't talking about the wrestling match and his bruising grip on her wrists.

"I know I did," he said with a hitch in his voice. "But what happened in Italy wasn't about you or me. It was about her. If you have to hate someone, go ahead and hate me. She did nothing wrong, because she never knew the truth."

Hadn't Eden told her as much that night in Italy? *"Jon wanted you and you gave him to Arie."*

"I let go of blaming her while we were still in Italy," Ciana managed in a thick whisper. "I could never hate her."

"That's good." He took her at her word. Ciana felt the roughness of his jaw on her cheek, then the tenderness of his mouth on her skin. "I loved you, Ciana. You were the one I wanted."

*Loved. Past tense. Once upon a time.* She slumped. His arms slid around her, but not in restraint. She didn't try to move away but leaned into his body. Caramel stared at Ciana and Jon, her ears pricked forward, her brown eyes calm. The space heaters hissed out warmth, and smells of leather, horseflesh, and fresh straw blended together. Outside the wind moaned, echoing the sadness in Ciana's soul. Arie was dying . . . dying, and there was nothing she could do about it. Nor had there ever been. She said, "I don't hate you, Jon."

"Good. Because I don't think I can take another beat-down from you. You hit hard. For a girl."

She managed a half smile and closed her eyes, and he held her for a long time, neither of them moving.

Eden crossed the kitchen, tossing her car keys and purse onto the new kitchen island. The clunking sound broke the quiet and made her feel even lonelier. Now that her mother had split, Eden found herself missing having another warm body in the empty house. Just then, the house phone rang. Eden started to ignore it but realized she'd like to hear the sound of another human voice. She answered, only to be asked, "Is Ms. Gwen McLauren there?"

"She's out, and I can't say when she'll return."

"Well, then, are you her daughter? She said I should ask for you if I couldn't reach her."

"Who's calling?"

The woman's bubbly voice said, "I'm Sharon Weber, an agent with Farm Care Realty. I have an offer on your house and need to set up an appointment to discuss it with you all."

Eden's chest tightened. What was she supposed to do?

"How about tomorrow at eleven?" the realtor pressed. "The offer has a deadline on it."

Eden agreed with the appointment time and hung up. She leaned against the counter, catching her breath and shaking her head. Why had Gwen cut out before the house sold? "Thanks a lot, Mom," she said aloud. "The perfect ending to a crappy day."

Today Eden had learned that her dear friend had no hope of recovery, her mother had left her no instructions about the house, and now she might soon be homeless. A triple play. A *trifecta* of rotten news. She wondered if it was even possible to reach her mother. Gwen rarely chose to answer her new cell phone. Eden left a message, but who knew if Gwen would respond, especially before the scheduled meeting?

Eden went up to Gwen's bedroom, still full of Gwen's stuff. Until now, she'd stayed out of the space. She looked again to where the missing blue duffel usually sat on the shelf. How was it possible to pack so few things in such a small piece of luggage?

Maybe she should call Ciana, take her up on her offer to move in with her. Maybe she should begin breaking down the house's contents before it sold. She was leaving the room, mentally listing her options, when she saw the large brown envelope on her mother's dresser. She grabbed it up, ripped it open, pulled out a sheaf of paperwork, and riffled through it. Several pages looked legal. A short stack paper-clipped together was headed DURABLE GENERAL POWER OF ATTORNEY.

Another short stack was labeled DURABLE POWER OF ATTORNEY FOR HEALTH CARE FOR GWENDOLYN MCLAUREN. Eden's hands shook, and her heart thumped hard.

She scattered the papers on the bed and saw a Post-it note in her mother's handwriting. It read:

> *Don't panic. I'm not dying. But I am handing over legal responsibility of my life to you, my daughter. I called Alice Faye Beauchamp and got the name of her attorney, a Mr. Boatwright (his card's enclosed). He's set up everything nice and legal, so if you have questions, call him.*
>
> *Mom*

Eden's knees felt rubbery. She eased onto the bed and skimmed the paperwork full of legalese. The paperwork did indeed put her in full control of everything—the house sale, bank accounts, tax matters. A thousand questions bombarded Eden, not ones for any lawyer, but ones for her mother. How could Gwen have done this without saying a word? She shook the larger envelope and another envelope fell out, this one smaller but also fairly thick. She tore it open and removed sheets of paper. Quickly she saw a letter in her mother's jagged handwriting. Eden's heart thumped like a drum. In all the years she could remember, Gwen had never written her a letter. Perhaps a note for school. Or words on special-occasion cards. Or scrawled mention of her whereabouts when she was on her meds. But never a letter.

Eden planted her back against the headboard. She turned on the bedside lamp with trembling fingers and began to read.

# 42

Eden drove to the complex where she had once lived with Tony, thinking she would check out whether they'd put anything into storage she might want. Not things of Tony's, but things she'd brought from home when he'd all but forced her to move in with him. Maybe she also wanted closure. She'd heard the word bandied about in these days of armchair psychoanalyzing, and wondered if she needed it to close this chapter of her life forever.

Merely driving through the gates had sent a shiver through her, but once there, she went into the office. A pretty brown-haired teenager jumped up from behind a desk. "Can I help you?" Her drawl was as thick as tomato paste.

Eden explained her reasons for coming and gave the building number and location of the penthouse.

The girl's eyes widened. "You're the one who lived with that drug lord? The guy who was shot to death in Memphis?"

Eden cringed. Was this how she'd be remembered in the town?

The teen didn't wait for an answer but just forged ahead. "After he was shot down, the cops looked for you. It was in the papers and on TV."

"I was out of the country at the time," Eden mumbled, wishing the girl would hush about her and Tony.

"You don't want to rent his penthouse again, do you?"

"I only want to know if some of my things might have been stored . . . afterward."

"You mean after he was killed?"

Eden thought the girl denser than a lamppost and with about as much tact. "I assume that's when his place might have been cleared out."

The girl's face reddened. "Oh yes, of course. Let me check my computer." She quickly sat down and tapped her keyboard. "Here it is," she said brightly. "His stuff's still in storage, but I think the property owners plan to sell it at auction come spring. To recover financial losses he left with them. You understand."

Eden's patience was wearing thin. "Some of the contents are mine and I want them back. My name was on the mailbox. I was a legal tenant."

The girl looked hesitant. "Well . . . I . . . I . . . Do you have proof?"

Pressing her advantage, Eden said, "You cannot sell my things without my permission!" Eden flashed her driver's license. "Is the unit locked?"

The gal leaped up. "Well, certainly!"

Eden held out her hand. "The key?"

The girl rummaged in an unlocked desk drawer and fished out an envelope marked master keys. "I have to take you," the cowed girl said.

They drove to the storage units in a golf cart, and the girl unlocked the door and handed Eden the key. "You can drop it in the outside box when you're finished."

Inside the unit, Eden sighed, dispirited by the furniture stacked and shoved into the space every which way. Boxes were stuffed with clothing, lamps, kitchenware, linens. Valuable rugs had been rolled up and pushed into corners. The bottles in Tony's expensive wine collection had been set upright, probably ruined. So many bad memories haunted her as she started through the contents, especially when she looked at the bed where she'd lost all innocence, all self-respect. What had she been thinking, coming here?

She saw Tony's desk wedged between the wall and the heavy mattress of the bed she'd shared with him. Suddenly she recalled the day Tony had had a carpenter come in to create a special feature for the drawer, a sliding panel that concealed a two-inch false bottom. If the cops had gone through Tony's stuff, as she suspected they must have, maybe they hadn't discovered it. She shoved hard against the mattress, inching it just far enough to one side to expose the bottom left drawer. She pulled it open and groped inside, fumbling with the cleverly designed panel. It slipped open and she closed her fingers around a stack of money. Her heart hammered. Tony's cash! Probably the results of drug transactions he hadn't had time to launder, and it was too late for that now. Who would know about this or even be able to ask about it? She shut the panel, stood and stuffed the cache into her purse, then resumed her search for her personal possessions, the things she'd come after.

The hunt was short, and she quickly filled an old grocery sack with the few things she wanted. She took one last look around, locked the unit, and left. She drove away in bright sunlight, with a cold breeze blowing through her open car windows, pushing the stink of the storage space's dead air off her clothing and skin. Somewhere in the big wide world, there was Garret. Somehow, someway, she would find him. And when she did, she'd find out if love, true love, was real or a romantic illusion. Eden left the condo complex knowing that along with a stash of cash, she had indeed found closure.

Jon was waiting for Ciana when she came into the barn to saddle Firecracker for her morning ride. Without preamble, he said, "I got a phone call yesterday. A bed's opened up for my father in Texas."

Ciana stopped short. News she hadn't expected. She held her disappointment tightly, determined to hide it. "When will you be leaving?"

"I have five days to get him there or he loses the spot to someone else. I'm checking him out tomorrow afternoon at the county place. May be easier to drive all night."

Tomorrow. So soon. Too soon. "I understand."

"He can't live alone and I . . . well, I need to go home." He walked to the tack room doorway, his quarters at Bellmeade for months. "I'll get my stuff packed up and out of your way."

Her world had been rocked. What would it be like to get up every morning and not have him come to breakfast in the kitchen? Or to not see him working the horses? She saw a hole in her life big enough to drive her truck through. "Taking your daddy home isn't the only reason you're going, is it?" Intuition drove her to ask.

She watched his back stiffen. He turned, studying her with his clear green eyes, drawing out the silence, as if gathering his words from a deep place inside. "I came here for the summer.

Just three months to help my old man and for the experience of working with wild mustangs. But not much went the way I thought it would."

Her summer hadn't gone the way she'd planned either. "How so?"

He jammed his hands into the front pockets of his jeans. "One night, I wandered into a dance saloon and met someone. Didn't plan on that."

"Me neither."

"Then I go to work and find I'm helping a girl with cancer to train her horse. I'd known her from a one-time visit years before. I liked her. But I couldn't get the other girl out of my head. And then, on a fluke, girl one shows up and turns out to be best friends with the gal I'm working with. Which was hard enough, 'specially when gal one asked me to keep a secret I never wanted to keep." He shook his head. "And then the damndest thing happened. I found myself in Italy. A European side trip wasn't in my plans, or my budget. But I went. And going damn near wrecked my life."

The old hurts grabbed at her. She shrugged them off. "You had help with that one," she said, meeting his gaze. "My fault too."

He walked to her and stopped, keeping his hands in his pockets. "And when I came back here, after having stayed away from Texas longer than I ever planned, I find out my dad's an invalid and that the cancer girl's sick to death. So no, Ciana, nothing's gone the way I planned it."

He paused, but after a few heartbeats said, "And so I'm remembering all the dreams I once had—following the rodeo, saving my cash, buying property for a little spread in Texas where I can work and train horses. And dreams die hard. I still want those things. But no one can make them come true except me."

His words struck like arrows. He'd told her the first time they'd met what he wanted for his life. She was a complication, an unforeseen liability. And all that had happened to him since coming to Tennessee was an entanglement he had never asked for, and mostly her fault. Her throat burned.

"But the hardest part for me, the worst part, is being around girl number one day after day, and knowing she's out of reach."

Ciana's eyes brimmed and her chin trembled. She knew what it was to chase dreams. She wanted Bellmeade, her inheritance, and her lifelong commitment to untold ancestors. And she wanted him. Even without the complication with Arie, the lines between them were clear—she wouldn't leave her land, and he must go after what he'd planned long before she'd come along. She had no right to stand in the way of Jon's dreams.

He again walked away but stopped and looked at her over his shoulder. "And, I might add, I have nothing in me that can stay and watch Arie die. So I'm leaving now, before her last dance ends. And I'm going over to tell her I'm leaving tonight. I think I owe her that much."

"Yes, she needs to hear it from you." Ciana's voice quavered. Her friend would be devastated, but Ciana certainly understood his desire not to be around when the inevitable happened to Arie.

Jon headed to the tack room, the distance between him and Ciana widening in every way. In the unlit doorway, he said, "I've caught up on most of the outside work. You'll be able to start spring with a clean slate."

"We . . . we owe you money. I can write you a check right

now if you come up to the house," she threw out desperately, hoping to make him stay with her a little longer.

"Mail it to me. Your mother has my mother's address, which is where I'll be staying until the spring rodeo circuit starts up."

She imagined him moving west, riding broncos, getting busted up. *Back off*, she told herself.

"I best get a move on," he said.

"Regrets?" she asked before he could leave.

"Life's too short for regrets, Ciana. So no regrets."

To his back, she flung, "We'll miss you, Jon. Me and Mom."

He didn't turn around but walked through the door of the tack room, into the dark.

# 43

Eden met with the realtor the next day. Sharon Weber was a vivacious young woman, eager to make a deal.

"It's an excellent offer," Sharon said with a cheery smile. "And in these hard times—it's a buyer's market, you know—offers don't come along every day. But the couple who want your house are delighted with the way it's been upgraded."

Eden could only think about the generosity of Arie's family to Gwen and herself. Without their help, where would they be? "Yes, the house was almost completely rebuilt on the inside."

Sharon opened her file folder and removed sheets of paper that she laid out on the conference table for Eden. "I think you'll find the offer generous, especially when you read the comparables of homes sold in your area over the last year."

Eden squinted at the papers and was surprised to see the letters and numbers squiggling on the paper before realizing that the movement was caused by moisture in her eyes. Shocked, she wondered how she could possibly feel sentimental over that old dump of a house? She didn't exactly hold fond memories of living in it. She cleared her throat, picked up the papers, and skimmed them. The bottom line sale price did look generous. "I . . . um . . . have an appointment with my attorney later. I'd like for him to look this over. Can I have an extension on the deadline?"

Ms. Weber's brow puckered, smoothed. "I'm sure I can ask my clients. They're motivated because they want to move in by mid-March, in thirty days."

*Thirty days!* "I'm motivated too," Eden lied. How would she manage? The house held a lifetime of accumulation and clutter. Gwen had texted her once about the house: YOUR HOUSE NOW. Perhaps Mr. Boatwright could counsel her. "I'll call you later," Eden told Ms. Weber, standing and shaking the woman's hand.

Outside in the bright light of the afternoon, Eden fished sunglasses from her purse. She got into her car but didn't start the motor. She merely sat and stared out the windshield and fought the desire to cry. What was wrong with her? Hadn't her fondest desire been to blow this stupid town? Now she had the opportunity. She had cash money, no entanglements. Except for Arie. She would have to stay until Arie died. Eden hiccupped and let tears slide down her cheeks. She would take Ciana up on her offer and live at Bellmeade. Together she and Ciana would help each other through the dark days ahead. Together they would hold on to Arie until life let go of her.

Arie checked herself in the mirror for the umpteenth time and realized that this was as good as she was going to look this evening. The pink sweater and extra blush could only help so much. She'd also taken her pain medication in order to feel her best during Jon's visit, even knowing it would make her drowsy. She planned to bring him into the living room, where her daddy had laid a fire that danced brightly. Her parents had already retreated to the den in the back of the house and to the wide-screen television. Swede would have cornered Jon and talked forever, but Patricia knew the score—Jon was special to Arie, and in the silent code between women, her mother had signaled that Arie and Jon would not be interrupted.

When the doorbell rang, Arie rushed to open the door.

"Hey," Jon said with the smile that always made her heart sing.

She wanted him to hug her but had to settle for him taking her hands in his.

"Come into the living room," she said, leading him into the softly lit space.

"You look nice," he told her, removing his sheepskin jacket and settling beside her on the couch. He gazed appreciatively around the room, then looked up, grinning, and pointed. "Who painted the Sistine Chapel up there?"

Arie had taken Jon to Vatican City once her tests were completed that day at the Italian hospital. She'd wanted him to sit with her in the chapel, see its beauty.

"My goofy brother. My 'chapel' is made up of posters he's pasted on the ceiling. I talked about the chapel so much when I returned that he thought he'd surprise me by giving me my own copy."

Jon laughed. "Clever guy, your brother."

What she didn't tell Jon was that soon the living room would become her bedroom, a better and bigger area to have family and friends visit her than her tiny upstairs bedroom.

A hospital bed was being set up next week. Her father had already mounted a track across the ceiling near the bay window where the ceiling-to-floor curtain would hang when she needed privacy. And of course, Eric had already installed his gift to her—God about to touch Adam into life, as painted by Michelangelo.

"I like it," Jon said.

"Me too." Arie could feel the heat of Jon's body. Her body held little heat these days. She was always cold. "Would you like some coffee? It's ready in the kitchen."

He shook his head and turned partway on the sofa to better look at her. "I came to tell you something, give you something, and ask you something. But maybe not in that order."

"Okay. Is this one of those good-news-bad-news things?"

He grinned. "Depends on what's good and bad news to you." He locked his fingers together and rested his forearms on his knees. "I'm going back to Texas tomorrow. A bed's opened up for my dad."

His words caused her heart to stutter step. For although she knew his father's circumstances, she didn't want Jon to go away. Knowing he was near brought her comfort. Seeing his face made her happy. "So you've come to say goodbye." It was a statement, not a question.

"I have."

Her throat tightened. She would never see him again, and the sense of finality bruised her. "Have you told Ciana?" *Dumb question.* Of course he had.

"Yes. Chores are pretty well caught up. She won't have too much to do except keep up with the animals."

*And her dying friend,* she thought, because Jon's catching up on the chores would free Ciana for that also. Arie sighed, knowing it was probably best in the long run. This way he would remember her in pink, not someone wasting away in a drugged stupor until death took her. "I'll miss you."

He nodded self-consciously but didn't say he'd miss her too.

She grabbed a tissue and wiped her eyes. "That's one of three. I'm guessing that's the 'tell-me-something.' What do you want to ask me?"

He cleared his throat, staring down at his big rough hands. "I want to ask you to let me buy Caramel. She's a good horse, and I'll give you a fair price. I want to take her with me to Texas. And on to summer rodeos."

"She isn't for sale, Jon."

He blinked, obviously surprised by her answer. "Not at all?"

"She's spoken for."

"Oh." He nodded, but his disappointment showed. "All right. Okay. I'm sure her new owner will be pleased with her."

Arie laughed softly. "She isn't for sale, Jon, because I'm giving her to you."

"What?" He shook his head. "But I can't just take her. She's valuable, so it isn't fair."

"It's fair. She's always been more yours than mine."

"Arie, I don't feel right—"

"You have to take her," Arie said. Unable to keep her hands to herself, she clasped his wrist. "There's no one else who'll love her the way you do. Plus," she added, "I've already written it into my will."

He startled. "Your will?"

"Everyone should have one."

The rims of his eyes reddened. He coughed, said gruffly, "I'll take good care of her."

"I know you will."

They sat in silence, listening to the crackling of the logs in the fireplace. After a few minutes, he reached into his shirt pocket and withdrew a small object. "I . . . um . . . I made this for you."

He opened his hand and she saw a small, crudely carved horse. Around the horse's neck, Jon had tied a colorful beaded string.

She took the horse, held it, imagining his pocketknife shaping the wood, his thick fingers sliding the tiny beads on the piece of string. She couldn't speak around the emotion clogging her throat.

"I'm not a great whittler," he mumbled. "But it . . . um . . . has a purpose." He lifted her chin, looked fully into her eyes. "The reason, well, the custom out west is that no Indian brave should go into the beyond without a horse to ride. Great braves always took their horses to the other side. And, Arie"—his hand cupped her chin—"you're the bravest person I've ever known."

Her arms flew around him and she cried, "Hold me. Please hold me." She loved him, loved him so much.

He hesitated briefly, but then his arms encircled her, and he rested his cheek on her head. "Thank you," she finally managed. "Thank you for the horse and for Italy and for being a part of my life."

"Same goes for me," he said gruffly.

She nestled in his arms until her eyes grew heavy with twilight sleep from her medication. After a while, Arie was aware of Jon easing her down on the sofa, of covering her with a wool throw warmed by the fireplace. At some point, Patricia came into the room, and Jon stood. Too groggy to rouse herself, Arie heard hushed goodbyes from the foyer, followed by a rush of cold February air as Jon left, and Patricia returned to sit with her daughter.

Arie clutched the small horse and floated back to the night when she had lain in Jon's arms, loved him and made love with him with unimaginable abandon—a night where he had, for a few brief hours, maybe . . . perhaps . . . might . . . have loved her too. Maybe just a little.

# 44

Ciana stood at the window in the front parlor watching Jon load Caramel into his horse trailer. The buckskin didn't want to go into the vehicle, but Jon was patient and coached her firmly with shoves and whispers and soothing touches. In the end, she went quietly. Ciana had told herself she wasn't going to go out there. They'd said their goodbyes at breakfast that morning. Now there was nothing to do but watch and wait. And ache.

A cold wind whipped Jon's sun-streaked hair and sheepskin jacket he'd failed to button. His expression looked somber, even from this distance. In moments he'd pull down the driveway and toward the open road to Murfreesboro to pick up his father, and then he'd be gone. She could stand silent no longer. Ciana grabbed her fleece jacket and hurried out the door. He looked up from examining the trailer hitch when he heard the front door slam. He asked, "Did I forget something?"

She pulled up in front of him. "Did you get the food basket I packed?"

"In the backseat of the truck."

"And the extra blanket? For your dad."

"I have it."

"Um . . . maybe during the drive, you could ask him why he doesn't like Beauchamp women," she said to keep the small talk going. "I still wonder about what he said that day." She shivered in the blustery wind and crossed her arms.

"You better go back inside before you catch pneumonia."

She didn't care if she did. "I'll be fine."

He nodded tersely. "Goodbye, then."

"Goodbye," she mumbled, willing herself not to cry. "Be safe."

He turned, walked to the truck, and scooted into the cab. He popped the truck into gear and slowly pulled up the long driveway. Ciana didn't move, just stood woodenly and held her head high, fighting tears. She saw his eyes watching her in the large mirror mounted on the side of the truck. Green eyes, troubled, uncertain. He drove partway, threw the gear into park, and opened the cab door with a loud, "Aw, hell."

He jogged to where she was standing, pulled her to him, and kissed her hard. Ciana met his kiss and gave back as good as she got. She saw stars, felt his arms slide around her. She threw her arms around him, melting into the rising tide of passion inside her like a tidal wave. When their mouths parted, they stared at each other in wonder. The pull between them had not abated one bit over time or circumstance. She wanted him. He wanted her. Jon was the first to blink. He backed away. Ciana felt rooted to the ground.

Jon stalked to his truck and, without another glance backward, drove away. Ciana watched, tears tracking down her face as the taillights of the trailer turned out of Bellmeade's driveway and fled the landscape of her heart.

Arie had raised her hospital bed, positioned near the bay window of the living room, and was staring outside at pummeling rain. She felt as if she'd worn out her welcome with life. She was tired, sick, and ready to have it all end, but life clung to her stubbornly. "How's Abbie's job going?" she asked.

Eric was stoking the logs in the fireplace. "All right. I'm sorry she has to work at all, but if we're going to buy our own house, she has to. Cabinet business is slow because construction is slow. Whole town is waiting to see how the big subdivision is going to go." He eyed his sister covertly. "Um . . . Ciana tell you anything about selling Bellmeade?"

"Why do you ask?"

"Everyone knows the deal hinges on whether the developer can get hold of her acreage."

"Is that what you want?"

"It would give this town a big boost. And mine and Dad's business too."

Arie sighed. "She doesn't talk to me about it, but I'd be very surprised if she agrees to sell. Bellmeade and farming is in her blood."

Eric looked disappointed. "This town will die without the project."

"It didn't die after any other disaster over time, so I doubt it'll die if Ciana doesn't sell." Arie was ambivalent, with split loyalties, divided between her family's business and her friend's wanting to keep her land in her family. She'd be long gone before it would be settled one way or the other.

Eric came beside the bed and stood gazing down at Arie, looking uncomfortable. She knew him well enough to understand he had more to say. "What is it?"

His face reddened. "I . . . um . . . want to thank you."

"You're welcome. What for?"

"Remember last summer, when you told me to not let Abbie get away? To tell her I loved her?"

Arie vaguely recalled the conversation. "You took my advice."

He nodded. "If I hadn't, she was ready to move on. Going out to Oklahoma for a job. If I hadn't said something that weekend, I would have lost her. And that would have been the biggest mistake of my life."

Arie loved her brother very much, and to have his gratitude meant the world to her. She took his rough, work-worn hand into hers. What she wouldn't have given to have Jon love her the way Eric loved Abbie. "Take good care of her."

Eric cleared his throat and glanced out the window self-consciously. "Who's that?"

They both watched as a long black limo pulled up in front of the house.

"The Grim Reaper?" Arie suggested.

"Not funny, Sis."

"I have no idea, then."

Together they watched the driver come around to the back door of the car with a giant black and white striped umbrella. He opened the door, held the umbrella open. Two people ducked under the umbrella's safety, a woman and a child. Arie's heart leaped in recognition. "They're friends from the hospital," she told Eric. "Let them in."

Eric went to the front door and ushered Lotty and her son inside while the driver said he'd wait in the car. When the visitors saw Arie, they burst into smiles. Eric's expression was of total disbelief. Behind the visitors, he mouthed, "*Is this who I think it is?*"

Arie nodded to him but said, "This is Lotty Jones and her

son, Cory. That's how I know her in the hospital." She opened her arms and Cory threw himself onto her bed and hugged her. Lotty grabbed the boy's shirt. "Let's not smother her, son."

Arie couldn't stop smiling. "Look at you, Mr. Cory. You've grown a foot taller."

"I miss you," he warbled as his mother helped him down from the bed.

"I miss you too."

Eric stood starstruck.

"Could you pull up a chair for Lotty?" Arie asked of him, amused at his reaction.

"Oh yeah. Sure." He jumped into motion, lifting the room's most comfortable chair and setting it beside the bed. Lotty thanked him, oblivious to his stares.

"I brought you a present," Cory said. He reached into a satchel Lotty had carried in and pulled out a sheaf of paper, bound by thick red string through holes punched in the top of the bundle. "I drew every picture myself."

"Oh, Cory, how wonderful." She scooted over, patting the spot on the mattress next to her. "Come up here and show them to me."

Eric lifted him in one smooth motion to sit by Arie. Together they flipped through every piece of paper, Arie praising, Cory grinning. When they were finished, Arie lay back, exhausted. Beads of perspiration had formed on her forehead. Eric stepped closer, but Arie held him off with, "Cory, would you like to go to our garage and see some of my brother's woodworking tools?"

The boy eagerly hopped down and followed Eric, who kept glancing back at Arie. When they were gone, Arie said, "He looks great. How's he doing?"

"Very well. His cancer's in full retreat. How about yours?"

"Advancing." Shortness of breath interrupted Arie. Lotty waited patiently. "You're so kind to come see me."

"Cory's talked of nothing else."

"Does he know . . . the truth?"

"Yes, but I don't think he quite gets it. Death is still a fuzzy concept for him." Lotty paused, caressing Arie's hand. "I want to do something special for you and your family."

"Like what?"

"I want to sing." Lotty's pretty eyes filled with tears. "A concert, something private."

Arie started crying too. "That's . . . that's so kind."

"It means I need a list of your favorite songs."

"Everything you sing."

Lotty laughed softly, wiping under her eyes. "Surely you have other favorites. I won't be offended, you know, if you like Reba, or Pasty, or whomever." She gestured to the empty air.

"I'll make a list."

They sat in silence, listening to the rain let up outside. Weak sunlight broke through dark clouds. Lotty said, "I can see you need to rest."

Arie made no apology. Pain was coming in waves. She needed another hit from the morphine pump set up on the other side of her bed. "I want Cory to remember me at my best," she said honestly.

"It's the only way any of us will remember you." Lotty stood, bent, and kissed Arie's forehead. She slipped a small envelope from her satchel. "This is how to reach me. Unfortunately, I have commitments through May, but after that have someone in your family call."

Arie knew she would never hear Lotty's concert. It would

come after she died. Still the woman's generosity touched her deeply. And her relatives would be blown away. The thought made her smile and brought satisfaction. Lotty gathered Cory and said goodbye. Arie pushed the button on the pump, and Eric held her hand until her pain-racked body relaxed and her eyes closed in dreamless sleep.

The signing and transfer of the house to the new buyers went smoothly. Eden brought Ciana with her to the closing, as much for courage as for company. The selling had been emotionally trying. There was something nostalgic and melancholy and scary about bidding goodbye to her childhood, as complicated as it had been. She'd donated all the house's contents to charity, and with no further communications from Gwen, Eden gave away her belongings too.

Ciana had asked, "Are you sure she'll never want any of her stuff?"

"A while back, she left me a letter filling in a lot of blanks in her history—our history," Eden had answered. "It explained lots of things to me, and I think it was her way of saying goodbye to her unnatural struggle against her illness. You see, she hated feeling what other people think of as 'normal.' When she took the meds, she felt like a stranger in her own skin, and no matter how hard she tried to remain on her meds, she just couldn't. She says she's happy now. Maybe so, maybe not. But she's who she wants to be." Eden's voice had broken. "And . . . and she told me that she loved me."

"Oh, Eden, of course she loves you."

Eden had offered a weak smile, then sagely said, "Well, love certainly wears a lot of faces."

A trip with Eden's car and Ciana's truck moved Eden's

clothing and a few boxes of sentimental items to Ciana's. Otherwise, she left her past and all that went with it behind.

At Bellmeade, Eden was given Olivia's old room, still full of antique Victorian furniture, old lace curtains, and outdated wallpaper.

Alice Faye welcomed Eden warmly, and when she opened the bedroom door, she said, "You can change anything you want in here. I'm not attached. I think whatever you do would be an improvement."

Ciana looked stricken by her mother's suggestion, so despite longing to change everything, Eden left the room as she found it. She didn't feel it was her place to intercede in their tug-of-war over Olivia Beauchamp.

Eden continued to work, but each night when she arrived at Bellmeade, there was a hot meal on the table and a warm fire in the parlor. It took getting used to, but she managed it far more quickly than she expected. So this was how regular people lived. *Amazing*.

In early April, she and Ciana were watching a video, a bowl of buttered popcorn on the couch between them, when Ciana said, "I went by to visit Arie today. She's so thin. Her mom says she only weighs sixty pounds."

Eden felt a nudge of guilt. She didn't visit as often as Ciana because one time after seeing Arie fading away and in pain, she'd gone to her car, knelt on the ground, and vomited. "At least she's surrounded by family," Eden said, picking up a handful of popcorn. "They agreed that she would never be left alone, that someone would always remain in the room with her. She told me they take shifts."

"So what do you think you'll do after Arie dies?" Ciana

used the word more freely these days because Arie's suffering would not be relieved by anything except death.

"Not sure. It's crazy, isn't it? I'm all grown up, I have a job, I have money from the house in the bank, but no place to go."

"Still no luck with Garret?"

"Not a lick."

"Your loneliness shows."

"So does yours."

Ciana scoffed. "Not true. I don't miss Jon one bit."

Eden tossed a kernel of popcorn at her. "No, not much. Tell me, what's so horrible about admitting to yourself that you love him?"

Ciana rubbed her temples, fending off a headache. "Can't afford to dwell on him. Too many other things on my mind right now."

"Like?"

"Arie. The Hastings buyout offer. Do you know that half the town is counting on me to sell, the other half swearing to hate me if I do? I overheard that gossip two weeks ago at the hardware store. I don't want my neighbors hating me. Everyone talks about the money. Heck, I could use the money, too, but I want my home more."

Eden saw worry lines pucker Ciana's brow. "Um . . . maybe I could help out some around Bellmeade. On weekends, you know. I'll bet there's something I can do to help and earn my keep."

Ciana offered an amused smile. "You could start small. How about turning the compost heap once a day? Or pick up pasture patties that the horses leave behind?"

Eden's eyes widened. "Manure?"

"Has to be done."

Eden sat ramrod straight and keeled over on her side in

an exaggerated impression of a cartoon character. Ciana burst out laughing. So did Eden. They laughed uncontrollably until their sides ached and tears ran down their faces. Weeks later, Eden would recall that night as the last time either of them laughed about anything.

# 45

On April fifth, Arie awoke feeling alert and without pain. She asked for pancakes and Patricia rushed to the kitchen to whip up the meal. Arie ate heartily, better than she had in months, getting up and going to the table to sit and eat with her mother and father.

When the hospice caregiver arrived, she beamed smiles, urging Arie to do whatever she wanted all that day for as long as she felt like it. Arie asked to be taken outside, and Swede bundled her up, tucked her into a wheelchair, and pushed her around the yard and flowerbeds already blooming with sunny yellow daffodils. The weather was cool but the sun warm—the month of April at its best. Something akin to joy bubbled up inside Arie during the stroll. The world was beautiful, too beautiful to leave, and yet she knew she was ready to go. Not resigned, but ready. She could tell the difference.

In the late afternoon, Eden and Ciana came together to

visit. "You look fabulous!" Eden told Arie when she saw color in her cheeks.

"It's been a good day," Arie said, bundled in a spring quilt on the sofa.

Ciana said, "I hope you have many more."

"No guarantee, but it sure would be nice. I'm sick of being *sick*. I haven't felt good since we were in Italy." Her expression went dreamy. "That was the best time of my life."

"Mine too," Eden chimed in.

For Ciana, it had been the best and the worst of times. "I loved being with my best friends," she said truthfully.

"Request time," Arie said soberly before quickly adding, "I don't want the two of you moping around and acting all sad and gloomy after this is all over for me."

Panicked glances darted between Ciana and Eden.

"I'm serious. Get busy with your lives and have a good time. Eden, go find Garret. Ciana, tell Jon Mercer you love him."

Ciana went wobbly, queasy, as guilt and shame coursed through her. "What are you talking about? I don't love Jon."

In spite of Ciana willing Eden to endorse her words, Eden said nothing.

Arie took Ciana's hand. "I didn't know how you felt about him until Eric's wedding. I never had a clue, I swear. Because if I had known . . ." Her voice tripped. Ciana started to speak, but Arie shook her head. "Let me finish. Maybe I didn't want to see, but that night when you two were dancing and the new year came, it was like scales fell from my eyes. The way he looked at you, and the way you looked at him . . . it was a blinking billboard. You love each other."

"I . . . I didn't. I never—"

"I know," Arie said, tears in her eyes. "You didn't want to

hurt me." Arie took short hiccuping breaths, pressing Ciana's hand tenderly to her cheek. "I wish you'd have told me." She looked into Ciana's face. "But I'm glad you didn't."

Ciana fought for composure.

Arie smiled. "It doesn't matter anymore. Truly. The heart wants what the heart wants. No regrets."

Arie echoed Jon's words, and Ciana realized she had no regrets either. Nothing could change the past.

"Now shoo," Arie whispered. "This room will be swarming with relatives soon. Make a clean getaway while you can."

She lifted her arms and Ciana and Eden leaned down to hold her one last time. This was goodbye, and all three of them knew it. A log in the fireplace, burned through its center, thumped down over the andirons and they glanced over in unison. A shower of golden sparks danced upward like spirit sprites, becoming a metaphor for Arie's life—intense and sparkling. And far too brief.

Arie was seeing her living room and the people clustered around her hospital bed from the most unique perspective—from above. She hovered close to the ceiling, marveling at how small and wasted she looked on the bed. Was she dreaming? People were crying. Her mother, her dad, Eric and Abbie, Aunt Sally and Aunt Ruth. They were all so sad. She wanted to tell them she was fine, light as a feather, like a bird with its hollow bones, rising, floating over the bed and looking down on the scene. And she felt . . . what? Safe and warm and peaceful.

The voices below grew fainter, and it was as if she were hearing them from far away, through a mask, or a tunnel. Ever so slowly, her air body began to turn over so that she saw the ceiling and the poster of the Sistine Chapel, so close that the ink pixels on the paper became geometric shapes. So close she saw the colors as vibrant flares. She watched, transfixed, as the poster turned translucent. And just as it began to fade into nothingness, Arie Winslow reached out and touched the face of God.

# 46

The *Windemere Journal*, the small hometown newspaper wrote in an editorial:

> Not since the July Rodeo Days has there been such a turnout of people as for the funeral of Arie Winslow, age nineteen and lifetime resident. Miss Winslow, daughter of Swede and Patricia Winslow, lost her brave, lifelong fight with cancer, and the town turned out en masse, closing down local businesses and the high school for three hours on Thursday to bury her.

Ciana wasn't surprised. The town felt invested in Arie, its sweetheart, a pretty little towheaded girl with generational lines that went deep and wide. And now she had been placed in a gleaming white casket lined with pale pink satin, dressed in her favorite pink jewel-studded rodeo jacket. Her head rested on a lace pillow, and her hand held a small carved wooden horse, a beaded string hanging from the neck; she had insisted that it be buried with her. Only Ciana knew why, recalling the day she'd first seen it, half formed, in the hands of its creator.

Early on the day of the funeral, Ciana rose, then washed and groomed both her horses. A sleepy-eyed Eden found Ciana in the barn and asked, "What are you doing?"

"Couldn't sleep, decided to come prepare the horses for the procession."

"You're bringing the horses? Why?"

"A sign of respect. I'll ride mine and lead Sonata. Before Caramel, Arie rode this one."

"Is there anything I can do to help?"

Ciana looked solemn. "Bring us some coffee. Mom should have it brewing by now. And come help me braid Sonata's mane and tail with this black ribbon." She reached down and lifted a silky spool. "I want Sonata to look her finest."

Eden looped the ribbon through her fingers, blinking away tears. "My honor. Back with caffeine in a minute."

Once the horse was ready, they went into the kitchen and a hot breakfast. No one felt like eating, but Alice Faye insisted. She looked red-eyed, and tired and said things like, "Arie's poor parents," and "How does a mother bury a child?"

Ciana showered and dressed in cowboy black—black jeans, black shirt, boots, and hat. Eden wore a simple black dress and jacket and pulled her hair into a severe bun. Ciana loaded the horses into her trailer and drove to the big Baptist church downtown. Her mother and Eden followed behind in Eden's car.

After a celebration of Arie's life, pallbearers led by Eric and Swede loaded the pearl-white casket into the hearse. From there the seemingly endless procession wound through the streets behind the limo holding Arie's immediate family.

Following that car, Ciana rode her horse and led Sonata, with the dressed-out horse wearing the ornate black and silver Mexican saddle, empty of the rider who would never return. The town would long remember the sight and sound of slow clopping polished horse hooves all along the slow journey to the cemetery.

At the entrance, Ciana dismounted, grasped both horses' bridles and walked them the distance to the graveside, a beautiful spot on a hill, near an ancient oak tree. The ground had been left wild, and bright purple and yellow flowers carpeted the hillside. Arie would have loved the space. Blue sky above was shot through with sunlight, and a soft April breeze ruffled the mantle of flowers across the casket. Eden came alongside Ciana, encircled her waist and whispered, "Reminds me of Italy."

Ciana agreed, pricked by unbearable sorrow but also comforted that at least one of Arie's dreams had come true. She also thought of her grandmother, buried in another part of the same cemetery, and her father and grandfather, adjacent to Olivia. Four people she had known and loved were gone before she would turn twenty in July. And one, Jon Mercer, was among the missing. *Life is better left to chance*. The song's refrain ran through her head, and she wondered what "dance" lay ahead for them all?

# 47

Rule of thumb: Don't plant until mid-April, when frost is most likely finished for the winter. Harvest in mid-October before the first killing frost of autumn. Farmers followed the rule faithfully, and Ciana was no exception. In the middle of April, she plowed the fields she meant to plant, turning the rich clay soil to ready it for seeding. As she made the furrows, she grieved for Arie but also found comfort in the smell of fresh dirt greeting warm sunlight. Therapeutic. And watching the soil turn into green fuzz as the seeds sprouted and grew delivered hope for the spring and summer months to come.

Ciana had several surprises over the months too. The first and best was when Alice Faye, still sober and faithfully attending AA meetings, broke the news that Hastings had hit a bump on his subdivision project via the Tennessee legislature. The snafu required an issue that the politicians would need to vote on, but since they wouldn't be reconvening until the fall, the Bellmeade Estates project was at a standstill. Her mother and half the town—the half that wanted the project—were disappointed, but Ciana felt as if she been handed a reprieve. "It just pushes our decision down the road," Alice Faye told her daughter. "Sooner or later, you'll have to decide."

Of course, Ciana had already decided. Her mother had just refused to hear her.

Ciana also rented out her empty barn's stalls. With Caramel gone, and with Firecracker and Sonata housed in two stalls, she wielded a hammer to new lumber and created two more. The boarding money helped cover extra and unexpected costs. She reopened pasture land for the new horses to graze, planted additional fields of alfalfa to sell after harvest, and hired Clyde Keating, a boy just out of high school and the size of a heifer, who was planning on attending University of Tennessee in Knoxville on a football scholarship. Come August, he'd leave for football camp, but until then she paid him for a prodigious amount of muscle power. Clyde took a shine to Eden, becoming tongue-tied every time she came into view.

"You have an admirer," Ciana teased Eden.

Eden just rolled her eyes.

One week, Ciana couldn't cover Clyde's cash-only paycheck. She was frantically hunting through cookie jars and under sofa cushions when Eden asked what was going on. Ciana told her and rushed off to the barn.

Eden followed her. "Good grief, why haven't you asked me for it?"

"You pay rent already," Ciana said, pawing through the change jar she kept in the tack room. "This is my problem."

"Wait here," Eden said. She returned quickly and handed Ciana ten one-hundred-dollar bills.

Ciana stared at the money, openmouthed. She threw up her hands. "I won't take your house money."

"It isn't my house money."

"Then where—"

"Tony's drug money."

Ciana's eyes widened. "When? How?"

"Don't ask. I can't stick it into the bank without accounting for it come tax time, so it's tucked away for rainy days. I think today qualifies as 'rainy.' Take it."

"I . . . I'll pay you back."

"No need. It may as well do some good after all the harm it's caused."

Ciana took the bills gratefully. "You're a lifesaver."

"It's a pinkie-swear secret, you know. Not even your mother."

Ciana hooked pinkies with Eden, then ran from the barn to find Clyde.

In June, Eden quit the boutique and devoted her energy to helping Ciana and Alice Faye with their giant home garden. She surprised them and herself as well, taking an unexpected interest in growing vegetables, in watering, harvesting, and even in pulling detested weeds. Every week some new food cropped up to pick and eat, each made more delicious because she'd nurtured it. She learned how to cook and how to can, putting up countless jars of tomatoes, squash, beans—a stash of food for the coming winter.

Eden liked helping Ciana, too, because seeing how hard she worked, how she fell exhausted into bed every night, also made Eden feel valuable and necessary and wanted. Eden didn't hear from Gwen, could only hope she was safe wherever she was living with her illness.

July brought the rodeo, but Ciana didn't ride in the opening ceremonies. Not this year. The flag corps all wore black armbands in honor of Arie.

August came hot and airless, along with an amazing special concert from a top country singer, exclusively for Arie's family and friends. Naturally, the crowd was large enough to fill the high school auditorium. The singer told stories about Arie between songs, and there wasn't a dry eye in the place.

Sometimes Ciana drove out to the cemetery and put wildflowers she'd gathered on Arie's grave, sat for a spell in the quiet, and wept. Her memories of Arie were everywhere; there seemed no escape, no respite, when the fingers of grief unexpectedly grabbed her heart. She saw Arie's face and sunny smile in the rising sun as she rode Firecracker across her fields. She heard Arie's laughter over Eden's childlike exuberance the time she ran into the kitchen from the chicken coop shouting, "Baby chicks! We have baby chicks!" Often when the long summer days were done, Ciana and Eden sat out on the veranda, sipping wine by candlelight, and reminisced about Italy. "I wonder where everyone is, all the people we met over there."

"You mean Garret and Enzo," Eden said. "Who else matters?"

They giggled. Ciana said, "I'm sure Enzo is bedding some countess."

"Do you think he scored every time with every woman?"

"Probably. He *is* charming."

"But not with you," Eden said. "You're the one who got away."

"I'm the one who was too scared."

"And in love with someone else."

"Ancient history." Ciana rested her feet on the porch's rail. "Which isn't the case with you and Garret. Have you given up looking for him?"

"I haven't, but I've been doing something for myself before I resume the hunt. Something special." Eden held out one of her arms so that the underside showed. "I've been going to a dermatologist in Nashville. He specializes in scar removal, and he's minimizing my scars from my days of cutting. After treatment, the ugly raised lumps should be reduced to thin white lines. It's a long process. When I see Garret again, I want my past to be as wiped away as possible."

"But you said he knows about your scars and didn't care."

"*I* know," Eden said. "And *I* care."

Ciana touched Eden's glass with hers in tribute. Beyond the porch, fireflies blinked coded messages, and a horse whinnied from the pasture. The night silence was broken by a cacophony of tree frogs calling to each other, underscoring the lost piece of their friendship circle. "I miss Arie."

Nostalgia for what was gone brought a lump to Eden's throat. "Know what she'd ask you if she were here? She'd ask, 'Why haven't you called Jon this summer? Asked him to come back?' "

"Phone works both ways," Ciana said, spinning the glass between her palms. "He hasn't reached out to me either."

Eden had struck a very sore spot. Jon had not once contacted her since leaving. The slight stung until the truth dawned on her: he was content in his old life. Yet, try as she might, she couldn't rid herself of his memory. The men she met on her and Eden's occasional venture into Nashville clubs were pale reflections of him, inferior to Jon in every way. She kept this to herself, of course. One of the Beauchamp rules of life: Be content with what you have, and don't bitch about what you don't have. Yet in the dark of night, when she was alone or standing under a full moon, she missed him all the more.

Ciana raised her glass. "To Arie. And to friendship."

"How about love?" Eden asked.

"A fool's game." Ciana rose, dumping the contents of her glass over the porch rail, and bounded barefoot onto the grass. "Have you ever caught fireflies, girlfriend?"

"Why would I do that?"

"Come here," Ciana commanded.

Eden scampered onto the lawn. "Why do they blink?"

"It's their language of love." Ciana twirled, raised her glass, and scooped it through the air, snagging several blinking insects and slapped her hand across the glass's open top. "Now your turn."

Eden attempted the same procedure but failed to catch even one bug. "Empty," she lamented.

"Practice!"

Eden captured two, but when she saw Ciana's full jar, she said, "How illuminating!"

Ciana laughed. "Glowing!"

"Flashing!"

"Incandescent!"

"Resplendent!" Eden shouted after a few seconds of thought.

"Luminous!"

"Now what?" Eden asked.

"We let them go."

"Why?"

"So they can live," Ciana said, removing her hand covering the glass. She lifted it high over her head, and together the two friends watched the fireflies slip from their prison in slow upward spirals one by one, to mingle with the stars.

# AUTHOR'S NOTE

I have lived most of my life in the South. Honestly, I enjoy the slower pace of life here. I like the South's sense of tradition, family, and history. I like the idea of inheriting land and place, of holding on to both, and of passing them along to future generations.

My new Windemere series is a deepening of my own Southern generational roots. The series is filled with imagined characters living in the fictional town of Windemere, Tennessee, not too far from Nashville, a place of plentiful farmland and beautiful horses, of seasons measured not only by sun and rain, but by a sense of ownership and respect for the past.

This first novel, *The Year of Luminous Love*, depicts love *of* people and *between* people, a love for the land, and a way of Southern life still embraced in a fast-moving, ever-changing world. It focuses on friendship, family, and heartbreaking love, on choices made and on pitfalls that cause people to stumble but also to overcome. In this book I launch three young women, best friends from high school, into the bigger world, each with hopes, dreams, and plans for their futures. They often face complicated, even controversial, situations. They have troubles with money, health, love, family. But through every crisis, they have each other.

You will share their struggles. One girl must fight to hold on to her beloved land, one must escape the stranglehold of a love relationship gone bad, and one must confront death. When given the chance to travel across an ocean, each girl leaves her familiar life and comfort zone for an adventure that helps her to understand her own needs and wants and to determine what she most values.

*The Year of Luminous Love* begins their journey. *The Year of Chasing Dreams* will continue it. I think of these two books as a love letter to my Southern roots and to you readers, who encourage me. As a bonus, I'm also writing two e-original short stories about these friends and their families. Watch for them online or check my website, LurleneMcdaniel.com.

I hope you will love Windemere, its past and present, its people, and their stories. Please come into their world with me and live their dreams with them.

# ACKNOWLEDGMENTS

My thanks for agricultural expertise for this novel go to John Goddard, Loudon County, Tennessee, Agricultural Extension Agent; Bart Watson, Loudon County, Tennessee, Farm Bureau Agent; and Jim Farley, a dashing young insurance man, and Martha Farley, his wonderful wife.

# ABOUT THE AUTHOR

Lurlene McDaniel began writing inspirational novels about teenagers facing life-altering situations when her son was diagnosed with juvenile diabetes. "I saw firsthand how chronic illness affects every aspect of a person's life," she has said. "I want kids to know that while people don't get to choose what life gives to them, they do get to choose how they respond."

Lurlene McDaniel's novels are hard-hitting and realistic, but also leave readers with inspiration and hope. Her books have received acclaim from readers, teachers, parents, and reviewers. Her bestselling novels include *Don't Die, My Love; Till Death Do Us Part; Hit and Run; Telling Christina Goodbye; True Love: Three Novels;* and *The End of Forever.*

Lurlene McDaniel lives in Chattanooga, Tennessee.

Turn the page for a preview of
the companion novel to
*The Year of Luminous Love*:

# THE YEAR OF CHASING DREAMS

# ONE

A LONE HORSE AND RIDER stood at the top of Bellmeade's long tree-lined driveway. Ciana Beauchamp had noticed the figure as she passed a window inside her house but hadn't paid it much mind. Horseback riders often passed her property on the road fronting her land. Yet this one had been motionless at the entrance for what seemed too long.

She couldn't see the rider clearly. Gloom from the darkening cloudy overhead sky had gathered from the west, promising autumn rain. She had been in a funk all day. It was October twenty-fourth. This would have been Arie Winslow's twentieth birthday—if she had lived.

Ciana's friend Eden McLauren had gone into town, and her mother, Alice Faye, was banging around in the kitchen. The final harvest was completed, and Ciana should have felt peaceful satisfaction, but she didn't. She was sad and on edge, and the horse and rider were adding to her tension.

She'd thought about Arie all day, remembering her trip to Italy with Arie and Eden the summer before, concentrating on the good times, glossing over the hurts. She missed Arie as much now as she had on the day she'd left her earthly life. What she wouldn't give to see her, talk to her one more time.

Through the window, Ciana saw the horse stamp, growing restless. She squinted, trying to see the rider more clearly. Exasperated, she stepped out onto the wraparound veranda of the old Victorian house. The rider urged his mount forward and the horse came up the drive under tight rein, almost as if it knew where it was going. The rider, a man in a cowboy hat, sat tall in the saddle, and as he drew nearer, Ciana saw that the horse was a buckskin, toffee-colored with a black mane and tail. Ciana's heartbeat picked up, and her lungs seemed to tighten in her chest.

At the front steps, the cowboy removed his hat and hung it on the horn of the saddle. He slid off the horse, grabbed a leather bag, and laid it on the top step. Ripe red apples rolled from the pouch, stopping at Ciana's feet. "Here's a gift," Jon Mercer said.

Almost overwhelmed by the sight of him and the gesture, Ciana felt her chin tremble. She kept her composure, squared her shoulders, and asked, "Who told you about the apples?"

"Arie. It was one of her favorite stories about your grandparents. She said it was how Charles came to court Olivia. Fresh apples were all he had to offer."

Ciana saw instantly that Arie had shared the story in a final act of kindness when she had realized the truth about Ciana and Jon. "Arie died in April," Ciana said stoically, feeling old resentments toward Jon rise.

"Abbie let me know. I had asked her to call when . . . after it was over."

Ciana felt slighted that Jon would have asked Eric's wife instead of her. "Arie was my best friend. I would have let you know if you'd asked me."

"I know. But I asked Abbie instead. Thought we needed the space." His horse, Caramel, once Arie's horse, wandered to the grassy lawn and began to graze. "How's Eden?"

Ciana needed space, all right. "She lives here now with me and Mom. Some changes around here too. I've taken in horses to board for their owners. I don't have an empty stall for Caramel." She added the last to let him know he couldn't just walk back into her life or heart without explanations, and certainly not without permission.

"I talked to Bill on my way from Texas. He'll let me crash at his bunkhouse and board my horse."

She glanced up at the sky and the gathering rain filled clouds. "Well, you might want to head back before the rains come. They look to be gully-washers."

Jon propped his boot against the bottom porch step. "Not until you tell me if you meant it."

"Meant what?"

"That last kiss you gave me. Did you mean it? Did it matter?"

Ciana blinked, conjuring up the heat from that cold March day when he'd loaded his horse and driven away. "Why?"

His jaw muscle tightened. "Because I need to know . . . why did you kiss me like that when I was walking away and leaving this place? I don't get it."

She felt a ripple of irritation. "And I don't get you. Seven months gone and not one word from you."

His neck reddened. "I didn't know what to say."

His answer was insufficient, annoying her further. "How

about a phone call saying, 'Hi. I'm fine. How are you? I miss you.' What's wrong with saying that?"

He swept her face with his green eyes, recited, "'Hi. I'm fine. How are you? I missed you.' Every minute of every day and night," he added softly.

She steeled herself from the effect he was having on her. "Why have you come back?"

"Because everything I want in my life is right here."

Just then the screen door opened and Alice Faye stepped out. "Eden's on her way and supper is—" She stared. Her face broke into a smile. "Why, Jon Mercer! You've come back to us!"

"Yes, ma'am."

Alice Faye beamed at him. "A sight for sore eyes, you are. How's your daddy?"

"Settled in at the county facility. Safe."

"Any recovery from his stroke?"

"Not much progress. Doctors say this will be the best he'll ever be."

Alice Faye shook her head, perked up and said, "Stay for supper."

His gaze found Ciana's. "I couldn't—"

"Tie your horse up in the barn before the rain starts." She glanced at Ciana, and the older woman's expression was challenging. "You're invited. I'll go set another place." The door slammed behind her.

"Mother's flexing her muscle," Ciana said, with a note of bitterness. Jon's look was questioning, but she wouldn't elaborate. Why had he intruded into her life now, when she'd almost put him behind her? God knows, she had missed him, but she had no idea what lay ahead for her . . . the fate of Bellmeade, perhaps the fight of her life to keep it from financial ruin, a possible permanent rift between herself and her mother about selling the land. And what of the things he'd said he wanted? How would they fit into the picture?

"What do we do now?" she asked.

"I don't know. I was hoping we could figure it out together."

On the lawn, Caramel grew restless, sensing the approaching bad weather. "You'd better tend to your horse," Ciana said.

Jon searched her face, nodded brusquely. "This isn't over between us, Ciana."

She wasn't sure if he meant the discussion or the relationship. She folded her arms, their shared past returning in a flood of painful memories. "Today was Arie's . . . would have been . . . Arie's birthday."

Jon's eyes saddened. "I didn't forget. Is there a statute of limitations on your forgiveness?"

Ciana winced. His question hit her hard, and she was ashamed of her reminder of the past to him. The simple words were packed with emotional dynamite, and it was unkind of her to have reminded him of what had almost torn them apart. "Eat with us," she said, offering an olive branch.

He nodded, turned and walked to Caramel, picked up her reins and led the horse toward the barn.

"Sorry," Ciana whispered, knowing he couldn't hear her, but knowing she needed to say the words. She fidgeted waiting for him to return to the house, watched the rolling clouds, heard the low rumble of distant approaching thunder. The smell of dampness lay heavy in the air, and dead leaves danced in eddies of swirling wind. The day, once bright and calm, had turned darker, cooler. The winds of change were blowing. An omen? Ciana shivered.

A storm was coming. . . .